Josefina emptied boxes, tossing aside her plain cotton pantaloons and camisole to try on undergarments of satin and lace, admiring the seductiveness of her newly molded form. Boxes emptied of hats, shoes and undergarments stacked up where they were opened like a child's forgotten blocks. Josefina felt like a child in a candy shop, indulging a new taste from each selection, then going through the ritual again because each seemed sweeter than the one before.

She slept that night, secure in a silk sleeping gown. Francois would not attack her. He was giving her complete freedom to make her choice. He offered the power, wealth, and freedom she coveted for the price of her virtue, this stacked against remaining an innocent and settling for Jacob's future of mediocrity. But she loved Jacob, and Francois had been like a member of the family, generous and understanding.

No one would ever know of the agreement, as long as Francois never told. And whom would he tell? The *Elders* considered him an 'outsider', valued for his gold alone. He would never tell Mother, chance breaking her heart, or Father, for fear of his wrath and losing his standing among the other members of the cartel, and any revelation in general would besmirch the heir Francois prized so dearly. No, Francois would find the telling worthwhile only to hurt her, Mother, Father, or Jacob, because the truth would destroy them all.

The choice rested with her alone, to live with for the rest of her life.

What They Are Saying About
The Pawn

Richly written, The Pawn is a compelling story of intrigue, danger and fame.

—Peggy P. Parsons w/as Evanell
Glimpse of Eternity,
Glimpse of Forever,
Glimpse of Never-Ending Love

Wings

The Pawn

by

Nancy Minnis Damato

A Wings ePress, Inc.

General Fiction Novel

Wings ePress, Inc.

Edited by: Leslie Hodges
Copy Edited by: Karen Babcock
Senior Editor: Dianne Hamilton
Managing Editor: Leslie Hodges
Executive Editor: Lorraine Stephens
Cover Artist: Christine Poe

All rights reserved

Names, characters and incidents depicted in this book are products of the author's imagination or are used fictitiously. Any resemblance to actual events, locales, organizations, or persons, living or dead, is entirely coincidental and beyond the intent of the author or the publisher.

No part of this book may be reproduced or transmitted in any form or by any means, electronic or mechanical, including photocopying, recording, or by any information storage and retrieval system, without permission in writing from the publisher.

Wings ePress Books
http://www.wings-press.com

Copyright © 2005 by Nancy Damato
ISBN 1-59088-602-X

Published In the United States Of America

August 2005

Wings ePress Inc.
403 Wallace Court
Richmond, KY 40475

Dedication

To Robert…

who gave me the freedom

to follow my dream

One

The Netherlands, 1852

Baron Josef von Taylor's fingers twitched as he suppressed an urge to pull his timepiece from his pocket for one more look. An exaggerated pretense of adjusting the vest girdling his girth quieted their restlessness. In truth, he need not see the hour to know the time had passed for any young lady mindful of her reputation to be home among family and friends.

He paced. Hours ago darkness had draped shadows on the empty settee across the room. The housemother, endorsed by Dusseldorf Prepatory Academie for Girls, sat reading in a straight-backed chair, effectively avoiding his glares. She dared not glance in the direction of the vacant seat.

A sudden draft chilled his neck, not unsurprisingly accompanied by a feminine wail. "Josef, you arrived a day early. Would you not allow a fiancée time to prepare herself for her promised?" The scent of roses floated with the sweep of petticoats and skirt. "Ah, my Josef, you have become more handsome since the last visit." Beyond the sitting room doors, footsteps could be heard ascending the stairs.

At least she adhered to essential propriety and did not go out alone. Josef peered down at a doll-sized creature of unnatural beauty whose platinum curls swirled into a design that would shame a fancy bonnet. Startling sapphire eyes twinkled in welcome above lips rivaling a rose petal.

"Have you waited long?" Her face softened with sincerity and a need to be forgiven. "I am sorry."

Josef's body itched with a longing so ardent he could not remain angry. "I have been waiting some time, my Louise. You were not at your studies. Your house companions seemed at a loss to explain your absence."

A wisp of concern veiled her eyes for only an instant.

"I suppose your unseemly absence has to do with that French boy in your letters?"

"Darling Josef, you know me so well. Yes, that is where I have been." She paused. "Did you consider my entreaty?"

"I did. More as a threat than a plea." Her avoidance of any explanation peeved Josef.

"Oh, drat and dumplings! You know very well I only hinted at calling off our engagement to force your hand. How else does a young woman of respectability win the indulgence of her betrothed?" Mischief backed by confidence sparked the darkened blue eyes.

Josef waited, choosing not to answer.

Louise pursed her lips in a pout, then rose on tiptoe and kissed his cheek. "I am thankful you came." Her lips widened in a beguiling smile. "Now, tell me your plan to save François."

"I came, as you asked. I promise nothing." He dared not let her know how easily she could manipulate him.

"Josef, he is quite bereft. The French are too terrified to offer any aid while negotiating peace with the Austrians. The new German Confederacy will not help him. Our own Holland denies him entry through our borders. What are we to do?"

"We? I hear tell the boy stole funds intended to buy arms for the French crown and then was accused of quite unspeakable acts with a number of royal ladies under his protection."

"Rubbish, François told me the truth. The royals concocted that history to buy his safe passage when the revolutionaries put a price on his head. Would we not do the same to protect one of our own secretly defending the royalty?"

"No circumstances exist where I would elect to become involved with a mongrel of such ill-repute." Josef lowered his voice, striving to sound grave with authority. "And, I advise you to extract yourself from this alliance. Now."

Louise's eyes stormed to a blue-violet as ominous as any thundercloud. Her fingers first clutched then twirled a heraldic ring circling her finger.

Josef sought to temper her storm. "By now, this... this scoundrel must believe you fight for him out of affection rather than dedication to our nobles' cause!"

"You cannot be jealous, Josef, it is so unbecoming for a man of your influence. François is but a child. Well, perhaps more an innocent youth, pursuing noble dreams of saving a kingdom lost to revolution." The cloak slid from her shoulders, revealing skin as flawless and luminous as a pearl. "We must help him."

Mindful of the head mistress dozing across the room, Josef lowered his voice. "Perhaps if he were to invest those stolen funds with the Bank?" Josef nodded toward the door leading outside.

"Oh, he would be forever grateful." Louise retied her cloak. "He has the gold you speak of, but without us he has no one trustworthy to turn to. He received word the French nobility disclaimed him today."

Josef scowled. "You see, it is as I warned. Even his own country steps away from him."

Louise narrowed her eyes. "If you cannot, or will not... I will undertake his plight myself." The tempered whisper carried the weight of promise.

François ducLaFevre. Josef's heavy sigh collapsed into an inflexible stance. *The lascivious dragoon will circle Louise like a wolf* after a lamb during my absence. Even now he ruins my chances to woo her."

"The Bank must approve any steps before I involve myself," Josef said. "The boy must produce proof of his innocence. At minimum, provide creditable witness of his loyalty to the House of Orange."

Louise smiled and clasped her hands. "I saw letters signed by the French cabinet, orders to act as their agent."

"I cannot act on your good word alone. Be practical, my love. Documents must be inspected, authenticated. These efforts take months, years, and I must leave for America within a fortnight. Too little time remains." Josef leaned into her, mindful of respectability so their shoulders barely touched. "Am I too brash to consider a walk in the garden? Leave thoughts of treachery this side of the door? Two weeks, then I am gone for a year. I dislike spending my last visit discussing another's misadventures."

"Come." Louise slipped her hand into his, moved toward the veranda door, then stopped. "One last plea. Allow me to take you to François?"

Josef nodded his acceptance with obvious reluctance. He needed to assess the young man, face to face. One must know the enemy.

Louise stepped out the door. "You will become as convinced as I of his innocence. If you care for me at all, you must free him. Accept his word, if that is all he can give."

Louise's plea troubled Josef. Her interest blazed too brightly. Even after his complaint, she talked of the fugitive. Josef stroked his chin, his anger hidden in the darkness, his jealousy building.

"I have a proposal, Louise. A civil ceremony here, marry me tomorrow. We will have two days, then return home together." Josef held up his hand, halting his fiancée's interruption. "Your partisan may accompany us, and I promise to find him safe haven before I sail. By the time I return, he will have retrieved his gold and be prepared to come to America with us."

Louise's visible disheartenment aggravated Josef. The situation had progressed further than he suspected. He had best press her decision. "I suggest your French patriot might enjoy serving as our witness, instead of hanging."

Louise looked up, eyes bright with tears. "If that is the price you demand, so be it."

~ * ~

From across the street François ducLaFevre could not see Louise's face, but she had stiffened, obviously upset. *One year until the dour banker returns. Time enough for me to see that she learns to find pleasure in living. She will forget this severe Dutchman.*

When the couple disappeared, François started back. He loathed the shabby hovel where he hid. Reeked of cabbage and mutton. Children papered the walls; the imps irked him.

Louise will want offspring. No sons to compete with for her affection. I will choose a daughter, the likeness of her mother, yes. But, I will teach the girl to laugh and dance and be a pebble in the shoe of pious tyrants the likes of banker Taylor.

Two

Taylorsville, Illinois
June, 1879

The stone mansion rose like a sacrificial altar in the midst of the green patchwork fields. Inside, shoulders squared, Josefina Taylor glared across the breakfast table into Father's cold eyes. "I cannot do what you ask." Her protest hovered at the open windows of the sunroom, threatening to destroy the surrounding serenity.

"Ask?" Josef Taylor bellowed. "Mine is not a request. You will carry out your part as I command, or you will remain locked in this house until your teeth rot and your hair hangs in wisps."

The danger of her platinum curls paling into transparent shreds seemed absurd. *I can never live the life Father and the church demand.* With Mother's increasing bouts of melancholia, Josefina had managed Father's household remarkably well, although he would never agree. No matter how hard she tried, he always furrowed his brow and directed her attention to a shortcoming on her part. Josefina stretched her small frame as tall as possible, her silence thickening the air.

"If that is your mind," Father rasped, "I can accommodate such defiance by withdrawing permission for you to attend François's banquet this evening." His eyes flashed, "And, for your furtive shopping trip in two days. Rid us all of the gloating you bandy about with such relish."

Josefina waited quietly.

"I should never have allowed Mother to convince me you had earned that foolish coming-of-age gala François orchestrated." Josef slapped his newspaper on the breakfast table. Accompanied by the clatter of nested china, the unfurled print announced BANKERS GATHER.

Josefina jabbed at the dark banner. "After this charade, I will be thought a fool, lacking the sense to make an everyday decision. Any other woman could portray the submissiveness you demand—and to your satisfaction. You know I choke on every word."

Josef rose, scowling, his stocky body forbidding.

"You brought in tutors from outside our community," Josefina reasoned, "to teach me law, history, finance. Pressed me to excel at my studies." Her words tumbled out in rapid fire, sharp and shrill. "Why now, when I stand on the brink of womanhood, do you demand I appear foolish and unschooled before your peers?"

Josefina knew she pressed too hard, and worse, with Father's least appreciated reasoning. In step with their patriarchal society, Father disapproved of women exhibiting ambition and ignored their competency. Josefina had given up her lifelong dream of serving in Father's bank after he killed her aspiration with one declaration. "No woman will ever be granted a chair at the table in my board room, nor on any other bank seat—unless she comes seeking mastery of her inheritance."

Despite Father's feelings, Josefina had no choice but to rely on his investment in her; she had exhausted every other reason to be freed of this pending humiliation.

Father growled, "I indulged your education solely to protect Mother, judging your brothers poorly inclined to protect the family's interests should I fall into decline. For that lapse, never prove me wrong."

He cleared his throat noisily. "As for this 'charade' as you refer to it, a widowed Austrian of title and an Elder of The Church seeks a permanent alliance with Worldwide Bank," Josef shrugged, "obtainable within the rights of a marriage contract." His voice calmed; his gaze appeared preoccupied. "There are children near your age. They will provide you with company."

The hard edge of the chair seat struck Josefina's backside before she realized her knees had buckled. *Widower? Elder? Father had said "provide you with company".*

Josef ignored his daughter's near collapse. "The gossips ruminate over your willfulness and aired ambitions. They warn The Elders I allow you too much privilege. You must prove them just that, rumormongers, without foundation." Josef grabbed up the newspaper and strode across the room. "As for this marriage offer," he declared, "I, too, wish to bind our interests."

"I have a right to choose my own future," Josefina called after his departing back.

"Your only 'right' is what I grant you," Josef countered over his shoulder. At the archway he stopped and turned around to face her. "Do not make a fool of me, daughter. You know very well I never engage in idle threats. Such folly would not be worth your grief suffered." His glacial blue eyes never wavered.

Josefina froze.

The smell of pork drippings, onions, and potato pancakes thickened the air of the cheery breakfast room. Father had added the lanai at his wife's insistence. In rare lapses of winter chores, Josefina lolled here in the warmth of the sun while the housekeepers worked around her.

These same domestic "do-gooders" saw to it Josefina caught her comeuppance for such idleness later at the "enlightenment" gathering conducted weekly by their forbidding Dutch Apostolic Church. Sequestered according to gender, men politicked while the women brayed their complaints, accusing others of sins and discontent that caused friction within their own household. The journals listed numerous infractions under Josefina's name.

In contrast to the Spartan houses of Taylor County, the mansion of Taylor Estates reached skyward, towering over miles of uninterrupted cropland. Other than his repute as an owner of high-priced horseflesh, the house had been the single due Father claimed for his vaulted position as founder of the sect and keeper of the bank.

Since Josefina's two brothers had moved out, with Father wedded to his bank and mother secluded in her rooms, the cavernous quarters echoed with emptiness. Normally Josefina's second-floor suite, with its bright easterly welcome of each new day, served as a refuge for her, but not today.

Josefina rushed upstairs to her rooms, tore off her morning coat and tossed it on the bed. Rage disabled her fingers while she yanked and twisted on a gown. Buttons grew too big for their holes, laces too stiff for the muslin chemise. Petticoats mushroomed into unmanageable tents. All the while Josefina clenched her teeth, determined to hold back the tears threatening to spill. *I will choose my own future.* And she would not waste a speck of sentiment on Father.

After triumphing over the intricacy of clasps and bindings, Josefina paused at the stair landing and studied the closed door of Mother's room. Louise Taylor slept, too powerless in her fight against melancholia to console anyone. Rumor, shushed by the aunts, claimed the sadness came attached to the plain, gold wedding band Father had slipped on Mother's finger long ago.

Mother had good days. She had persuaded Father to consent for his younger partner, François ducLaFevre, to sponsor Josefina at his sister Marianne's debut. For that Josefina felt immeasurable gratitude, but now she needed an historic effort of support. Josefina stomped down the stairs, one step at a time, sourly mulling over Father's calamitous news.

Maybe a year, she decided, before the vile husband-to-be made an appearance, if she behaved and Father allowed her forbidden fling. She had spent the last months scouring Marianne's mailings, secretly devouring her best friend's every publication addressing fashion, fantasizing over the possibilities. Josefina despised being unworldly and untested.

Ever since she officially became a woman, Josefina dreamed of a life-long prodigal fling befitting a mutinous "sister". She hardly believed half a social season could provide memories enough to last her lifetime. At least the weeks in St. Louis would give her unfettered time to develop a better plan.

Father had relented to Josefina attending Marianne's St. Louis debut scheduled for the winter holidays, then, after a week of celebration, accompany her best friend on a social season beginning in Chicago, continuing through late winter in New York with a brief sojourn to the Adirondaks.

Father had dictated one stipulation—all activities must occur well away from the meddling range of their restrictive Dutch Apostolic community. Although a member of the highest level of the church's priesthood, Father would not rub The Elders' noses in Josefina's transgression. The coconspirators, Mother, Josefina, Marianne, and François, had all been warned not to discuss their violation of the 'laws of righteousness living' within hearing of others. "If the Elder's call at Taylor Estates to lodge objections," Josef had declared, "Josefina will remain here."

Father had rejected spring in Boston and Philadelphia prior to the traditional 'callings' in Virginia and the return sailing through New Orleans, preaching the folly and expense of the whole venture.

The much-publicized cities teased Josefina with freedom and glamour, bolstering her want to begin. Their severe community labeled celebrating, other than to pray over events of the church or gatherings to recognize personal industry, as self-indulgent and a lapse of faith, which caused Josefina to doubly rejoice in Father's limited generosity. Their Dutch forefathers arrived in America sermonizing that singing be reserved to praise the Lord and merry-making be denied as opening a door to the devil. Joy in hard work and striving to achieve spiritual grace was all the reward needed in life.

The thought of missing the coming pleasures of "the season" stilled Josefina's anger. *I must adhere to Father's command. Convince him I accept his terms. Besides, what choice do I have?* She owned nothing. Ink squiggles in Father's ledgers constituted her only funds. A few pennies lay in her reticule for trifles. No one, neighbor or family, would step forward to help.

But, if Father escalates this marriage plan and forces me to forego my whirlwind and flee now, I want no forewarning of my intent.

One person offered escape. But, if she followed her heart, abandoned her family to join Jacob in his trek West, she faced lifelong poverty and unfathomable hardships.

Jacob Levinia Broderick, handsome, daring, absolutely free of constraint, delighted Josefina's heart and soul. I want him as my own, her heart sang. *I want to feel his touch,* her virgin flesh murmured. She ached to hear the music of his voice and melt with the accidental brush of his body, to look up and see his hazel eyes gazing at her.

Luxury and laughter is truly what I desire! Without warning the traitorous wantonness shattered Josefina's pondering with such fury it drove all else from her mind. Josefina moaned. The battle of needs clashing in her mind, she reached the front entrance of the house weighed down by invisible shackles of hopelessness.

Josefina stepped out onto the porch floor and scanned the warm, blue sky. More fitting to have darkness, and rainfall of thorns and thistles. She reached back, and using all her might slammed the heavy, walnut door as hard as she could. The bang rumbled, swelling into a thunderclap filling the foyer. The cavernous house quickly swallowed the announcement of her anger, allowing her very little satisfaction.

Robins' trills, mixed with the fragrance of roses sweetening the air, grated against Josefina's foul mood. Nothing could cheer her. This morning's futile battle had set her mind. *Whatever the sacrifice, I will not allow Father to rule my life one day longer than I must.* In the end, Josefina vowed, she would not submit.

While crossing the wide porch, Josefina's festering sulk dipped ominously. A broad-shouldered figure lurked in the buggy at the bottom of the steps, the outline too vague within the shadow of the canopy for her to discern if it was man or woman. *Father?* She would not suffer his company.

Josefina started to turn back at the precise moment the figure leaned forward. A straw hat bright with green ribbon and buttercups followed by a shawl of coppery hair poked out into the sunlight.

Josefina bristled. "Marianne, what on earth are you doing here?" Josefina wanted to wail. The injustices kept piling up. *The last thing I need, my best friend witnessing my ruination.* The only thing worse was if the concealed passenger had turned out to be Jacob. The tight corners of Josefina's mouth softened at the thought of the dazzling engineer.

"I tell François I prefer riding to town wiz you." Marianne's French accent dripped thick and cloying, mimicking words snuggled in sugared crêpes. "He told me to extend you his wish for good fortune today." Her green eyes twinkled saucily.

Josefina climbed up onto the seat, righting the plain, saucer-like hat that topped her mass of curls. François seldom bothered with good wishes. Marianne had made that up.

"I thought I would be the only woman appearing before the consortium." The words erupted grumpy and accusatory even to Josefina's ears.

"Woman?" Marianne chortled. "Two years less than I? You wish for much." Marianne fluffed her yellow lawn dress indifferently, smoothing the colorful embroidered violets.

Josefina's blue cotton dress suddenly imprisoned her in its plainness. She kicked the brake loose with a zealous thump and slapped the reins across the horse's rump.

"François arranged a luncheon," Marianne said. "I am to hostess. Some gentlemen from Mizzouri cannot remain for zee banquet tonight." Marianne gripped the canopy's frame as the vehicle veered around a series of dips. "No one could ever compel me to endure a roomful of men engaged in boring talk about money and law."

"Nothing but a closed-minded, tyrannical father like mine." *Odd, François holding a private meeting.* Under any other circumstances, Josefina would be thrilled to share in the bank's deliberations. Her mouth crimped flat as an iron. "I envy your freedom, the playfulness in your life, the glamour," Josefina sighed.

"And I you—having charmed Jacob. I would trade what you envy happily."

"Which comes of no use to either of us with Josef Taylor serving as sentry."

"You spoke again with your father?" Marianne's prying remained friendly.

"Yes, earlier this morning." Josefina turned down the lane.

"Your plea went unanswered?" The wide green eyes wavered between sympathy and acceptance.

"Hardly." Josefina raised her chin defiantly. "Father gave his answer, all right." Her shoulders slumped. "I have begged, cajoled, promised everything in return for freeing me of this dreadful exhibition."

"I warned as much." Marianne shrugged. "Thou shalt honor thy Father..."

"I am sick to death of 'thou shalt' and 'thou shalt nots.'" The fire of Josefina's voice damned.

"Your father only seeks what eez best. You admitted your appearance today eez a real plum. No female ever address zee cartel. Enjoy your celebrity." Marianne's long fingers snatched at the arm of the seat as the buggy jarred across several rocks.

"Not an 'address,' a performance akin to a street hustler." Josefina felt the need to unburden herself, confident she could choose no better ear. She flicked the reins again before turning to Marianne. "I have learned much worse. What I am sharing is not to be repeated."

Marianne nodded her assent.

"Father announced a husband snips at my heels. Some unknown who feels uneasy with my reputed "willful" nature. That is why Father demands I portray a simpleton before the bankers today, to win the wretch's approval."

"For a woman to be too clever eez not endearing." Marianne's words exploded like pebbles from a slingshot as the buggy bounced along the dirt road.

The admonishment did not surprise Josefina; Marianne practiced pleasing.

"A new home, a husband." Marianne smiled broadly, eyebrows raised in anticipation. "The leave-taking you wish; accept your Father's plan as a welcome gift."

"Trading one heavy hand for another—of whom I know nothing? If I am not valued enough to enjoy a proper position at the bank, I will assuredly never serve as its pawn."

Josefina leaned forward and absently flicked the reins, urging on a horse that already raced. The wind rushing beneath the canopy attempted to make a kite of her hat, but did nothing to cool her temper.

"I am as familiar with the banking world as any one of the men who will be present," Josefina continued. "Father molded me to his likeness; now he regrets his success." Josefina's round jaw quivered as she fought mounting anger and misery.

Venting her frustrations using the only weapon available, one of Father's prized thoroughbreds, Josefina snapped the reins with a sharp crack. She pressed the high-spirited animal with the aggressiveness of a man, a man pursued by the devil himself, so decent folk claimed.

Marianne gripped the swaying frame with both hands. "Zee field hands witness your recklessness."

Rigid, dark forms scattered across the landscape watched, some with hands on hips, elbows jutting. Any other day Josefina would accept the distant disapproval as her penalty for not abiding by the Dutch community's suffocating law of "everything in moderation." Resentment pushed aside Josefina's usual resignation. Ignoring the visible warnings, she flicked the reins again.

Another censure to endure. Josefina imagined the Elders flailing her soul into a shriveled dreg-like being. *If a centipede modeled the calluses I have from kneeling in penance, it would resemble a fat pincushion.* And still, she failed miserably, unable to forge the strength to obey.

"I will not allow Father, or this dreary place, to kill my spirit." Unwittingly, Josefina mumbled.

"Remember your duty," Marianne chided. The words peppered the air as the wheels jolted across a series of ruts. When the road leveled, Marianne became adamant. "Your Father eez granting an unheard of indulgence. You will lose that privilege if you defy him. You must obey." Marianne stressed, "In every respect."

Her fervent insistence surprised Josefina. She turned to face her companion. "Are you suggesting I abandon Jacob?"

Marianne would not look Josefina in the eye.

Surely, Josefina thought, Marianne would not let desire for Jacob goad her into betrayal. "We entered into an agreement to be fair in winning Jacob. Are you advising me to ignore my feelings? Free Jacob for you?"

"Josefina, please, we are like sisters. I only think what eez best for you. I worry over zee disgrace you will suffer, and zee bank, too, if you fail today."

Troubled by her inclination to mistrust her friend, Josefina bowed her head in shame. "Please, forgive me, of course, I feel the same bond. Father has me all adither." Still, Josefina could not let Marianne's protests die. "You know well enough I would never scandalize the bank, even over this debasing appearance and my ongoing battle with Father."

"Allow this," Marianne said. "Your Father acts with zee wisdom of a man. He must have excellent reason to request theez of you."

Josefina itched to disagree, but realized no point to it. "Rest assured, I will be my most charming, if only for spite. You know full well I can be." Josefina's conciliatory tone took on the biting edge of a fine wine soured to vinegar. "But I am not a possession, and I will never allow the Chairman of Worldwide Bank to use me to barter with in the manner of one of his prized thoroughbreds."

At the mention of Father's pastime, Josefina realized the staggered pounding of four hooves had gelled into a single beat. Foam lathered the flanks before her. The horse bound from one full stride to the next, risking a broken neck. Leather rubbed against exploding muscles, leaving evidence of emerging chafe wounds.

Knees locked, Josefina braced her slight frame against a wooden crib nailed to the floor. Her shoulders stiffened. Doeskin gloves, straining at the seams, clamped the reins with viselike pressure and tugged. "Whoa! Whoa!"

Shame and remorse replaced Josefina's anger. No one possessed the right to abuse this magnificent animal, or any other, especially someone who admired their strength and grace as she did. *The anger I wrestle need be directed at my own timidity.*

Josefina mentally scolded herself while a calming cadence, resembling the secret code of crickets, clicked from her lips. But the horse, having tasted freedom, continued to race at a furious pace.

Josefina yanked harder, called out again. "Whoa!" Then judging they raced far enough from town, the road clear of conveyances, she suddenly felt no desire to check the freed spirit. Instead, the reins fell slack against her knees. Her heart sailed with the horse, unrestrained, sharing the animal's seeking of its potential.

Marianne, eyes shut, hung on in silence.

The buffeting wind plumped with the sweet smell of fertile earth. Tilled with the withered stalks of summer's labors then left to winter, the rich soil hugged plants that stretched in perfect rows as far as the eye could see. The land lay before Josefina as black as if night rested upon the earth. The fields spread in a flat horizon, disguising loamy clumps that sifted easily through thick fingers, a rich element in need of constant purging and feeding.

Feeling more grave than resentful, Josefina studied the passing miles of Taylor Estates, acre after acre, greening tracts that bridged the distance to town and beyond it. Her birthplace. Barefoot, uncertain and awkward, her first steps had united her with this land. She had tasted sweetness and death in the soil, secretly wallowed in rain-filled hollows that turned her pale skin dark then dried to a grayed crust of armor deserving of any knight.

With Father's revelation, the obsession of being separated under any circumstance from this property and the prestigious standing accompanying such holdings heightened Josefina's anxiety. The thought brought almost paralyzing fear. Without her family's standing, dependent on an outsider's generosity, she would be wretched, impotent, without merit.

Moreover, Josefina had spent years dreaming of riches enough to savor the luxury the Elders forbade. She planned to experience extravagance to her heart's content. Such desires hardly fell within the dictate of the church's mandate to live a simple life with charity.

Josefina's teeth nipped the inside of an already savaged lip. *I have no hope of ever achieving the pure heart required of me. Worse, when Father hands me over to this husband of his choosing, that stranger, not I, will control my inheritance and everything I know of this world. And with Father's blessing.*

The buggy slowed before entering Main Street, then swayed to a bumpy halt before the largest building on the village square. Three story Corinthian columns balanced a granite slab announcing Taylorsville Bank.

In one graceful move Marianne's narrow slippers touched the ground. Josefina flipped down the stairs that had been added to the buggy to accommodate her diminutive size, then stepped down, airy as an angel, careful not to reveal a peek of ankle or show of petticoat.

"*Bon chance.* Good Luck at zee meeting," Marianne said, giving a flippant wave. "By the by, François invited Jacob." The supple redhead sauntered away, not waiting for a response.

Marianne's quip blindsided Josefina.

Nausea rumbled in her stomach. The words crippled formerly agile arms and legs. Josefina leaned against the buggy, unable to steady herself.

Why had François invited Jacob? Marianne had delivered the news much too casually. Had she some part in Jacob's invitation? A flush of renewed anger warmed Josefina's cheeks. Hiding behind the buggy, she struggled to regain her composure, splashing cool water from the trough onto her flaming face and throat.

Josefina had to trust Marianne. They had shared Josefina's dreams of becoming part of high-society, of laughing and singing in public, of being able to find joy in living, and even more so, her ambition to return one day a successful financier challenging the power of the custodians of father's "inhospitable" bank, and yet, Marianne had proposed Josefina abandon all that, and Jacob. Her best friend seemed to have lost sight of their agreement.

Several minutes after hearing Marianne's distressing tidings, and as calmed as possible, Josefina jammed the escaped ringlets up under her hat and approached the bank's entrance.

The brass-clad door failed to open at her hearty tugs. *One of the two wealthiest families in Taylorsville County, and no manservant to assist me.* Another of Father's slights, Josefina fussed.

A sharp ping sounded when her boots finally crossed the metal threshold and she stepped into the lobby. Josefina stopped and inhaled the musty, hushed air. "Ahhhh," came a decided sigh. Her shoulders softened; head tilted submissively. Josefina felt she had arrived home after being absent on a long journey. A welcomed calm, comforting as the stroke of a mother's hand, flowed over her body and soul. She knew her entire life she would always experience the same feeling whenever she stepped into a bank.

Abruptly, Josefina's neck stiffened. She would not surrender, no matter how hypnotic the setting. This privileged arena could never be hers. Still, Josefina's body strummed with an undercurrent of excitement while she contemplated the power contained within these walls, the lives controlled. Her own included.

The room rose skyward like a cathedral. Gray marble floors soared into massive columns that stretched to the ceiling, their polished strength offering welcome to the members of the moneyed class. Brass cages, bars darkened from years of touch, separated aspiring clerks from the everyday clientele, the barriers gifting their imprisoned with the capacity to intimidate.

Nearby desks accommodated a myriad of males suited in very proper black wool. They waited like false gladiators, guarding stacks, drawers, cabinets, all crammed with slim black ledgers scratched with columns of figures that chronicled secret histories. Everything precise, accounted for, balanced in neatly recorded black ciphers.

Of all places ever, Josefina loved best being here, in Father's bank. Unique to its grandeur, she relished most the scent, the sweet, potent essence of riches. A sniff confirmed the presence of wealth, but Josefina's thrust of chin addressed a trickle of annoyance that robbed her of total pleasure.

What did she care if Dieter and Marianne, her two best friends, chided her? They could ridicule all they wanted; she could smell the unseen gold. The intoxicating perfume eased her raw crankiness, rendering her confident and bold. The accompanying taste of the precious metal pulsed through her veins.

"Good Morning, Miss Taylor." Without invitation a young clerk boldly approached and bowed. A fainthearted smile preceded his address. "You look especially blessed this morning." Her head dipped in modest acceptance. He continued. "May I remark on your stylish costume."

Josefina smiled primly, then nodded blindly, dismissing him. She loved parading across the lobby, admired for her presentation. Months had been invested secretly copying delicious designs from a borrowed Godey's magazine. A sin of vanity. *Well, not the first, nor the last of my sins.*

No time remained this morning for lolling in self-indulgence. Her steady climb up the stairs slowed near the main chambers. All the morning's previous displeasure returned swift as a sleet storm on a sunny day, poking holes in the bloom of her good humor.

Father's exhibition would make a fool of her.

Josefina breathed deeply, wanting to concentrate on the rich scent, but her brow furrowed with the recollection of Father's scorn. A fish on a hook had more free will than she.

Stubbornly Josefina rehearsed. *I will be obedient. I will play the role assigned. I will be the perfect daughter.*

Three

The gathering consisted of the wealthiest members of the banking community ever assembled within the borders of America. Worldwide Bank, an Americanized arm of a Deutsche financial institution, had authorized the Taylorsville facility to launch an investment program boasting of a secret pact with the federal government.

The invited members would form a consortium to act as agent to buy and sell all lands publicly held or under dispute. Ultimately, they would control the disposition of all land the rest of the world so eagerly sought to own.

Businessmen, holy men, teachers, farmers, gamblers, whoever aspired to becoming a member of the landed class, would be able to purchase grants only through this cartel. If the aspirants defaulted, the land would be seized and returned to the cartel. By agreement with the government, any property within the jurisdiction of federal officials, whether condemned, confiscated from rebels, foreign peoples or governments, claimed by Indians or deeded abandoned, would come under the exclusive disposition of this group of men.

The promoters speculated the value to be in the hundreds of thousands. At a time when ten dollars a month signified a goodly salary, such contemplated wealth was incomprehensible.

Although concerned by the cartel's opportunity to swindle the public, Josefina worried more about Father's personal agenda, neither openly nor covertly publicized, to utilize this event to market her.

Josefina surmised the contemplated contender would not be in attendance; however, she knew word of her public submissiveness would spread in advance of Father's anticipated overtures.

Father had directed her to act as a distraction, a muff to legitimize an indoctrination slanted to educate, but not belittle, his Board and guests. A farce, Josefina determined, like the crafty medicine man and his shill who promoted vile concoctions as healing balms.

Just last month she had toted chamomile and peppermint purging brews to aid a poor and trusting family poisoned by the likes of such a street vendor. A stronger fear attached itself to this like attempt of Father's. Josefina had no experience providing healing potions to the moneyed class.

"For a girl who supposedly submits to a closefisted father and follows his allegiance to plain costume, you look splendid as always, Lil' Jos." The velvet-smooth voice leapt from the shadows.

Startled, Josefina jumped. Her hoop snagged on the overhanging step above, revealing an underskirt trimmed with row upon row of prohibited lace. Josefina's arms waved in the air as her back arched precariously.

From the darkness of the windowless stairwell, a young man, his hairless face squared with a blonde Dutch bob, smiled and steadied her with a light touch. "May I say, the blue of your dress falls short of the beauty of your eyes, especially when they darken with such fury."

"Dieter," Josefina snapped, her balance restored. "Must you forever slink about, sneaking up on the unsuspecting, like... like a disgusting stable rat?" She had labeled him the vilest of all creatures. Yet even as her heart pounded, the soft spot in her being would not allow her to further belittle him.

"Shush," she warned, "you know better than to show disrespect for Father. Someone might hear you." When Dieter downed his head, Josefina felt guilty that her reproach had put him so out of sorts. Even though Father expected him to one day manage the bank, as the son of an indentured domestic and a horse trainer who served Taylor Estates, Dieter had always been particularly sensitive to Josefina's judgments.

Josefina strove to breeze away her snippiness. "You look very handsome this morning. New suit?" In spite of her good intention

Josefina challenged him. "Father's suggestion I presume." Unlike her, Dieter only exercised one independent thought, which had become a refrain.

"Marry me," he had begged, more than a month ago. "When the time comes, control the bank through me."

A childhood friend, Dieter had always known what Josefina desired, more than anyone else, sometimes before she knew. But he had not guessed how much she desired Jacob.

That day her escape had come easy. "I am about to join Marianne in her debut. You would rob me of a winter of partying, parading about the country costumed as I have only dreamed of. Free of this cheerless place?"

"Enjoy the season. Announce our engagement next spring," Dieter wheedled.

"You have too far to rise to consider marriage. And, I will not humor you by being used to ease your way."

Jacob's name had not come up that day or since then. If Dieter turned a blind eye to her dalliance, so much the fool, and she would never align herself with a fool.

Gathering the freed skirt about her, Josefina topped the stairs. Male murmurs like thunder under a blanket came from the nearest doors.

"Off with you," Josefina whispered. "If Father catches you skulking about, he will have you working sixteen hours a day like an unlettered bondsman."

"You know I already labor more than any other. Your father's opinion of me suffers." Dieter smiled crookedly, shamefaced, his ears reddening.

Josefina instantly regretted calling attention to his standing. "We share his same poor regard, I fear. But, I shall not disappoint Father this time."

She squeezed Dieter's arm affectionately, freed herself, then quickly pulled apart the nearby French doors and swirled into a crowded, smoke-filled room.

~ * ~

Dieter watched Josefina strut away, the landing dismal with her going. Even from the back Josefina displayed pride and grace. She had been born beautiful and nothing in that respect had changed. Her gentle manner reflected heartfelt caring, and she acted on her perceptions in her own way, independent of the strict canons of the Apostles.

Josefina never let the difference in standings interfere with friendships. She had often suffered reprimands and additional penance for her unapproved cavorting with outsiders. Dieter knew she coveted finer things, the dazzle and pomp denied her, public merrymaking and dress balls, but her heart stayed pure. He loved her for that, among other things.

At an early age, they had assumed the airs and manners of bankers and wielded power over the cows and chickens. Many days, hidden behind the grapevines with a goat serving as judge, Josefina distributed the wealth of vegetables in their fabled kingdom so the lamb, bovine, and poultry shared equitably.

The frustration and disappointment began for Josefina later on, when she realized her father would never allow her to use her talents within the chambers of the banking world.

Josef Taylor educated his daughter well, particularly in law and finance. In Dieter's private opinion this dedication came not from the Chairman's respect for his daughter's ambition, but from the Elder Taylor's sole intent to assure that his wealth remained intact to protect his ailing wife. Josef swore publicly that Louise Taylor would never have need to depend on anyone, especially the likes of his partner, François ducLaFevre.

The day Josefina discovered her Father's aims unlinked to her own ambitions, the only time Josefina ever cried for her own wants, Dieter dedicated his life and love to her. He vowed he would deliver her dream, whatever it took and however long. In the meantime, he would serve her best by staving off the hounds.

Four

Josefina stood inside the doors of the exalted, private chambers she had never dared enter. A long, cherry table offered its uncluttered surface in the center of the room. Matching chairs clustered in small groups or waited invitingly along the paneled walls, enough places to capably seat the thirty-odd financiers who stood about, arguing, crowing, their hawkishness rifling the room.

Standing head and shoulders above the majority of stocky Teutonic bankers, François ducLaFevre, Father's young French partner, challenged Josefina's entrance with a penetrating stare, aping a ferret spying its prey. François moved to the far side of the room, his eyes never leaving her.

Josefina caught the attention of her adored, older brother, Louis. He hastily elbowed several men aside to come to her aid. Father had insisted Louis take the day off from the farm to lend support, but the nearby presence of Stuart, their blackguard sibling, surprised Josefina. She would not have given him a thought. She wondered momentarily what had curtailed Father's talk of evicting Stuart from the St. Louis townhouse, banishing him to the German countryside for his antics.

"You are a most welcome sight," Louis said. "Add some spirit to this cheerless gathering." Infectious laughter accompanied the words. Louis was as jovial as Father was dour. Sliding an arm protectively under hers, Louis began to squire Josefina through the crowd. "Mr. Stern, may I present the bank's secret weapon. No, more like our armada. My sister, Miss Josefina Taylor." Pride colored his overture.

"We refer to her more readily as 'Little Jos', the Chairman's namesake."

Louis repeated the introduction dozens of times while they circled the room, allowing Josefina time to direct a personal query or special comment to each man, penetrate their reserve, form the bond Father demanded.

François, his showy attire conspicuous among the somberly dressed puritans, performed an identical courtesy, circulating in a course that assured their paths never crossed.

An hour passed before Josefina came face to face with Father. His waxed collar and black suit appeared impenetrable. "You arrived on time, daughter."

She bristled; she was never late.

"You have asked each of his family?" He whispered, turning his back to the room. "After his wife? His health?"

"Yes, Father. But I..."

"No prattling. You know your duties. Go about them."

"Father, must I go through with this?"

"You have exhausted my patience." A red flush crept above his white collar, then his voice hammered. "Do as you were told! Carry out your part as ordered. Do not embarrass me, or yourself, with any exhibition of common influences." Josef turned sideways, flashed a brilliant smile, one arm outstretched to greet a recent arrival. "Your mother birthed you with beauty and gifted you with charm, that is all the world seeks." The words snaked out menacingly from between clenched teeth before the Chairman turned his back to Josefina.

The bankers greeted new members and recounted competitions with old friends. Set adrift among the self-absorbed men, Josefina stepped to a tea tray and filled a delft cup, inhaling the vapors of steam. For a few moments the liquid's sarsaparilla infusion lessened the stench of the nearby spittoons.

A knot cramped at the base of her skull, threatening more to come. She reached up and tugged harshly on a curl, the pain distracting while her eyes searched the room. Thankfully, Jacob had not appeared. Eyes closed, Josefina pleaded silently. *Please, Lord, keep Jacob away.*

"Harrumph," her father cleared his throat, "if we might all be seated?"

Josefina claimed a delicate settee alongside the head chair, in contrast to the expansive chairs of the members seated at the table. Other more recently arrived men formed a deep well around the room.

"You have all been introduced to my daughter, Miss Josefina Taylor, who will favor us with a presentation demonstrating the need for our proposed consortium." Father remained standing while she curtsied. "We all know that women, especially ladies of consequence, seem unable to attract responsible men to manage their affairs."

Father's steel blue eyes darted directly at her when he emphasized the word 'responsible.' Josefina's thoughts went immediately to Jacob. A flush warmed her cheeks. Her patent smile shriveled as if she had bitten into a sour plum.

"As dutiful business men, we are obligated to step into that absence. We cannot allow ill-informed women to flounder about with their insufficient capabilities, inviting undesirables to bilk them of their fortunes." The Chairman offered his hand. "If you would?" As he assisted Josefina up to the podium, he leaned near, speaking confidentially. "Regard my warning."

Josefina squelched the burning retort that sizzled on the tip of her tongue and curtsied masterfully. She struggled to extinguish the flush that hinted at hidden anger while her eyes swept the room in an artful motion. Halfway, a churning, reminiscent of a taste of rancid bacon, turned Josefina's insides queasy.

Jacob Broderick stood in a far corner, engrossed in conversation with a man not previously introduced. God have mercy. The throbbing of Josefina's heart pounded erratically as if a sack of toads had taken residence in her chest. She swallowed dryly and struggled for breath. *I must be perfect. I must obey.*

Josefina could think of nothing except Jacob's liquid, amber eyes and the strength of his hand guiding her waist. The words Father demanded flowed by themselves. "Mr. Taylor, I have recently come into a rather large sum of money, and being uninformed in the ways of the world am in need of a gentleman's counseling. If you would relieve me of this worrisome burden?"

Josefina glanced up just as Jacob's head turned away. He had been watching. Trembling knees barely registered a tremor in her voice while she buried her torment and vexation in the role. Eyes focused on the reflective sheen of the tabletop, Josefina fought to channel her mind to her charge. "Having no capacity to understand the workings of the world, I fear in my foolishness I may well lose all my capital." Father frowned. "My inheritance," Josefina corrected.

"We advise everyone of means," Josef emphasized, "to consult an experienced executor. It is to your benefit to employ a qualified agent dedicated to preserving your resources."

Josefina's attention was drawn to Jacob again. He gazed across the room, away from her. "Easily impressed by a well-turned phrase," Josefina continued, "I find myself incapable of judging a well-intended executor. Could you suggest an appropriate financier? Uh, advisor?" Josefina tried to swallow her error of education.

Josef rushed on. "Worldwide Bank holds the interest of its client at heart. Entrusting your funds with us would guarantee you a life free of worry. Open your days to the teas and womanly interests you so enjoy."

"And these assets, would they remain intact, protected?" The question bulled its way out. Josefina, too aware of Jacob's lithe body leaning against the wall, had faltered.

Josef scowled. "Worldwide Bank is embarking on a revolutionary investment with our government that will capitalize on the great adventurous spirit of our nation. In a short time we will hold title to all of the lands of the developing West."

That meant an end to Jacob's dream, perhaps hers. Josefina's incense erupted. "Why not purchase this property on my own? Deal directly with the government. That would save commission, would it not?" At this invention Father's eyes bored into Josefina like nails in a coffin. His hand gripped the gavel, blue veins bulged.

"Ours will be an exclusive agreement. Acting alone would invite scalawags and thieves to abscond with your holdings. Let me explain our acquisition opportunities more thoroughly."

Josefina concentrated on Father's cravat, fearful if she met Jacob's glance, she would come further undone. The Chairman droned a list of towns. In Josefina's mind, Jacob's voice recited the names of the legendary frontier, properties soon to be inked into the bank's ledgers. The prospect of Jacob braving pauperism loomed before Josefina.

Josef Taylor's invitation promised his listeners a washing of the hands. Clean. Deliberate. Harmless.

Across the table, François appeared agitated, watching the theatrics with the relish of a hawk, so much so he appeared prepared to pull flesh from limb at Josefina's slightest offense. Of late he studied her every move, more so than in the past, seemingly to Josefina determined to expose her weaknesses. François exchanged conspiratorial looks with Stuart. Imagining them in cahoots, Josefina labored, determined to disappoint them both.

After an hour, Josef turned to the assemblage. "Do any of you have questions?" As the Chairman anticipated, shrugs greeted his inquiry. No one would dare challenge the plan put before his colleagues, or voice concern, after sharing in this spirited young lady's obvious welcome of the investment. "Then, gentlemen," the Chairman continued, "we tackle the more practical task. Asset disbursement."

Feeling mentally bruised and drained, Josefina retired to the settee. She finally looked directly at Jacob's corner. Following Stuart, Jacob nudged his way to the doors without a backward glance. Josefina suffered no feelings of abandonment. Two unfamiliar men preceded him. The men of François and Marianne's private luncheon she suspected. Even though Jacob had gallantly avoided drawing her attention during the charade, his departure came as a godsend.

Young, broad shoulders led the easy swing of Jacob's body. He nodded across the room to François. Had Jacob turned toward her, Josefina feared she would swoon under the gaze of his pensive eyes, but still, she felt cheated when he disappeared without a backward glance. The loss triggred reflection of those same amorous eyes pleading with her, infecting her with the merits of fleeing West with him.

An hour later, legs locked like a grapevine, Josefina awkwardly straightened her cramped back. She had been leaning forward, so hypnotized by the slight of hand to be perpetrated by the cartel, the time flew by quickly. The movement of enormous profits to be controlled by this roomful of moneylenders awed her. Their power would prove staggering.

Josefina felt more alive than at any other time she remembered, but with each pulse forced through her veins she felt robbed. The core of her would be forever seeking, her skills untested, on this pursuit or any other such financial venture.

Eyes narrowed, lips parted, pent-up excitement dampened Josefina's brow. Her normal refined poise had evaporated, laying bare all the longing and exasperation she felt. Her body twitched like a rabbit eyeing the tender sprouts of a newly planted garden.

Josefina realized, much too late, her raw, covetous feelings had been easily read. With a quick tap to the arch of his eyebrows, François's probing watchfulness saluted her weakness, her vulnerability. He smirked, then shrugged indifferently at the dilemma. Cheeks burning, Josefina turned her attention back to the chairman.

Josef Taylor stood like a reigning baron at the head of the table, palms open in generous invitation. "Remember, we expect you all to attend the banquet at 'The Chateau' of Monsieur ducLaFevre this evening. Be forewarned," his lips puckered, "the Monsieur owns one of the most luxurious properties in our country. My daughter spent days begging for an appropriate frock, proposed scattering my money like fodder for a mare in season." A smile inched away his smirk. "May she generate as good a return."

The mushrooming laughter left Josefina disheartened, chastised, like an unruly child. A swaddled sob choked her. In the end, Father's wit marked her place and her price.

Josefina waited alone while the men mingled, debating their ruination or possible profit. She had hoped someone would approach her. No one, not even her own Louis, sought her out to praise her presentation, and assuredly, no one favored her counsel. As she began to work her way out through the crowd, a studious appearing gentleman came forward. "Miss Taylor, may I congratulate you..."

Josefina smiled her most charming. *At last, a man who recognizes my contribution.*

"... on your endurance. And may I extend apologies for us all. I am sure it was most difficult for a lady of your esteem to be receptive to this boorish discourse. It would be unpleasant for any woman of refinement to be exposed to such base dialogue. When I speak with your mother I shall be most explicit on your behalf. Mrs. Taylor must understand how genuinely well you managed your sacrifice."

~ * ~

Josef Taylor's face remained passive while he watched his daughter make her farewells. She had done well. The test had not been of her intelligence, of which he had no question, but of her ability to control her strong will, to set aside her temper and submit in a most grievous role. Yes, she had probed, some, but in the end deferred. He felt satisfied.

No one else would guess from the courtesies Josefina extended that she seethed inside—with one exception. François had noted Josefina's every leaning since the day she had been born. Some days his partner seemed able to assess Josefina more accurately than he.

Mentally Josef ticked off his schedule and set aside time to meet privately with his wife. He must instruct Louise not to speak of the arrangement he had divulged concerning the future of their daughter, particularly within hearing of François. Only a dunderhead would not have the good sense to realize that, as usual, his partner had begun moves contrary to his own.

Josef thought back to his first experience with François's opposition and the Frenchman's attempt to seduce his beloved Louise. Losing to a country banker had wounded François's pride severely, forcing Josef to plan well, confirming his family would never have need to depend on the Frenchman.

~ * ~

The buggy pinged and clattered as Josefina raced back to the estate, veering recklessly across ruts and around rocks. While she sped by the painstakingly tended acres, her noisy passing another intrusion on the somber workers in the fields, her thoughts ricocheted between the land speculation and her own future.

Marianne seemed prepared to contest Jacob's affection. Am I imagining it? Of course, we have been like sisters for two years. Marianne said so herself earlier.

Concern about the debate of the men of the cartel intruded. The discussion of the amount of profit and how soon they would start receiving a return on their investment occupied most of the discussion. Not a half dozen members of the cartel voiced unease over the working public who might be victimized. The charter of the National Land Company was signed, sealed, and constituted, prepared to take advantage of the public's need.

The urgency to possess property to prove their worth needled most members of the landless class, driving them, not unlike the resolve Josefina felt. Some of the unfortunates craved ownership of expanses like Taylor Estates, others would settle for less covetous wants, a small measure of the world deeded to their name, a claimed square of earth of any size or shape, no matter how barren.

The corners of Josefina's lips drooped in heartfelt scorn. How convenient that Worldwide Bank of Taylorsville's newest scheme fed upon this universal hunger, how unfortunate for Jacob, herself, and the other dreamers of the world.

The miles of fields passed unnoticed. Nettled, frustrated, preoccupied with the less than fruitful reception her portion of the presentation had received, Josefina felt further mortified about Jacob's presence. She fretted over facing him at the banquet tonight.

Deserting the vehicle at the entrance to the mansion, Josefina barely missed crashing into the chess board set up to continue Father and François's weekly competition. Her dash up the staircase ended at her mother's bedroom door.

Josefina knocked tentatively. "May I come in?"

"For a few moments," a voice answered indifferently.

When Josefina entered, Louise Taylor, wearing a gray day coat, platinum curls ironed flat into a sleek bun, sat at a rosewood vanity. "You appear disheveled. You promised you would not tire yourself before the banquet. You have decidedly inherited my delicate constitution, and Father requires we be attentive tonight."

"Mother, how could you forget? My presentation?" Mother's expression remained blank. "At the bank?" Josefina knew Mother had no recollection of the unwelcome humiliation.

"Please? Do as I ask." Louise shook her finger in Josefina's face. "Take better care of yourself. I will depend on you all too soon."

Josefina threw her arms in the air and staggered toward the chaise. "I squabbled with father. He promised to curtail my privileges if I embarrassed him, behaved unladylike."

"And suitably so," Louise answered.

Josefina twisted a curl around her finger. "They ignored me at the Bank. High-hats. Behaved as if a pesky gnat had fluttered under their noses for all my significance. Thieves of honest wages, land pirates, that is how they will go down in history."

"Enough!" Louise ordered. "I will not allow such talk!" The natural blush and comeliness of her face had faded, leaving behind edges resembling a stonecutter's first chiseling. Sapphire eyes warred. "I will not tolerate your crudeness, such profane name-calling. Thieves? Pirates? Your Father is quite right about your erring behavior. I pray you obeyed him."

Josefina quickly sought a salve. "One gentleman promised to tell you how gracious I remained during such a common public display. He suggested I should feel crass, tainted by my appearance." A forlorn moan leaked out. "Humiliated and foolish is how I felt. Not by my presence, but by portraying the role of the addled woodenhead Father demanded."

With a forbidding look Louise stared her daughter down.

Josefina leaned her chin on her fists. "Father offered Louis the choice to enter the banking world. I understand Stuart's standing, considering his misdeeds. But not consider me? On top of that arranging a marriage without my yea or nay. Father treats me unfairly."

Louise primped, staring gloomily in the mirror; buffed nails probed a velvet case. "As long as you brought up fairness, your father requests that you wear the ruby tonight. His attachment to that stone goes beyond my understanding. I accepted the jewel as a wedding gift from François, never believing Father would demand I display it. My gold wedding band, within keeping of the Elders' approval, and permission to adorn myself with my mother's pearls or great-grandmother's scrimshaw in the company of outsiders, that's all I require."

Josefina slumped down onto her back and flopped her arm across her forehead.

A squawk rivaling a scalded hen pierced the air. "Josefina Louise, ladies do not sprawl! Posture... back straight, feet flat, hands tidy!" The mirror reflected a face aged and twisted with displeasure.

Ashamed, Josefina quickly righted herself. "I spent months scouring the periodicals of the fashion houses to alter your blue batiste so I might wear it. I already promised to accept a nosegay from Jacob that complements that dress." Josefina's peevishness increased. "He will feel embarrassed, knowing his favor ill-suited. He will think I hold no respect for his intentions."

"Do as Father requests. Bring down your celebrant white dress. Here, take the ruby." Setting the gem aside, Louise's attention wavered as she aligned the vanity set perfectly. "That young man certainly created a stir. Marianne appears sorely captivated. Such a shame. He shows no future."

"Oh, but he does. Jacob thrills everyone with tales of going West, exploring all the strange, exciting places, striking out whenever he chooses, testing his strengths against the land's challenges."

"One must. To avoid starvation and affliction."

"Living off the land, yes. But more rewarding sides exist, founding a town, the wonder of being free to control your future, perhaps finding gold." Josefina sighed. "Jacob will leave soon, for Santa Fe."

Her mother remained indifferent.

"François told me Jacob is the brightest man he ever hired," Josefina added in defense.

"François would say whatever he thought might please you. He is a most accommodating gentleman."

"Well, he did. And if I must turn over my inheritance to some unknown, barred from exercising any influence, I would be equally well off to flee West, like Jacob, and make my own way."

"Aaagh!" Louise's pain-filled screech pierced Josefina's self-pity. "Leave? Abandon me? Run off with an 'outsider'? For sinfulness and the poor house is what. I will not endure such ravings. Understand, Josefina, you are too young, too inexperienced to choose or dismiss. You will be content with your father's decision. Until that comes about, you will remain here, in this house."

Louise plopped down hard on the bench, her breath ragged and shallow. "Do not test your father's affections," she wheezed, "nor mine."

Josefina felt guilty, and a little afraid. Her selfish ranting had caused another of Mother's spells. Not a muscle of her body moved. She dared not breathe until Mother's tremors stopped.

Within minutes of her opposition being spent, the afflicted woman drifted to the armoire, her passage effortless. "Father knows these young men for what they truly are. He will do what is best for you. Your only duty is to show him respect. Never challenge him. I can promise you, you would live to regret it." Her child-sized fingers smoothed the cincher of the drab garment. "Later in life you will grow content enough with overseeing a fine household and providing children. Now go. Rest. Take the ruby."

Closing the door quietly behind her, Josefina headed for the attic stairs up to the wardrobe where the celebrant garments hung. *The white gown is woeful, childish, high-necked, long buttoned sleeves. It will need freshening, perhaps repair.* Josefina's foot paused, suspended above the first tread.

Jacob's feelings for her came ahead of his concern for any other, Josefina felt sure. *He must have shared immeasurably in my suffering today.*

She mused, unable to rid herself of the evil speculation that Marianne had orchestrated Jacob's invitation. Father's debacle provided a perfect opportunity for her friend, begging François's aid, to attempt to drive the sweethearts apart. Whether such betrayal had occurred or not, Josefina made her decision. *I will not test Jacob any further.*

She turned from the attic stairs. Back straight, hands tidy, Josefina entered her room. She plunked the ruby alongside the fashionably styled dress fanned across the bed, then lay down.

Father's back would be up, irritated by her choice of costume. François would hide his resentment at her wearing the prized jewel that she had never seen adorn Mother. Josefina closed her eyes, smiling in contentment. Unaware of the tensions swirling around him, Jacob would be pleased.

Five

Lights from a hundred lanterns played hide-and-seek along the tree-lined driveway leading to the entrance of François ducLaFevre's chateau. The flames flickered, unheeded by moths, June bugs, and white flies that ventured too near the flame, their dying sizzles uncelebrated by the noisy gathering.

Lines of red-coated servers, arms burdened with delicacies, dashed from the unattached summer kitchen, across the backyard, then disappeared through four tall veranda doors. The original path to the rear door began to develop arms where the matted grass shredded, then clung to the shoes of the waiters. Pans wiped clean, their subtle odors unable to record their former contents, began tilting in shoulder high towers alongside the outbuilding.

The great hall vibrated.

Josefina emptied her plate of the last morsel of spritzel and veal, leaving enough kale, potato, and beets to attest to good manners. Surprised she could eat, Josefina sat in amazement, loving it all, her eyes, nose, and ears absorbing every rite and subtlety of the opulent pageantry. Taylor County had never been the setting for such hedonistic and joyful celebration. Josefina had never experienced such extravagance, Christmas with a house overrun with relatives being her nearest comparison, and certainly she never heard tell of such immoderation ever occurring within shot of the Elders.

Laden tables creaked under the weight of wild duckling glazed with current-raisin sauce flecked with candied orange rind and fresh asparagus served alongside roasted pheasant and chestnut stuffed goose, trophies of the hunt enjoyed by the guests who had arrived early in the week. Butchers had sliced and sawed for weeks, smoking hams crusted with an ale-soaked mustard seed and maple sugar paste and boning pork chops to be stuffed with caraway weinkraut. Father sacrificed only one spring lamb, preferring to serve tender beef flooded with bock blood gravy. The guests dined with gusto.

When François took charge of hosting, simply because of the need to accommodate such a large assemblage, Mother's ease in coordinating preparations for the festivities surprised even Josefina. Since François cherished his bachelorhood and Marianne had not yet been "introduced", Mother served as hostess. Josefina hoped she took heart in the numerous compliments.

The gardens of Taylor Estates furnished tiny new potatoes and spring sugar peas. Mother had prayed over the plants in the hot house to produce the scarlet tomatoes. The vegetable cellar provided pickled watermelon rind, clove studded peaches, and cherry tomato chutney stewed with hot peppers and onion.

Around the table, eyes drooped with the satiation of overindulgence. Then, François paraded his heritage. After clearing the gold-rimmed plates, the waiters returned with delicacies from François's cold cellar. Carts shockingly overflowing with lemon and chocolate filled croissants, Napoleons, cherry topped cheesecakes, apple and peach tarts, fresh strawberries and cream, fruit sorbets, and Black Forest tortes sealed in dark chocolate ganache tempted the diners beyond reason.

Not to be outdone, Josef produced dozens of gold embossed boxes of Dutch chocolates. The guests shared the much-loved candies reluctantly, occasionally secreting a gold wrapped delicacy or two.

In ladylike fashion, Josefina left a small lump of pie plant, puzzled how anyone could not appreciate the rhubarb custard, then gazed down the long dining table. A barnyard hen among peacocks, her whirling mind-set stalled. Poverty and the frontier offered nothing to compare.

I want to live like this. She basked in the opulence that unfurled in the expansive room, platters sticky from imported fruits, tumblers slick with François's profanity of Chiquot champagne, exotic perfumes riding the smoke of candle fire. Unknown luxuries for Josefina, all diminished by the lavish costuming and coifing of the guests.

Up and down the table jewel-dyed silks, embroidered satins, shimmering brocades, and sheerest lawn glistened and rippled, their luster outperformed by the flash of gems and sheen of gold fingered and flaunted by the guests. Josefina smiled. The diners glowed like a rainbow of mortal jewels, mincing and sipping. Their chatter centered on how to spend the new wealth of the National Land Company.

Father had glowered when Josefina arrived at the chateau, but too many guests were present and, by then, it was too late. She had done her best to liven her blue dress. Jacob's favor of white roses and baby's breath looped with blue ribbon boosted her confidence, but these endeavors did not compare to the richness of the gowns around her. *One day, I, too, will swirl and tempt in like fashion.* Mother's ruby, however, rivaled any jewel at the table.

Josefina scanned past sixty settings of sparkling crystal and silver to a smaller, intimate table where mother's platinum head bobbed demurely. Identical as twins others said of the mother and daughter, but Josefina knew they saw only the outside. Mother's far set of rosebud lips parted in an engaging smile in response to something the Governor said. Louise Taylor was a natural hostess, beautiful but unassuming, nothing contrived, not humbugged by a sinful nature.

François sat alongside Mother, his green-gold eyes blank. His fingers tapped, then twirled the wine goblet. He fidgeted. His downcast eyes purposely avoided any contact.

Halfway down the long table, Marianne and Jacob leaned toward each other. Josefina could not tear her eyes away from them. Candlelight bounced golden glints off Jacob's shoulder-length chestnut hair, chiseled his angular jaw and prominent nose. His eyes were deep set, protected by full-feathered lashes. Against his white evening shirt Jacob's sun swept face and throat appeared bronzed, radiant, as magnificent as a native god. A yearning like Josefina had never believed existed swelled her heart. *The handsomest man I have ever seen. I will not lose him.* Josefina smiled, remembering. Jacob was a traveler who had stayed, seduced her with his levity, tantalized her with tales of adventure, then taunted her with his freedom to stay or go. Her eyes narrowed at the thought of his ease in leaving.

Jacob shifted toward Josefina, as if he sensed her watching, his mind tuned to hers. When his gaze met hers, then studied every inch of her from waist to temple, her stomach pitched and somersaulted with the spin of a capsizing schooner. Dampness beaded the flesh of her upper lip, her breasts tensed against sheerest lawn. Her breath stuck, hot, billowing in her throat. Sense of time, place and reason abandoned her.

~ * ~

The Secretary of State leaned forward across Josefina and quietly inquired of Josef. "Surely, Mr. Chairman, you anticipate repercussions from the issuance of these land bonds. On your word alone tens of thousands of citizens will risk their life savings without guarantee."

Josef frowned. "The fleeced lambs' cry be damned. It is the reason for their existence." Although his voice barely carried beyond himself and the Secretary, he assessed the attentiveness of the nearby guests, inwardly relieved no one had witnessed his cursing. Their stern community forbade profanity.

"We are righteous," Josef paused, "laboring in the name of all that is sacred and good, profiting in the name of the Almighty. We serve who stand in his stead. If these fools are not of our mind, they would be shorn anyway. Should we not be the ones to wield the knife? Petition my daughter, you agree as to her innocent nature?" At the answering nod, Josef continued. "She supports our position. Hear what she has to say."

The Secretary blotted traces of strawberries and cream off his mustache. "And just what are your thoughts, Miss Taylor?"

Josef saw that his daughter's interest stretched beyond the tight trio. A smile teased the corners of her mouth, and her eyes sparkled with dizzying brightness. "The Secretary asked a question." When he, too, was ignored, Josef traced her stare. A flush of heat swelled up his thick neck. "Josefina!" he barked.

Father's voice hung at the edge of Josefina's mind, nudging her. The imagined warmth of Jacob's sun-toasted hair brushing her throat in teasing wisps while he held her close blocked out all else. Suddenly the pointed toe of a boot whacked her ankle.

Josefina hastily turned to the man beside her. "My apologies, Mr. Secretary." She struggled to bring her attention back to the discussion at hand. "You took me by surprise." Her nose fought to ignore his sour breath, while her veiled eyes cast their charm at his bushy eyebrows. She would not allow a single line of her face to betray the silent threads of slander that stitched through her mind: *charlatan, traitor of public trust.* Aloud, she purred. "Would you mind repeating yourself?"

Warming to Josefina's interest, the object of her secret maligning preened like a peacock. An audible sigh caved in his sparrow-like chest. "Who could not respond to s-s-s-such a c-c-charming young lady?"

Josefina turned coyly from his stammering predicament to allow him time to gather his wits, using the moment to steal another peek down the table. The smile brightening her face disappeared. Her eyes clouded as if malice seeded a storm that gathered in full fury behind her pale lashes. Jacob's full attention centered once again on his dinner partner.

Josefina recovered her cheeriness and turned back to her companion, her gaze welcoming the Secretary's attention. "My Father and Monsieur ducLaFevre's banks command the world's respect. They control here and in Europe sufficient assets to support your proposed western land acquisitions. More importantly, their knowledge will reap profits a hundred times above what your investors envision." She leaned closer, batting her lashes. "I think you test me," she challenged.

As Josefina teased, her curiosity again strayed, eyes drawn to Jacob's calm, manicured hands erecting bridges of wafers on his companion's plate. A sigh escaped Josefina as his fingers manipulated the fragile delicacies. *How would he touch a woman?* Josefina wondered. *With the same gentleness, fingers teasing?* Or recklessly, like the eagerness she felt.

Marianne leaned into Jacob, her mouth gaped in open laugh, green eyes sparkling, dark full lashes fanning flirtatiously above blushed cheeks. Her crown of red hair seemed aglow with a disarming vivacity.

What a fool she makes of herself. Josefina struggled to cool the hot circles of anger that burnished her cheeks. *Surely, Marianne realizes Jacob chose me.* While Josefina watched, the conspirators' shoulders touched and remained, a cocoon of laughter isolating them from the gathering.

Josefina shifted on her chair, her body taut as if fitted out in battle armor. Under her breath she muttered a promise. "I will have him." In spite of Marianne's feelings, Father's objections, and mother's warnings.

Josef Taylor, although middle-aged, retained perfect hearing.

When Josefina rose and retrieved her nosegay, Josef dragged his chair backward on the thick rug, eyes riveted on her. Josefina guessed his intent, first the inattention, then the dress. Before Father could reprimand her imprudence, Dieter Vandemere bumped the older man's elbow.

"Lil' Jos," Dieter called, "come with me. I heard some astonishing tales." His growing reputation as town tattler appeared justified.

Josef stood, glowering, his elbows protruding sharp as a steer's horns. "We have important guests. Josefina has duties." Josef's body separated Josefina and the young apprentice, his voice menacing. "Do not disappointment me, daughter. Remember your charge. I have not indulged you to have my investment wasted."

Outwardly, Josefina appeared serene, her curtsey graceful, her bearing rigidly correct.

"Before you commit elsewhere," Dieter began, "may I sit with you during the performance later?" His question trailed after Josefina as she sailed past her father and halfway down the length of the long table. Her arrival came just in time to block Marianne and Jacob's exit.

Facing her best friend, Josefina kept her eyes leveled at the tall girl's emerald brooch, which she pretended to examine, and whispered through a fixed smile. "Jacob, meet me at the stable. After my duet with father." She nodded sweetly at Marianne. "You guard the path." At the unconcealed shock on Marianne's face, Josefina snapped, "must you be so priggish?" Curtsying regally to them both, Josefina hurried off to clasp the Secretary's offered arm. That, she affirmed, would most certainly take care of Marianne's silliness.

The guests rose slowly, the men assisting their dinner companions, claiming their feminine prize for the evening as the crowd fraternized with unrestrained gaiety. The huge dining hall easily accommodated two hundred people, although anyone familiar with local history could count on one hand the number of times the Chateau had welcomed more than a carriage full of visitors.

The banquet hall, originally designed as a ballroom, occupied a wing of the third floor. The guests had ascended on marble stairs whose garnet walls exhibited valued paintings. Heated discussions had erupted among the diners who debated the genius of the well-known Dutch solemnity of Weir, Pyle, and DeLand with the undisciplined experimentation of the displayed canvases of Degas, Manet, and the childlike disfigurement of Cézanne.

At the top of the stairs, the latter's artwork introduced a stained glass dome of such brilliance that every jewel of the earth appeared trapped overhead. A remarkable artistic endeavor accomplished by Mr. Luvres, famed worldwide. Framing these pieces, rubescent nudes languished on contrasting chalky cornices, their naked white bodies embellished with gold leaf. François ducLaFevre had indulged his every whim.

In the midst of these splendors, decked in a thick choker of pearls, their luster contested by her own pale skin, Louise Taylor led the guests from the festive dining hall to a more intimate music room below it. She gestured erratically as she chatted to the cluster surrounding her.

In the middle of a sentence Louise abruptly nodded at François walking beside her. "I know you too well, François. This shopping excursion to St. Louis shouts of your opportunity to orchestrate mischief. First you solicit me, promoting Marianne's fondest desire that Josefina accompany her for the debut. You knew marrying Jacob prohibited my 'coming out,' and I would not deny Josefina taking advantage." A fragmented hum accompanied the disjointed message. "As for your escorting the girls to St. Louis in two days, there is talk of ague, cholera and plague ravaging the city."

Several members of the party injected, "Yes! Yes! So we heard." A rotund gentleman announced, "like many others, our party circumvented St. Louis. Crossing upriver reaches Jefferson City equally well."

Louise talked over the interlopers, ignoring their support. "Equally troublesome, I feel very uneasy not providing a proper chaperone, even though Stuart's residence under my daughter-in-law's direction will provide proper guardianship. I shall continue to scour the countryside the next two days to find a suitable woman companion for the girls' trip."

"I am devoted to Josefina as I have always been devoted to you, Louise. You know I would never allow anyone else to harm her. I am bringing one of the women from here at my Chateau with us. I will see to the girls' protection."

Without warning Louise covered her cheeks with her hands. "Poor Dieter, and you, my adoring François." Her faint voice tinkled with distress. "We must all protest. Josefina is willful, but barely sixteen, too tender to undertake the strain of Father's proposed arrangement." Louise shook her shoulders as if ridding herself of a constraint. "But as Josef proposes," she murmured with an ethereal quality, "she will make a quite remarkable Baroness."

François's head snapped up. The muscles defining his jaws twitched and knotted, his ears bobbed.

Josef stepped up and hastily interrupted. "Dieter still needs years of apprenticeship before heading the bank. Besides," he laughed heartily, "Josefina is armed for wealthier game." He bowed as if to remove an imaginary top hat from his head in salute to his daughter.

Only Father's grandstanding reached Josefina. His mockery frustrated her; embarrassment flushed her face. Tightly reined indignation burned beneath her poise, forming clinkers of smoldering resentment, impossible to dislodge, slow to cool.

Must he crow so meanly of her, insinuating she stalked wealth with the appetite of some gold seeking guttersnipe? Josefina struggled not to speak her incendiary thoughts. *Hypocrite, you molded me to your liking. You have no complaint.* Her outrage flared, but not so quick as to miss Father's next warning.

"Any candidate will need to prove exceptional before I hand over Josefina." The sneering patriarch patted a bulge beneath his waistcoat. "Or, I will see to it, by my own hand, that he suffers a father's reckoning." The nearest guest involuntarily stepped back.

The coldly delivered threat did nothing to cool Josefina's temper or dampen the angry fire that banked within her.

Josefina moved among the guests, her voice lively with practiced interest, face alight with studied eagerness. But under the surface her mind stood on another path, the single lane leading to the stable.

While Josef and Josefina tuned their violins for the evening's announced recital, the convivial spark of Josef's eyes flattened. He pressed Josefina. "Finesse the Secretary. Extract a promise to invest more in our venture."

"I did." A smile swift as a drifting smoke ring lifted her lips. She had anticipated Father's need, as she so often did, and felt a notable satisfaction at having already accomplished his demand. "The Secretary said 'the plan appears worthy enough to invest additional funds.' But, he must first get approval."

"Then do more." Josef showed no pleasure in Josefina's foresight, upbraiding her at the level of a novice. "These land certificates require massive investment. Our bank stands insufferably indebted. More government monies must be obtained to ease our financial strain."

Josefina fidgeted under the potency of his dressing-down.

"When foolish adventurers, like your Mr. Broderick, become impoverished, we will have siphoned off all their funds and still own the land. Concentrate your girlish yearnings elsewhere. Do not chance making a fool of me, or I would be forced to curtail your freedoms." Father glowered at her. "I will withdraw your much anticipated celebratory season." Smoothly he turned away, nodding to the prestigious gathering. Josef's smile addressed only the waiting audience.

Josefina stepped up next to Father, violin poised. When the bows crossed the strings, enchanting melodies floated throughout the room.

Tears dampened many eyes. Eventually the music began to ease even Josefina's seething soul. *Why,* she mused, *only with the violin do I ever come near meeting Father's expectations?* A melancholy as leaden as wet sand weighted her, the burdensome ache enhancing the plaintive notes.

An hour later, the duets completed, Josefina dispatched the fawning Dieter for fruit punch. After he disappeared into the crowd, she sidled out the music room doors and hurried toward the stables. Along the way, the despair kindled by her father's slights evaporated, as easily as water boiled over a flame.

Six

When the violins' haunting notes stopped, Marianne stood at the library window staring out into the darkness. Tears washed down her face, their salt tweaking the tip of her tongue. *I have never in my life known such a friend. I treasure Josefina. But, I will have Jacob for my own.*

Marianne remembered when he had stood alone on the stone veranda of this very chateau, waiting for François to receive him. The handsome wanderer presented less than impressive credentials, but had a winning way. She had desired him from that very moment.

She stood in François's stead and welcomed Jacob, then set out to win his heart. François, at her pleading, found "a project worthy of Jacob's talents." Additionally Marianne extracted François's promise to "employ Jacob as long as it took for her to win the young engineer's heart."

She needed not waste time worrying. François had not denied her a single request since her arrival from France two years ago. They had not known each other in her childhood, and he worked faithfully to make up for this void. To redeem his soul, he explained.

While Marianne watched, a figure approached the flickering lanterns. Bypassing the softly lit footpaths, Josefina darted through the rose garden. Giving a defiant sniffle, Marianne turned away, anxious to return to the gathering and find help. François would unleash a way for her to capture Jacob.

Moments after Marianne left the window, a second dark form paused outside in the dancing shadows, to all appearances expecting someone, then veered furtively down the path bordering the rose garden.

~ * ~

Josefina neared the stables. A full moon outlined Jacob's boxy shoulders and bold profile as he lounged against the building. The sight of him patiently waiting sent her heart skipping.

"Here," Jacob reached out, "let me help you step inside."

Their fingers touched, sending ripples of pleasure through Josefina. When Jacob guided her through to the other side by a possessive grip on her waist, the press of his hand fanned Josefina's maidenly fancy into desire.

The rattle of the latch under the fallen weight of the wooden beam startled Josefina. She looked back to see Jacob wedge a rake beneath the bar to warn of tampering.

Holding tightly to Josefina's hand, Jacob picked his way across the paddock using the ghostly glow of a well-placed oil lamp.

Grasping Josefina by the waist, Jacob lifted her high in the air, twirled toward the open door of a vacant stall then fell with her down onto fresh smelling straw. The weight of their bodies smashed a trough in the layered stalks. Josefina felt as heady as if she had drunk pitchers of François's forbidden champagne.

Sharp stubs snagged her dress and pricked her skin leaving scratches Josefina blissfully ignored. Jacob hovered over her for an instant, then slowly lowered his body alongside hers. The musk of wintered stalks vanished when his distinctive male scent filled her senses. Josefina sat up quickly.

Jacob sat up, brought her hands to his lips, kissing first the palms, then the tip of each finger. His chin nuzzled her neck, before he traced her cheek with slow pecks that felt cool on her hot flesh. Swift nibbles sweetened the corners of her lips before Jacob kissed her fully, with a fervor Josefina had never imagined, a heartfelt telling of need.

Bathed in the lamplight, Jacob's amber eyes extended an invitation that beckoned Josefina, their bottomless depths baring a passion that appeared endless. Josefina responded involuntarily, her kiss releasing a hunger that responded to his.

"You are the most bewitching girl I ever met." Jacob's voice was breathless. "There is no one in the world I desire more." One arm cradled Josefina while he lowered her, and nimble fingers flicked open the buttons of her gown.

The neckline scrunched down, exposing shadowed cleavage. Jacob moaned, his breath warming her bared flesh, flaming her body into a fire of its own. A hot wave flowed beneath her chemise, across her breasts, then ignited the secret niches of her belly.

Josefina murmured, "My heart is yours, my love." Her voice sounded foreign, husky, of another world. "We will marry. First, you must prove to Father you are worthy."

"First," Jacob sank into her, the stubble of his face scraping her neck, "this." His gentle kisses roamed over every exposed pore of Josefina's body. Currents of anticipation raced up from the hollow behind her knees, sailing past her hips, settling into the basin of her body.

When the chemise bodice broke free, gooseflesh prickled her half-bared breasts. Josefina felt she would explode from impatience. Jacob's lips and tongue caressed the revealed flesh while her body simmered in wakening passion. "Father found a husband for me."

Jacob continued his pursuit. "Forget him," Jacob whispered. "Come with me. To the gold fields. We will make our own place in the world. Somewhere we can be everything we want to be." Jacob tugged Josefina closer, allowing her barely air to breathe.

"Father would track us to the ends of the earth, then ruin us." Josefina pulled away. "A few days after I leave for St. Louis, go to him." Gasps fleeting as butterfly wings punctuated the urging. "Promise to act honorably, ask for my hand."

"You know he will never accept me." Jacob's tone became terse. His legs fought the layers of petticoats between them.

Josefina writhed beneath Jacob's weight, her voice trembling. "You must present your intent."

"Your Father broadcasts his warning at every turn. My ordinary wage is not 'worthy,' and beyond that I have only my love of adventure to offer, and your freedom." Jacob's kisses increased in urgency. "The man gives us no choice. We will leave, regardless. I will show you how to live off the land, carry all you need in a knapsack. Our days and nights ruled by our passion." Jacob kissed her long, full, a temptation beyond Josefina's reason. His hands fumbled beneath the petticoats. "Come, seal our love now."

Floundering in the desire firing her body, Josefina feared Jacob spoke one truth. Father would not listen, would never allow them to marry. "The cartel? You could solicit..."

"He would never allow me a proper position. I would be treated as a foundling." Jacob's irritation showed. "Fed scraps. Besides, I want to make my own way. Easing the way for others to do what I dream of? Josefina, you know I could never endure that."

Jacob's powerful hands gripped Josefina with increasing urgency, inviting the fulfillment she imagined for so long. Her wantonness flooded her, more powerful than rain eroding a dam, tearing down her inhibition. Jacob's insistent lips caressed her flesh, each kiss drawing her in, the torment heavenly. "What of our future?"

"A contract awaits me in St. Louis. My work can provide for us. Not with luxury. But, you can rest assured, I will take proper care of you." Pink welts trailed down Josefina's chest. "While you are away, I will promote my skills across the country. When you return I will have everything readied for us to leave."

"How can I abandon my mother when she is so ill?" Then, Josefina dared ask. "What if Father disinherits me, disowns me?" She feared the question. For all the confidence she bandied about, what if Jacob considered Father's fortune part of her charm? She wanted to tell Jacob how she loved him, but it was not "their" way to speak of love, except where it concerned church doctrine.

"My work on François's hotel is nearly completed. You must choose. By the time you return, I will be ready to leave. I must, with or without you. I will not abandon my dreams to remain in this stifling place."

Josefina's fingers toyed with the lushness of his chestnut hair where it feathered across her shoulders and trickled into the dusk of her cleavage. Shivers rippled across her partially hidden breasts then swelled into a flush that filled her body.

"Think, my lovely," Jacob said. "We will be free. Living our lives as we please, without the censure of others. One day we will claim enough gold to live in the manner we both want."

Josefina's vigilance faltered when Jacob addressed her weaknesses. "See Father," Josefina murmured. "I will find the means for us to go West in style now." She had no idea how, but the unreasonableness of the vow fled her mind as she gave in to the desire sweeping over her.

Beneath four petticoats the ties of her bloomers loosened. Jacob's fingers trailed gossamer strokes across her bottom, then feathered slowly up the inner tenderness of her thighs. Her legs parted of their own accord while quivers raced up from her toes and gathered like honey bees swarming beneath his touch.

Strong jostling felled the bar holding the latch. The rake handle snapped; the door slid open, its rasp lost to the lovers. Footsteps entered, one, two, three, then stopped. Moonlight glazed the tangled bodies for an instant before the footsteps retreated. The door closed.

Dieter's feet pounded clefts in the path as he tromped away. Both hands clenched, his fists longed for a target. Josefina had failed him. Dieter knew his spying had passed unnoticed. The secret of the lover's tryst would be his—until he had need of it.

~ * ~

Josefina's fears gave way to an appetite that saw only the mirrored urgency of Jacob's eyes, the longing of a besotted man who desired her. She ran her fingers down his arms, kneading the powerful muscles that waxed and waned as Jacob struggled with his clothing, her only concern tuned to the frantic need she felt. No one had ever loved as much.

A second dusting of moonbeams shimmered across Josefina's slack dress for a brief moment before a long silhouette darkened the paddock. "Lil Jos, are you there?" Marianne whispered. The shadowy form moved closer.

"Go away," Josefina said. The lovers scampered apart.

"Hurry! Now!" Marianne warned, "Someone comes. I think eez your Poppa." Her slippers shuffled softly like the crushing of dried leaves as Marianne stepped back outside. The stable door stayed ajar.

Jacob rolled away from Josefina.

"Quickly," Josefina prodded. "Father stands ready-armed always. He will kill you."

"Leaving you is impossible." Jacob rolled back to face her. "I cannot wait. We must go. Tonight." The tips of his fingers teased at her breasts while she struggled to pull up her dress.

"Father would hunt us down, if only to salvage his pride. Then he would cast me out, disown me." Josefina ached to feel Jacob's touch where no other had been. She wanted to lie to herself, accept a future of deprivation but filled with passion.

"Come with me tonight. Your father thinks of you on the same rung as his mares. He will auction you off to the highest bidder."

The bite of Jacob's words stung Josefina with their truthfulness. "I cannot dishonor him," Josefina persisted. "The public shame would kill him, and me." Her lips formed a soft, moist kiss before she hurried out the door.

Josefina rushed alone up the path to the house, fanning the frothy yards of blue skirting to dislodge the clinging debris. Picking the last stubs of straw from her hair, she slipped in the side door, blending with the meandering guests.

~ * ~

François, surrounded by a circle of women, stood slightly off to the side of the door. In a single glance he apprised Josefina's state, the rumpled dress and flushed cheeks. He raised his voice and began loudly repeating an age-old dictum.

"I swore not to marry until I found a wife as exquisite as the woman Josef won. I fear I may never find another." François's voice grew more persistent, louder, drawing attention to him. He blocked the guests' view of Josefina. The girl had raised many a hubbub with her feisty conduct, but he would not allow gossip of loose morals to sully her reputation.

"Before you stands one of the richest men in the country." François threw back his head and cackled. "Some prudent Miss may have to sacrifice herself." The maids swarming around him fluttered and cooed, nudging each other aside for a better position of notice. "My years close quickly. I must choose soon." The answering squeals and bumping elbows successfully drew attention from Josefina who busily adjusted petticoats and straightened combs while François watched and waited.

Carefully, Josefina stepped from behind the circle, her eyes scanning the room. She sauntered up to the lanky man. "François, have you seen mother?"

"Your father went looking for Dieter to take her home. She was not feeling well." François stepped closer, studying her.

"Dieter took mother to Taylor Estates?" Josefina was distraught. "I was afraid mother would not be well enough to stay. I should have been here to go with her."

"No one could find Dieter. Louis took her." Leaning down, François lowered his voice. "Have you seen Jacob and Marianne?"

"Marianne and I took a stroll. The night is beautiful. She is still out in the garden. I have no idea of Jacob's whereabouts."

The lie darkened Josefina's sapphire eyes to an inky blue, a telltale sign François had learned to recognize since her infancy. *So, she feels compelled to deceive to me.* Marianne had told him of Josefina's order. The anger he buried so well lay hidden smugly under the satisfaction of his plans. *Well, Josefina, enjoy. You have seen the last of Jacob Broderick.*

"Thank you, François, for your help," Josefina said smiling. "Please, excuse me. I must find Father and see if he needs me." Josefina walked away, then suddenly turned back and studied François. Her eyes narrowed. Tiny teeth nipped the edge of her swollen lips while she slowly wandered away, her fingers tugging a platinum curl.

François dismissed his eager admirers. His attention focused on the troubled cornflower eyes that had turned away. His evening was over.

~ * ~

After Josefina rushed away, Jacob lay still on the straw, his young body aching from longing. Josef Taylor would never grant his permission. Even so, Jacob would keep his word, do as promised. When that failed, he would have arrangements completed for Josefina to join him by whatever means available.

Josefina's beauty rose beyond any he had ever enjoyed, but her honesty and trusting way set her further above others and had won his heart. Josef Taylor humored Josefina, objecting to her self-mindedness and freewill, the same attributes Jacob admired at length. Her life at Taylor Estates demanded responsibilities, but only minor endeavors a refined lady need know. He wondered how she would fare on the rough trails.

Jacob stepped from the stable's shadows into the starlit night. A cough startled him. Marianne stood waiting in the darkness. Jacob offered his arm. "May I escort you to the house?"

Marianne leaned into his body and wrapped both arms cozily around his. "A stroll, perhaps? The evening eez too beautiful. Give 'Lil Jos' time to be seen. Besides, I wish to hear more of California. Perhaps I could approach François to guarantee employment for you along your travels."

Jacob admitted a tenderness toward his companion he had not realized he felt. He had known from the beginning she cared for him, and he appreciated a warrior who gave up a losing battle graciously.

Marianne sighed, nuzzling her head in the crook of Jacob's neck. "I, too, love to travel. My sailing from France was exciting, but I have not yet gone beyond St. Louis, and I am dying to see more of this wild country. So tell me, where eez theez place you wish to see?"

~ * ~

Josefina lay in bed, touching her face, breast, and shoulders where Jacob's kisses had caressed her flesh. The heat of that moment crawled through her body, warming her with desire. The smell of a stable, the whinnies of horses, the uneven flame of lantern light would always remind her of Jacob and this night. She slept with the confidence of a reigning queen.

Seven

Two days after the sumptuous banquet, the gray light of dawn silhouetted the horizon when Josefina, Marianne, and François rumbled down the lane in an opulent coach. A thin, fair-haired old woman sat next to the red-coated man on the driver's seat. François did not bother to introduce her. Josefina speculated the stranger was to serve as chaperone.

Although consumed with excitement about exploring St. Louis to choose finery previously denied her, Josefina still watched eagerly behind them as their vehicle lumbered away. She had not seen Jacob since their clandestine meeting in the stable. She had hoped he would make a special effort to say good-bye, especially since this shopping trip would last at least a month.

At the head of the lane, as she looked back, the mansion of Taylor Estates appeared lonely in its abandonment. Fronting the house, adding diversion from a lush lawn, empty paths wound through colorful beds of roses. Father preferred the scattered red blooms, rich as freshly drawn blood. Mother partitioned her favorites, baby cheek pinks, corals bright as a robin's breast, whites pure as milk glass. Their subtle perfume fought to command notice over the smell of freshly mown grass, the bouquet of emerging corn, and the "black gold" of the stables. As the carriage sped away, the gardens cascaded into perfect symmetrical swipes of color. *Just as the inhabitants,* Josefina thought, *not a single bud dares venture from the rigid pattern of Father's design.*

Josefina rode facing the mansion. Her arm held the waxed rawhide curtain from the window while her eyes searched the grounds for signs of Jacob, but the coach had gone too far. The mist of the waking morning's labors shrouded any form beyond the end of the lane. A heavy sigh accompanied the drooping of her shoulders when Josefina realized Jacob would not come.

They had not seen each other since that blissful night in the stables. He had eluded her. She had searched daily, going so far as to invent excuses to visit the hotel worksite and dawdle with Marianne over packing at the chateau last night nearing evening meal time. She yearned for Jacob and wanted desperately to hear his voice, to be near him when he reaffirmed his promise, and to kiss him good-bye. Perhaps, she considered, she should pretend to be ill and stay behind today. But bearing in mind the hundred or more who had died in Tennessee last week from the fever, such playacting would be a cruel infliction on her family.

Perhaps, though, Jacob was wiser and had made the right decision; to flaunt their love too soon would invite opposition.

On the other side of the carriage, Marianne sat quietly, almost sullen, her body rigid. Josefina speculated her corset was bound too tight. François dozed on and off, with the ease of a man accustomed to bumpy rides, able to place his safety in the hands of the driver.

The three passengers had traveled for several hours when Josefina suddenly patted the bench beside her. "François, come sit next to me. I spent two fitful nights and need a sound pillow. Your shoulder might provide me with a small square of comfort."

François shifted from one seat to the other. His arm spread across the top of the bench, his fingers splaying Josefina's platinum curls. "Do you always get what you want, little one?"

"Is there another way?" In spite of Jacob's absence, Josefina felt too expectant to be offended.

"Life will not always come to you so easily." François seemed pleased by her spoiled acceptance, mocking her.

"Why not?" Josefina leaned away from the seat back, looking up to observe her companion. She needed to see his shock if he thought ill of her. "Tell me, how does a lady obtain funds of her very own?

Enough to feel secure, to be free to do as she pleases?" She settled back, just far enough away to easily read François's face.

He smiled, a seldom genuine event. "That would clearly depend on the woman and the degree of her love of luxury. A loan, perhaps, a maid might marry wealthy, a matron would sell her jewels. Not many options for most."

"What would your answer be, François, if that woman were me? Would you loan against my future inheritance? And what if, in the end, that legacy might possibly not be forthcoming?"

"Your collateral would have to be highly valued. Very dear indeed. I shall have to think on it."

~ * ~

Two days later, the coach entered St. Louis and turned north, causing Josefina to scold. "Stop the driver. He is obviously lost. This street does not lead to my brother's. Stuart lives much further south." An unnerving apprehension floated like a feather in the hollow of Josefina's chest, its tickle annoying.

"My orders," François explained. "I took a townhouse more suitable to our station. Stuart's ill-gotten reputation need not taint the contacts we develop during our stay." He flitted his gloves at the tip of Josefina's upturned nose. "Besides, we will be much too engaged for his modest household. I have made plans to provide every avenue for my charges in their quest for womanliness."

Josefina hugged her body in anticipation. As the carriage sped along, her apprehension quieted by François's explanation, she wallowed in fantasies of more fancy dinners and an armoire crammed with beautiful gowns. Josefina loved the obscene display of riches, the gluttony of wealth, and thought the Elder's barring of such splendors unreasonable. Her father's dour insistence that the family maintain an austere position in keeping with the community wore like an iron collar and cuff on her.

Mandatory presence at church services three times a week, daily prayer circles, weekly attendance at dull bank reviews at which she was not allowed to give an opinion, classes in languages, finance, history, and law. None of these tedious hours spent of her choosing. She had thrilled at François's vulgar display of riches at the banquet, whereas Father commanded they not divulge the extent the sect's rules had been violated. A life corrupted by such merriment and laughter, the showy indulgence of aristocracy, seeded Josefina's thoughts day and night. But, she wanted Jacob, too—hopefully, not with her life crammed in a knapsack.

~ * ~

The afternoon following their arrival, François escorted the girls to a private shop. "Madame Saugveau, my charges wish gowns to transport them from young ladies to women at the wearing." He touched his finger to the tip of Josefina's nose. "My sister knows what is befitting. This one I discussed with you before. You made some suggestions, and, I presume, followed through with my requests?"

"*Mais oui,* the creations left France many weeks ago. But, we have others here to consider. Please, look about."

Josefina danced in her skin. The shopkeeper's conversation sounded so mysterious, and it certainly pertained to her. She was about to inquire when François disappeared into the attendant's lounge.

The dress on the saleswoman draped and hugged her frame like nothing Josefina had ever seen. The lavender fabric was unadorned, yet shimmered and flowed in a manner that accented the woman's delicacy.

"May I help you make a selection?" When the woman came from behind the counter, Josefina was astonished to see she wore no hoops. The bustle was, in fact, a simple darting and gathering to accent a naturally plump derriere.

The woman brought out azure blue lawn that captured the freshness of a sunlit sky. "I will take this," giggled Josefina. "Perfect for an early fall picnic." A bolt of linen invited Josefina to finger embroidered blooms of such magnificence only the absence of fragrance revealed their falseness. "What do you think, Marianne, too colorful? This would certainly brighten any Bank's boardroom." Josefina regretted her reference to the lost aspiration.

Marianne glanced at the cloth unfolded on the worktable. "Too heavy. Weigh your petite frame down worse than a monk's robe."

Spotting a cerulean silk, Josefina hurried to the bolt. "Look, Marianne, fit for a goddess." Josefina spread the few feet of loose fabric across her chest. "My Dutch sister's would have apoplexy."

Precariously stacked bolts of fabric tumbled onto the floor in colorful chaos. Josefina did not move as the silk unrolled. Truly, the cloth appeared richer. She stepped to a mirror and held the blue against her pale complexion, her restless eyes reflecting its liveliness. Surrendering her choice to the shopkeeper, Josefina admired a stack of pastel eyelets.

Marianne picked up somber fabrics, testing their weight, holding lengths against her tall frame, selecting moderate to midnight shades of melon, wines and greens. The sun turned a russet velvet of short nap into a shimmering coppery pool. "What do you think? For evening dinner parties? Most of our season will occur during the cold of winter."

Josefina ran her fingers over the sensual pile and nodded with enthusiastic agreement, abandoning the pastels and eyelet.

A matte satin of embossed ivory invited Marianne's test. The shopkeeper produced a cheesecloth sample of a design of simple lines. Its chapel train would barely swish when the adorned walked, which pleased Marianne with the simplicity. Similar suggestions emphasized the same fluid lines, no ruffle or fluff to distract, only sumptuous fabric and clear color to announce richness and modesty.

For three consecutive days François bustled his charges from shop to shop. The imposing escort appeared on familiar terms with the shopkeepers, which astounded Josefina, and Marianne more so.

On the third day Josefina lamented, "I will never find something special for the coronation. Marianne has already had a fitting."

"Be patient, little one." François patted her head. "Plenty of time still. We must not settle for anything less than the spectacular entrance you deserve."

Later that same day, charmed by François's interest, a seamstress wheeled out a bolt from a private room reserved for established clientele. Gossamer silk shimmering with unearthly blue-white starlight unfolded, sporadically adorned with a barely discernable splash of pinhead-sized crystals and pearls. Sparkles danced in

Josefina's eyes. She had never seen anything so lovely and dramatic, yet dainty. Before Josefina could speak, the saleswoman produced a drawing of her recommended design.

Long sleeved with a deep décolleté stopping at a tightly cinched waist in the front, the sketch showed a flat skirt topped by a separate panel that swished free as angel wings in the back. Josefina had never seen a gown so beautiful, and daring, in all her searching.

François pounced on it immediately. "Exquisite. I will buy the entire lot. This is to be an exclusive."

The seamstress simpered. "Absolutely, as you wish."

François began issuing orders. "Design a brocade for tea, a subtle fabric, nothing dowager looking. Her tiny stature requires a walking suit of elegance. Something soft that brings attention to her regal bearing. Perhaps in a blush."

Josefina groaned. "You know I dislike pink, roses, washed-out, lame colors." A navy or black would be more suitable for the bank were she to ever gain entrance to their hollowed walls.

François continued as if she had not spoken. "She will need a warm, fur-lined coat. Lastly, a sapphire blue velvet gown, sumptuous, for nighttime events. A featherweight cloth. And a matching cloak. Specifically, nothing voluminous or too heavy."

He turned to his young companion. "One 'lame color' to call attention to your flawless skin seems little enough sacrifice. And, we must not offend your Elders too soundly if you are to save anything from your celebration. Come, enough for today."

When they left, Josefina's head was spinning; she did not feel the floor beneath her feet. Father would throw a tirade seeing all this sinfulness.

At Ledyard's, a nearby outdoor café, François remarked to his sister, "The shopping seems to have overly tired you. I suggest we linger over our lemonades, watch the people promenade."

On their return ride, Josefina could not remember if she tasted of her drink or not. After they entered the townhouse, she realized Marianne had said nothing of her own selections.

For two days the girls squirmed and squeezed into pinned and tacked gowns. Josefina had not owned as many dresses at one time ever, perhaps altogether in her entire life. The very thought was more than she could absorb.

As the two prepared to leave for yet another fitting, Marianne complained. "*Mon Dieux*, my head eez like a battlefield. 'Lil Jos,' I think you must go alone."

"Not today," Josefina protested. "The dressmaker promised a peek at our competitors' coronation gowns." Her lower lip extended in an exaggerated pout.

"I feel I might faint right here at zee table." Bright red splotches burnished Marianne's high cheekbones. She appeared to be fighting to stay conscious when her glazed eyes grew alarmingly fixed. Josefina jumped up and dashed around the table, then brushed Marianne's forehead with her palm. "You have a fever. Up to bed with you." Josefina called loudly for the chaperone eating in the kitchen. The woman was mute and had poor hearing. "Bring cloths and a crock of cool water."

Josefina studied her friend, dabbing Marianne's face with a napkin cooled with water, then gently patting it dry. Josefina spoke softly. "I will stay with you. You cannot be left by yourself."

"No, please, we look forward to this for a year, besides I will not be alone." Marianne's voice first sounded angry, then she gently pleaded. "Go without me. Do not make me feel zee worse for spoiling your day. Tell me of your venture tonight. Your stories are more entertaining than what ah'pens anyway." Marianne's voice sunk lower. "I have many here to care for me. I just need zee rest."

The chaperone arrived with wet towels and a full basin. "Go, go. You can see I am well cared for. Call François to accompany you."

"Your brother does not need to escort me; I am quite capable of finding my way. Besides, he works much too hard to waste time on my boring fittings." Josefina's tone first sounded sharp, then kinder. "You are sure you do not mind? I could stay, read to you. Watch over you while you sleep." Her reluctance overshadowed her attempt at sincerity.

Marianne tried to shake her head, but clung instead to the edge of the table. "Have one of zee serving girls go with me upstairs." She pecked her friend on the cheek. "I will be all right. Come wake me zee minute you return."

"I do hope your malaise leaves quickly." Before Marianne disappeared around the stairway arch, Josefina marched to the hall mirror and adjusted a straw boater on her curls. "I am sorry you will miss today, we have so much yet to see. I promise to come back early, filled with delightful tales."

An extended palm offered a hastily blown kiss as Josefina stepped out the door.

~ * ~

Josefina had fully intended on returning directly back to the townhouse. However, a gauzy yellow sky foretelling the end of the hot, humid day crept up the windows before she flounced in through the front door. In the dining hall, a girl-in-waiting held a single clean plate in her hand and was removing the remaining unused set of silver lying on the table. François, chin resting on clenched fists, sat hunched over at the head of the long table.

With the bang of the foyer door closing, François sat up straight and watched Josefina enter. "You stayed away so long I sent a runner to search for you. I feared, like my sister, you had collapsed." A sputter escaped when he sighed. "The boy found you, safe, and well occupied." Sarcasm failed to mask his concern.

"I am sorry." Josefina pouted prettily. "There are so many things to do. So much to see."

"Speaking with strangers at a sidewalk café? And the boardwalk? Your reputation suffers." The sternness in his voice failed to reach his eyes.

So, François had spied on her. But, he spoke the truth. The unprecedented freedom had carried her away; word of her unchaperoned adventure would demand severe condemnation from Father. Josefina rushed to François's side and bussed his cheek, hoping to distract his displeasure and lighten his bad temper. "How is Marianne?"

"The doctor arrived a few hours after you left. He promised to return later tonight."

"Is she that ill?" Josefina frowned, feeling miserable about her inattention. If a doctor had been called? She remembered her promise to Marianne. "I am truly sorry to have wandered. Especially to have worried you so. I will sit with her. Shall I take up some soup?"

"The service girls tempted her with every morsel in the house. We even sent to the market for fruit. It was closed." François's eyelids shut, then scrunched tightly, as if to ward off some upsetting thought. "Marianne carries an unnaturally high fever. The doctor diagnosed her illness as quite serious." François opened his eyes.

Josefina saw his pain and could not hide her distress. She went to his side.

François tensed. "Whatever this sickness is, be assured I will get the best of care for all of us."

"All of us?" Fear deflated Josefina's irritation at the likelihood of missing their anticipated amusements. Before she could think sensibly, a rewarding possibility slipped into her thoughts, home to Jacob. Perhaps the doctor would order their return immediately. A smile tipped up the corners of her lips.

"You find Marianne's plight amusing?" François's eyes narrowed as they watched, his jaws flexed.

Concentrating on a vision of Jacob, the question momentarily startled Josefina. "I was thinking of someone else, at home."

The crinkles at the corners of François's eyes deepened into barbed slits seconds before he strode from the room. Each thud of his footsteps thundered as he climbed the stairs, two at a time, to the bedrooms above.

~ * ~

Late that night, in Marianne's bedroom, an officious mannered man snapped a black bag shut and wiped his brow. "Fifty died today. Twenty yesterday, I expect more tomorrow." His tired voice droned. "The sheriff will tack a quarantine notice on your door which will be strictly enforced. I will arrange for food to be left on the doorstep. Keep a sharp eye out, the street urchins will steal anything that is not brought in at once. Who else stays here?"

"All the servants, except the woman in my employ, disappeared after dinner," François replied. "Now, just myself and another young lady remain."

"Is either one capable of caring for the sick girl? I may be able to arrange for an attendant to come a few hours each morning, but all reliable help is committed."

"You need not trouble yourself. The woman experienced the French-Austrian war." François shook his head, his voice confidant. "Besides, I always find the means to get whatever I want." Then his assurance faltered. "How long might our confinement last?"

"A minimum of thirty days for the quarantine. For your sister, much longer before her strength returns enough for her to travel. Even so short a distance." The young doctor rubbed his purple shadowed eyes. "I will return as often as possible, but the epidemic has touched every house. Five hundred died in Tennessee. The constable sealed off our entire city just before nightfall."

"Thank you. Your services are most appreciated." François's eyes glazed like polished stone. "You have, then, officially quarantined us. Only your staff is allowed to enter?" At the doctor's nod of agreement, François dismissed him. "Please, be kind enough to let yourself out."

François chaffed Marianne's hands while he perched alongside her on the bed. His parents had trusted her to his care while they sought invalidation of a contract arranging her marriage to an older man, a spendthrift neighbor of nominal sobriety who sought only her dowry. When Marianne became smitten with Jacob, her quick affection surprised François. He had wished her well and helped in whatever manner he could. But then, like most people, Marianne had underestimated Josefina.

He spoiled Marianne too much, giving in to her slightest whim. He had not been there for Marianne's birth, her growing years. Banned as he was from ever returning to his homeland. In truth he had no desire to share in the domesticity of child rearing, but now he felt regret that he'd had no part in her history.

The two years she had lived at La Chateau with him had pleased him immensely; the time passing too quickly. Like Josef and Josefina, father and daughter, Marianne's likes and dislikes mirrored his own, giving him all the more reason for the remorse he suffered now.

François remained by her side for nearly an hour before returning downstairs to tell Josefina the news. The promise of a month, and probably more, locked together in the house only served to solidify his decision. His footsteps dragged under the weight of Marianne's burden, but a flicker of eagerness sparked the emptiness of his heart.

Eight

Nine days confined. Josefina swiped at the hairs damping her forehead and flung herself onto the window seat, feeling impatient and irritable. Marianne's green ribbon fit nicely tied around the frizzy curls, pulling her hot hair away from her face and off her neck, but the updo was not the stylish pompadour she had envisioned. Josefina brooded, her dreams of banquets and fancy dress abandoned.

Why had François not yet announced dinner? She heard him fussing around downstairs. The food basket generally arrived at five, but the clock showed after six. She had cleared the dining table immediately after the midday meal and reset it, just to have something to do, everything readied in answer to François's request they maintain a semblance of social dignity.

However, the question of which irked her more, the heat or the quarantine, did not baffle Josefina. Definitely the confinement.

Not hungry for food, rather famished for companionship, Josefina watched out the window endlessly, hopeful of recognizing someone. Gratefulness for the anticipated meatless stew and dried up biscuits would not come. She starved, not for sustenance, but for diversion, for people. All of Marianne's acquaintances had undoubtedly already escaped north to Lake Geneva or east to the Adirondacks and the frosty Canadian waters, at minimum to St. Charles summer retreats. Josefina knew absolutely there had never been a worse time to be in St. Louis, and although the fever and trauma had grown no worse, Marianne lay as if in a trance, showing no signs of improvement.

Empty days. Josefina read and reread tedious books on electricity, the wireless, railroads and phrenology, and learned to gracefully lose games of chess to François. He always won, taking full advantage of his use of the pawn, steadily moving it one square at a time in whichever direction he chose, forcing her to react. She tended to rush to seek advantages and lost.

Too many days trapped in this stifling house, each longer and drearier than the previous. She left the window to go downstairs with her letters. Scratching notes to Mother and composing furtively conveyed letters to Jacob offered her only opportunity for pleasure. *First time free of Father and The Elders and this happens.* Resentful, Josefina stewed.

If I could only return home to Jacob. Not one letter had arrived. No word came of Jacob's discussion with Father, or of Father's answer.

The thought of Jacob warmed her blood. Josefina closed her eyes, smelling his scent, hearing his voice. She imagined the night air, the stable, chestnut hair, hooded amber eyes bottomless with desire. She felt him stroke her arm. Bold tingles traveled from neck to knee in repetitious waves like pepper red poppies caressed by a sunny breeze.

Suddenly, thumps and bangs exploded from the foyer, startling Josefina out of her musing. She listened apprehensively. A thief, a madman crazed by fever? Few people moved about the streets any time of day, and this late, only carts piled high with bodies passed. The inns had closed, the sparse food guarded, water restricted. People huddled in their houses.

Loud thuds, crashes and cursing interspersed with unintelligible French mutterings bawled from the floor below her. Frightened by the clamor, Josefina jumped up and took a position at the balustrade to get a good look at the entry.

François wrestled a wooden cabinet almost as tall as he through the doorway, his brown hair clumped in tangles. Moth-like flutters of laughter slipped from Josefina's throat at the sight. His slight frame, bent under the weight of the ponderous article, seemed in danger of losing the battle.

When Josefina's giggles reached him, François looked up, amber eyes eager, a grateful smile brightening his face. "If I had known my distress was all it took to dash away your gloom, I would have played the buffoon days ago."

Josefina stepped so quickly she almost skated down the stairs. "A Victrola," she sang. They were not allowed in Taylorsville, but she had heard one before in St. Louis. "We have music." She spun a little pirouette before grabbing François's hand, attempting to help pull him and the box across the doorframe. "Quickly, I want to hear it."

Wedged against the casing, François gave a gigantic shove. The machine scudded across the threshold into the foyer and stopped. "Where do you suppose we should put it?" François looked to Josefina for direction.

"The dining room, we can listen to the music with our stew."

"Excellent. But before we eat, perhaps you might favor me with a valse."

Josefina's jaw dropped, her mouth watered as if she sucked taffy. He invited wickedness. "You know dancing violates church law." Before the sound of her protest faded, an involuntary smile spread across her face. "Could we? Would you teach me?"

"Ah, Josefina, my sweet, I plan to teach you everything you will ever need to know." François wiggled the player onto a wool carpet then tugged the goods step by step into the dining room.

The arched lid of the square oak box opened to reveal various lengths of metal strings resembling a miniature harpsichord lying beneath a tubular wooden arm. François opened a door on the side and extracted several brass cylinders riddled with bumps and holes having no definitive pattern. After selecting and inserting a cylinder onto the arm, he cranked the handle near the top. After several rotations, a tinny melody peppered the air.

François clamped his arm tightly around Josefina's waist and began twirling her from room to room. Their boisterous cavorting soared noisily up the stairs, but there was no shushing, no complaint, no other sound in the house, except the metallic ditty and their own laughter as the hours passed.

The gold of dawn crept along the horizon before Josefina finally quit dancing. She had had enough. A quick bite to brace their energies, periodic cranking, and exchange of cylinders had been the only interruptions in their nightlong dance. Pangs throbbed through her exhausted feet and legs; her arms hung like limp noodles on a body that could barely move. Josefina knew she should feel wicked, had been racy—the church would rule sinfully. But in truth, she had lived a wonderful night.

"Think of what Father will say," Josefina said. Not that she really worried, but she should prepare. Father's infamous temper frightened her, too. "What shall we tell him?"

"I suggest we tell him nothing," replied François. "Your debut has begun. You stand with one foot across the threshold into womanhood. No longer a child. As a woman, you will encounter certain occasions when it proves best to keep your own counsel. This is one of those times." Like a cat caught in the cream, his upper lip curled under as his tongue licked across it. "One warning, however, from personal experience. Never give Josef Taylor reason to distrust you, or you will pay dearly."

Josefina reached up with a quick hug. "François, you are the most wonderful man in the world. I never knew you had such understanding. I wish Father could be more like you." Her eyes relayed all the admiration she could convey.

"Whatever happens here will be our secret, just you and I," François continued. "After all, Marianne has no idea what occurs outside her bedroom, and by the time she feels well enough to join us, we will be preparing to return home."

Like lightning a prospect penetrated Josefina's thoughts. Home, to Jacob. The pleasure of seeing Jacob's amazement when she showed off her dance skills made her giddy. The gleeful tilt of her mouth broadened into an engaging smile. "We are agreed."

An answering grin turned François almost handsome. "And so, we have begun your introduction to the world." Reaching his arm out wide and clasping her hand, François raised Josefina's arm up high, spinning her around with the tempo of a lackadaisical top.

While Josefina watched, his eyes traveled the length of her body, from platinum head to slippered toe, resting on the plumpness of her backside. "You are as beautiful and gracious as your mother. Better. You add a freshness, an allure for the worldly appetites of a man. A man would be a fool not to want you." The compliment crept deep from François's throat.

"I do hope so, for I want a man who is no fool, and he has another woman interested in him." Josefina dropped François's hand and hugged herself while she continued to twirl.

François's eyes narrowed. "You know very well, Josefina, I, too, am no fool." He stepped closer, his face stern above hers. "You know Jacob is not worthy of you." The words growled from rigid jaws. "You need a strong man, a man who possesses the knowledge to encourage and guide your ambitions. A man who can provide you with the means of obtaining that seat at the bank you long for, teach you discipline, introduce you to the exhilaration of exercising power." A haughty challenge invaded his words. "You know I can do that—Jacob cannot."

Josefina stepped backwards abruptly, as if his words physically punched her. What he said was true. But she did not want him; she wanted Jacob. "Jacob is eager to have me. He will do anything he must to make me happy."

François bent forward, pursuing her, his body a barrier. "Untested. Appearing at my door without letters of introduction. Presenting less than flattering credentials. Full of his own bravado. Hardly a peer, more likely a wastrel."

"First, you flatter yourself, then imply I am ambitious and greedy. Inventions of yours, thrown out as obstacles to my happiness. Lastly, accusing Jacob of fortune hunting?" Josefina held her ground, voice trembling. "All this spite amounts to nothing! Jacob will become my life. He is the most wonderful man I ever met."

The reasoning seemed ungrateful, childish and whiny, but Josefina did not care. All the luster of the night was tarnished. She felt betrayed, her spirit drained. Worse, she realized her protests sounded unremarkable, lame. A growing alarm accompanied the tiredness of her body before she turned to leave.

François chuckled. "You assured me, not a moment ago, I was the most wonderful."

Josefina paused, then spun back toward him. "You are wonderful. You have been part of my life, our family, since I was a baby. I care a great deal for you." She looked up at him, caution softening her voice. "But, Jacob is—special." Her lips lifted into a fixed smile as her voice swelled, strong with affection, and determined. "I love him more than anything." She marveled, up until now she had avoided speaking the word love. Now, the unique expression and all its implication fit the feelings in her heart. "I will not give him up."

"What of Marianne? You know her feelings."

"I did not deliberately set out to stand in her way. I shared all the feminine wiles I knew to help her entice him. After I realized Jacob was not enamored of Marianne, I told her I wanted him for myself. We agreed to be fair, let Jacob make his own choice."

François threw back his head and cackled. "An untruth you most probably believe. When he presented himself, you could not resist the challenge. You always set out to catch what rests just beyond your reach. The contest, my darling, the test of your powers, that is what you relish most. Once obtained you see only fool's gold. The thrill disappears."

"You sound like Father. Well, you are both wrong. I love Jacob, and I will share his life no matter what I must sacrifice. Even now, while we delay here, he asks Father's permission for my hand."

François paced, then stopped so his long torso towered over her. "Listen to me carefully, I can give you everything you want. At my death, France requires a son be identified from my bloodline to preserve the property and privilege entitled to my family. I desire an heir who is brilliant, handsome, ambitious. A child who embodies the traits we both admire." He bent closer, his tobacco-flavored breath hot on her face.

"If you are the woman you advertise to be, give me that heir. We will couple, so that you might produce a child." François's eyes had grown bright, his body a barricade. He shrugged casually. "In the process, even if you do not learn to care for me, I will provide that generous income you seek. Enough to last your lifetime. A princely sum, sufficient to make the way for you to marry whomever you choose and still live in luxury. The means for you to fight for the position on the bank's board that you seek." His face showed no emotion, his voice flat as if he spoke before the Elders of the church, shoulders hunched, shielding his heart.

Josefina stood in stunned silence. The deafness of the house engulfed her. The smell of François's sweat mixed with a smothering odor of decay, the disease of a house shut up too long. The sweet morning song of the birds welcoming the dawn warbled into jabberwocky and screeches of complaint. Blood pounded through Josefina's body, carrying poisonous bile that fed on greed and threatened to drown the sweetness of her youth. She wanted the bank, the wealth, and the freedom to pursue her dream.

The minutes passed like decades. She envisioned herself, splendidly attired, sitting at the table in Father's sacred boardroom. "We will couple," François had said. Was there no one to hear his madness? No one to protest? No one to come to her aid, to right the terrible wrong proposed? Her hands covered her ears shutting out the shrieking of François's barbarous proposition.

She looked at his long frame, then shuddered from head to toe, seeing him as a man for the first time. She felt trapped, an animal with nowhere to hide. When she turned to flee, he grabbed her elbow, tugging her against his body. She pulled away and turned to escape. He blocked her path. She shoved him aside and raced up the stairs.

François had deceived her. The dancing she had enjoyed had been a night of pretense. Yet he knew her too well, for she did indeed desire riches, the bank, and Jacob. At a premium cost? François had stolen her trust and wanted more: her innocence, the theft of her purity. The tears of a child plopped across Josefina's breast, staining her dress with the weakness and corruption of a woman's earthly desires.

Heedless of Marianne's illness, Josefina made no attempt to enter her friend's room quietly. She dared not sleep in her own room. François's boldness alarmed her. Pawing through the drawers and trunks like a crazed person, Josefina tossed a cape, a robe, a pillow, petticoats, everything she could gather onto the floor to make bedding. Muslin, linen, and seersucker, ruffles and feathers alike piled into a jumbled heap. Afraid to risk changing into a sleeping gown, Josefina wound the tie of her dress tightly around the leg of the bedstead before lying down on the floor. François could not move her without disturbing Marianne.

The remainder of the sunless day Josefina dozed fitfully, waking at each sound, imagining nearing creaks on the floor. She woke at midday, bruised, feeling she had lain on a mountain of platter-sized rocks, then stumbled vacantly through her toilette, dazed, knowing her world a prison. All day she read steadily, without rest, to the semiconscious Marianne, any print she could put her hands on without leaving their suite, including the boring texts from the library.

For days, while she avoided François, Josefina mastered the physical phenomenon of electric current, the theories of Thomas Edison's telephone, the birth and expansion of railroads, and phrenology.

François labored behind the closed door of the library or remained inside his suite on the floor above theirs. But his shadow lurked by the archway when Josefina bypassed the dining room, choosing to bring soup and cracked bread up to Marianne's room instead of remaining downstairs. His silhouette darkened the parted curtains at the windows each time she stepped outside the house.

Since the beginning of their confinement, Josefina had faithfully placed daily notes to her mother in the emptied food basket. Up until now, bulkier envelopes containing all her longings in passionate letters to Jacob had gone by more furtive means, wedged between the posts of the iron gate or flung into a vacated carriage when she retrieved the food basket, sometimes tossed to passersby from the upper story window. Josefina no longer cared. So what if François thought her racy and bold, she kept no secrets from him. The letters to Jacob lay alongside the ones to Dieter and Mother; they would travel together.

~ * ~

Six days after François proposed his idea to Josefina, loud, repetitious rapping thundered against the front door.

"François, please, the door." Her voice quaking with panic, Josefina called out, "The door, there must be more trouble."

When he passed the girls' level, François saw Josefina flattened against the wall at the rear of the vestibule, near Marianne's bedroom. *So, she fears the sight of me. She will soon feel differently.*

François opened the now silent entry door. Dozens of parcels tumbled in. Behind those another stack of boxes rose to a height as tall and wide as the portal itself, and deep enough to shut out the light. François looked up at Josefina watching from the top of the stairs. "Well, do you want them?"

Josefina's eyes widened in surprise; confusion crinkled her face. She stepped to the banister but kept her distance, purposely not looking at him, seemingly aware only of the boxes.

She thinks me a rascal, a scoundrel. François's festering impatience exploded. He began hurling the packages into the hallway, slamming them against the stairs and walls, bursting them open. Splendid things began to billow, float, and slither in the entry. Clothes of vampish red, witching black that slinked, a gauze as sheer as a cobweb. Only the thud of the paper boxes as they hit the walls broke the silence.

His anger spent, François beckoned to Josefina, making his voice inviting. "Take them. They are yours. All this finery was designed for you, for your debut, to shepherd your introduction as a woman. I ordered the designs from France months ago, sized to fit the woman you have become, to complement your fairness, your body." He beckoned again for her to come down, then waited as Josefina slowly edged along the steps. Of course, she could not resist the temptation; he had always known her hungers.

When Josefina reached the last few steps, François turned to leave, but not before triumph wreathed his face. "I do hope you are pleased?"

Josefina consumed the rest of the day emptying boxes, tossing aside her plain cotton pantaloons and camisole to try on undergarments of satin and lace, admiring the seductiveness of her newly molded form. Boxes, emptied of hats, shoes and undergarments, stacked up where they were opened like a child's forgotten blocks. Every gift was tested, measured for its effect. Colors matched with textures, purpose, rearranged, then more creative touches added. Josefina felt like a child in a candy shop, indulging a new taste from each selection, then going through the ritual again because each seemed sweeter than the one before.

Josefina slept in her own bed that night, secure in a silk sleeping gown. She felt no compulsion to tie herself to the bed. François would not attack her. He was giving her complete freedom to make her choice. He offered the power, wealth, and freedom she coveted for the price of her virtue against remaining an innocent and settling for a hollow life of mediocrity.

No one would ever know of the agreement, as long as François never told. And whom would he tell? The "Elders" considered him an "outsider", valued for his gold alone. He would never tell Mother, chance breaking her heart, or Father, for fear of his wrath and his standing among the other members of the cartel, and any revelation in general would besmirch the heir François prized so dearly. No, François would find the telling worthwhile only to hurt her, Mother, Father, or Jacob, because the truth would destroy them all.

And the offense in the doing? Not adultery, that was lust indulged outside marriage, and neither of them was married. Their act would be without passion, a coming together to satisfy a legitimate necessity. A breaking of church law, definitely, but surely, the presentation of the gift of a child outweighed the transgression? A harmless deed? Josefina considered the truth. No. And the responsibility of the choice rested on her alone, to live with for the rest of her life.

Nine

The next morning François stirred the coals of the baker's oven before tucking the meal inside the bread bin to warm. Within minutes the pleasant aroma filled the kitchen and drifted up the stairs. A week had passed since Josefina had been down to eat with him. At breakfast, when he entered Marianne's room with broth, he found her alone.

But, Josefina could not resist the aroma of a fat hen and fresh bread after all the meals of potato and cabbage stew and cracked corn loaves, any more than she could resist his gifts.

Within minutes Josefina appeared in the doorway fitted out from ankle to shoulders in carnation red hemp. She could not have chosen anything bolder. François chuckled inwardly at the thought of the Elders' response. Subtle hollows beneath her eyes attested to her sleeplessness, and she acted skittish with the wariness of a cornered kitten, but she did not retreat. François felt his battle half won.

"You make the dress more beautiful. Come sit." François bowed politely, pulled out a chair, then seated himself at a distance. "Marianne's health shows a little improvement, her sleep seems more restful when I enter her room. Perhaps in a few weeks we may begin to make preparations to return. Would that please you, Josefina?"

"Seeing my mother and father would be very nice. There is, however, another's presence, as you know, that would bring me more pleasure."

"You are foolish to persist in your childishness." François shrugged his shoulders. "I warn you, Jacob is not worthy of your charms. You require a larger audience, a more prestigious stage, a better part to play." François kept his voice deceptively calm.

"I would be content to share the rest of my life with Jacob no matter what the circumstances." The half-truth died before it reached Josefina's eyes; she could not look at François.

"And a position on the board of the bank, travel, the gowns and other luxuries you yearn for. What of all that? And what of my need?" He smiled invitingly, seeking her personal counsel, as if he depended on her, as if they shared a future. "Have you considered all you would be giving up? And about my property, my family, Marianne, if there is no heir?"

A napkin fell across the arm of the chair when he stood. "I apologize for leaving you alone." He bowed extravagantly. "If you will excuse me, I have work waiting." Josefina appeared disappointed at his leave taking. François believed more fervently in his plan.

Later that morning, Josefina's door was cracked when he passed. Her boots topped the stairs at the same time he brought in the food. Lunch consisted of tea, potted meat and crackers, and Josefina, wearing a navy pleated skirt with a white dotted Swiss blouse, as delicate as a snowflake.

"You have chosen well," François remarked. "Perfect selection for a serious lunch. Tell me of the books you so generously read to Marianne. What have you learned?"

Their conversation remained impersonal, revolving around the reliability of trains, electricity and telling fortunes by bumps of one's head. Eventually, Josefina began expressing her feelings about the staggering amount of profit prophesied for the cartel and their opportunity for swindling the public.

Josefina knew she expressed her opinions well and enjoyed having a listener. Her insights obviously impressed François. She decided those boring meetings Father demanded she attend and the readings of the past weeks might yet prove fruitful.

Later at supper, champagne satin crafted an illusion for Josefina of leisurely dining before rushing off to attend a cotillion, her dance card full, admirers fighting for a chance to be near her. Alone with François, Josefina concentrated all the implied carefree excitement of her imagination on her dinner companion. She had never before had the freedom to live out her fantasies.

In anticipation of showing off her new acquisitions, Josefina's frenzies mounted before each meal. Which gown to choose? It mattered not. Armloads more remained. A black chiffon gown left her shoulders bare, cinched her waist and rounded her breasts into mounds like twin pearls. An oriental dress of milk white trimmed in red and gold, slit from thigh to ankle on each side, exposed sinfully silk-clad legs. A navy and white linen day set that fit like a second skin slimmed down into a pencil thin skirt not full enough to wear with more than a single silk petticoat. Josefina could not get enough.

At the following night's dinner, Josefina wore a glacial blue organza. They had already dined, as usual, on stew and biscuits, when François dangled a sapphire pendant as dark as the ocean and as large as his thumb before Josefina. The reflected light cast spiked violet rainbows across the table, up her arms, and onto her throat.

"The day after you were born I purchased this, to match your eyes." He swung the precious jewel to and fro, an arm's length beyond Josefina's reach. Sprinkles of brilliant sparks climbed up and down her body and circled the room. "In my wild youth, an eternity ago, I hungered for a woman as beautiful and gifted as your mother. When she chose your father, I vowed to never marry until I found a woman her equal, or more so. I chose you. I bought this to be worn on your wedding day."

Gesturing, his arms flung wide open, he pressed her for an answer. "Tell me you can live without all of this." His breadth encompassed an entire imaginary world. When she failed to answer he continued. "Convince me you can reject this life, the excitement of having more than you ever dreamed of, the arrogance of abandoning anything that has grown tiresome and boring, the insolence of greed, the titillation of shocking behavior. The freedom wealth buys."

Josefina sat silent.

"Jacob can never provide this for you. Without my support, or your father's blessing, you will be locked into genteel poverty.

Mediocrity. As confining as a public stockade. Enough to eat, a roof over your head, a new gown for special occasions. A place of worker bees. And then, the children will come. " He paused. "If you can say truthfully that is the life you desire, I will leave you to it. I will say no more."

Josefina's nails dug into her palms with the need to scratch the truth from his throat. The corners of her mouth twitched, words accepting the poverty he described pricked her throat, but when her mouth opened no sound came.

"I take it then that you agree. This is the life you desire, the world of wealth you were born to and covet."

"I have thought long on your proposal," Josefina said, hoping to flatter him. "Fear of knowing that others would think badly of me should they discover my transgression discouraged my acceptance."

"No one need know outside you and I, and Marianne."

The mention of his sister surprised Josefina. "Marianne?"

"She would, of necessity, accompany us and aid you during your 'confinement'. She would stay with the child. Then if you wished, you could return within the year, fashionably attired and worldly traveled." He paused for effect, "and wealthy beyond your fondest dreams."

Josefina lowered her eyes, her troubled thoughts hidden behind a veil of pale lashes. "You know me too well, François. I cannot ignore my desire to have what I feel life has open to me." She paused, her mouth dry, her mind a battlefield, her ambitions imprisoning her mores. "If you promise, on your honor, to never speak of this agreement. Never ever, to anyone. And to protect me." Josefina could barely believe what she was about to say. "I will give you your heir."

His breath made a whistling sound when it rushed out, like a teakettle, as if something had boiled inside him for a long time. "You have that promise, Josefina. I will never, ever, even upon death, reveal our bargain to anyone at anytime."

"And, you must pledge to guarantee that no gossip develops alluding to my condition, or later of my relationship to the child." A shiver, like a dog shaking off muddied water, scampered across her skin.

François bowed deeply, took Josefina's hands in his own, then bent to one knee. "Our contract as you said! And since I am to be your first, you must promise to remain faithful to me. You must bear *my* child."

Josefina felt appalled by what he implied.

"I will choose the times to come to you. Once you have proven fruitful, I will provide for you while you carry my child. Somewhere in seclusion. I, too, do not wish to damage our son's future with malice. I suggest you retire to my family's chateau in France. As for gossip, I can stop that immediately upon our return. I will announce that you will join Marianne on an extended European tour to compensate for your missed debuts." His voice had grown husky, intimate, and more affectionate than Josefina had anticipated.

"The arrangement would be temporary?" Josefina asked. "I would still be free to return to my home, or wherever I wished, after the child?" He must pledge that.

"In time, you might learn to care for me." François's voice softened, the words as tender as if he wooed her. "In which case we will raise our son together. Were that to happen, I would be more than pleased." He touched his fingers to her lips to stop her interruption. "If you cannot learn to care for me, or do not wish to share in raising our son, you will have your freedom. In either event, you may rest assured you will have everything you covet. I pledge, if my heart's desire is fulfilled, I shall settle an income on you worthy the Baroness you might have been."

Josefina stared down at the food in her bowl. Her appetite had gone the way of her mores. "Agreed." She deliberated. "Surely, other women who made such a sacrifice earned forgiveness from those who loved them?" Anxiously Josefina awaited François's answer. One fear unnerved her: Jacob's understanding and pardon should this agreement ever be aired.

"If you should choose to leave your son, any arrangements you make after his birth will be none of my concern. And you have my promise." François rose from his knee, and sat down heavily in his chair. "Your plate has not been touched." He picked up a decanter, his hand trembling with the effort. "A glass of champagne, perhaps? I secreted a magnum for celebration."

"No, thank you," Josefina declined. Her heart weighed heavy with her guilt. She would not be able to swallow. Regret stuck in her throat. *Have I made the right choice?*

"Some music? Let us wind up the Victrola."

"Thank you, but I wish to be excused."

François nodded, then bowed. "I will give you time to prepare yourself before coming to you." François's smile appeared boyish, nearing good-humored. "Would you like me to help in some way?"

Josefina winced visibly. She had not anticipated his thirst for an heir needing to be quenched immediately. "I have watched horses breed since I could walk. I doubt the differences between a man and woman coupling carries many surprises." Her lower lip trembled as she spoke. She tugged at a wayward curl. *Besides, I will be thinking only of Jacob.*

~ * ~

Within the hour François rapped on Josefina's door hard enough that it swung open. Josefina lay on a narrow bed facing an open window with her back toward the entrance. Although the night was sweltering, a light covering was pulled up to her chin. A moonbeam tinted her hair silver and cast a shimmer on her flesh that made François want to believe in angels. His heart leapt into his throat at the sight. He wanted to crush her to him and never let her go. Gently, François schooled himself. *I must utilize all my skills, be patient.*

He stripped off his shirt and slippers, removing his knee britches after he sat on the side of the bed. Neither François nor Josefina spoke. The room smelled faintly of roses.

François reached down and toyed with Josefina's hair, thrilled by the fineness fed through his fingers. He turned her face toward him, caressing her cheeks and throat's smooth surface. His fingertip traced the arch of her brow.

"Josefina, you are lovely. There is no one else as fine in Taylorsville County, or anywhere else." He tasted of her neck, her brow; finally pulling her toward him, he tasted the sweetness of her lips. "Will you open your eyes? Look at me?"

Josefina rolled her head from side to side. Eyes pinched tighter in her pale face.

A ribbon gathered the neck of Josefina's gown into a nun's collar. François untied the bow and began kissing her throat, carrying his passion to her breasts. He moved the coverlet without removing his hand from her. He sensed her unyielding stiffness, a lump of clay, waiting to be brought to life under the skill of his experience.

François lay down on his side behind Josefina. She turned away. His tall frame circled around her, his knees cupped under her thighs. His hands, mouth, fingers, continued to test, explore, lingered with gentle touches, then grew more demanding.

He could no longer hold himself back. François thrust inside her, spending his passion, riding a crest that made him explode. Again, and again. He triumphed in the taking.

Not until his hunger for her was satisfied, and he leaned forward to bury his face in her curls and taste her neck, did he discover the tears. They bathed her cheeks and throat, hanging like cheap beads on her rounded chin.

François felt more content than any time in his life, but a phantom, not of his liking intruded on his happiness. His Josefina had undoubtedly imagined Jacob despoiling her. What matter, the absent engineer had not been here. *But I, François ducLaFevre have, and I will not allow my pleasure to be ruined by the lackluster vagabond.*

For well over twenty years revenge had simmered in François's belly, waiting for this chance. Anytime he chose, the news of Josefina's dishonor could destroy Josef, who would protect Louise from any harmful gossip. But, François knew, Josef would never regain his aplomb.

Jacob worked somewhere in Missouri awaiting word from his sweetheart, word that would never come. One of François's own men or Dieter intercepted Josefina's letters to Jacob. More satisfaction would come for him on the return home, reading her secret delights, knowing she would never belong to Jacob.

After Marianne vanquished this plague, she would be free to pursue Jacob and win his love while Josefina languished. François felt sure, in time, after the child's birth, Josefina would grow to care for him and forget Jacob. After all, Josefina had said he was "wonderful," and she had been created of the same mold as Louise, who'd loved him, until Josef demanded they marry.

Josef had earned this due, the deflowering of his only daughter. François groaned. He had been within days of having Louise for his own. He had been a youth, championing noble platitudes, when Josef, too keenly, judged he must marry Louise quickly or she would no longer be his. François dabbed at his eyes. Louise had submitted only to keep him from the guillotine. The gold stolen from the French nobles had allowed him to remain at Louise's side, and sealed his separation from France forever. For François, the gold, flaunting his obscene wealth and indulging his contemptuous lifestyle, which all grated on Josef's soul, shrunk to the size of a grain of rice alongside the taking of Josefina.

Tomorrow he would come again, in the daylight, so he might enjoy Josefina's beauty fully. And the next day, and the next. For however long she took to realize only François ducLaFevre could give her what she desired most in life. He could wait.

~ * ~

Weeks later, suffocating within the confinement of the carriage, miserable and repentant, Josefina rode silently beside Marianne, not looking at François, not seeing the countryside. She thought only of Jacob and the fear that curdled her food and throbbed in her head. He must never know. She would convince him to explore, find the perfect place for them in the West and allow her this teeny indulgence, a grand tour of Europe, before she joined him. The money would be explainable, from a great-aunt who read those nickel western thrillers and wished the best for the couple.

The tale seemed plausible, only Josefina knew she would never be able to look Jacob in the eye during the telling, perhaps not after either. She had been foolish to accept François's offer, but she would have the money, and with it the power to buy her way, establish Jacob as a man of consequence should he choose. And, after all, the child came as her gift to François; such devotion as hers could not be too great a sin.

Roasting in the heat of an August afternoon, the trio finally returned to Taylorsville after a three month absence. The carriage reached the end of the lane at Taylor Estates when Josefina spoke for the first time in three days.

"I am indisposed. The heat and jostling has sickened me. Please, I would see my mother, then rest. Perhaps, François, you would put off explanation of our trials until tomorrow?"

François smiled broadly. "Anything you wish. Please, have a boy send us a note of your disposition this evening, so I have no worry of the fever. I will be quite preoccupied where the matter of your health is concerned."

Josefina sprang from the carriage the minute it stopped, not wanting François's hands on her to assist her descent. Racing to the parlor where Mother served tea, Josefina hugged the frail body and sank her face in the sweet scented shoulders. She longed to yield to Mother's gentleness and divulge the shame eating at her, expose the guilt killing the joy of returning. Josefina hungered earnestly for understanding. Surely, Mother would forgive her desperation. Instead, Josefina was calmly relating the tragedy of Marianne's illness when Dieter entered unannounced.

Grateful for the diversion, Josefina beamed. "How wonderful. You came to welcome me home before I had time to shake the dust off my clothes. Quickly, sit down, tell me all the news I have missed."

Hat in hand, Dieter stood stiffly before her. "Jacob is gone."

To Josefina's ears Dieter's voice implied permanence.

"Two nights before you left, Jacob packed up his things and disappeared." Dieter turned his face away, unable to look Josefina in the eye, his pending lie wedged between them. "No one has heard a word from him since."

The day after we met in the stable. The cup slipped from Josefina's hand, slopping its contents onto her lap. She felt woozy, eyes blurred. A moan snuck out.

"Goodness sakes, child. Look what you have done." Her mother popped up and vainly attempted to mop up the liquid. "Hurry upstairs and change. We must soak that dress or it will stain." Bony fingers prodded her ribs while Josefina automatically rose from the chair.

"Go, quickly." Mother's gentle push headed Josefina toward the stairs. "She is exhausted," Louise warned Dieter. "She endured a horrendous situation. Come back in a few days. You can tell her everything then."

"There is nothing more to tell."

The words, driven by a howling wind, knifed their way through a wall of fog. Josefina believed them the mutterings of a demon.

Dieter caught Josefina before her head banged the floor.

Strong arms cradled her, but Josefina did not know anyone was there. She struggled alone in a black hole, her soundness of mind drowning in the lie of Jacob's repeating promise.

Ten

August's heat had cooled to the crisp, cool air of September. Josefina judged each field critically while she drove past, calculating the labor spent against anticipated profits. The fresh green smell of robust birth had died, replaced by the peppery dust of tired earth.

The road snaked past fields that had spent the summer warring nature's best weapons. Corn bowed in formal stance, relinquishing succulent juices to a toasty sun and drying wind, the kernels toughened for the cracking of cows' teeth. Long broad leaves, parched into white pennants, scuffed across the ground rustling with the rasp of sandpaper.

Beans rattled like castanets, their misshapen stems lining the horizon with death, as if a war had ended. Only the cotton stood silent, the crunching of the weevils muffled by the white soft bolls.

Some acres lay stripped bare, fallow, shreds of leftover vegetation protruding like hands from a grave, waiting their turn to be interred. The plow had already cultivated and disked a few acres, punching sleeping seeds into sheltered beds beneath the surface where they waited to sprout green with wheat as the snows melted. The mental acrobatics of profits and costs of the ever-changing fields helped relieve the worry and tension that plagued Josefina.

François had stopped his casual visits to Taylor Estates within days of their return, appearing only on formal occasions with business associates, then remaining attached to her mother or occupied with Father and their infernal chess game. Josefina's frustration had climbed well past annoyance. Now, she feared equally Father's discovery and the punishment he would inflict. Banishment to some secret place, a lifetime of shunning. Perhaps a hasty marriage to some accommodating dolt far away?

François's evasion frightened Josefina. Four days ago Mother announced, "We have guests from the bank for dinner this evening."

"Will François be coming?" Josefina asked.

"How silly. Whenever do we not include François if he is available?"

Josefina rushed to her rooms and spent much of the afternoon filling sheets of water paper with carefully constructed pleas addressing the severity of her situation. She prepared to confront him, determined this would be her most persistent of many such attempts.

The debaucher arrived late. She had loitered near the entrance to be first to greet him. "I must speak with you. I have a matter of importance..."

François patted the top of Josefina's head while looking beyond her. "Ah, Louise, as lovely as ever." He sprinted forward and took both of Mother's hands in his. "My youth hardly seems so long ago whenever I see you. What a mistake for me to give you up too easily that you might marry Josef."

"Your flattery still causes me to blush." Indeed, pink tinted Louise's cheeks. "You were not artless then, and your charms continue to improve over the years."

"Sadly, my best was not good enough. But, perhaps one day, I shall find another who touches my heart as you do." François tucked Louise's fingers under his arm and proceeded toward the other guests.

Josefina lingered in the foyer, her heart heavy with grief. Mother would never believe François a lecher. And, after all, if the terms of the bargain were revealed, who would take the part of a young woman seduced by riches, no matter how innocent her nature?

Unable to intrude on the business that engaged her adulterer without appearing discourteous, and possibly alarming her parents, Josefina burned her note by candle fire later that night. Her fear of ruination grew with each sputter of the flame.

Other duties had occupied her since that evening, the insistent worry infecting everything, often erupting at most inconvenient times and muddling her mind. She stewed continually. The bargain must be honored. He had promised. But, without deviation, François continued to offer no more than formal greetings and exchange public pleasantries.

Josefina's hands became all thumbs; she grew clumsy and inattentive. The abundant harvest demanded care, the canning and drying of apples and grains, salting of meat, clearing of root cellars for storing vegetables and herbs for winter's use, all tasks now under way.

In the kitchen, women stood shoulder-to-shoulder, steadily washing, slicing, measuring, seasoning, and stuffing until the overflowing bushels emptied. The workers shared womanly chatter and veiled gossip, making light of their labors. Josefina felt unable to join in, preoccupied by the horror that she stood alone on the brink of a lifelong fall.

This morning Josefina had placed the burden of her share of the work on another's shoulders by inventing a lie about Marianne suffering a relapse and a pressing need to offer assistance. Josefina despised what she had done. Guilt weighed heavily on her, dulling further her normally cheerful disposition. She never shirked her duties. Adding further insult, unsure of her position and bested by François's avoidance, this venture promised no enjoyment.

The darkened lane up to the Chateau gave Josefina goosebumps. Heavy leafed oaks and maples that lined the drive held onto their red, orange, and gold dresses. Their frenzied dance of shadows blocked out much of the sun. For over a mile only speckles of light brightened the lane, as if a party guest had sprinkled a handful of starlight confetti.

When her rig emerged from the parkway, three stories of pink marble blocked the horizon. Lacy, white metal balconies trimmed dozens of narrow windows creating thin, grimacing faces.

The surrounding grounds rolled in acres of decorative parkland as far as Josefina could see. Father warred often with François over the wastefulness. The shrubs and grasses remained.

No one lounged on the emerald carpet or wandered about.

Marianne should be waiting. Even in adverse weather, guests to the Chateau were always greeted at the steps. Guilt taunted Josefina. Perhaps her lie had turned to truth; her heart would stop if she had hexed Marianne. A stable boy suddenly appeared out of nowhere and led the horse away. Still no one came out to welcome.

Josefina's rap on the entry door echoed, weak and ineffectual. She turned the knob and stepped onto the cool, Italian marble floor. The door closed with its weight. The snap of the latch faded in a descending hollowness, clicking its way up a staircase that had consumed an entire forest.

Josefina peeked in the adjoining rooms, searching for a servant or Marianne, praying not to be confronted by François, not yet. The ornate rooms served like royalty without a populace, perfect pageantry, waiting to be needed.

"Marianne, it is Josefina. Are you here?" The echo disturbing the silence sounded frail, frightened. Josefina climbed the stairs determinedly.

"Marianne, where are you?"

"Come in, Little Jos." The voice sounded from above, from François's suite. Josefina froze.

"Entrez! Come, I am in zere," Marianne called out.

Tentatively, Josefina pushed on the half-opened door and braced for the sight of François. Marianne sat alone at a gold leaf secretary. Worldwide Bank ledgers stamped with years past towered neatly on the desktop; others dated more recently were strewn like fallen leaves across the floor. Marianne stood waiting, her arms open in welcome. The empire tea dress of pumpkin linen emphasized Marianne's height, making Josefina feel small and vulnerable. The hug felt brief, polite.

"What a surprise," Marianne said.

"You did not receive a note arranging my visit?" Josefina could hardly believe such ill fate.

"No. When did you send this note?" Marianne's brow creased in obvious concern.

"Two days past. We have been so involved with the harvest I could not come any earlier. One of our workers brought the note here, on his way to the fields. He said he handed it to the lady standing by the front door. I assumed that was you."

"I received no note," said Marianne.

"I have no reason to doubt his trustworthiness." Josefina scowled. "Did you have visitors?"

"Of course, that is what happened. François has been viewing candidates. He seems to be circling, as you colonists say."

"Going in circles. You mean to say he is very busy."

"Ah, yes, that is zee case. Perhaps your note was mislaid by mistake. Anyway, you are here now."

"If you were not expecting me, are you free?"

Marianne glanced at a gold clock chiming musically on a nearby table. "*Mon Dieux*, I am to go out for midday. François has narrowed his selection of a designer and wants my presence. Not that he would value my opinion anyway."

"François is hiring someone new? He has given up then on Jacob's return." Josefina's voice faltered. "Has he heard any news, anything at all?"

"François sent a recommendation about Jacob to a colleague who needed to hire an engineer after our project was to be finished. Seems our Jacob interviewed with this associate in St. Louis, then turned down a proper offer."

"Why would Jacob turn down a good offer?" Josefina was stunned. "Did he apply elsewhere?"

"He only stayed there a short time. Told these people new gold fields had been discovered in Canada, and that was where he was off to."

Josefina sucked the soft flesh of her cheek between her teeth, biting hard, willing herself not to wail. This second-hand report, worse than ever imagined, had flung a boulder into her midsection. "When was Jacob in St. Louis?"

"Supposedly, he stayed with friends but a few days then left town within hours of making this announcement. We have seen zee last of our lovely engineer." Marianne stared steadily into Josefina's eyes, seeming to measure the depth of acceptance.

Josefina could not believe Jacob had not intended marrying her. Her body ached to have him near, to feel the strength of his arms. Surely, she had overlooked a clue somewhere. Someone else plotted to ruin her life, or more simply devised a scheme to separate her from the man she loved. She would welcome any reason, except Jacob's desertion.

"Are you going to meet François or stay? I have a serious matter to discuss with you. An unpleasant situation, involving a friend of ours who needs help. The delay would be inconvenient, but I can return another day."

"Oh, Josefina, who is it? Of course, I stay. Let me send a note I have been detained." Marianne quickly scribbled across a paper.

Josefina saw her name mentioned, the French easily translated. According to the message, François would be gone for the remainder of the day.

Marianne, beckoning Josefina to follow her out the door, called for a maid and handed over the message. Instructions flowed rapidly in French fractured by an accent Josefina found difficult to understand.

"To my suite, quick. We will enjoy tea while you tell me who is this poor darling who seeks our advice?"

Josefina waited until they had seated themselves comfortably at a table. "You must pledge to keep what I tell you secret."

"As always, I promise. Now, tell me your story."

"A young girl, inexperienced, finds herself in the family way. No one knows except the man involved."

"And now you, Josefina. She has confided in you. What an honor, to be confidante! Tell me of this person?" Marianne twittered with the thrill of conspiracy.

"First, let me tell you the circumstances." Voice hushed, Josefina began. "A man of standing asked this young woman to bear his child."

Marianne interrupted. "Ah, a kindness. And zee girl was poor, without a bed. The barren family gives her nice home and take care of zee babe."

"Harrumph! You speak of charity and romance. I am not telling some sugarcoated melodrama, but a cause of injustice and deceit. Be serious."

"That is my nature, to be serious. But, zee story is so titillating."

"Listen sensibly to what I say. She is unmarried, I neglected to mention of quite proper standing, whose life will most assuredly be ruined. This child will be scarred by the scandal of illegitimacy. Both will pay the penalty of unnatural sin, and the man escapes scot-free."

"To make baby is not unnatural. All come zee same way. There is an evil twist here?" Marianne acted surprised. "Yes?" She hesitated, waiting for a response that didn't come. "Zee man commit a crime?"

"Something like that." Josefina averted her eyes and gazed out the window.

"Zee young woman screams, scratches, fights to be free?" Marianne's green eyes lit with an unnatural brilliance, narrowed, then widened. "I must be told zee truth, Josefina. She had no desire to bear zee babe?"

Josefina squirmed in her seat, her mouth dry as five-day-old bread, a lie sitting on her tongue. They had been best friends since Marianne arrived, almost inseparable, closer than sisters, sharing every part of their lives. What if Marianne chose not to believe? Or worse, was repelled.

A storm brewed, Josefina could taste the salty air while excuses somersaulted in her head. "The girl ran from the man, rebuffed him. But he seduced her with a proposal she could not refuse. Her heart was not in the contest."

"If she ran away, how did this babe come about?" Marianne's voice became unnaturally sharp.

Josefina remembered the pain of the taking. Burning the bloody linens while her body still ached. But, the heartfelt anguish came later, with the realization no one, especially Jacob, would celebrate her newfound wealth should they ever discover the price paid. And now she had to share that knowledge. "Initially, the girl rejected him. Later he appealed further, and when gifts came to entice her and he made more promises... She did not protest." Josefina fingered a fold in her skirt, then spoke rapidly, though unemotionally. "He agreed to provide sanctuary for the mother until the birth, raise the child as his own. There was a promise made to protect her reputation. If, in the end, she did not love him, she would be free to marry a man she truly loved."

"Such a fool," Marianne snorted. "Zee nuns warn us. Men agree to anything. Theez girl arrange her own trouble. Does she have no decency? Where is this *fille de joie*?"

The scathing name-calling of harlotry maligned and branded with disgrace and disapproval. Josefina felt her hope waning. Marianne gave her no choice. "I am that girl, and I need your help." Her fear of scandal weighted the words as Josefina spoke rapidly. "You must find out why François avoids me. Never answers my notes. Makes no attempt to provide the protection and haven he promised."

A breeze ruffled Marianne's red hair, spinning fine wisps into a fiery crown. An angry blush reddened her cheeks. "You cannot be speaking of François? And you?" The cold words whipped out as if driven by a befouling glacial wind. Green eyes narrowed to slits resembling a viper, no rattle preceded the strike. "This is why Jacob was not here for our return. To escape your insult." Her voice was pitiless. "You bed them both, then accuse a ducLaFevre of fathering your child?"

"That is a vicious accusation. You of all people know Jacob and I love each other. We shared nothing more than a harmless romp. Exchanged nothing more scandalous than kisses and teasing airs." Josefina spewed indignation. "We dallied in the stable but minutes before you arrived cautioning us Father was coming. An erroneous warning. You stayed behind, with Jacob, while I ran back to the house."

"How stupid of me. Of course, I was there." Sarcasm coated the words. "Did you bargain with Jacob, too, then or afterwards about secretly becoming lovers? And with François, did I intrude there also? Or did you mimic the Holy Mother with some miraculous conception?"

Josefina cringed at the vehemence. "No, you lay upstairs, knowing nothing. The tryst happened during your illness." Josefina's voice became soft, seductive, like her tale. "For weeks François behaved kindly towards me while we prayed for you to overcome your fever. He entertained me with music, taught me to dance, told me stories of myself I did not remember. We were companions sharing secrets and joy. Other than occasional visits by the doctor and a nurse, François and I spent every day solely in each other's company."

"And you found that grievous? To be so entertained while I lay desperately ill?"

"His attentions were flattering. He trusted me with his plans for expanding the bank out West, sought my opinions, treated me as an equal."

Marianne's ill-tempered expression hardened. "And you think him insincere?"

"Your brother spoke of his wish that I bear his heir. Initially, the idea shocked me. For days I felt so wronged I could not eat or sleep. He assured me he had wanted our union since soon after I was born. More so after I grew into a woman he truly desired. When I told him Jacob and I had promised to marry, François offered me a proposal."

"And what could he possibly offer that appeared too delicious to ignore?" Marianne folded her arms over her chest.

"He pledged to settle a fortune on me if I would bear his child, to protect me, and to keep my sin secret. If François fails in his promise, my life will be ruined." Josefina stopped, the whole story told. Nothing said about the shame that filled her, of his paraded triumph, of her growing heartbreak.

"And?" Marianne stood stiff as a shock of wheat.

"I am carrying François's child."

"You drove Jacob away from others who loved him," shrieked Marianne. "You seduced and now profane François, and you fear losing your reputation?"

"François promised to take me to a place of solace and secrecy, to shield me from public censure, to provide for me and the child." Josefina was desperate. She could not find the words to convey her terror. The devil does not pop up dressed in red with horned head and hoofs; he arrives with a temptation so seductive it overrides any objection. Marianne would not understand.

"And what has that to do with me?" Marianne's voice was merciless.

Josefina knelt before her best friend. "You must help me. Please? I beg you. Convince François to talk with me. Tell him you know of the agreement."

"Why should I?" After the question, Marianne's slender body seemed to wilt.

"This child will be his heir, a son to protect the title and property belonging to your family. François spoke of taking me to your chateau in France for sanctuary. He planned to announce a world tour for both you and me as a token for your missed debut. Later, he would bring the child here, as his own." Dropping her head onto Marianne's slippers, Josefina wept. Body-racking sobs dulled the happy pumpkin cloth to a murky brown.

Several minutes passed before Marianne knelt and patted Josefina's trembling body. "There, there, you must stop wailing. I have known other women such as you, and I cannot harden my heart against you. It beats not as stone." The weeping quieted to whimpers. "Much as zee honorable path displeases me, your request is justified. If, what you tell me is true."

"I have no reason to lie."

Marianne pulled Josefina into her arms, quieting the hysterics. "If François made such a promise? If your carry his seed? He must fulfill his obligation to the child."

A rap sounded on the door.

"*Entrez,*" said Marianne. A servant entered, carrying a large gold tray with sweets, sandwiches, and fruits. Marianne cleared off space while Josefina moved nearer the warmth of a sunny window.

The domestic arranged cups, saucers and table service while Marianne thumbed through *The Chronicles of Einhart and Collins*, a well-worn collection of western maps of America, as if she sought immediate distraction. Abruptly, Marianne addressed the maid. "I will finish. You may return to your duties." She motioned for Josefina to sit down.

As soon as the door closed Marianne began. "Your situation seems clearer now. You have been treated cruelly." Her voice deepened with sincerity. "I know François to be a man of honor. I have experienced that loyalty. He would not mistreat a true friend without just cause, especially someone to whom he promised his protection."

Josefina choked on a nibble of scone. Quickly she washed it down with tea. Childhood fables told to her by Louis, and later by Stuart, of François's dubious honor popped up in unsettling fragments. Scary tales of unchivalrous acts. Boys' imaginations, she prayed.

"François, in his letters inviting me to come and stay with him, wrote glowing details of your charms," said Marianne. "Of how he admired you. I saw from the first day I arrived how deeply he cared for you."

Josefina blinked. What little hope she had mustered before leaving Taylor Estates barely survived. François did not love her. He wanted only an heir. That would disappoint Marianne.

"I will speak to François. I am sure there is a misunderstanding." Marianne plucked at Josefina's platinum curls and straightened her collar. "Do not fret so. Everything will be righted. Leave everything to me, I will make sure everybody gets what is deserved." A smile carried up into twinkling emerald eyes. "Do not worry so. Eat, eat. Little mother must feed her perfect babe. I do not wish to be related to crooked sniveling goat." She chucked Josefina's chin playfully, then rose, placing her arm around Josefina's shoulder. "Please, my friend, everything will come out as it should. Sit, let me tell you of the French countryside so you may prepare." She smiled broadly, returning to her chair. "Our debut *fini*, I shall return to France with you. I would like to see you safely away. Now, tell me how you fare. What else I might do."

Josefina ached to ask for Marianne's help in locating Jacob; instead, she settled for companionship.

They talked until late afternoon, sharing lunch and strolling the parkway while settling a number of questions. Marianne remained in charge, offering advice on how best to travel, the climate, clothes appropriate for provincial Marseilles, visiting the Vatican, and later for shopping in Paris and London.

One conflict remained a thorn, impossible to prick loose. "You must agree to have François accompany us," Marianne persisted. "That is without question. I understand that you agreed to try to care for him. Fulfill that commitment, perhaps, over time, I might find a real sister in zee bargain."

Josefina did not recall mentioning that portion of François's request. Beyond delivering the baby safely, she had only one commitment and that was to herself, to spend François's initial settlement searching for Jacob. After finding her vagabond engineer, she planned to join him and share the fortune. A gift, she would explain, for all her suffering and kindness during Marianne's illness.

Josefina kept her silence, not committing to anything. Although the outcome appeared much brighter, she saw no reason to test Marianne's loyalty. After all, her almost sister had used every means available to win the handsome Jacob for herself.

More importantly, the thought of sharing a household with François frightened Josefina. She feared if she ever again submitted to him, she would never get free.

Eleven

Taylor Estates, October 31
All Saints Eve, a day of demons and ghosts.

Three weeks passed without word from either François or Marianne. Soft rose of daybreak, chilled with misty dew, colored the rug, duvet, drapes, walls, everything in the room, including the emaciated woman in the bed.

When Louise's eyes opened at the gentle tug, Josefina blurted out. "Mother, I am having a child."

Within the confines of the dozens of pillows that supported her, Louise Taylor sat up straighter. "Stupid girl. Dieter has years of work ahead of him to earn any..."

"It is not Dieter."

"That accounts for your despair these past months. Jacob leaving without a word..."

"Not Jacob either. The father is François."

"I cannot believe you." Her mother showed amazing vigor, rising dramatically. "Must you add lying and defamation to your long list of sins. The man is a saint, part of our family."

"He seduced me with a promise of..."

"Do you wish to send me to my grave? I will hear no more. Get out! Go to your father. With the truth, or I will tell him of your lies myself. Leave me."

Behind the mansion, cornstalks stood broken, dried and browned, giving sustenance and harbor to quacking ducks and honking geese, hiding the stanchions of the hunters. Surrounding tracts of sorghum and oat stubble lay dormant, waiting for winter's wrath and spring's rebirth. A dozen nearby outbuildings bristled with busy bodies hurrying through their morning chores, like giant ants silently foraging in the predawn light.

In the solarium, blue stripes with sunflowers trimmed the windows of the room stocked with wicker furniture. Josefina had been allowed to choose the decor since Mother never came down for breakfast. The morning hour had always been one belonging to Josefina, her father, and numerous newsprint.

She sat silently at her place, watching Father read, waiting for his eyes to travel the length of the page and stop. *Dear God, if I could be anywhere else, doing anything else, I would be forever grateful.*

Josef licked his forefinger and reached up.

"Father, I am with child." The words hung in the air, polluting their very breath. Josefina wanted to pull them back, swallow them, shove them down to her poisoned womb. The possibility of dying by her own hand loomed invitingly.

"What?" Father's hand froze halfway of turning a page. "I did not hear you correctly."

"I am with child." She rushed. "François is the father. It happened while we were quarantined in St. Louis."

"Josefina, you speak the truth?" All color drained from his face. The paper crumpled with sharp crackles as his hands clinched into fists.

"François promised to protect me, to take me to Europe for the birth of the baby. He pledged to return me home then, my reputation intact. He would come back later with the child, claiming it as a relative's. I feared telling you. But now he has deserted me, I think..."

Josef bellowed with the pain of a bludgeoned bull. The newspaper fell to the floor, ripped in half. The sturdy chair toppled backwards when he jumped up from the table. "I will kill that devil with my own hands." He dashed from the room roaring his threats.

"Father, stop! Wait, please, I must tell you of the agreement." Josefina chased after him. She arrived outside the stable in time to barely escape being trampled when her father raced from the stable astride his fastest warmblood stallion.

~ * ~

Overnight dew sparkled in the shade at Taylor Estates, caught in its struggle to exist just a moment longer. A faint scent of rose mingled with the mildew odor of rotting foliage. Inside, in the library, hundreds of books crammed shelves that covered the walls from floor to ceiling. The oily aroma of the leather bindings saturated the humid air, the normally comforting scent ignored by the room's single occupant.

Josefina, perched on a tall gilded chair, twisted a handful of curls through her fingers while sticky streams of perspiration slid down her sides and seeped into her tightly laced camisole. Her body registered nothing, numb, unfeeling. She had sat for three hours on the hard, uncomfortable seat.

Without warning the French doors to the veranda burst open. The frames slammed against the paneled wall shattering the silence. Glass inserts cracked into a downpour of misshapen slivers.

Eyes wide with fright, Josefina pressed her fist tight against her mouth, stifling a scream when her father stomped before her. His short legs hammered the floor like pistons. Dark stains smeared his shirt; more smudges crusted the side of his thick neck and matted the hair lying on his shoulder. When he slapped a coiled whip across the palm of his hand, the blouse of his sleeves carried the fumes of opiates and fire to Josefina's nose.

"Get out!" he bellowed. "I cannot stand to look at you." His nostrils flared. "Liar! Trollop! Your sainted mother would die if she knew." An angry red welt creased his cheek from temple to chin.

"I did not lie! I told the truth." Josefina rose, filled with terror. "You must believe me!"

"You have made a murderer of me," Josef thundered. "You and your filthy tale. I will not have you here in my home, within my sight." Hate edged each word. "Get away from me. I want you far enough away to never cross my path. Go to—go to Stuart's. Your brother's acquaintance with the sordid side of life should serve you both well. From there go wherever you wish, cast your seed as the wind blows. I shan't give a damn." He pointed a rigid finger at her midsection. "And, get rid of that bastard!"

Josefina's body swayed as if Father had dealt a reeling blow. She had not anticipated the second part of his command; she reacted automatically. "Father, I am keeping this baby. He is a part of me, a part of you." Her hands clenched, nails digging half moons into her palms. She cringed under Father's spewed hate, as if she were some pestilence befouling his beloved land. Her blood flowed cold and sluggish in her veins. How could his caring have vanished so quickly? "He will carry on the vein of our family," Josefina said.

"Now, harlot!" Josef's jaw muscles knotted like a rope. "Out of my sight. Out of my house!"

"Please, let me stay. I need your help..." Josefina begged, "or let me stay with Louis, near you and Mother."

Josef's head bowed. "Out! Away from here." The whip wagged in his clenched fist.

"Be assured," Josefina struggled to keep her voice steady, "I will not give up this baby. François promised me a lifetime stipend for bearing his heir. I will not concede that." She could be just as stubborn as Father. She would not yield. The blood of her body warmed.

"You," Josef shook a spearlike finger at her, "are a liar and a whore. Your 'Mr. Broderick' came to me. Sniffing after you, but I sent him on his merry way. Little did I know you had already given him what he wanted." He hesitated, studying her hard, then barked. "Did you lie with him in François's stable?" His eyes glistened like chunks of blue ice.

Shocked by the question, Josefina faltered, unable to respond.

Before she could gather her wits, Josef snapped, "your sorry face reveals the truth." The butt of the whip whacked the burnished desk. Papers flew, a pen fell from its well and rolled noisily across the flat surface. A stained-glass lamp teetered precariously near the edge of the reverberating wooden top. "Out, whore!"

Nausea swelled, subsided, and boiled again in a huge wave up from her belly to her throat. She felt her face sicken as the blood drained away. She fought unsuccessfully to clear her muddled thoughts. Who had told him of the stable? Only Jacob and Marianne knew. And what of the stains on his clothes, the odor of burned flesh? 'Murderer' he had said. She must make him believe the cause was just. "Father, I carry François's child. I am telling the truth. On the life of my beloved mother."

"My God, have you no heart?" Josef roared. "To curse the woman who gave you birth. Get out! Now! And I forbid you to speak to your mother, a decent, God-fearing woman—unlike you." Josef pounded his bear-like paw on the desk with each indictment; his expression thundered revulsion. "Unless you rid yourself of that cursed offspring," air hissed between his teeth warning of the strike of a viper, "you are forbidden to ever contact anyone of this family! I expect to never hear of you, nor your ill-begotten bastard."

His words hacked at Josefina's heart like an axe, the blade lodging deep. She trembled. "The child matters most. My son. François's heir." Everything had gone awry.

"I will house neither a liar nor a harlot under my roof. And you are both." Josef swept the desk clean with an arc of his arm then turned his back on the daughter he had molded to his liking. The lamp shattered as it hit the floor. Glistening splinters of colorful glass sliced the soft Aubusson carpet beneath Josefina's feet.

Driven to the brink of madness, Josefina took dead aim at her Father's heart. "Then you shall never see me again." Her young body seethed with all the malice it could hold as she lashed out. "And do what you may, I will never give up this child." Turning away, she ran from the room and the wall forged by her father's back.

Josefina dashed across the echoing foyer and up the wide oak stairs. Father had never raised his voice in this manner at her, ever. But then, she had never given him strong cause. *This banishment will be his undoing.* The stairs held steadfast under her angry feet that stomped noiselessly, like a pair of powder puffs. "I will survive," she promised aloud. "Father will live to regret this."

Stubbornness hardened the round jaw; lips crimped to the bloodlessness of a landed fish. When she reached her rooms, Josefina screamed at the chambermaid straightening the bed. "Pack, pack all my things! I am leaving this house and never coming back." Anything to escape Father's loathing face with its ugly revulsion.

Josefina grabbed everything in sight, slamming new and old into the hastily gathered trunks. She stopped once, to send a message to the stables to harness a buggy and ready her foal Contessa.

An image flashed through her mind of a calendar crammed with years of racing schedules arranged in the many animated discussions she had with Father. A ladder of escalating competitions aimed at securing unprecedented sums for breeding privileges for Contessa, the animal that had been her sixteenth birthday gift a few weeks ago. The foal was a lineaged, prized creature, its future assured.

The groom returned. "Mr. Josef says that animal's a breeder. It stays." Hard eyes showed no questioning of authority, no hesitancy.

Josef Taylor bought no Negroes to labor on his property. He did not believe in owning darkies and always preached, "Want no tar heels carrying the Taylor name." He did instead initiate his own form of slavery, paying the way for indentures to come from Germany, Austria, Belgium, and the Netherlands. These adults spent their entire lives laboring to buy freedom in the hopes of securing a better future for their children. For the owner of Taylor Estates, those dreams bought absolute loyalty.

Josefina charged off to the stables, her body heaving with barely controlled fury. "Listen to me." She reached up and grabbed the foreman's shirt. "I have five trunks. Bring me a vehicle equipped to make St. Louis. Now!" Then she added as an afterthought, "and ample provisions for Contessa." Her youthful voice, quivering on the brink of hysteria, carried its demands across the yard, throughout the stables.

"I do as Mr. Josef orders." The foreman's head and shoulders braced for an onslaught. "He tells me the horse stays here. It stays."

Months of controlled fury erupted from Josefina. "Damn you," she cursed. "I am taking Contessa. The horse belongs to me!" Both feet planted firmly on the ground of the ancestral estate, hands on her hips, Josefina shouted toward the palatial house. "And I will never, never give up my child! Damn you to hell!"

Dark clouds swirled across the midday sky, closing off what sunshine existed, bringing a chilling rain. Suddenly, turning away from the public curses spreading their poison through the air, Josefina watched a figure with bonnet flying and skirts twisted around long legs sprint across the slippery lawn. Relief surged through her when she recognized the advancing figure. "Marianne, thank God! You are all right. I was afraid Father had hurt you, too."

Clothes askew, smoky eyes sunken into a bloodless face, the girl babbled excitedly in French. Each breath sucked up in a rasping gasp. "*J'ai ne sais pas...*"

Josefina commanded, "In English! *Anglais!*"

Marianne clung to Josefina who used all her strength to keep them both from toppling. "I know not what 'appened. Your father storm zee room, raving about Jacob. I could not lie to him of your tryst. Before I can stop him, he lock me in zee room and run out shouting curses."

Marianne's puzzled look changed to exasperation. "When zee upstairs maid unlock zee door, I find my brother in zee care of his confidante. When I step up to help, theez *roué* say I must go, leave zee tending to François's intimates, that I am not needed. Go where, I think? I come here, to you."

Josefina led her distressed friend toward the stable, all the while shouting instructions at the stablemen. "Fetch Contessa. Get feed. I want lap robes." With François's death, had his cavalier retinue dispossessed Marianne? And the blame for her best friend's dilemma, Josefina admitted, rested squarely on her.

Men scurried about busily. One dragged a trunk from the house; another feverishly harnessed a horse to a carriage; several loaded trunks; one loped back and forth from the stable, tossing equestrian equipment onto the floor beside the trunks.

Marianne's accent grew more pronounced. "I am at fault. I did nothing to defend you. I never go back zere. I sail home to France." The panting ceased while Josefina stroked the long, heaving back.

"No, do not reproach yourself. Father would not have listened anyway." Josefina stared unseeing at Miss Vondyken, her tutor, who first spoke to a groom, then hurried forward, balancing an armload of boxes, several tins and a violin case.

A wall of disbelief seized Josefina as the weeping woman first hugged her, then thrust a box at her. "Take care, if you ever need me..." The older woman's voice evaporated into a series of stoic snuffles.

Josefina turned abruptly to face Marianne. "Come with me! Together we can decide what to do." Grabbing Contessa's lead from the reluctant groom, she lashed the foal behind the vehicle then pushed Marianne up onto the bench. Before a driver could mount, Josefina disengaged the brake, clicked the reins and began a headstrong flight across Illinois.

They dashed heedlessly into a wintry front storming its way across Illinois, leaving withered, lifeless roots in its wake.

~ * ~

Josef watched the departing buggy from the library window. This offspring had quite possibly turned him into a murderer. The shooting had happened quickly.

François had stood in the open behind the chateau. Josef recalled riding down upon the stupefied man without warning, his guns cocked. "Traitor! Cad! Judas!" he had shouted. Other, more vile curses had been eclipsed by his rage. The rifle fired, then one pistol shot; he did not remember taking aim.

François had first turned to run, then staggered to his knees. When the horse reached François's side, Josef had dismounted and stood over the man, prepared to kill. One shot remained.

François begged. "The child is not mine. Josefina lies. Jacob already bedded her. Ask Marianne." Then his unsteady frame collapsed face forward. The still torso displayed wounds, a slice along the side of the neck and a clean hole in the lower back.

People quickly converged on them. Josef shouldered his way through the bystanders and headed to the house. Only seconds passed before he barged into Marianne's room.

Josef felt ill even now, picturing the conviction Marianne bore when she corroborated François's allegation, adding further the damning proof that Dieter would support her allegation. She contended that Josefina had bedded Jacob Broderick then seduced

François out of her anger at the proposed plans to marry her to some unknown.

Before he left to learn the extent of François's injuries, Josef locked Marianne in the room, protecting her from witnessing the tragedy his daughter's lies had caused.

At the place of the shooting, blood covered François from neck to knee. The workers had cut his clothes away, revealing a large and deep hole exposing tendon and bone in the back. The neck wound appeared less deep, but blood flowed freely.

Josef carried the unconscious man indoors, then waited for the doctor's arrival. He stayed through the cleansing, then stopped at the workers' huts edging Taylor Estates to confront Dieter before returning to face Josefina.

Then she had the audacity to embellish her previous lies. What obstinate folly! Did she really think he would believe her preposterous tale? A promise of lifelong support without a marriage contract from a man of François's character. What nonsense.

Reliving the destruction of his trust in Josefina fired Josef's anger again. Two brothers had preceded Josefina's birth. Yet, when this daughter arrived, he immediately declared her the pride of the litter and ignoring the laws of male lineage named her Josefina, after himself. He instilled in her his own passions and strengths, had driven her to be her best. Before today she had never failed him. Never.

Now she had done much worse: she had betrayed him, rejected his life's dreams and ambitions. Love of commerce thundered in their veins, riches fueled their pumping hearts; the exercise of power strengthened their bodies. The challenge of making and keeping their fortune consumed their life. He had set her on the throne beside him, coached to reign in his absence.

A lifetime of lessons wasted. Josefina had not learned, had not seen the foundation under the frill, ignored the power of the woman behind the throne. She had been his choice. She held promise. Now she fled in the grayness like a slut creeping from her lover's bed. Well, he would have none of it. He would instruct Stuart to rid the family of the bastard, send it to a workhouse, ship the whore to France with her artful friend. Let the harlot make her own way.

The decision made, Josef dismissed his daughter from his mind, as one would discard an imperfect rose.

In his rashness, Josef ignored a wisdom practiced by his wife. Cast off the thorny stems of the rose, arrange the perfect blossoms for display, and salvage the abused and unappreciated petals to scatter their sweetness among private things.

Twelve

Josefina and Marianne endured three days and nights snatching sleep in turns while crossing Illinois. On the fourth day, night fell quickly, as dark and impenetrable as widow's weeds.

Josefina cracked the whip, slicing the air with razor sharpness inches above the thoroughbred's flanks. As the buggy lurched, she flicked the reins again, urging the horse on. She had never touched a whip to any animal, perhaps tonight would be a first.

A frozen grip sealed Josefina's gloved fingers to the leather straps, their protesting tingle long since ceased. Her shoulders, spasming from hours of tension, ached as if she had carried a kicking mule on her back for days.

Pain throbbed into a Herculean pulse beneath her skull and lodged grating spikes behind her eyes, yet giddiness simmered beneath the aches and fatigue. A single new revelation carried her on. Jacob had presented himself to her father; he had not deserted her. Jacob Broderick had asked to be considered.

A full moon, the only blessing of the night, allowed Josefina to urge the exhausted steed through the darkness. The radiance ricocheted off the gleaming silver trappings sending dimples of light prancing across the snow. Any other night she would have admired and remarked on the wonder, but this night Josefina's mind remained rooted on the stench and measure of bloodstains that had smudged her father.

"Dieter brought on this entire debacle," she said aloud. Josefina glanced sideways. On the bench next to her, seemingly oblivious of the ongoing chatter, Marianne pinched a lambskin wrap tight about her throat with one hand. Her other arm woodenly hugged the buggy frame.

"If he had not pressured me unduly. Last night he suggested to Mother that she and I consider a trip to Tobins to select a pattern for my trousseau from the newest china and silver offerings. I have no idea what encouraged him to make such a presumptuous statement. Our friendship certainly did not give him any such claim. I had decided months ago when and to whom I would give up my heart. Dieter Vandemere was not an aspirant then and is not now."

Josefina scowled, her throat emitting a soft guttural noise as she observed her companion's gaunt face. Splatters of rusty specks contrasted starkly against the pale complexion, the sprinkles resembling the orange berries of the pyracantha that had fallen along the road onto the dusting of snow.

Perhaps the decision to take only brief stops on the road to rest the horses had been too extreme. They had fostered a better than normal speed, two brief stays at inns, while cramped together in the enclosed buggy for three days. "Racing against what?" Josefina chided aloud. "Nothing." Simply to get as far away as possible from her father's loathing.

Aimless thoughts toyed with her tired mind. A messenger traveling cross-country probably would have already arrived at her brother's house. Stuart would be waiting. She would guess he knew about Marianne. There was no escape facing him.

Before they left Taylor Estates, Josefina vowed personally to keep Marianne safe. The horse could be destroyed, and she could succumb in the process, but her best friend would not fall ill again. Perhaps the route chosen had been too ambitious. "We will rest here by the creek, Marianne. Get out and walk about a bit."

When the buggy halted, Josefina surveyed the naturally frisky foal tied on behind it. The white head nodded impatiently above the reddish hairs of an Edwardian script "T" that blazed across its white chest. Steamy breath bellowed from its nostrils as it demanded attention. Shame flooded Josefina at the brutal run the young animal had endured.

The remorse faded when a slight thump in her midsection diverted her attention. *One day, this child will win back what François has withheld.*

Worry trenched her mind. *How soon will I be so misshapen others will guess my predicament? I must find Jacob well before that time. What if he has left for California? Will he desire the heiress of Taylor Estates or will he still want me?*

The cold winds trifling with whirling skirts and petticoats almost overpowered Josefina when she reached up to help Marianne down from the trap. The two girls struggled to maintain their balance, clutching at each other as their numbed bodies threatened to give way. Josefina ordered, "Move about. Get your blood flowing."

Marianne nodded dumbly as she tucked strands of red hair firmly under her bonnet, then coughed dryly, draping a muffler tighter across her face. "How much further?" Marianne asked, her voice raspy, fingers twitching across a pearl and onyx rosary dangling from her muff.

"This is our last stop. The Chain of Rocks Bridge crosses into St. Louis at the bottom of this hill. After that we have only a few miles to Stuart's."

Josefina broke a skim of ice on the creek, then opened a sack of oats. Her frozen hands probed among the trunks, then fumbled across the floor of the carriage searching for a feedbag. Irritated, she removed her bonnet, waving away the platinum curls that sprung about her head. Dumping a few handfuls of feed into the hat, Josefina hastily fed and watered both animals. The rest had passed too quickly when she beckoned Marianne back to the carriage.

Over and over Josefina blessed the numerous trips she had made to the riverfront town accompanying her father on business. He had forced her to captain their rig on many jaunts. If not for that, she and Marianne would both be at the mercy of the elements and the jackals of the countryside.

Father had demanded she be as accomplished at handling firearms and horses as her two elder brothers. Minor endeavors on his long list of absolutes, but now those perfected skills had put a satisfactory distance between father and daughter.

If only—Jacob had waited, François had kept his promise, or Father had loved her enough to provide sanctuary. Josefina daydreamed, costumed in the wishfulness of an actress whose play had gone sour.

The well-tramped road broadened into a wide thoroughfare whose rutted surface had guided numerous travelers on their way. Immigrants flooded St. Louis. Most were swallowed up by the burgeoning city, some floundered deep in its underbelly, others lived like kings on the crest of the four hills. Most existed somewhere in-between, longing to rise to the crest, grateful to be free of the bowels. Nearly all arrived at the banks of the Mississippi unsure of their rightful place.

In the city the road turned black as licorice, the darkness almost impenetrable as buildings blocked out the moonlight.

"Almost there," Josefina announced. "A warning first. Stuart is the rogue of our family. Among other things, he never cared for me. I usurped his hold."

"I will be happy to be in a bed, near a fire, and out of this buggy. I do not care if he is Lucifer himself." Marianne scrubbed at her face. "My eyes feel as gritty as silver polish, like peering through filthy windows."

"Perhaps you should not have come. Father would have protected you. You have Dieter and all the bank officers who are indebted to François."

"Ah, yes, but to François, not me. And your father may well pay a heavy price for his wrath."

Josefina spotted blazing gas lamps and candles flickering in the windows of a large Victorian townhouse. The two girls cheered spontaneously. As soon as the golden arcs of lights touched on the vehicle, several people rushed out. Their calm assurances welcomed the weary travelers.

Stuart stood framed by the doorway. His ash blonde hair clumped like a spider on each shoulder. The lamps caused yellow slivers to rim the murky irises of his eyes, creating a menacing obscurity as they darted about.

The servants quickly separated the girls. One woman hurried Marianne through the entrance and up the stairs. Without a word of concern, Stuart yanked Josefina through a door, pinching her arm and bruising her shoulder as he shoved her into a library.

Even with the gaslights Josefina had difficulty seeing. Large furniture crowded the dark room. Hideous heads of beasts with dead eyes glared down from the walls; grotesque pieces of lifeless limbs shrouded every available space. Josefina stumbled on the carpet, nearly collapsing onto the lap of a rotund, bawdy appearing woman. A flabby arm darted out and grabbed Josefina's elbow, then pushed her into an empty chair. The rouged and penciled face gazed at Josefina with indifference.

The click of a lock pierced the silence before Stuart joined the woman on the settee and addressed his sister. "You need not go into detail about your predicament," he sneered. "This is Madam Vlydovski. She came here to rid the family of your indiscretion."

Exhausted, Josefina listened without hearing. Her shoulders and arms throbbed; each spasm brought more pain. Her eyes burned, blurred from peering through the blackness, navigating the narrow lanes, picking out obstacles, trying to avoid the jolting ruts that seemed to turn into mountains before her. She wanted only to shut out the night, to lie down, to sleep.

The older woman peered into Josefina's eyes and shook the girl's limp wrist. Dirty nails poked at her tiny chest. Josefina roused storming. "Get away from me. What are you doing? Who are you?" She pulled away, not so done in as to allow such personal invasion.

Stuart curled his lip and gestured for the woman to continue.

Josefina shrank back against the leather seat. Fear pummeled her anger to the background. *Stuart had always resented my getting Father's attention. Is he getting even?*

Hate glazed her brother's narrowed eyes. "You have no say in this. Father directed me to take care of your problem. You are in my hands now." Dark shadows cast by the flickering lamps danced across his face, distorting his features into an eerie disjointed mask.

Josefina would not allow her child to be taken away, dumped in some horrible workhouse. Harnessing her remaining energy, she demanded, "How take care of my problem?" Nervousness dampened the palms of her frigid hands. Her knees trembled. Her heart pounded.

Stuart towered over her. "Do you think I would allow your bastard to live? Eligible to someday walk into our lives, claiming to be an heir, absconding with our hard earned profits?"

Josefina guessed at the nature of what he intended to say. She had heard talk of such grisly goings on, but her family could never be involved in such indecency. She would not believe Father's anger had pushed him this far. Perhaps crazed, a murderer, and had believed she lied, but nothing led her to accept that Father ordered this. Distraught, she screeched, "Who told you to do this?"

"Listen, Josefina." Stuart deliberately mangled the pronunciation, his resentment pronounced. "If you wish to survive, you will do absolutely as you are told. This woman has performed the procedure many times." Stuart seemed to stare through her while he delivered the ultimate blow. "The excision comes by order of our father. To rid our family of any reminder!" Stuart's eyes danced.

Delicately, Josefina turned her head and involuntarily spattered the bile rising in her throat onto the rich carpet. Her brother watched in horror before half dragging her shuddering body from the library.

He shoved his exhausted sister at a waiting housemaid. "Take her to a room. Make sure she stays there, or it will be your hide."

The servant helped Josefina up the stairs into a dimly lit room and toward a bed. In complete silence the house girl removed the soft kidskin boots, motioned toward a basin of water, then withdrew to sit outside the bedroom door. The water undisturbed, Josefina lay across the bed, her clothes matted in lumps under her depleted body. She slept.

~ * ~

Downstairs, Stuart ushered the feathered and flowered Madame out. "I will send my card at the first opportunity. I expect our business to be concluded at that point." When he returned to the library a self-satisfied smirk slashed his portly jaw as he poured a glass of brandy.

Strutting across the library, he contemplated the situation aloud. "First Louis, then this girl child. I got nothing. Well, not now." He lifted his glass of Kirschwasser in salute as he congratulated himself. The cherry liqueur blazed red in the firelight.

His decision went far beyond what the letter had requested. Someday father would approve. Still, no one must ever learn the full extent and finality of the procedure. "Not only will father satisfy my overdrafts," Stuart boasted aloud to the empty room, "he might feel charitable enough to pay off some of my other debts." His sharp cackle drilled the air.

And what of the other girl? A short-term impediment, Stuart decided. He had already sent a message informing Father about Marianne's presence. However, Stuart decided, it might be in his best interest to postpone the mischief until after the uninvited guest departed.

If the excision worked as promised, accepting Josefina survived, he would have no worry of her ever producing another heir. Stuart knew through experience that his own bloated bride, with often enough thrashing, failed to carry full term. Only Louis's uninspiring progeny remained. All dolts content to muck about at the farm. There would be no others to protest his taking the throne. Stuart rose and sauntered to the cabinet. His exuberance demanded another drink.

Thirteen

The morning after arriving at her brother's house, Josefina stood at the bedroom door listening. The house was a tomb; the servants stirred like mourners at a wake. She opened the door and pounced on the dozing girl guarding her. "Master Stuart, is he about?"

"No, Missy. He's off. He said you must keep to the house. He will return late."

"And, Alexandria? She did not greet us when we arrived."

The maid cowered. "She is of importance?"

"I want to greet my sister-in-law. Where is she? Has she already gone out, too?"

"The mistress is in St. Charles with the Reverend. She lost the baby before the quickening." At the later information, the girl's demeanor suggested less of fear and more of compassion.

Josefina's body chilled at the telling. "I seem to recall four times Alexandria failed to carry her child to term. Is that correct?"

"Yes, Missy. She is sickly. The doctor told her to leave here, visit the countryside until her strength returns."

"Alexandria did not ask to come to Taylor Estates? To recuperate under my family's care?"

"I cannot say. The doctor is old friend. Maybe he advise rest, from family." A trace of fear slipped back into the girl's voice. She began to edge away.

First, Josefina decided to attend to her body's needs, then the next task must be to devise a plan. Judging by Alexandria's predicament, Josefina feared the previous night's attendant might have already proven too efficient. "Fetch some bath water and tell the other guest to come to my room."

After indulging in hot baths, Josefina and Marianne shared grits with bacon drippings, then dozed for several hours before inspecting the rooms. The house wore dismal and severe trappings. Deep purple, almost black, drapes hung at the windows creating somber borders around heavy shutters that allowed little light to penetrate.

The stale cigar odor of the grim house soured all the rooms. Heavy mahogany, stained blacker than normal, planked most of the rooms. Any walls without the prison-like trim sported dull, flat paint. No decorative paper, no flowers.

Oppressive furniture overpowered each of the public rooms. No stained glass lamps existed, no pretty pillows or colorful pictures. Even the portraits boasted austere people Josefina did not recognize. Not a hint of a woman's leanings appeared anywhere.

"It is like a dungeon," Josefina said. Marianne agreed. If Josefina had not known Stuart's history herself, she would have guessed her brother a bachelor, and a macabre one at that.

Later that evening, after the rest of the house slept, the girls retired to Josefina's room. Josefina felt it time to broach a concern that had troubled her since leaving Taylorsville. "Marianne, I am thankful you chose to come with me. Your friendship means everything to me. But, I am responsible for what happened to François, and your absence from the Chateau worries me."

"I can do nothing. François's staff caters to heez every desire." Marianne sighed. "François and I shared two wonderful years. But from birth 'til zee day I walk off zee ship I know of François only through my mother's tales."

To Josefina the explanation sounded callous. "But surely you feel pain for him. And for your own loss."

"My own loss?" Marianne sounded thoroughly confused.

"No one told you?" Josefina felt unsettled, popping the bitter news without preparing Marianne. "Father said he killed François. I am so sorry."

Marianne sat quietly for several minutes. "Josefina, all your life you know and love Louis, but with Stuart, theez absent brother, affection did not exist. That speaks more to François and me. We are blood relations, but we shared no history. I will return to Marseille."

"François is dead. What will happen to his remains? His property? To you?" Josefina doubted Marianne's unconcern. Her friend was being gracious, not faulting Josefina for François's death.

"When I speak with zee solicitor, he will tell me what I am to do." Marianne dabbed at her eyes. "Provisions are in François's papers."

"I feel so awful." Josefina grabbed her friend's hand. "Can I do anything to make this up to you?"

"Do not ever abandon zee child. You must make theez sacrifice for the little one, François, and me. I will arrange everything before heez majority. We will make heez claim and introduction together."

Marianne's kindness did not lighten the burden of blame Josefina carried. The short time with François, the missing familial memories, all meant to ease her guilt, only made Josefina feel more regrets. Marianne's heartening forgiveness moved Josefina to the brink of tears.

"You are the only person I have left," Josefina said. "Soon you will be gone, too. I feel desolate already, as if my whole reason for living is being snatched from me."

The thought brought Josefina back to Stuart and his butchering conspirator. "You need to know what Stuart divulged after the servants led you away." The story spilled out with all the pain, fear, and loathing Josefina had boxed up inside.

"Surely you exaggerate," Marianne exclaimed. "Stuart, your father, they are men of principle. How could they suggest such a deed?"

"This vile woman assaulted me," Josefina protested. "She tore at my clothes, poked filthy fingers over my body. My brother hired her to perform a procedure that would take the baby." Quivers of fear slurred Josefina's words; tears welled in her eyes. Several pillows puffed hollowly as she slammed them at the floor. "Stuart said Father ordered it." Knees hugged tightly against her chest, the shattered mother-to-be rocked back and forth on the bed.

"Little Jos, we arrived late at night," soothed Marianne. "You were exhausted. You must be mistaken. Your Father would not be so cruel."

The rocking stopped.

"My father has no heart. His own position, that is all he cares about." Josefina's voice rose angrily. "And don't call me Little Jos. Not ever again! I will rid myself of the shame of being his namesake." Josefina paused. "I will be known as Josie, and I will make no claim to the family surname either."

Her supple body hardened, edged with a brittleness as stiff as confectioner's icing. Patting her stomach, Josie spoke to her unborn. "We need no familial ties, you and I. Someday you will know your ancestry. But, until that time, you will belong only to me. Not linked to any treacherous family line."

"Josefina, come to France as François proposed."

"You are to call me Josie. My name is Josie."

"All right, Josie. Zee chateau has many rooms empty for years." Marianne protested as she had for days. "Zee Duchess is old, the village isolated. You and zee baby would be safe, not tormented by sly winks and whispers. They were very kind to me. I beg you, especially now with zee life of zee child at risk. Take my ticket. Go to France. I will stay behind. Finish François's business and speak with your mother."

Josie calmed at the thought of her mother. "When Mother recovers from her illness, she will convince Father to allow me to return. In my heart I know." Her response came instantly and with confidence.

Mother's probable true reaction suddenly struck Josie. Because of what he subsequently deemed a lie, Father had murdered François. Mother carried an extraordinary affection for François; her concern for a licentious daughter might not be as tolerant. "If Mother's health declines further, Father will need my help even more." Josie hopefully saw her shoes under that bed.

"Your father sent you away. You have no one. Please, Josie, come to France."

Banished forever was the truth of the matter. "Jacob will take care of me," Josefina said. "He loves me." The pain in Marianne's eyes did not stop the revelation. "Father said before Jacob left, they met. Mr. Jacob L. Broderick requested permission to marry me." Josie cheerfully persisted. "He had already confided that his next assignment would be here, in St. Louis. I am sure he is waiting for me to come to him. You must help me search the city for him."

Marianne stared off into the dimly lit room, her green eyes thoughtful, as if she had something to add. Her reply came after a lengthy silence. "I will do what you ask." The hollows of her cheeks deepened, like the sinking of a grave. She said no more.

~ * ~

The following evening Marianne tiptoed across the rug and knocked lightly on the library door. No response. She rapped again, harder. Within an eye blink the door ripped open and Stuart's steeled body filled the frame. Annoyance plastered his face, suggestive of having swallowed a bitter pill. "Yes?" he demanded. Severe creases dragged his mouth downward. "What do you want?"

Marianne stared directly in his eyes. "Last summer," she began, "my brother open zee accounts for me. Now I arrive without zee proper dress. Pleez, to provide a buggy. I would visit the shops." Her exaggerated accent was meant to disarm.

"Why would I do that?" Sarcasm sculpted his voice as his irritation visibly flared.

Marianne exhaled deeply. "I am going home. To return without distinguished appearance would dishonor François, which would bring much grief for us all. Would you want me to leave from your care without properly prepared?"

"Ah, yes, I see." Stuart remained fixed, warring with his scowl. Some time passed in silence before he finally spoke. "Leave a schedule with me. Take the house girl with you. She will report directly to me upon each return."

"I will take Josefina. She knows zee city and zee shops." Marianne dropped the comment as nonchalantly as possible.

"By no means will I permit that girl to cavort about!" Stuart's brows drew together, his eyes glared.

"It eez necessary. To be done quickly for sailing."

Quick as a bubble bursts Stuart's face relaxed. "On second thought, if her assistance hastens your departure, so be it. But, you will take my driver and housemaid with you. They will report everything to me."

The girls traipsed throughout the city, confusing the naïve housemaid and guard with excuses of being lost, dissatisfaction with the materials presented, or out of fashion designs, bribing and soliciting information. Late on the third day of exploring, their inquiries proved fruitful. They discovered where Jacob Broderick resided.

Josie insisted, "Marianne, now that we have found Jacob, you must confirm your departure date. Please, find someone to travel with you. Plenty of girls must be seeking a way back to their homelands. You do not need chaperoning, I know, but after your calamitous summer, I fear our hasty trip may have sapped too much of your strength."

"Bash. My health is splendid."

"There is another reason." Josie grinned. "If your companion uses my name on the registry, Stuart will believe I went to France with you. He will not come searching for me and my son."

The following morning, yellow dawn added the only color to the drab bedroom as Josie patted her rolling stomach and munched tasteless flatbread. Jacob's boarding house had returned her letter unopened. *What to do now?* Josie suspected Marianne would not sail until confident mother and baby would be looked after.

Josie fingered the note that had been attached. The message stated tersely: *Mr. Broderick has been called out of town indefinitely.* If Marianne discovered this news, she would cancel her return to France, and Josefina wanted her friend safe with family who cared about her.

Josie slanted notepaper at an awkward angle, cocked her left hand and scratched out a few words immediately.

The paper secreted up a sleeve, she slipped out the kitchen door and beckoned at a ragged street urchin. "A penny to deliver this paper at four o'clock." Josie pointed behind her to the richly appointed town house. "It must be delivered to the rear entrance." She prayed Stuart would not have returned.

Fingers caked with filth grabbed first the coin, then the note. The child started to dart away. Josie grabbed his collar. "There will be others," she promised, "if, you do this delivery properly." With the boy firmly in her grasp, she added, "Tell no one how you received the note."

At four o'clock Marianne and Josie nibbled on yesterday's muffins and sipped tea in the dreary sitting room when the kitchen girl entered nervously. "A gutter waif dirties the stoop. Wants the misses."

Josie accepted the note with feigned surprise. "From Jacob," she whispered. Quickly the girls retreated upstairs. Josie read aloud:

> *My Beloved Josie,*
> *Send word when it is safe for me to come for you.*
> *Waiting anxiously.*
>
> *Lovingly yours,*
> *Jacob*

As Marianne read the note in turn, her finger traced the flowery signature. "How strange. He addresses you as Josie."

"I think I explained in my note. I am sure I signed the message Josie."

"We can meet him tomorrow." Marianne smiled slowly. "After my fitting at two."

Josie bowed her head. "Too dangerous. Stuart probably has more ruffians watching us." She smiled contentedly. "I warned Jacob of Stuart's treacherous leanings. As soon as you are safely on your way, I will meet Jacob at a prearranged place."

With outward reluctance Marianne confirmed her voyage. Sadly, she had missed the Philadelphia sailing of the steamboat British Crown whose brochure advertised less than ten days to cross the ocean. Her sailing would take considerably longer.

~ * ~

Two days after Josie's faked receipt of Jacob's note, Stuart peered out the window while his sister and her friend supervised the loading of a carriage. They looked smart in their fashionable winter coats. *Lord*, he thought, *that French girl had a passel of trunks*. But that was not his worry. Somehow he felt pleased that François had paid to have them all filled.

As soon as the girls and the carriage departed, Stuart sent a card off to Madam Vlydovski requesting her attendance that same evening. Each day that passed Josefina had grown bolder. Stuart scoffed; she would lose that insolence soon enough. Mares broke easily if treated to a stick, and he had beaten them often enough to know. Breaking Josefina would be glorious; he ached to witness her comeuppance. She would learn to be obedient. But to what end? No one of their family would ever know, that he would assure. Stuart smirked; if the madam completed the procedure tonight there would be no reason for him to miss the hunt scheduled for this weekend. If Josefina survived.

~ * ~

The driver deposited the girls, along with the mountain of trunks, on the wharf. Marianne addressed him, "Thank you, *monsieur,* for your kindness. A cabin boy can load my belongings." She included a generous gratuity with a warning. "Please go quickly, find shelter. I sense a storm coming."

When the low moan of the Mississippi paddleboat's horn belted the air, Marianne looked down at Josefina. Vision blurred by tears spared Marianne witnessing the agony that mangled the upturned face. The girls clung to each other.

Josie buried her head in the older girl's chest, reveling in the affectionate embrace. In spite of Jacob, the contest for his love, and her willing duplicity, Josie cared deeply for her friend. "I will miss you." Boulder sized loneliness wedged its weight beneath her breastbones bringing heaviness and despair.

"You must write to me," Marianne handed Josie a paper. "No matter what happens. I must know how you fare. And about zee child."

"I will. I will write often. Such long letters you will shudder at the postman's whistle."

"I shall tell my family of you." Regret filled Marianne's eyes. "You can still come. My mother would welcome you, and zee little one. I could stay here, finish your affairs."

"I have Jacob." Josie wondered at the curtain of doubt that veiled Marianne's eyes. Josie did not want her friend worrying. "I am sure mother will send for me soon. She and Father shall need me more." She had failed to tell Marianne of Father's ban and the savage hatred he displayed. "When that hour arrives, Jacob and I must be prepared to return." Josie mustered all her courage to smile confidently.

In spite of her bravado Josie felt hollow inside, fragile as a spun sugar shell. As Marianne walked up the gangplank, Josie feared the depth of pain yet to come from this separation, feeling her spirit straddled a blunt dagger. Additionally, an alarming disquiet prophesied that if she ever saw Marianne again, the meeting would not be favorable.

After Marianne safely disappeared into the ship, Josie hailed a shabby appearing vehicle, loaded the remaining trunks and instructed the driver where to go. Clouds blocked the sun, and a film of ice glazed the buggy's iron fittings. The frigid air knifed Josie's bones and clung to her clothes robbing them of any warmth. A harsh wind shrieked its winter howl. Josie scrunched in a dark corner. She felt abandoned and longed for familiar arms to hold her and tell her everything would be fine.

After arriving at the stable, the grumbling driver, addressing his body's wish to warm by a hot fire, swiftly dropped Josie and the baggage outside the horse stalls. Josie reluctantly gave up one of her few coins.

Frightened of what lay ahead, but more fearful of what awaited her at Stuart's house, Josie hastily smeared muck on the silver trappings of Father's carriage to disguise its value, tied Contessa on behind, and disappeared into the bowels of the city.

~ * ~

Inside the dark foyer on Lafayette Square, a thick walking stick cracked down once again on the cowering shoulders of the hack driver. Stuart snarled. "Tell me again how you allowed those two young women to leave this city when I instructed you to deliver only one, then return here directly."

The old man shuddered under the stinging blow. He'd be damned to a life with the devil before he'd give any information to this blackguard. And poor and ignorant as they were, word would pass among his fellow drivers; Stuart Taylor would receive no help from them or their kind in his search.

Fourteen

Along the St. Louis streets, shopkeepers hurried from their locked doors. Josie followed the slower girls, whose feet plainly ached in their thick boots, heads down, backs seemingly permanently bent. The way led into the bowels of the city where pushcarts became beds and crates served as shelters.

Josie chose a stable that stood upright and sported iron latches on its stall doors. She lay gingerly on the straw, unable to find any comfort on the prickly stubs. The stuporous man who had taken her money kept his establishment as untidy as himself. The rotting, mashed stalks stank with use, surely stirred only by the weary hooves of cabbies' drudges.

Drifting from wooden beams scarred with horse bites, fine piths spun through the moonlight, swirling and whirling in a dance to the dirt floor, only to be fluffed into a repeat performance whenever the animals stamped or Josie moved.

Contessa crowded the mare, rump turned out to the wintry draft, the shape of her blanketed silhouette lost in the darkness of the filth stained planks of the wall. The gentle foal's moist breath rose in transparent clouds, a false welcome in the miserable stall.

Occasionally another animal's snort broke the silence, like a bomb, momentarily startling the animals and disturbing Josie. She listened for voices. Footsteps. Halos of light announcing a search. The alien creaking and popping of the weathered wood made her goosey.

Layers of petticoats and the cape blanketing her captured the acrid odors and muffled the scurrying sounds that traveled along the crude spattered walls. Josie's throbbing head had calmed to a knotted pressure; her soured insides quieted. Disgust with the foul conditions weighed a great deal less than the fear of discovery that kept her from sleeping.

A lump poking Josie's hip gave her some sense of security. Before embarking, Marianne had slipped a handful of coins into the pocket now safely quashed beneath Josie. In a generous mood, almost celebrant, her best friend had gifted the money as a wedding present, willing the aspiring bride to select something pretty for herself.

The minute Marianne stepped onto the boat, Josie had counted her money. She had remembered to bring along the few pennies Father considered an extravagant allowance that she had saved in a music box, tucking Jacob's dried nosegay alongside. Her more extensive capital, accumulated as part of her dowry, consisted of digits in a black book possessed by Father.

Josie's meager pocket money limited shelter and food to only a few days. Unfortunately, the timetable for her escape had not turned out favorably. The hours spent preparing for Marianne's sailing, reloading Josie's luggage, then plodding through the wharf traffic had consumed most of the day. After retrieving the family's buggy and the horses from the Lafayette Square stable, Josie had been forced to harness the mare and reload the luggage again by herself. By then gray clouds curtained any sunlight and bitter cold seeped into Josie's bones. Her last errand, to find an inconspicuous place where she could hide and bed the animals, took until nightfall.

Only one vacancy remained. The shabby owner, more interested in his wine and finding warmth than in her predicament, accepted Josie's initial offer of a pittance before fleeing into the darkness. She suspected by daybreak he would set upon her in plausible sobriety demanding more payment for the putrid shelter.

She curled up in the foulness of the corner, but sleep evaded her. A heartfelt but wistful prayer willing Jacob to find her played over and over in Josie's head, sometimes muttered aloud, more often felt silently in her heart.

Without warning a rodent scurried up her petticoat. Josie yelped and jumped up in fear, flopping her skirts around, hopping about, first one foot then the other. Her frenzy frightened Contessa and woke the sleeping giants in the nearby stalls. Striking hooves jarred the wobbly plank walls. Iron latches jiggled. Loud whinnies slashed the cold night air. *This will not do.* Josie could not imagine occupying such poor quarters another night.

Planning to skip from shelter to shelter for the next five days, stretching her funds, Josie hoped Stuart would truly believe she escaped to France with Marianne. Josie felt barred from going straight to Costello House where Jacob had lived. The ease with which she and Marianne had discovered his past whereabouts made her anxious. If the coarse woman in Stuart's library indicated a sample, her brother's world encompassed extensive resources of ill repute.

Finally, the fellow stable mates settled down. Josie, her skirt tucked tightly behind her knees, squatted against the door and listened for voices while she envisioned tomorrow's escape.

She had parked her buggy in the paddock, on the other side of the stall wall, not trusting to leave it out of her sight. Shuffling sounds, like feet dragging, forced her to stand on tiptoe to peek through the iron bars and reassure her of the rig's safety. The moon lit up only a small portion of the buggy.

The silver trappings blinked recognition, as if the property of Josef Taylor welcomed the scrutiny of its mistress. Josie gasped at the thought. Father could claim she had stolen his property, have her arrested as a horse thief. A crime punishable by hanging.

One hand involuntarily reached up, rubbed the muscles and sinews of her neck, testing their wellness. She quickly tied the hood of her cape snugly about her throat. Stuart would not find her tonight, she felt sure. Her heart stilled a little. Still, she started at each unrecognized noise.

The next morning, when the rest of the city first stirred, Josie had already rolled up her belongings, harnessed the horse to the buggy and tied on Contessa. Her private parade disappeared into the city before the domestics set out for the other side of town.

By midday, frigid air blustered. Few people moved about on the streets, only the hungry and working poor clustered about in tight little cliques. Anyone with sufficient resource kept close to a home fire, using the miserable weather as an excuse for undertaking ignored household duties and sharing family fellowship.

Josie longed to return home. Mother would be instructing the kitchen help in the final tasks of uprooting turnips, rutabaga, and carrots from the frosted earth, then going off herself to haunt closets and drawers for neglected mending. Mother had not believed her, had not wanted to accept the truth. Josie was broken-hearted and felt unloved, knowing she was alone. All she could depend on to survive was her own will.

Father, she knew, already sat at his desk in the bank, having traveled the road often enough to find his way in the merest dawn. For just a moment, anger warmed Josie. She despised him, not for killing François, but for not loving her enough to believe the truth.

François's bones rested cold in his grave. She felt no remorse.

All the people who had witnessed the shooting or heard her curses would have told their story by now. Some would want her returned, an example to be whipped and rid of the Devil; others, passing on rumor, would applaud she had been banished so they escaped the effort of shunning and having to face her sin. No one would grant her a chance to prove she spoke the truth, and that she was sorry her greed had shamed and dishonored them all.

Josie shook herself, frightened by her morbid thoughts. It would do no good to break down because of what could not be undone. She must concentrate on surviving each day, hour by hour.

On the other side of the iron bars of the stable door, the buggy stood too prominent, too fancy for dingy neighborhoods, as was her dress, and her hair much too recognizable. Something must be done about that. Hunger plagued her midsection. Food had held no taste for her for weeks. She wished she'd had the foresight to stuff herself at Stuart's. Josie shook her head hard. Such wishes and worries would never end—she needed to confront today.

While her mind had been occupied, the horse had drifted. Their wandering ended at the river where a knot of complaining passengers waited to board a steamboat, their bundles neatly ticketed and stacked while they stepped aside for recent arrivals to disembark.

A tall figure wrapped in a green wool cloak aroused Josie's attention. The same shade Marianne had worn. Josie's arm shot up instinctively, waving wildly from shoulder to wrist. Prepared to call out and attract the passenger's attention, Josie suddenly realized the absurdity of her mistake. Marianne would be nearing New Orleans, preparing to transfer to a sea vessel to travel further east and board an ocean-going ship.

The errant hand returned to Josie's lap. Her best friend was lost to her, Josie suspected forever, certainly until the son now squiggling within came of age. Flustered over mistaking the girl for Marianne, feeling hopeless and more demoralized and once again facing her lonely future, Josie fled the wrestling, cranky mob.

~ * ~

Marianne pulled the hood of her cloak further toward her face, hiding her head. The combination of dress and red hair could lead Josefina—Josie—back to her side. The sight of her best friend half-standing, waving erratically had been startling. *If only Josefina had given up Jacob, let him follow his heart to me, we could have all been happy.*

A cabby slowed a few feet away, then stopped before Marianne when she waved a greenback at the driver. She almost fell headlong into the vehicle in her rush.

If Josie, with her trusting nature, came nearer, Marianne was prepared with another lie to justify returning. She would simply say she decided the child would be better served if she went back to Taylorsville and convinced François to adhere to his promise. But then—Josie thought François was dead. Marianne had to remain at the Chateau anyway. She was in charge now, until François recovered. Or at least until a message arrived from Jacob.

~ * ~

At the intersection just past the docks, a sign identifying Park Avenue tipped heavenward. The street of Jacob's boarding house. Josie's heart skipped a beat in anticipation, just to be near where he lived.

A peek, a quick drive by for familiarity's sake, dare she chance exposing herself? No one followed; her repeated backward glances had assured her of that. What if someone watched the house, waiting for her to appear? Not a soul loitered on the walks; no vehicles parked along the steep street. One buggy slowly rolling past would not arouse suspicion. She would take the gamble, keeping her eyes alert for Stuart's spies.

After a few blocks the boarding house came into view. Comfortable appearing, she judged, a bit shabby as old money should be, not through neglect but history. The horse slowed enough to enable Josie to look in a window and observe a fleshy woman supervising the passing of plates. Josie thought she saw steam rising in thin drifts from delicate cups.

Her stomach grumbled. She gnawed on a poxed carrot found in the stable and sipped water from a foraged flask that left metallic flavored flakes on her tongue. *I must keep going. I must.* Only a few more days hidden from Stuart, and she could safely return here. She prayed Jacob had left instructions where to join him.

A lurch of the buggy nearly toppled her. She looked around again. No one was nearby. *I must stay alert, be more careful, for the safety of the child.* Within weeks she would be unable to hide her condition. Jacob had said he wanted her above all things. And with child? She was sure he would take her as she was. Jacob loved her.

The temperature plummeted. Icicles hung from Contessa's eyelids, nose and mouth, every place moisture collected. Josie's little group rounded the block and descended the hill, coming upon a stable near the river. Josie entered and saw clean straw, shiny equipment, mangers stuffed with hay, troughs inches deep in dried corn.

"Excuse me." Josie curtsied prettily to a boy. "I am a visitor to the city. Have you room for my animals?"

The groom eyed the hand-tooled leather, the silver clasps. "Can find room. I'll get the bossman."

Before he turned to go, she asked, "The fee?"

His face showed obvious bewilderment. The lad eyed the carriage again, then the fine luggage. "One dollar. Boss man takes cash, in advance." When Josie fumbled with her moneybag, his eyes narrowed. "You steal these things? You look mighty pert, but cain't never tell." He tucked his bare hands in his armpits. "Don't make me no never mind. Just you should know, Johnny-law beds their critters here."

Josie felt the blood drain from her face.

"You might wanta chance Devon's, on River Street, nearer the wharf. Take anything off your hands, for a price."

Josie marveled at the boy's craftiness. She had not considered selling the buggy, but why not? The vehicle was too easily identified. And the horse, she could trade for a less distinctive animal, a plodder, healthy enough just to get about the city. Besides, Jacob would undoubtedly buy her whatever she needed.

"Would you mind repeating the address? I am looking for another animal, perhaps your friend might know of a possibility."

"Sure lady, and I'm standing here in the cold waiting for the queen to pass by."

"My husband, quite impossible man, squandered my earnings." Josie lied without regret. "I must get a satisfactory price for my possessions or face the street."

"You never worked a day, lady. But if you wanta git a fair price, dicker with Devon, then tell him you'll go to Hannibals. He'll come around. One block, at the river turn right."

Josie wanted to hug him, buy him some warm food and a place by a fire. But first, she must find a place for herself.

The transaction went smoothly. Mr. Devon asked no questions and quickly found a rickety cab that leaned cock-eyed on a broken spring and had lost most the stuffing from the bench. He offered only a pittance of Josie's buggy and horse's value. After giving Josie the coins, he begged repeatedly for the colt, offering increasing amounts to buy the animal.

Josie declined politely. She would never sell Contessa. Such a prize would someday be mated with a stallion of equal pedigree, the base for the future of a notable stable. She had forgotten some valuables in Taylorsville, but the battle for Contessa had reminded her to grab the foal's registration papers.

The proprietor plopped a sack containing a few handfuls of oats on the slatted floor beneath her feet. "In case you have a change of heart," he explained, "remember my kindness."

Josie kept near the riverfront, stopping for bread and cheese at a neighborhood store where she rubbed elbows with fancy-dressed street girls, housemaids, and rascals.

A girl wearing a poppy red dress and thin coat argued with a second woman layered in blouse, sweater, jacket, and shawl over the merits of a particularly interesting glass pot, discussing the disadvantage of bleaching hair. Their cigar smoke and cheap perfume took over the store.

The conversation fascinated Josie. "Excuse me?" She kept the hood of her cloak tight about her platinum curls. "Would you be kind enough to explain how one would go about darkening hair?"

"Pretty classy for a river gal," the poppy girl remarked, her voice low like a man's.

"Uptowner, seeing what life's like for working lasses," quipped the other.

Both turned their backs to Josie.

"Please," Josie begged, "my hair brittled and is as parched as a weed. If I uncover my head, I look like a hag. My lover avoids me, spends his evenings with others. A few months more of his sponsorship, for my coming child, is all I ask. Enough to buy us food and shelter to last the winter." She wiped imaginary tears from her cheeks, tore a thick sob from her throat.

"Here, now," spoke the woman of layers. "We won't have any lass throwed out carrying a babe." The two searched through the pots, arguing the rightfulness of each choice.

"Something dark. Maybe black, to interest him with a new look."

The poppy one smiled. "Might offer another wile, too." The girl tugged up her ill-fitting skirt. Underneath, tattered red satin showed the stain of much use. "For the wool cloak."

Josie was shocked, offended by the familiarity.

The poppy girl snipped, "Well, you don't hafta look so prissy. I'm good enough to foller that broken down nag of yourn and take yer feller afore he knowed his own mind."

"Forgive me," Josie implored. "I am sorry. Your generosity surprised me." She was determined to get their help. "Do you come here often?" When the girls failed to answer she went on. "Before losing interest, my lover promised to marry me. If my fortune turns up, you can have my coat. I will come back in a few weeks."

"Don't be counting on no john's words. They say anything to gets what they want."

The same truth had come from Marianne.

Josie reassured them. "But he does truly love me. I know he will take good care of the child, and me. You will see. In a few weeks, I will return, and you will be the warmer for your kindness."

The layered woman held out a pot. "Brown—the dye. Your face is too wan for black, look fake, like a walking corpse."

"I have no idea what to do."

"See, what'd I tell ya." Layers did an "I told you so" look to the poppy girl. "Cheesy, we borrow your back room?" At his okay the girls hustled Josie behind oilcloth curtains.

A sink, hand pump, and some rags provided all they needed. The change amazed Josie, adding years and a subtle hardness, not enough to offend but instead made her appear older, more worldly.

"Right fine job," said layers. "Don't know why you would want to give up the look of an angel."

"He finds me too prissy looking. Not 'woman enough.'"

The girls laughed loudly, helping Josie with her outerwear, then stood aside and waited for Josie to leave. Just as Josie stepped out the door the poppy girl spoke. "Did you see that fur? Last we see of that coat."

Near dusk Josie purchased a bag of roasted nuts and a hot slice of fat-soaked cornmeal at a pushcart near the skating park.

"Wind's picking up. Frigid as the North Pole." The vendor wrapped some bits in paper, generously handing her two of each. "Shame to waste on wild dogs."

"Bless you," Josie said. Her fingers hugged the warmth.

The kind soul folded away his awning and tossed the crumbs to heeling strays while watching Josie gobble one corn patty in three bites. "Got a Northerner coming. Best head for home, mam', likely be couple days afore any young man comes hunting company here."

Embarrassed and stinging from his crude insinuation, Josie failed to find an adequate reply. She turned away and looked around her. The frozen pond was empty of skaters, the benches unoccupied. Even the street hovered in soundless anticipation as a heavy snowfall began.

Josie took her appeased appetite and headed toward a nearby stable. No vacancy. She tried another and another. All full. It seemed everybody in St. Louis had already turned in for the night.

Fearful of being left in the cold, Josie directed the creaking buggy back to the stable that had shown her such disservice the previous night. The stalls were all occupied. The vulgar drunk, however, after several indecent propositions, offered the storage section of the paddock at a highly inflated price.

Josie sheltered Contessa first, then stacking enough trunks to be able to reach up and remove the trappings, unhitched the mare and led it in. She left the dilapidated buggy where it stood outside.

The cubicle, open on the paddock side, allowed any passerby the opportunity to indulge their curiosity. Stuart would not bend to look for her on a night like this, but any stranger could easily invade her privacy. Josie searched for her handgun. When she had fled Taylor Estates, the tutor had tucked the weapon, an ax, kitchen knife, some herbs, and hand tools in a satchel under the seat box. Josie fished the chunky piece of metal out. Only capable of chambering two bullets, the gun felt heavy and awkward in her cold hands.

Crouched in a corner, resting against Contessa's warm coat, Josie slid the gun alongside the nearest trunk before she settled in to wait out the stormy night.

The wind howled in glacial gusts that whipped down the long paddock tunnel as if the walls were made of bride's netting. Snow filtered through the cracks of the outside walls with the carelessness of spilled tins of baker's flour, turning the weathered beams into an ice palace, the splits and burrows packed with flakes of iridescence. Josie shivered too often and too hard for the beauty to please her.

Battered by the icy gale, Josie labored unsuccessfully to pull the buggy into the paddock to serve as a wind block. Her arms and back ached. Sweat chilled the marrow of her bones while she struggled for almost an hour to stack her trunks into a fort. Finally, her hands deadened, she lay back down near Contessa on the thickest straw she could find, praying they would not be found frozen into a single heap by morning.

Although physically exhausted, sleep came in spurts. Josie dozed, fearing waking to find her extremities black and cracked, or perhaps not waking at all. Each time Josie stirred she forced Contessa to get up and step with her in a tight head to tail circuit to warm their blood. She gave no thought to strange sounds, spies or Stuart.

By dawn the cold licking at her bones had settled in; she thought only of warmth and fire. When she gathered her belongings and rode away from the stable, not another creature, two or four-legged, ventured on the streets.

Well away from Lafayette Square, two squat buildings framed a narrow alleyway, lessening the bluster of the gale into a shrieking tunnel. Josie parked awhile in the imperfect shelter before moving on. By late afternoon, Josie knew she and Contessa could not survive another night under these circumstances. *I will not give up.* She fought with only her will to hold back the tears. The arctic winds whistled and moaned so harsh ice crystals draped her forehead, coated her lashes and cracked her lips. The icy air stung her throat making swallowing painful, and the howling created a buzzing in her ears.

Her belly seized by sudden wrenching cramps forced Josie to reconsider her five-day plan. Three coins, enough for one more night in that frightful stable. Impossible. She must beg food and a fireside, or she would not live to bear François's heir and deliver her vengeance.

Fifteen

Bundled from head to toe with limbs scarcely showing more life than chunks of frozen fish, Josie prodded the nag to cross Washington Park. The animal staggered under the labor of pulling the ladened buggy through ice capped snow. Sleet-peppered gusts whipped across the open parkland, hampering their progress, forcing the solitary band to endure hours of biting winds.

The direct route proved a wrong choice. The tall buildings of the commercial district would have blocked the wind, provided a less fierce passageway, walled off drifting snow. Driven by Josie's will, the horse trudged on, toward what Josie prayed would be asylum.

Temperatures registered near zero, setting a record for the end of November. The night burst in blacker than usual, a perfect backdrop for spikes of brilliant stars that peeked from behind layers of storm swept clouds. Swirls of dancing snow dropped flakes so plump and ethereal they heaped into pillows both bizarre and beautiful.

The mother-to-be saw nothing to admire. Josie's thought dwelled only on herself and her unborn child, of their freezing to death, now, or anytime too soon. The means for survival existed, especially protection for her growing son. Josie was determined to fight her way to it.

~ * ~

All about the city, glazed trees, fences and light poles glistened with a magic of reflected white fire blazing in a layer of frozen water. Having seen enough of nature's picturesque production, Mrs. Costello exited the front entrance of her ordinary house to be certain the steps showed no slick areas. She would never excuse laziness, including her own, if one of her guests fell because of someone's neglect.

One large foot tentatively poked at the top step while the wary proprietor judged the stair's safeness. Absorbed in her task, she gasped when a shadow leapt between her feet. Startled, her body stumbled backward, her heart pounding erratically, her thoughts fleeting. Sturdy arms flailed the empty air like windmills as they sought something to grasp. Her sideways glance perceived something dark and ominous nearing. She heard no crunch of shoes on snow. The figure, silhouetted against the snow by the gas streetlight, hinted at an unnatural phenomenon.

Within seconds, the stout woman regained her balance. She sensed that the dark shadow closing in bode nothing formidable, most likely a billowing cloak covering someone. From the size, she speculated a child. Her thumping heart returned to normal. When the creature neared the stairs, Mrs. Costello asked, "May I help you?"

The blue muffler muttered something unintelligible then led an enormous shiver that shook to the hem of a cape. Mrs. Costello squared up to shield the wind, then shooed the quivering bundle up the landing and into the foyer, fussing continuously. "Quickly, quickly. It's frigid. You cannot stay out here. Come in, near the fire."

Forcing the door closed against the wind, the proprietor surveyed her companion in the glow of the oil lamp. The cloak draped in luxurious wool; expensive detail embellished the frivolous hat squashed beneath the hood of the outer garment. Before shutting the entry door, Mrs. Costello had peered beyond the porch into a circle of lamplight. A vehicle waited, brass twinkling in the snow covered stack of trunks.

Bustling with efficiency, Mrs. Costello propelled the girl through the front hall toward the kitchen. "This way. I am sorry, my house sleeps. I just banked the kitchen fire. Sit, while I stir up a flame."

All the while her apologies swirled about in tune with the blizzard howling outdoors, she fussed. "I was on my way to bed. Since I have several guests expecting morning courtesy calls, I came back downstairs to settle my mind that the entrance was clear of any hazard. You are fortunate to have arrived when you did." Her voice softened, sweet with kindness. "I am Mrs. Costello, owner of this ordinary house."

A frail voice mumbled, "My pleasure. I am Miss Josie... Louise." The words came out garbled, as if unpracticed, or muffled by the bulky hood. The ice-coated cloth offered no further information.

Fleshy, comforting arms guided the shapeless form onto a kitchen bench, then vigorously stirred and fed the glowing embers in the fireplace before turning up the flame in the kitchen lamp.

"May I offer some tea?" Mrs. Costello asked, her curiosity grown beyond containment. She prodded. "Such a fierce night. Extreme weather for St. Louis. You must be on a very important mission."

No reply came from the thawing lump.

The landlady continued to prattle while gently removing the ice-glazed cape, delighting in the weight of the rich fabric. Silver sable, wet and matted, but with a luster rarely seen, lined the hood and spilled extravagantly down the inside of the front placket. Grunting, the plump caretaker stooped down to pry loose the girl's frozen boots, judging them to be as fine and soft a fawn as any she had ever seen cross her threshold.

The stranger sat listlessly, seemingly accustomed to having someone take care of her, definitely unafraid of a stranger taking such liberty with her personal items.

Crackling flames revealed a young girl with such a translucent complexion she appeared to be an ice princess sculpted from the frozen panorama outside. Mrs. Costello studied the stranger. She guessed an age, possibly fifteen, sixteen. Absolutely heavenly. Thick swatches of tangled dark curls slipped from a lopsided ornamental hat; seventeen, maybe younger, certainly an innocent, much too young to be traveling alone, especially in this treacherous weather and so near the riverfront.

While the tea brewed, Mrs. Costello chatted on without pause. "A peculiar day it is. All the streets empty, the businesses vacated. No one moving about the city. St. Louis seldom suffers such happenstance. Never before this early in the winter. We usually see no more than a dusting of snow before the holiday season. Are you familiar with our weather?"

When no response came Mrs. Costello continued. "The entire town shut down. Every man, stray dog and peddler elected to stay near the fires today. Fortunately, at Costello House we have the luxury of central heating." Pride colored the comment. "Our guests enjoyed a comfortable, leisurely day." Mrs. Costello's mind digressed. *Too bad Mr. Broderick went away. He had hopes of such fascinating adventures incorporated in intriguing tales. Probably invented, but of no harm.*

A command interrupted Mrs. Costello's musing. Haunted sapphire eyes blinked at her, waiting. One plump drop of water slid slowly down a cheek. A tear or thawing?

The girl spoke again, louder. "Someone must look after Contessa!"

Jumping up, Mrs. Costello barked, "Lordy be! Is there someone else? I saw no one." The landlady searched her memory for a shadow, a strange shape, some movement in the carriage.

"No. Not a person," uttered the girl. Her agonized face turned up, seeking the widow's attention. "But my foal, Contessa, is extremely valuable. She is not a delivery brood. Please, she must be bedded down safely, watered and fed."

Rattled, Mrs. Costello peered into the damp, pale lashes, "But, but, you cannot stay here. I have no room to let. Every space, even my dormitory, is occupied."

Hopelessness hardened the delicate structure of the girl's face. "But that cannot be. I have nowhere else to go." A tinge of impertinence sharpened her declaration.

"I am truly sorry. But, my house is full." The older woman sympathized. "If you have friends, acquaintances nearby, perhaps I can arrange for someone to take you there, then stable the horse."

Josie sniffled and downed her face, averting her eyes from the woman. "You do not understand. Mr. Broderick, Jacob, my intended, I promised to join him here. He is a boarder."

Mrs. Costello plopped down on the unyielding bench and gawked, astonished at what she had heard. Her thoughts jumbled. Mr.

Broderick had presented himself as a bachelor. The man made no mention of a fiancée. Could he have acquired a young lady while away? But then this girl should know her betrothed was not here, and certainly that Mr. Broderick had not returned from his assignment.

Well, we have a person of quality here, but a child just the same. And children's tales are suspect. "Fiancée indeed!" Mrs. Costello muttered while she moved about the large kitchen.

Her sensibilities protested. *What about the mound of trunks? The valuable animal? The girl had definitely set out in this miserable weather with a purpose. And, the child is such a lovely, forlorn creature.* Mrs. "Cos", as her guests referred to her, pondered the situation, her heart already gone out to the abandoned young lady.

Guided by a maternal instinct she usually ignored, Mrs. Cos replied impulsively. "I will wake my 'free' man to help. Your animals will be cared for. While I run about, you warm yourself! Don't worry, we will think of something." The girl's radiant smile greeted her announcement. The burdened landlady felt kissed by an angel.

When the innkeeper left the kitchen, the newly anointed Josie Louise slumped on the sturdy table, head buried in her arms, relishing the warmth of the fire. Several times Josie raised her head a few inches, but lacked the initiative to sit up. At each attempt the room reeled, her head bobbed, unable to steady itself.

Mrs. Costello returned, red faced and breathless, having rushed up and down several flights of stairs. She studied the waiflike girl, noting the blue tint still evident around the bowed mouth and the goosebumps percolating along lace cuffs.

Gathering her wits about her, Mrs. Cos clasped her hands against her generous belly and addressed the stranger. "Tell me again why you came here." She watched with a sternness that allowed no denial.

Josie pulled her weary body up straight, shoulders squared. The pluckiness born of desperation appeared an act of respect and acquiescence. Without hesitancy Josie started. "Mr. Broderick and I became engaged. I have come to St. Louis to marry him. He did not expect me so soon, but I was able to secure a chaperone for the trip and took advantage. Unfortunately, my companion became ill on the way and went directly to her family."

With lowered brows Mrs. Costello watched every movement of the despairing face, pondered the steady clear eyes, listened to every nuance in the lilting voice. Her judgment wavered; perhaps the truth, her cynicism born of experience spoke up, or more likely the girl lied extraordinarily well.

The proprietor turned her back and rested her palms on the kitchen table. She felt awkward and bumbling; a guilty flush crept up her face from her doubting, needles of apology bit her tongue. She must think. She felt embarrassed, humbled, as if she had accosted nobility and was being put in her place, here, in her own kitchen. The girl had not been rude; in fact, she was charming and tragic.

Shaken over her ill-suited response, Mrs. Cos considered the situation. The caliber of clientele she had been soliciting for years sat across the table, that pedigreed haughtiness of the wealthy. Manners, persona, attitude that spoke of years of pampering and the uppishness of gentlefolk. Perhaps, the landlady reasoned, her aspirations had been a mistake, and she should settle for less titled gentry. Or perhaps... her time had arrived.

Mrs. Costello turned toward the distraught stranger. "I will allow you to temporarily occupy Mr. Broderick's room. As soon as practical, and certainly before he returns, you must make other arrangements." She did not offer even a hint of Mr. Broderick's whereabouts or expected arrival. After all, Mrs. Cos reasoned, one could not divulge personal information concerning one's tenants, no matter what the interest. She dared not risk being accused of impropriety.

Her household would be warned to keep their eyes open; she could not afford to be bamboozled. The minute any trouble popped up, she would call the constable forth-with and the girl would be thrown to the street. "Come with me," said Mrs. Costello.

Josie climbed the stairs, one leaden foot in front of the other. Her toes tripped on the treads as she followed the shifting rump up three flights. Overwrought, her mind floundered, wanting recklessly to confess everything to the landlady, give up this pretense and rid herself of the protective burdensome armor of her lie and find peace.

While preparing for bed, Josie cautioned herself. *I must remain aloof, until Jacob returns. He will take care of everything.* But for now she desperately needed a friend, and Mrs. Costello owned such a good-hearted soul.

But Josie knew forging a heartfelt, comforting friendship was impossible for her right now.

Such familiarity might break down her guard, pressure her into divulging the truth; her story might come out. Experience had taught Josie well. Others would think ill of her and perhaps be led to conspire with Stuart. Josie buried her face in the sweet smelling pillowcase. *I will not give in.*

~ * ~

Inordinately puzzled by the arrival of her mystery guest, Mrs. Costello lay awake in her room, embroiled in seeking answers to her growing list of personal concerns. Five years ago, when the widowed Mr. Costello had discovered he was gravely ill, and at his solicitation, she had agreed to be promoted from housekeeper to wife and care for him until "death us do part".

The value of his promise that she should inherit this impressive piece of property in exchange proved questionable after he passed away and the reality of his poor financial judgments emerged.

Adding further insult, to pay for community necessities the city enacted a tax based on the number of closets within a private residence. The homeowners bought armoires and sealed off the closets. Then came the window tax, draining Mrs. Costello's limited cash reserves. Perhaps, the windows should be boarded up next.

Having suffered a lifetime of demeaning, demanding work, the widow Costello faced the need of earning a substantial income or lose her ten-bedroom mansion and her dream. Her decision came easily enough: establish an "ordinary house", a private home that provided accommodations for the overflow of the wealthy fringe of society. The venture began with limited capital, but her choice proved fortuitous.

The estate faced Park Avenue, where the frontier industrialists had originally erected their residences, near the town square, between the business district and the riverfront, and within several blocks walking distance of all. Over three acres originally surrounded the four-story brick mansion known as "Costello House". In the past two years Mrs. Costello had sold tracts on each side to pay taxes.

Recently, the new industrial magnates began building their estates further north, on Forest Hill. The fear that a declining neighborhood might reduce her establishment to an everyday boardinghouse, not the quality guest house anticipated, and not with income enough to provide well for her old age, kept Mrs. Costello awake most nights.

Imported French Victorian furniture graced the interior of the house, and not a speck of dust was allowed to settle on the glossy finishes. Mrs. Cos kept an immaculate house, a well-organized kitchen, and served a breakfast of notable quality. The problem arose not out of location, or rendering acceptable or even flawless service, but of her inability to create that luxurious aura of "privilege", that indefinable unique style people born to wealth thrive on.

Her weakness further revealed itself in an inability to deal with demanding guests. Intimidated by their arrogance, and in her desire to please, Mrs. Cos knew she behaved too commonly; point in fact, she groveled.

She simply did not possess the haughty deportment that made ladies and gentlemen of wealth feel privileged to find lodging in her establishment. Those kinds of accommodations became jealously guarded, their existence passed by word of mouth among those who could afford to be selective.

For Mrs. Costello these financial straits bred nightmares of homelessness and begging excess from neighbors' tables. Her worry normally robbed the hard-working entrepreneur of the much-needed rejuvenation of peaceful sleep. Tonight, however, she soon fell to slumbering like an innocent babe. Her snoring channeled under the washed out quilts like a runaway trolley speeding downhill.

Sixteen

After an excellent night's sleep snuggled down in Mrs. Costello's fresh smelling feather tick, Josie rose early and joined the other guests for breakfast. Her witty stories of a large and energetic family entertained them, while social politeness guarded her privacy. Casually observing the affairs of the house, Josie noted Mrs. Costello remained too burdened with supervision of the kitchen to appear as hostess at the table.

Later in the day, after a much-enjoyed nap, Josie returned to the parlor. "When will tea be served?" she inquired of one of the maids.

"Sorry, Miss," the Negro volunteered, "ya have ta go ta town for tea. The Grand Hotel dishes up a middling good service with them fussy little cakes. Tain't far up ta hill."

Unhappy, Josie inquired further. "Supper, then, is it served early?"

"No, Miss, only morning vittles in this house. You might get the kitchen girl ta fix you a plate. Seeing as to the weather."

Josie thought of the trips she and Mother had taken, and of the superb accommodations they enjoyed in many private homes. She remembered the gracious personal attentions that gave them particular pleasure. The tarnished elegance of Costello House convinced Josie that with a little bit of effort this ordinary house could be of similar caliber.

Entering the kitchen, Josie addressed a colored girl mending linens while sitting on a stick chair near the fire. A toddler sat absolutely still between the young woman's feet. "Would you have some chamomile tea or ginger? My stomach seems to dislike this winter storm as much as I."

The woman rose, tumbling the baby dangerously near the fiery cooking hearth. "This here's the elixirs," she answered. She pulled out a tin from beneath a hutch. Pointing toward a cupboard, she said, "Them there's the tea fixings." The girl returned to the chair, poked the baby into position with the point of her shoes, then clamped her legs tight around its shoulders while Josie fixed a cup of tea.

"You must be extremely busy with the house full of guests," Josie remarked as she fiddled with the makings. The woman nodded. "Are some staying in their rooms for the storm's duration or is there a special celebration elsewhere? I noticed empty chairs at breakfast."

Two pairs of black eyes followed Josie's voice, the woman's dull and lifeless above a broad flat nose, the baby's bright and inquisitive above a thin angular nose surrounded by a café au lait face. "Mr. Broderick, he done gone 'til spring. Everybody else, they is comin' and goin'."

Josie dropped her coyness. "Do you know where Mr. Broderick went?"

The woman curled her foot under the baby's rump, giving it a hearty push. The toddler rose on wobbly legs then followed the mother's swishing skirt across the kitchen.

Only then did Josie see the definite protrusion of another child on the way. She was about to repeat her question when the girl spoke.

"Man took his work tools." The woman added as an afterthought, "Left a valise of evening dress and drawings. One da girls took them to da attic." She stopped any further questioning by entering a pantry and shutting the door after her. Left alone, the toddler stumbled around the kitchen poking dirty fingers into every opening in the wall along its bumpy path.

Josie stood between the child and the fire, brewing her tea, until she heard the rasp of the pantry door opening.

After listening to the woman's indifferent explanation, Josie felt more confident Jacob would return after the thaw and began to address the fact she must find some means of support until then. Since holiday festivities beckoned from the calendar, Josie began to feel rather smug. Her jewelry should command a substantial amount.

Up in her room, Josie dumped the contents of her jewelry satchel in a heap on the bed. Sorting the glittering objects, Josie moaned; in her haste to flee, she had grabbed mostly sentimental pieces. If she had only made time to retrieve the pearls given to her by her mother.

"Pearls warmed by the caress of bare skin bring radiance to a woman. They announce the indulgence of a lady without being crass. The Elders overstep their authority by banning such adornment," she had told Josefina in private. Mother remained discreet, wearing her finery outside the confines of Taylor County when in the company of "outsiders." Having been schooled under the auspices of the more liberal Dutch Reform, she might secretly fault the didactic Elders, but never embarrassed her husband with her "wild spirit" by dropping her mantle of reserve.

Acutely aware of his wife's unhappiness, Father had responded by presenting her with pearl and diamond earrings designed to match the lauded rope of contention, further qualifying his gift with, "Pearls on a bare throat may be imposing, but diamonds get attention."

Josie twirled a brown curl; the scatterings on the bed appeared dismal. A silver pin, shaped like a basket of flowers, had been given to her by Louis as a bribe when she started day school. Tiny sapphires colored each petal, jade formed the leaves, and citrine chips outlined the bow on the handle of the basket. The gift had rested inside a pocket, unseen by any but her, saving its consoling radiance for times of uncertainty and suffering.

She hated the cosseted, primary school that punished her daily for her failure at godliness. Father eventually tired of his daughter's public chastisement and hired a tutor to live in, a spinster who dwelled on the ways of the world and left the espousing of godly laws to Josie's own interpretation. As expected, she progressed swiftly, as long as the lessons dwelled on the "outside" world and left the workings of the godly world to church meetings.

Bank officials had presented her with a scrimshaw ivory miniature of a sailing vessel hung as a pendant on a gold chain on her first trip to Holland with her parents. Josie's fingers moved up to massage her temples when she recalled the pride her parents had shown. Father's associates congratulated them repeatedly on having such a bright and charming daughter. How had she fooled them all? Tears smarted behind Josie's eyes, but the image of Father's recent revulsion seared them before they dampened a single lash.

Josie quickly wrapped tissue around an obligatory black onyx mourner's broach in the shape of a gloved feminine hand dangling a kerchief, and pushed it to the bottom of the bag. Why had she chosen such a gloomy ornament to rescue?

Dieter had given her the tortoise hair comb topped with a miniature angel on her sixteenth birthday. One of the times when he had foolishly provoked her with repeated requests to allow him to announce their betrothal. A dozen other ornate hair combs and pins lay on the bed, each adorned with chips of precious stones, each salvaged from some contentious occasion when Josefina needed spoiling.

Nothing of real value lay before her. Other than a pair of pearl earrings, Josie had only trifles to sell. Except for the promising warmblood. Josie felt her desperation returning. Even upon threat of death, she swore never to part with Contessa; that horse would protect her future and the future of her son.

Finding a pen, inkwell, and paper, Josie stretched out on the bed, prepared to list all the income generating resources at her disposal. As the page remained blank, her distress grew. Her usefulness showed little to recommend. *I should have acquired skills instead of wasting my time dreaming of a bank seat.*

Mother was not at fault; she had trained her well. No question that Louise Taylor's preparation had been the best instruction available anywhere for managing a household. Farm life in a household of means required light work of Josie during the harvests and polite service as a substitute hostess during celebrations. Josie had never labored at the level required of a farm hand or housemaid. Her chores had been carefully selected for becoming suited to a woman's place in the home, not for livelihood.

Father had educated her like a son, knowledgeable in all the fundamentals of finance, hunting, law, languages. If she had been born male, she would have already begun her training in bank management. Her own bank would have come at her majority.

Matters were worse here than in Taylorsville, Josie could never aspire to banking here, not as a woman, especially an unmarried woman, and certainly not without her family's influence. Besides, Stuart's threat must be considered first in every decision she made, which prohibited her from ever relying on family connections, no matter how indirect.

Mother instructed her well about how to make any surroundings pleasant, and how to be charming. Josie knew nothing about factories except for their squalid conditions and long hours. And less about restaurants, although she could order from either a French or German menu. She could plan gatherings, set a beautiful table, shop with thrift, and drive a hard bargain. She had seldom held a broom, never scrubbed a floor and only once washed anything other than her own fair skin.

That time Josie had sparked some trouble for blaming a broken vase on the housemaid. Mother forced her to polish all the silver in the house for three days for the lie. Another time Josie beat all the rugs in the house for a week for switching the sugar and salt tins as a joke on the cook.

Although brewing ale, beer, and sweet drinks were tolerated, the "Elders" condemned drunkenness. One Christmas she stole Father's best ales and proceeded to drink herself blotto, along with four of her cousins. Father had meted out her worst punishment ever, mucking the stalls in the stables, as much for the public display of indulgence as for the theft.

Josie knew how to tat and embroider, simple tasks she learned to pass the time on rainy days. But with the Elders' discouragement of personal adornment and Father's prohibition of her dream, her disinterest in any requisite household skills was evident in a quality that only a mother would appreciate.

Perhaps, she could serve as a hostess or a companion. That, too, was out of the question Josie realized. Her figure would blossom soon. Already she wore fewer petticoats so her dresses could button around a thickening waistline. The bleakness of her predicament grew grimmer.

On the up side, Jacob sought to marry her. She must simply find a way to provide for herself until he returned. He would surely be back within the next few months, well before the baby's scheduled arrival. And he would have her, she felt sure, and the child, after she explained her generosity in helping François's need of an heir then his despicable behavior.

Josie wadded the blank paper into a ball, then smoothed each wrinkle flat again while she traced the ornate "C" crest on the top of the page. A smile plumped her cheeks and eased the weariness from her head. She had one means, at least, to keep a roof over her head. *I am about to ingratiate my way into Mrs. Costello's kindly heart and her household.*

Later in the afternoon Josie approached Mrs. Costello. "My mother set tea everyday, and being away from home so recently, I miss the custom. Might I have permission to conduct a late afternoon tea in the parlor? Since an unescorted lady is limited in her forwardness, the diversion would give me an opportunity to visit with the other guests without appearing vulgar." Josie's casual reference to convention brought a smile from the landlady.

Pen scratching across paper, Mrs. Costello happily organized teas for the next several weeks. "I must admit, I pray Mr. Broderick will not return and take you away too soon."

Josie assumed Mrs. Cos would collect an additional fee from the other guests for this extra attention. Once her complimentary service became a ritual, Josie would press to receive her share.

The two women supervised rearrangement of the parlor. A sideboard of black walnut descended from the attic. Along with several silver bowls, a silver tray displaying a matching tea set came out of storage. Lace trimmed linen napkins were washed and pressed. Meanwhile, Josie accomplished the crowning touch by persuading a neighbor along the route of her daily walk to contribute cuttings from his prolific greenhouse.

Josie welded herself to the household. With kindness and persistence the young woman floated in and out of rooms, chatted with the workers while they completed their duties, encouraging small details that made the difference between simply completing a chore and demonstrating exemplary work. Praise and pocketed tips brought the maids back for additional guidance daily.

Within days guests competed to share the company of the accomplished hostess, reveling in the mystery of Josie's sponsors. Such speculations added to her charm. After a very successful week, Josie waylaid the landlady.

"Mrs. Costello, not anticipating Mr. Broderick's extended absence, I do not wish to exhaust my funds. Would you have any advice on acquiring a genteel position, at least until my fiancée returns? I know nothing of the city. "

Mrs. Costello had no option. "Would you consider remaining here?" she asked. Careful to avoid any implication that the position would be of a service nature she quickly added, "Perhaps taking over my obligation as hostess, and keeping household accounts?"

Josie demurred. "I have been blessed that we have become more than acquaintances. I would not wish to impose. If my needs became a burden for you, I would feel wretched." Stepping beyond the bounds of civility Josie spoke hurriedly. "I sense that your income is wanting just now." Josie hesitated dramatically while Mrs. Cos sized her up.

"Perhaps, if I were to have room and board and give up Jacob's room? If you have room elsewhere?" She knew an unused nanny and nursery suite upstairs had been turned into a storage facility. "Then you would not be subjected to additional expense on my behalf. And I would have found a suitable haven." The necessity of having to discuss private economies was deplorable for Josie, but she did not want to encourage the woman to expect housekeeping services in return for a pittance.

"You would," Mrs. Costello chirped, "of course, continue to conduct tea. Quite possibly until after the spring thaw." Her wrinkled features softened.

Josie assumed columns of profit multiplied in Mrs. Costello's head and felt satisfied they would both benefit.

"Perhaps, we might add an optional late supper for any guests not invited elsewhere?" suggested Mrs. Costello. "And if you moved up to the vacant governess area on the top floor, near my rooms, Mr. Broderick's room would be free to let, only until his return, of course."

Josie smiled broadly, a second hint Jacob would return late spring. "Agreed." One more item needed cleared up before Josie completed her bargaining. "Like the housemaids, I assume any gratuities I earn for filling minor requests for the guests will be a personal remuneration." Josie felt an explanation due. "For additional expenses I might incur."

"I might have concern over accountability." Mrs. Cos's hesitancy was apparent.

"In addition..." Josie interrupted. Early on, Josie had discovered that most of all, Mrs. Cos hated bartering with the suppliers and facing recalcitrant guests. Josie kept her eyes on the proprietor's face while delivering the clincher. "...if I were to organize the guests' billings and do all the marketing, that would free you to oversee the house and prepare meals."

A smile wreathed her portly face as Mrs. Costello quickly agreed. By noon Josie had all her things moved up to the top floor next to the kind proprietor's bedroom.

~ * ~

The following morning fists pounded Josie's bedroom door. Josie gagged, stifling her urge to retch. Hair coloring darkened a basin of water sitting next to her in the dry sink. Struggling to right herself, Josie staggered and fell sideways against the bed just as Mrs. Costello pushed her way into the room.

"What is this?" Mrs. Costello demanded. "Are you ill?" She scrutinized the pale face, obviously searching for pustules, rheumy eyes, or an odor of spirits. Mrs. Cos's squint grazed Josie's eyes with displayed impatience and displeasure.

Josie, weak and nauseous, quivered. "I am not feeling well." She wanted the woman to leave. Just get out of the room. Not enough energy remained in Josie's convulsing body for her to be combative. "I will feel fine shortly." The eyes facing her darted about, wild with fear.

Shaking her finger vigorously Mrs. Costello interrupted. "What do you mean, 'not feeling well'? For how long?" So much energy went into gesturing that an elbow sleeve slid down into a bracelet around Mrs. Costello's thick wrist.

Josie gasped. *Good God! The woman suspects I exposed her to the fever.* "My malaise is not catching" Josie explained quickly. "I would never jeopardize you or your house. Never bring in any illness..." Josie bent over the chamber pot, steadying herself while her stomach gave a dry heave.

"Merciful heavens!" Mrs. Cos backed away. Panic raced across her face. But then, with the rush of river current, understanding sparked her eyes. Hands on her hips, Mrs. Cos brayed, "You are anticipating! You're carrying his child!"

"It is not what you think. Jacob wants to marry me, I know he does." Fumbling with her clothing in an attempt to erect a barrier to conceal the hair coloring, Josie's hand slipped. Mrs. Costello's flabby arm shot out and grabbed the basin from behind Josie.

"And this?" Mrs. Costello held the bowl. "What else are you hiding?" The older woman pressed Josie, looking about the room as if a demon might jump out. The dye slopped in the pan.

"The disguise is to protect Jacob, and me, too. My father threatened to kill him." Josie only half lied. "I must not be found."

Mrs. Costello sank down onto the bed. "Well, now, this is a horse of a different color! I think you had better tell me the whole story." Mrs. Costello's alarm vanished, replaced by indignation as she observed Josie trembling.

"Jacob asked for my hand in marriage. But my father ran him off, threatening to kill him." Not a complete lie, Josie suspected it near true. "We planned to elope later on. I ran away to join Jacob, but, as you know, found he had already been called away."

Mrs. Costello breathed heavily, her brows knit in a black vee. "Does Mr. Broderick know about the child?"

Josie's mind raced, trying to choose the right response. "Yes, Jacob urged me to come with him." The lie forced her to avert her eyes. Josie found one more point necessary to make. "I will not give up my child."

Mrs. Cos fiddled with the coarse gray hairs escaping from her tight bun while she paced the wooden floor. Her sturdy boots clomped steadily. Josie could smell the older woman's fear.

"I cannot be responsible for a girl I know nothing about and her chargeling. What if your young man does not want to care for you? What if Mr. Broderick decides not to return? I have not received one word from him. Someone else bound his room. Your man boarded here but a short time, leaving hastily, and that all occurred months ago."

While she protested, a selfish idea invaded Mrs. Costello's thoughts. Too late in her husband's life and as a widow, she had never had a chance to bear her own child. Mrs. Cos searched the girl's form looking for signs. *Such a tiny thing. If the girl does not survive the birth, what will happen to the baby?* Mrs. Costello's thoughts returned repeatedly to that single question. *Who would care for the orphaned child?*

"Does anyone else know?" Mrs. Cos questioned. "Tell me again, about the hair dye?'" Fleshy arms folded tighter across her chest.

"After Jacob left," Josie explained, "my father ordered me confined and made arrangements for the child to be ripped from me." Tragic eyes addressed the inquisitor. Josie threw her arms around Mrs. Cos's hefty body and buried her face in its soft strength. "You must help me protect my unborn child. No matter what, I will not endanger my son."

The whole drama sickened Mrs. Costello. How could anyone want to harm a baby? Her sympathy returned, the margin in Josie's favor increased. But first, Mrs. Cos insisted on knowing the strength of the opposition. "You have not yet answered my question." If she allowed the girl to stay, she must know who might lay claim.

"My father, a wealthy man, is well-known, so I disguised myself to keep him or anyone from finding the child and me. But, after Jacob and I are married, Father will have no rights." Desperation drove her words faster. "The child belongs to me. I know it is a boy, an heir to a fortune. One day my son will head the world's most prestigious cartel, and..." Josie faltered. She had revealed too much. The struggling proprietress could contact her father. *Blackmail,* Josie thought. *And Stuart? The exposure. What have I done?*

For several minutes Mrs. Costello did not speak. The ponderous body rocked back and forth from one foot to the other.

Josie clutched Mrs. Cos's pristine apron.

The proprietor deduced that no one knew the girl had come to Costello House. If Josie failed to survive the birth, if the errant fiancée did not return, out of charity some respectable person would be forced to keep the child, provide a home, guardianship. Mrs. Costello's uncertainty was brief. "If, *if* you remain here, there is a great deal of preparation to do. Tell me, when is the child expected?"

"Not for another six months." Josie stammered her lie. "Sometime in June." Relief crept up her body on cat's paws.

"The truth, now. Have you informed Mr. Broderick?" The voice, folded arms and poker back demanded honesty.

"Jacob knew I would follow him wherever. But he expected me to wait until spring. About the child." Josie acted shy. "I thought it best to wait until we were together. I can, however, let him know now. I shall need a forwarding address."

"No need to write him right away," said Mrs. Cos, dashing Josie's hopes of eliciting Jacob's whereabouts. "He will learn of the event in time."

"How did Jacob secure his room?" Josie asked. "Did he pay ahead?"

"Payment in advance is always required for reserving a room. Another young man, a visitor to the city, stayed one night then paid a large sum to hold the room through spring. He did imply someone might come to join Mr. Broderick. But I thought he spoke of a foreigner. A woman perhaps?"

Josie felt at a loss. Could that have been Dieter? Stuart's woman? Perhaps Jacob's mysterious employer. A foreign woman? Not Marianne. He had left St. Louis before she could have known of his whereabouts. She would need to snoop more among the maids.

~ * ~

Days later, when a pushy and persistent investigator knocked at the door of the ordinary house, the satisfied proprietor felt no qualms concerning her answers.

"Mr. Broderick left St. Louis months ago. As for the girl you describe, no one named Josefina Taylor resides here. I have never heard the name. And, I have certainly not entertained a young lady with blonde curls recently."

After the door squeaked shut, Mrs. Costello thanked the angels above that she had stabled Josie's distinctive foal behind the mansion. From the very first night, accepting Josie's estimate of value, Mrs. Cos had installed Contessa in her own private barn.

Several inquiries of kind followed. Mrs. Costello speculated the truth Josie promoted probably lay somewhere outside what Josie had revealed. Guests overflowed the house. Mrs. Costello had no time to dwell on Josie's mysterious circumstances. Besides, she needed to direct her energies to preparing for the child. A baby demanded extra attentions.

After the bustling holidays passed, Josie could no longer disguise her swollen body. How she came to be alone, without friend or family while awaiting the birth of a child became a topic of speculation for employees and guests alike. Josie and Mrs. Costello did their best to keep the mystery alive.

Seventeen

The snow had long since disappeared. Lacy crocus and lavender hyacinths scattered their scent of spring, daffodils bobbed heavy heads. The quick and uneventful passing of winter amazed Josie. The guests had accepted her and, in most cases, been enjoyable, her duties easy and rewarding. Fortunately for Josie, Stuart had not appeared on the doorstep.

A protruding belly dwarfed her body, causing Josie's walk to lose its grace, her stride awkward and labored. Each time she climbed the stairs or answered the bell of a guest, she arrived breathless and testy. Her time drew alarmingly near.

Josie created and discarded plan after plan of how she would care for her son until his majority. Noble families allotted stipends at an early age; she could only provide shelter and food, and that came by way of Mrs. Costello's kindness.

Her son would not be entitled to inherit, of course, until proving his bloodline. When that day arrived, Josie felt confident Marianne would step forward and demand that the ducLaFevre family be generous. Until then, Josie must use her wits to provide for their needs.

Stuart's threat, an issue she resented more each day, prohibited Josie from contacting solicitors to investigate her legal rights. The warmest day of winter occurred when Mrs. Costello had assured Josie she could enjoy free room and board at Costello House as long as she wished to stay.

Josie deliberated hourly, tossing aside ideas, inventing multiple means to not only secure income for the necessities of raising a child, but in addition, enough earnings to obtain the more costly incidentals required to maintain a satisfactory standing, even on the fringe of society. She would never allow even the minor members of society to find her or her son undeserving.

Soundness of body and enthusiasm drew the guests to her, after which Josie determined to captivate them, charm them into using her services and validating her standing.

Sadly, her son would have to attend public school at the start. The measure of his finer education would be afforded at the expense of François's estate. For now, she must see to it her son demonstrated exemplary scholarly credentials, and she would train him in the proper social graces, courtly enough to be included in society's more celebrated activities. He must appear in the listings of society, no matter how near the bottom. Should she use the family name? How, without exposing him to Stuart's henchmen and still maintain the family link?

No one questioned Josie's role as a waiting wife, especially since Mrs. Costello acknowledged having known the errant husband. Since the gold fever rush ten years before, St. Louis had grown accustomed to making exception for the wives left behind, normally tended by relatives for lengthy periods, more often than not, for years.

Even without the expected accusations, whispers, or rude affronts directed at an unattached woman displaying the results of intimate association, Josie personally suffered under the weight of her transgression. The upbringing of the church faulted her daily, reminding her of commandments broken, flawed intentions, and the promise of retribution. At least once a day Josie wondered what price she would pay. A dozen or more times she thought about Jacob.

She grew more reserved, within keeping of her station others judged. In truth, Josie had never witnessed a child's birth. What lay ahead frightened her. Normally during those times, children escaped outdoors, retreated to wood forts, skating ponds, or swimming holes if the birthing event was short-lived. Relatives or neighbors scuttled them off to homes further away if the birthing hours stretched too long.

Horses, pigs, cows, and a variety of pets had introduced the physical basics to Josie, but her involvement with women had consisted of boiling water, piling up stacks of clean cloths and seeing to the thirst and hunger of the waiting family. Worried faces, screams, whispers and a hurriedly packed valise meant difficulty and that she would be sent somewhere to care for the younger children.

Booklets on midwifery stacked up in the Costello House kitchen. Notes scribbled on scraps of paper without signatures were found tucked in odd places. Friends and guests alike shared publicly and furtively what knowledge they carried with the keepers of Costello House.

Josie and Mrs. Cos studied the manuals carefully.

April arrived. Wild violets dotted the lawn. Yellow forsythia formed a golden waterfall fence. Josie and Mrs. Costello sat on the back porch where a wooden crate holding small pots, soil, pebbles and herbs created a table between them. The purple cover-up Josie wore drained the natural flush of her face, casting lavender reflection onto her pale cheeks.

A housemaid had sewn drapes stored in the attic, grape tucked cotton and green moiré, into two cover-ups. Pleats arranged along the shoulders of both robes gave Josie the appearance of a partially extended accordion. Josie hated the unflattering design, the colors, her clumsiness. After the tiny flutters of the quickening six months ago, the unpredictable prodding and lurching inside now bruised her ribs and forced her to grab furniture in support. She wished the whole process were over.

"The writings on midwifery are straightforward," Josie said. She passed a sprig of rosemary under her nose and inhaled. "I have seen a variety of animals drop their young. Most gave birth without incident. There were times I have seen difficulty, but not often." She did not want to think about those times.

"Animals come by reproducing naturally," said Mrs. Costello. "A lady is not of the same disposition. The first time can be especially unpredictable." Mrs. Costello touched Josie's arm gently. "I read these other accounts noted by friends who worry about you, about your petiteness." The sheets of paper numbered twenty or more. "These tell of dire situations, lingering unconsciousness, stillborn deliveries, and deaths. Besides your own well-being, this child is too dear to me to risk its life. We must find a skillful midwife."

"I find no reason why I cannot do this on my own," Josie paused, "with your help. By then, Jacob may even be back."

"A man is of no help. I waited until I felt you strong enough, now I want you to read these revelations." Mrs. Costello handed Josie a dozen sheets of papers. "I resisted sharing them, so as not to alarm you. But, if I am to be responsible for you and the child, I will not jeopardize your lives nor my sanity."

Josie put out her hand for the personal notes. The handwritten letters detailed horror, sorrows, and unimaginable calamities. The more Josie read the more distressed she became. The accounts presented harrowing experiences. Josie realized she had been naïve in thinking the same problems animals experienced in delivery did not occur in women. How stupid to have closed her mind to the dangers, not addressed the tragic possibilities.

"Something else." Mrs. Costello gently touched Josie's shoulder. "Originally, you said another two months before the birth. I do not believe that. You have difficulty climbing the stairs. You constantly doze off. The least exertion makes you breathless. I expect the birth soon." Mrs. Cos leaned back onto her chair. "By now you know you have nothing to fear from me. I want the truth."

Without replying, Josie rocked up from the chair and shuffled indoors. Shamed was not strong enough to say how disgraced she felt. Her lie to the woman who continued to be so important in her life and who wished her only good things had come about from fear, not a wish to deliberately deceive. Her deception had been badly misplaced.

Minutes later Josie returned to the porch and gently dropped a flannel bag in Mrs. Costello's lap. "My gratuities. Please, engage a midwife. I never wanted my troubles to burden you. You have already treated me with more kindness than I deserve."

The older woman stood and embraced Josie. "We might possibly manage well enough together, but I will be relieved to have a midwife by our side." Mrs. Cos hugged Josie. "Just in case your son, like most men, brings us heartache right from the start."

"I am due within a few weeks, as you guessed." Josie said. "I apologize for having lied."

"I just want to be prepared; we both have much to do."

The guests spoiled Josie. Compassion for the young mother-to-be, who spoke so highly of her adventurous husband and showed such courage, brought almost daily gifts of baby clothes, a cradle, and a secondhand feeding chair belonging to a spinster who predicted she would never have the need.

A peddler, who stopped each week to sharpen knives, and who enjoyed most dickering with Josie, left behind a magnificent grinder to ease their preparation of baby food.

One guest, having discussed the plight of the charming Josie at a private dinner, returned to Costello House with a generous gift marker endorsed by a local cabinetmaker. Josie ordered a maple rocking chair and a primary bed.

The guests slept when Josie felt the first pang. A fiery knife divided her body in half with the disemboweling slicing of an earthquake. Beads of perspiration popped out on her face and body instantly. She breathed deeply, waited, then made her way across the hall with all the vivacity of a slug. Mrs. Costello opened the door after the first knock and quickly hustled Josie back to the bed.

One of the chambermaids had rigged up a bell between Josie's bedside and the attic. With the first pull, footsteps could be heard stumbling across the ceiling. Another pain began a paralyzing crawl up Josie's back and wrapped its tentacles around her midsection just as a young maid pushed opened the door. She did not waste time asking if the time was near before she backed out, crying, "I going. I going."

The midwife arrived after Josie lay on a sheet drenched in embryonic fluid. "Get up," she ordered, "walk. I want the bed made again with fresh sheets." A tub of hot boiled water, soap, and a tower of clean toweling sat on a table. She told the maid, "keep boiling water until I tell you to stop." She reached for Josie when a pain brought the pacing girl almost to her knees. "Onto the bed, let's have a look. Mrs. Costello, wash up, I may need you."

The examination lasted only seconds. "The baby has already entered the birth canal. With the next pain, push."

Josie felt the rolling contraction begin and pushed. As the pain grew stronger she clenched her teeth, her hands fighting to find something to grab onto. Mrs. Cos offered her stout arm, bracing herself by gripping the frame of the closed window. The torturous grabbing and pushing went on for two hours with periods of rest hardly enough for Josie to regain strength between episodes, but each pain drained more than that peak of her strength. At the end of the two hours, the young mother-to-be had spent her energies and became fearful.

Mrs. Costello massaged her back and shoulders, held her down. "You can do it. We have waited a long time for this child."

"The baby has descended," the midwife claimed. "I can see the head. Push hard."

Josie pushed until she felt her face swell blue with the effort, her heart racing, her body consumed by pain and waves of contractions. The midwife merely shook her head.

Another two hours passed with the same process repeated.

"A little more... doing fine. Push harder." The midwife leaned toward Mrs. Costello and whispered. "The baby is too large. We should send for a doctor."

Josie heard one word: 'doctor.' "No, I can do it. Mrs. Cos, push down on my stomach when the pain begins. Help me force it out."

The midwife nodded her assent. "Stand alongside her. Keep her legs in the air, when the spasm begins bend each one over an arm and hold tight."

Josie felt depleted, but she would not give up. Sweat made her body slippery and clammy. Her mind worked in a detached sense, noting the vibrancy of color, the rawness of odors that filled the room, and a vision of François ducLaFevre looking beyond her, ignoring her pain.

"The head is out." The midwife lathered her arms up to her elbows and wiped them with a fresh towel. "Push. No, Josie, push harder than you ever have. The baby's right here, use every ounce of strength you can find and then some. Push—push. Yes, I have shoulders. Another push."

Josie could feel nothing. Her body had numbed with the pain and strain. Josie heard the encouragement in the midwife's words, the excitement of Mrs. Costello exclaiming, "I see..." before the exhausted mother blacked out.

~ * ~

The baby arrived late April, in tandem with unusually hot temperatures and tornadoes, a full two months before the date Josie had originally stated. The timing, oddly enough, satisfied the inquisitive Mrs. Costello.

Seven months before that day, not a person for surprises, Mrs. Costello had inquired about the employment expectations of Mr.

Broderick prior to his departure for a meeting. He readily volunteered that after he had offended one of the company's principles, his employer in Illinois had found a temporary position outside of St. Louis that suited Mr. Broderick's skills. The job completed, Mr. Broderick had come to St. Louis to meet a representative of this same employer to consider another offer.

Later the same day Mr. Broderick had ridden away. That evening a young man attired in black wool, blonde hair styled in Dutch custom, paid to reserve Jacob's vacated room until spring.

Mr. Broderick's history and Josie's scrambled tale had taken months to gel for the wary proprietor. When the tallied events finally came together, Mrs. Costello had figured the child's birth date within a few weeks. Content, now, that the child favored belonging to Jacob Broderick, Mrs. Costello celebrated quietly to herself.

The baby, however, was not the promised heir of Josie's plan.

The fair, auburn-tressed girl weighed in over eight pounds. The delivery had ripped the tiny mother apart. An embroidery needle pulled a line of catgut up then thrust down as the midwife stitched the most severe tears closed.

The ravaging confined Josie to bed, where she berated herself hourly. Disappointment spawned scars more damaging than the body's needed repairs. A girl child held no hope of ever inheriting a foreign title or appointment to a prominent position in this country or any other. The most allowed would be a minor stipend, determined by François's solicitors, if they accepted proof of bloodline years from now, and perhaps a dowry.

Father's banishment, Stuart's tormenting, the suffering of menial circumstances, all endured for nothing. Josie berated herself for the sin of dishonor on her parents and betrayal of the pious community. François's rejection proved to be the most accurate measure of her worth after all. The plans for a wealthy life, a child who would someday be a member of even dispossessed royalty, all lost. Josie writhed in her failure.

Jacob would never come for her. Josie felt that was what she deserved. *And the child? Why would Jacob care to share his life and riches with a wife of no accounting and a girl without worth?* Josie mentally chastised herself; the sacrifice had been too dear, the reward forfeited.

Everything she and the child needed for the remainder of their lives would rest on her shoulders. At what cost? How could she ever rise above the status of a person of service? The questions without answers tumbled through Josie's mind without pause, dashing any glimmer of optimism. Each day the new mother withdrew more into herself.

Even as her body healed, a black despair consumed Josie, robbing her of any hope. A sinner and a bastard, survivors without a future. A girl, how in God's name could she ever bring up a girl properly? Curtains pinned tightly shut, Josie slept in the dark day and night, not leaving the room. Eating little and speaking not at all.

For two weeks following the birth, Mrs. Costello divided her time between the household, Josie, and attending to the sweet-tempered baby. Finally, in desperation, the weary proprietor dedicated a cook, who had recently undergone a stillbirth, to wet-nurse the baby and look after the dark souled Josie. Except for feedings, Mrs. Costello alone cared for the baby.

Three weeks passed before Josie's zealous will erupted, parting the angry seas of her guilt and hate, and redirected those energies. She sat up in her bed, "Bring me my baby." The wet nurse brought the child in immediately. Josie laid her on the bed, inspected every inch of her, then picked up the naked infant and cradled her. *This innocent baby is mine, my daughter.* Josie looked deep into the green speckled eyes, searching for something. No malice appeared, instead a penetrating wonder accompanied by flailing arms and an enchanting smile locked onto Josie's empty heart. She held her lips alongside the baby's mouth and breathed a bubbly gurgle of milk. Fingers caught her hair and tangled, the pull strong and steady. She had created and bore this being. *This is my creation.* She would never, never let François lay claim to her and would protect her from Stuart and the Taylor family with her own life if need be.

"Call Mrs. Cos. Tell her I have an errand for her." When Mrs. Costello entered the bedroom Josie began issuing orders before the woman sat down. "You must go today, record her birth officially. Taylor Louise Marianne Broderick, that is my instruction."

"I cannot register what is not so." Mrs. Costello's eyes widened in astonishment.

"In truth, you do not know what is so, or what is not. My daughter will be registered under that name. And you will list on the line for the mother's name, Josie L. Broderick."

"I cannot. You ask me to falsify testimony of record."

"Do you wish to be recognized as the legal guardian?" Josie's voice showed a hint of impatience. "Without a parent's declaration, the state retains the right of deciding custody. With no recognized guardian, the nearest relative may make claim. François..." Josie stopped, swallowed, then went on.

"Jacob has no surviving family. That leaves only my father and brother, both who wish the child dead. The papers we prepared designating you as guardian should I be incapacitated would be worthless."

~ * ~

Mrs. Costello walked the five blocks to the courthouse. Leaning on the scarred counter, she smoothed the form flat and carefully penned each line.

Name: Broderick, Taylor Louise Marianne
Born: April 23, 1880 Place of birth: St. Louis, Missouri
Mother: Broderick, Josie L.
Place of birth: Illinois
Residence:_____
Father: _____Place of birth:_____
Residence:_____

Not until closing time, many hours after the woman had departed, did the clerk note the mother's address and lines designating the father's identity remained blank. He applied a stamp. Bold squared black letters obscured the last lines. UNKNOWN.

~ * ~

Two weeks later, her health greatly improved, her mind more readily coping, Josie prepared to deal with the results of the fateful choice she made almost a year ago. She enjoyed excellent health and had high regard for her beauty and charm. However, her strong will would become her weapon. With a quick mind, industry, and ambition, and the indulgence of Mrs. Costello, she and Taylor would forge their future. She felt stronger than ever that even if she never found Jacob, she could never depend on a marriage of influence to make her way, and she was determined neither she nor Taylor would ever surrender to their enemies.

Josie felt one more detail needed attention. Someone must know about Taylor, a person outside Mrs. Costello, someone in a position to offer sanctuary should her daughter ever have the need.

Josie penned a brief note to her eldest brother.

> *My Dearest Louis,*
> *A daughter, born April 23.*
> *Both safe and well.*
> *Lovingly, Josefina*

A courier from the union bank carried the message among others to Taylorsville, to be handed directly to Josie's treasured tutor, Miss Vondyken, the only other inhabitant of Taylor County Josie trusted not to tell Father.

~ * ~

In the library at Taylor Estates, Louis huddled in the corner of an armchair, mesmerized by the waning light distorted into piecemeal lances by a cracked glass in the French door. When he had arrived earlier in the evening, a square envelope sealed with an ornate "C" was furtively slipped into his hand before he dismounted. His Father had kept the tutor on to write letters, read, do whatever matters of the sort that comforted Mother.

Louise Taylor had not left her bed for months; her condition monitored from dawn to dusk by healers and doctors. No conversations occurred, no pleasant exchanges, no dying wishes, just the brewing of tea and a silver spoon lying next to the vial of numbing laudanum.

Louis waited a day, until he decided the tutor knew no additional information, before he approached his father. His intentions were good, but he proceeded cautiously. "Father, have you news of our Josefina?"

Josef erupted with volcanic rage, throwing his arms in the air, spewing damnation. "Your mother lies dying because of that Jezebel. Her sin destroyed us all. Her treachery will wrack everything I hold dearest." Bitterness turned his words swift and lethal as a cavalryman's saber. "Never speak of her again in this house. Or anywhere within my hearing."

Louis judged the contempt of Father's command, the flat, hate-filled eyes. Turning his back to his Father, Josefina's beloved brother hurled the ivory paper into the fire. Louis watched sorrowfully while the carefully formed letters curled up black and brittle, then evaporated in the flame. "Peace go with you, Lil Jos," he muttered.

Late that evening, alone with Stuart in the library, Louis approached his brother. "Father believes Josefina sailed to Europe. Is that true?"

"I am the one who told him so," said Stuart.

"I know what you told Father. Now I want the truth."

"Why would you think otherwise?" The question challenged; his eyes turned hard as granite.

Louis conveyed all his anger to his eyes, tightened the muscles in his face to appear as fierce as possible and waited.

"Josefina sailed to France," Stuart answered swiftly. "I gave a confirmation of the ship's register to Father. We found no report about her arrival. She vanished. I suspect she and her bastard died in some French hovel." A self-satisfied smirk brightened his face. "Fittingly so."

"French?"

"Josephina booked passage to Marseille, expecting Marianne to join her. But Marianne put Josefina on the boat in St. Louis. She gave me the names of the shipping companies." Outwardly insolent in his recounting, Stuart slapped his brother on the back. "Besides, Father and I say good riddance."

Louis snatched the hand from his shoulder. "Marianne, you address her, without the propriety of Miss duc LaFevre?" Louis pondered the unflattering familiarity. "Why should I believe or trust you? You have never earned anyone's confidence." Knowing he would learn nothing more, he glared contemptuously at Stuart, "If I ever discover our sister suffered at your hand, or Miss ducLaFevre's, or you knew anything of her distress, I will see that you pay dearly."

~ * ~

Several weeks later Josie sent a message again. The second note lay among others ignored in a stack of condolences regarding the death of Louise Taylor. All awaited the services of a hired mourner's calligrapher, the tutor having been let go.

Shut off from the world, Josef Taylor grieved alone over the loss of his wife.

The St. Louis Republic published the simple, black bordered notification of the death of Mrs. Josef Taylor.

Sobs racked Josie while she waited for the world to stop going about its business, for all mortals to protest and beat their chests, acknowledge the pain and loss of Louise Taylor. Her tears ate wet holes in the newsprint covering her lap. The smell of cheap ink stung her nose. She clutched her daughter and rocked furiously. "I should have been at her side." She hugged Taylor tightly, tears darkening the sleeping baby's red tresses. She whispered in the tiny ear snuggled against her mouth, "I can do it. We will make our way together. There is no going back now."

Eighteen

St. Louis, 1887
Eight years later.

 August humidity accompanied by suffocating heat tempered the group gathered at the breakfast table. Josie feigned a freshness that ignored the petticoats glued to her body and the pools of sweat staining her collar and midriff. The latest trend, iced tea, ill-favored as she found the idea, might win her over today. Everyone moved as sluggish as a bee fat on nectar. The lazy sunrise, despite its intensity, failed to burn off the morning's soggy heaviness.

 Ruby hobnail plates, cups, and glasses cast blood-tinted shadows across the white cloth of the dining table. Eight of Costello House's fifteen guests indulged their ravenous appetites on Mrs. Costello's apple pancakes this morning. The empty serving dishes taunted the glutinous diners as their nondescript faces, devoid of interest and energy, studied their soiled plates, and they toyed with fragile cups.

 "The street noise is most annoying, Mrs. Broderick. Must we suffer through this?" clucked Mrs. Larson with boorish disdain.

 "That thumping and banging from the riverfront tests my character, most unsettling," added the finicky solicitor's wife. "With the windows closed, we would not have to endure such a raucous onslaught." The husband seemed unaware of any sound, including his wife's complaint.

 Trees lined the boulevard leading down to the river and muffled the racket of the waterfront barges where grips unloaded the wares.

The thunder of stacking crates softened into puffs, like gunshots into goose down. The bellows of the deckhands droned into unintelligible burps. Still, all that unwelcome commotion hovered like a thorny mist beneath, what was to Josie even more irritating, the shrieks of hundreds of hungry gulls feeding on the leavings of the market place.

"I apologize," Josie said. "I, too, find the noise annoying. However, Mrs. Costello insists that in keeping with healthful hygiene the house be aired daily. We certainly do not wish to fall ill or lose our excellent housekeeper over such a minor inconvenience, now do we?"

"And the odor? Something quite rank seems to have taken up residence nearby." The complaint came from a singular gentleman who reeked so of rum Josie questioned his ability to differentiate any other smell.

"Close the windows. Be done with it," ordered an older man. "Put a stop to this harping."

Josie twitched her nose, rankled. The wine colored drapes hung open, secured by rosettes. Their luxury framed windows raised to the fullest in invitation to any passing breeze. On such a day as this, Mrs. Cos's futile attempt attracted, instead, the musky odor of the river, the smell of fish, and the soot from the river steamers. Along with this, Josie suspected the overriding foulness came from the horse droppings dotting the gutters. Was it any wonder? The thoroughfare had not been cleaned by a slopsweeper in days.

The burden of the guests' displeasure rested on Josie, and she disliked being subjected to placating guests for reasons she also found offensive. "I am sure tomorrow will be better. We share each other's company for such a brief time each morning, surely we can endure this inconvenience with some charity. Tell me, what have you enjoyed during your visits?"

"Well, not the noise and stink." The rum smelling guest seemed set on stirring up dissension.

On Josie's invitation, a quaint Louisiana mother and daughter set, visiting St. Louis for the first time, launched an enthusiastic accounting of their excursions. Their calm voices and new outlook during the telling delighted and distracted the other guests.

While the women chattered, Josie looked about the dining room, inspecting the elegant details that heightened the guests' pleasure in the genteel surroundings.

A huge bouquet of roses filled a crystal vase on the sideboard. Finger bowls at each place setting held potpourri. Even at that, the flowers' fragrance and the sugary smell of maple did not sweeten the air. After breakfast, she would hang wreaths of dried lilac and fresh rosemary.

The lace-covered table, weighted with ornate silver pieces, stretched half the length of the dining room. The buffet exhibited sparkling crystal and glowing silver pieces. When everything met her approval, Josie returned her attention to the guests.

In the midst of pouring coffee around, Josie cocked her head to one side, suppressing a pique that threatened to intrude on the now sedate breakfast.

Several soft thumps and a swooshing tumble sound announcing her daughter's arrival came from the kitchen. The noises passed unnoticed by the self-absorbed guests, but Josie's ears would have picked up the flick of a rabbit's whiskers had the sound come from the back stairs.

I must admonish Mrs. Cos again not to undermine my rules. Encouraging Taylor's boorish behavior.

Josie continued pouring, courtesies rolling off her tongue from habit. "Mr. Manning, I have the jeweled combs I promised. Mrs. Manning will be delighted. They match her evening dress as if designed especially for her." The old man regularly ignored his wife.

"As usual, Mrs. Broderick. Your attention may well win back my wife's appreciation. I will be generous in return."

Addressing the nearby clucking matron, Josie's nose rose noticeably as if a rod poked her chin upwards. Her voice became haughty. "I discovered five jet buttons. A perfect set to replace the plain bone on your moiré gown. Of course, Mrs. Larson, if you are not interested, I had originally chosen them to enhance a gown of my own."

The lady in question gazed down her nose. "No, no, darling, they would be an absolute perfect touch. You will need to look elsewhere for your own."

The last of her ministrations completed, Josie mentally calculated what today's extra attentions had earned. She rose gracefully from the table, coffeepot in hand. "Ladies, gentlemen, please excuse me."

With minimum effort, Josie shouldered the swinging door to the kitchen open without a squeak. Mandy was loudly berating Taylor's laziness. "Who you think you are? Queen Uppity face." The undefinable speech pattern mingled a highborn nasal twang, the drawl of Negro influence, and Italian song.

Taylor deserved a comeuppance, Josie agreed, but name-calling was unseemly for Mandy's position. Orphaned at age three, the mulatto chaterling was cared for by Mrs. Costello and engaged in service. In contrast, everyone knew Taylor's circumstances were only temporary.

For a moment Josie waited just inside the door, listening to the two girls. Not quite two years older than Taylor, Mandy with her high cheekbones and pert nose, stood on a wooden box at the sink. Her elbows sloshed in dishwater while she chided the tardy child. "Your Momma already quit serving. Went upstairs. You missed your outing."

Taylor, her coppery hair still tousled, sat down before a plate covered neatly with a warming cloth. "Liar, liar, pants on fire. You're just jealous 'cause I got cakes." Taylor elaborately spooned a trickle of maple syrup onto the apple pancakes.

The truth was unkind. Taylor often enjoyed treats denied the normally easy-going dishwasher. The heat had heightened everybody's temper, magnifying everyday slights.

Mandy's mother, who had birthed a stillborn then wet-nursed Taylor, passed away at the same time Josie's health returned. Josie's first outing had been to take flowers to the crowded Negro cemetery across town and dish up food at the church. The rundown planked church and Negro singing gave Josie her first glimpse of religion since leaving Taylorsville. She had enjoyed the noisy services, more so because she knew the Elders would condemn the happy setting. That had not been her last visit.

Josie quickly stepped further into the kitchen. "My, my, I hear tell when a person lies, her tongue turns black and falls right out. If it were to roll across the floor, someone might snatch it up and run away with it." She flung her arms toward the floor as if grabbing at something. "What would the poor speechless child do then?"

"But," Mandy said, "she popped in here baying like a newborn puppy, wanting her way." At Taylor's astonished look, Mandy gulped down giggles cropping up between her complaints. "I just got everything all clean." The young girl managed to maintain an air of superiority.

Josie would tolerate no uppishness. "Mind your place." Josie smoothed Taylor's unruly locks and tucked them behind an ear. "I promise, after Taylor finishes, she will help you clear the dining room and arrange the tables in the courtyard." Mandy gave a snort; Taylor pouted.

Josie felt satisfied. Such a small penalty taught Taylor responsibility, and more to the point, like similar chores, kept Taylor from running about like an unrestrained calf. Her daughter must learn rules were meant to be followed if she had any hope of success at becoming a proper lady.

Josie's reproach to Taylor struck more deadly. "You indulged your laziness. And against my repeated wishes, you again dusted the stairs with your derriere. All very unladylike, certainly not suggestive of someone I would wish to accompany me uptown."

Lips scrunched up, clearly the scolding paining her, Taylor pleaded. "I'm sorry. Please, this is our only day out. I promise to do whatever you say."

Josie believed the sincerity. Regardless, she would not set aside Taylor's penance for any cause. "Then, young lady, you had better be on your best behavior. If your chores are not completed by the time I come back downstairs, you will stay behind." Josie puckered her brow and set her mouth in a hard line, dulling any twinkle that might spark her eyes. "Those knickers are for cycle riding. If you are walking out with me, you will dress properly."

~ * ~

On the other side of the closed the door, the guests gossiped about their absent hostess. The Louisiana daughter asked, "Mrs. Broderick seems so tragic. Do you suppose she is a descendant of royalty, a victim of some crown's indiscretion?"

"More likely she aspires to such lineage," Mrs. Larson said. "Ambitious, I would judge."

The rum-smelling man placed his elbows emphatically on the table. "A week ago, I was privy to an unusual happening in regard to our mysterious hostess. A lively occasion."

"Please, tell. I love flights of fancy," said the Louisiana set together. Other murmurs of encouragement traveled the table.

"Would that this be fantasy." The man leaned toward the center of the table. "I had been invited to sit at the table of Mr. Yettes, our local undertaker, on board the Goldenrod. That is of no consequence, except our own Mrs. Broderick just vacated the chair offered. Seems she had wagered and lost a large measure of money."

Whispers dotted the table. Heads bobbed and tongues wagged in furious fashion. The speaker shifted his weight pompously. "She then pursued this streak of bad luck by losing an additional significant sum, advanced by the undertaker. Gossips tell Mrs. Broderick owes a substantial amount to our local embalmer. We were probing her unfortunate turn of luck when a stranger joined us."

"Did I tell you she is lax?" commented Mrs. Larson loudly. "Trouble ahead for that girl."

"Well, Mr. Yettes welcomed the outsider." The storyteller's rum breath lingered in crossing the table. "Introduced him around as part of that new banking group." The speaker arched his brows. "Young man, squarish face, dull-witted appearing. Not at all the bearing one expects at a high stakes table."

"Probably with that private cartel backing the new bank," someone said.

The storyteller stuck his thumbs in his waistcoat. "Well, I digress. When I expressed my regret over Mrs. Broderick's bad fortune, after this stranger joined us, he became quite agitated. Asked me directly. 'Are you a personal acquaintance of Mrs. Broderick?' Of course, I explained. 'Mrs. Broderick is the proprietress of Costello House where I am residing."

"The man's agitation grew profound. 'Where is her husband?' he questioned. Well, let me tell you, he was all but foaming at the mouth like a rabid dog, he appeared unsuitably shaken. 'Presumably out West, I told him.'"

"I hardly think so," another male guest commented. "Her husband got killed in California looking for gold, I heard." At the matron's raised eyebrows he went on. "Well, I inquired as to her eligibility." He scowled at the tsking women. "Got good business sense for a woman, besides being attractive. Wanted to know my chances."

The speaker glared at the kibitzer before continuing. "Before I could explain any further, this stranger jumped up, began ranting. Something like, 'petite women, blonde hair, blue eyes, like mine! Well, his eyes were glazed as a wild donkey, in no manner comparable to our composed Mrs. Broderick."

"Besides, Mrs. Broderick's hair is quite dark," protested the Louisiana girl.

"Dyed, my guess," said Mrs. Larson. "Which alone should raise suspicion."

"Anyway, who was I to argue?" said the rum-man. "This stranger knocked people over in his haste to get away. Rushed out before I could correct him. Seemingly, all because our own Mrs. Broderick lost considerable wagers. A most unsettling incident, and I still have not decided if..."

Josie entered the dining room, catching the tale end of the conversation. His back to her, the old man scoffed. "I question if it was the beauty of our hostess or her indebtedness that held his interest."

Josie felt her cheeks redden. Her bustle barely covered the seat when Mrs. Larson addressed her. "I understand some rather alarming mischief occurred on the Goldenrod recently. The favor of this house would decline cruelly should its reputation suffer from your frequent attendance."

Josie peered down her nose in like fashion. "Society championed the gaming boats years ago. Only recently have the less fashionable elements appeared. I am sure, in time, they will find us quite boring. After all, our paltry wagers offer them no real challenge."

The lawyer interrupted. "We were not addressing the Johnny-come-latelies. I was led to understand that you risked quite a significant sum on Saturday last. Lost the wager."

Josie nodded in agreement, simultaneously flipping her hand nonchalantly in denial, as if shooing away a bothersome fly. "That was but one sorry happening among many more successful plays."

"There was a question of your ability to settle the debt," pressed the rum perfumed man.

The storyteller Josie had heard, and his comment carried an obvious slur.

He paused dramatically, then hurried on at the deadly squint of Josie's eyes. "Of course, as proprietor of this elegant establishment, there is no doubt of your access to funds."

Josie did not correct his misinformation. Few actually knew who owned the ordinary house. Instead, she dabbed a napkin at each corner of her mouth, then rose. "I remind you, no tea served today. Since most of the house received invitations to the Governor's Reception after the Fair this evening and to his races in the morning, I welcome you to a light breakfast a half-hour earlier tomorrow, five-thirty. Please, inform the housemaids if you are not appearing at the table."

Josie speculated nastily there would be few. They probably preferred lolling in bed like bloated cows, ruminating on ways to malign a person. Indecent, their gossiping. She must put a stop to these tales turning her social standing into a topic for public mockery. She would insist on civility at the table; manners never lent credence to bad taste.

"Before you go, Mrs. Broderick. I have a request." The maligning matron heaved her buxom chest. "I have a gentleman guest arriving midday. Please instruct the kitchen to prepare a fruit and cheese plate for me. I have need of wineglasses, also. We plan to inspect Costello House. He finds he may be in need of quarters for fall."

"Of course, Mrs. Larson, we welcome anyone you endorse."

The question of reputation weighed heavily on Josie's mind while she straightened the room and prepared for her outing. The undertaker paid her well to sit at the head table, her losses trivial, her winnings her own. Now, she must bow out. More important than the dreaded loss of income, Josie would not permit any gossip that might interfere with Taylor's future acceptance into high-society.

~ * ~

Josie lingered in the courtyard, suffering the sun heated stone. The warmth grew uncomfortable through the thin soles of her kidskin shoes. Her mind busied itself with how she should approach the undertaker this evening. One hand busily plucked dead buds from the potted topiary, masking the wait for her overdue daughter.

A brief shower had pelted St. Louis yesterday. Gnats swarmed in clouds around the hedges, and mosquitoes paddled like matchstick nymphs in shaded puddles. Contemplating the situation at Costello house, Josie bent over to attach her wooden pattens. She could not afford the expense if her delicate footwear were mired. Stepping into each clog, she tied the ankle laces.

Months ago Mrs. Costello reluctantly paid the closet and window tax for community services. Unlike their neighbors, they could not board up windows or wallpaper over sealed closets to discharge the tax. Still, the city neglected servicing this neighborhood, sending their workers instead to newer, more prosperous areas. Animal waste littered the streets and trash accumulated along the walk. Rarely did they see a slopsweeper these days.

When Taylor reached her majority and received her due, they would be able to occupy a more suitable residence, one without indifferent workmen and riverfront clamor. If attention to niceties and the society trade began to decline sooner, Josie already decided, she and her daughter could not gamble on the wait. She must finagle a part-ownership, then leverage Costello House into more suitable holdings.

Without thinking, her daily wish crossed Josie's mind. If only Jacob were here. Eight years, and not one sign he searched for her, or that he still lived. Her hopes for Jacob's return had begun to dim. Incidents that reminded her of him popped up less frequently, and when the recollections did interrupt her life, the images were less vivid. Her most grievous mistake: she had lied, had told Taylor that Jacob was her father. The child would not give up on his return.

The high-pitched farewell of her daughter drifted from the house. Josie stepped off the stone terrace as if she had just prepared to leave. Taylor's hand slid quickly into her own.

"Sorry, Momma, I hurried best I could."

Their strides matched step for step as they strolled. Josie felt flattered by the young girl's earnest attempt to copy the graceful swaying it had taken her a lifetime to cultivate. She felt mildly amused at the resultant bumbling.

They paused before crossing the street. Taylor looked back at the mansion, waved to Mandy in the garden, then crooked her neck as far back as possible to view her fourth floor window. The child repeated the habit at the beginning of every outing, as if she feared each departure might be her last.

The well-preserved brick mansion rose impressively above the surrounding walnut trees. White shutters bordered windows that sparkled among the shadows of the leafy trees. Along each side of the structure a quarter acre vegetable garden bowed in humbleness behind showy flowerbeds, compromising Mrs. Costello's frugality with Josie's choice of a more stately entrance.

The estate presented an enticing welcome, one that encouraged the fringes of society and the overflow entourage of the wealthy to stop for accommodations during their stays in the riverfront town. The new elite of St. Louis owned few homes in Lafayette Square. The wealthy Ferguson and McKinney's newest estates, establishments of obscene proportion, Josie judged, were situated on Forest Hill. Fortunately, the area near the river and amidst the uptown circle still continued to advertise a prestigious address.

During their saunter down the cobblestone street, Josie recognized one of their guests. "Step up, Taylor," she urged, "remember your manners."

Taylor curtsied. "Good day, sir. It is a pleasure to see you looking so well."

Josie nodded. "Lovely day." She had barely remarked on the weather when a line of greeters as fluid as a cotillion began to break from the walkers. After several blocks of similar interruptions, Taylor's boredom, bordering on impatience, began to show.

"Come forward. Be of consequence," Josie ordered. "You must exhibit the manners of a lady. Be prepared to fit into the rigors of society."

"Momma, I am going to stay with you forever," said Taylor. "I have no need to learn to be a lady."

"Hush, child. Do you wish me to faint dead away? Such nonsense. Not important being a lady, and you expect to live with me?" Josie knuckled the child's head. "We have breeding. Do you think I wish to appear in public with an insulting cur?"

Taylor hung her head, shame reddening her freckled cheeks. "Sorry, Momma."

Mother and daughter walked in silence for several blocks until they approached a stable. A corner stall window stood open where a magnificent white horse bobbed its head impatiently. "Even Contessa shows breeding. Look, she nods her head in agreement."

Josie, face glowing, gripped Taylor's hand tighter while she hurried toward the animal. She lifted the child up beside her onto a wooden crate, pulled a piece of apple from her pocket and quickly thrust it between the huge yellowed teeth before sharing a section of the apple with Taylor to do the same.

"Morning, Mrs. Broderick!" A boyish groom gripping a worn leather bridle approached them. "Goina' be a winner a'gin today."

"Good morning, Peter." His comment surprised Josie, and she was not pleased. "Contessa races today? When did Mr. Yettes make these arrangement?"

"Uh, not sure," the groom coached his answer. "Well, uh, real late. Near closing the undertaker dropped by. Got Contessa runnin' this afternoon. You goina' be there?"

The news troubled Josie. Her partner had promised to hold back on the racing until Contessa's foal arrived. "In her condition?" Josie flushed, embarrassed by her implied doubt of her partner's knowledge and the delicacy of the discussion.

"Contessa runs easy. Got another month or so," the boy assured her.

"Please, Peter, when you bring Contessa back, feed her some extra oats." Josie attempted to place a copper in the boy's hand.

Peter twisted his hand away. "No need for that, Mrs. Broderick. Yours is a fine animal. I see she gets good care."

Josie forced the coin into his fist.

"Thank you. Now don't go aworryin'. Go on, enjoy your day." Peter smiled. "You've never seen Contessa race, sure you won't come?"

Josie shook her head side-to-side, then turned away. Any connection formed between her and the uniquely marked horse compromised Taylor's safety. After all these years, she still shuddered at thought of her brother's threat. Stuart would kidnap Taylor and send her to a workhouse if not kill her, if he ever discovered them. Josie had no doubt.

Her brother had appeared only once, a year after her narrow escape. He had attended the Grand Opening of the Golden Showboat. Propriety demanded members of society go masked, daringly incognito, until the Dames of St. Louis deemed it chic to patronize the gaming boats.

Josie wore a blue feathered mask attached by self-fabric to a mushroom-shaped head covering. Preoccupied, she walked near the wagering at a gaming table. Stuart's wild gestures creased her hat, which bounced crooked. Luckily, in his anger over his loss, Stuart raced out, entirely unaware of the mishap.

In that moment, Josie's terror grappled with the rage that had lain dormant for so many years. Anger with Stuart, Father, and François flooded her. She jerked away from her brother, thinking to escape, but equally wanting to pursue him and punish him for the unhappiness he had created. She hungered to show him she had survived, to kick until blood flowed, feel his flesh bruising and renting beneath her pounding. But years of good manners hammered into habit caused her to hesitate, and in that instant Stuart disappeared. Her foolhardy desire to pursue him lost to a more rational fear. She must protect Taylor; they were all each other had.

For months afterwards, Josie refused to go near Lafayette Park. One afternoon, while on a carriage ride, she enticed a guest to tour Stuart's neighborhood. Josie discovered the stately townhouse closed, windows boarded, a chain and padlock secured the brass door handles.

A crypt, Josie thought, entombing her bitter memories. She hadn't seen her brother again. But every few weeks, she revisited the area, bile dripping in her stomach when she turned the corner onto his street. During the eight years of her vigilance, the house remained deserted.

~ * ~

Leaving Contessa, mother and daughter changed direction and walked down Water Street along the waterfront. Huge gaming boats teetered restlessly in the clear flowing waters. Late at night, with the oil lamps reflected like hundreds of blinking stars in the black water, with the music and gaily-costumed women dancing in their sparkling jewelry, the vessels did indeed appear to be floating palaces.

In the daylight, without the reflective glamour, the abandoned decks rotted under swaths of black soot and peeling paint. The faded flourishes of gold molding trumpeted off-key. Dozing deckhands sprawled about in their tattered work clothes and personified the overall appearance of shoddiness and neglect.

Josie trod quickly past the sleeping giants while she entertained Taylor with abbreviated tales of the society patrons she met during her riverfront excursions. What she did not tell Taylor concerned the money squandered at the tables, tossed on the inviting velvet cloth to be snatched up when the cards failed.

Many evenings Josie had returned unescorted to the house, grateful to escape the humiliation of watching guests' coins disappear with regularity. Increasingly, she felt satisfied she had settled for a finder's fee from Mr. Yettes for the participation of guests from Costello House and not the more lucrative percentage of purses lost. She felt no reason to question Mr. Yettes's honesty, but wanted to practice prudence on her part in connection with his gambling activity.

Leaving the troubling reminders behind, Josie approached the riverfront market. Many of the vendors waved, some circled cloths above their heads, others made catcalls, all vied for attention.

Josie displayed her most charming smile. Opening her eyes wide, she first approached the fish vendor. Smothering her amusement, she watched him, distracted by her gaze, fumble with a customer's package. When a rubbery black catfish slid from the newspaper wrapping, his chubby fingers grabbed the slippery fish in midair, but his eyes strayed from hers for only an instant.

After he bid the customer goodbye, he reached into another tub and produced a pair of large bass. "Saved these for you Mrs. Broderick. Best I got. And, I have fresh Louisiana crayfish."

"How thoughtful and kind! Our table stays the envy of the city, in particular from your excellent fish. How can I thank you?" His eyes danced, his mouth gaped as she batted her pale lashes.

Taylor squiggled her eyes, mimicking her mother's behavior, uncertain of her own powers as she watched the befuddled man slip extra mussels in with the bass.

Next, Josie shamelessly flirted with the fruit man, leaving his stall with unblemished grapes, the sweetest smelling peaches and the only coconut in his bin.

After inspecting her list and arranging delivery, Josie sang out. "Thank you. *Adieu. Au revoir.*" Whenever Josie spoke French, Taylor perked up. *Strange,* Josie thought, how the child seemed attracted to her heritage. Fanning a hanky in the air, Josie turned to her patient daughter. "And now, *ma cherie*, we begin our adventure." The day would turn out fine.

"Momma, tell me about your home," Taylor pleaded. "Tell me about my grandmother."

Josie sighed. "Once upon a time, there was a young girl just about your age, who would run barefoot through the lawn. Always careful to stay out of her Mother's sight." Josie could almost feel the damp, cool grass skim between her toes. Her nose filled with the nostalgic scent of roses.

Taylor interrupted, "Grandmother thought barefoot unladylike."

"You are right. My rooms occupied the third floor of one wing. Aunts, uncles and cousins lived on every road for miles around. Someone visited daily, to join in the breaking of bread, to show off a fiancée or a new baby."

"Someday I will be part of a big family," Taylor quipped. "When Poppa comes."

Josie ignored her daughter's wishfulness. "Every Sunday aunts, uncles and cousins arrived for morning worship then remained until after evening devotions. Wednesdays they came for prayer services. On holidays, we all bowed to your grandmother's wishes and joined together sharing the most splendid feasts in the county to celebrate."

Wistfully, Taylor asked the same question as always. "Which holiday was your favorite, Momma?"

"During winter days we built huge bonfires and all the children came. We skated on the frozen lake and roasted corn or potatoes. Sleds would be brought out and teams harnessed, and we raced across the countryside."

"Your favorite was Christmas, huh, Momma."

Josie's face took on a ruddy glow, as if spanked by cold. "Relatives from all over the country, even the world, came. Cousins, four, six at a time, sometimes shared my bed. All day, everyday, for weeks, the house smelled of roasted nuts, cinnamon, apple, cranberry. So many women would crowd the kitchen that no one could walk through. We would wait for the right moment, sneak through the kitchen and swipe some sweet, then hide in the stable with our treasures. The ladies clustered around pots of tea comparing stories of all our misdeeds, almost challenging each other over which of us was the most tiresome. Later on they spoiled us with taffy pulls, fudge boils, and cookie bakes."

"Tell my favorite part again. You know, the dress." Taylor's eyes danced.

"For the Christmas celebration when I was just your age, I wore a special dress. Sewn just for me. It was velvet, blue as a cloudless summer sky. A lace collar as big as a bib adorned my chest and miniature silver bells trimmed the hem. Whenever I moved, tinkles rang through the air like an angle's song."

Josie's voice broke as she leaned over and tweaked Taylor's nose. And, that was the first time Dieter Vandemere informed her he would do whatever it took and, if he must, wait forever to marry her. *What had happened to Dieter? And Marianne?*

Momentarily, Josie studied her daughter, searching the green eyes and oval face for some imperfection. The high cheekbones rose softly then blended into a gentle curved jaw. The nose extended stronger than her own, but still acceptable.

If Josef Taylor ever saw this face, he would know the truth immediately. Taylor would call him Grandfather. Nothing could be more prized, except to a man who wished his granddaughter dead. Josie shuddered.

"Momma, tell me about summer, too?" Taylor's face beamed, as if she shared a seldom-enjoyed sweet.

"Summers brought picnics by the lake, boat regattas, and always, horse races. After dinner in the evening, he would bring out his violin and play so sweetly that women wept." Josie emphasized the 'he', refusing to speak of the man as grandfather. "Most every night, before I was sent to bed, we played a duet. Your Nana ordered my violin special, an Armati, made in Italy. The one stored under my bed."

"Promise me," Josie only had to tilt her head down slightly to look her eight-year-old daughter directly in the eyes, "one day to be as queenly as your grandmother." Without waiting for an answer Josie straightened up and stepped out resolutely. "But first, you must learn to behave like a woman of quality. I will claim no ragamuffin."

Josie grew quiet thinking of the danger, of how she had tempted fate. Her impetuous decision to name her baby Taylor had increased the risk of being found. But in desperation she had reached out to connect, however fruitlessly, with family. If her father had really sought to find his granddaughter or Stuart had employed more detectives, such mulishness could have cost her everything.

Except for that one close encounter with Stuart on the boat, Josie had not seen nor heard from any of her family for over eight years. Josie fussed with her mitts and hat, then resumed her idle chatter, the brightness of her eyes clouded beneath lowered lids.

Striding quickly up Washington Avenue, Josie flaunted her disdain for the less hardy who rode by in the cool shade of horse drawn cable cars. At Fourth Street, the longest gaper's fence ever erected encompassed almost a city block. A recently posted sign attached to the planks announced the coming of Worldwide Bank.

Gossips had guessed correctly. Josie had listened to the rumors for weeks, squirreled away her fear, but she could no longer avoid the truth. Before the structure's construction drew near completion she must choose; confront the villainous masters of her fear or flee. The indecision that had gnawed at her too long must be faced.

Nineteen

At Twelfth Street, Josie faced a plain, frame building, the workingman's depository. Hand-painted, sun-bleached block letters announced Boatman's Bank. Josie stooped to remove her pattens, smoothed her dress, then her daughter's, and again tucked Taylor's copper strands back under her bonnet. "You must not hide behind me. Step up and greet Mr. Helmut. Show good manners, remark on his health or the pleasant day."

"Yes, Momma!" In one breath Taylor prompted, "Then can we go to Lindo's for fruit ices?"

"Today, there may be a special treat. If, a certain young girl in my charge remembers to behave like a lady."

When they entered the bank, Taylor obediently curtsied. "Good day, Mr. Helmut, you are looking well."

"Good day to you, Miss Broderick." Flakes drifted down as he bowed his head. Long johns drooped below his pant's cuff.

Josie puckered her brows tightly, stopping short Taylor's precipitous giggles. Her own amusement sailed into a lilting greeting. "I am pleased to see you and the property doing so well. The bank governors certainly chose well when they put you in charge." Each blink of her eyes mesmerized the poor, socially handicapped clerk.

Mr. Helmut fumbled with the bankbook she handed him, comparing the figures with his updated ledger before dipping his pen. Cramped, perfectly shaped digits followed a brief notation in Josie's book.

"Mrs. Broderick, you have a significant sum in your account." Mr. Helmut kept his eyes downcast. "Perhaps you would be interested in an investment with us." The clerk raised his head and attempted a smile. "We have just today attracted a new agent. A Frenchman, he is excited over recent information about gold mining opportunities in the Mexican Territory and is quite anxious to have you become involved. He is just visiting St. Louis two days. I would be pleased to arrange a meeting. Perhaps tomorrow, if you are free?"

"Well, thank you, Reuter." Josie fluttered her lashes. "I am not too forward addressing you in such a familiar manner?" Josie needed time to collect herself. The mention of a mysterious Frenchmen fanned the hate Josie thought long dead, flaming her fear of the vermin who had driven her onto the streets and her daughter into poverty.

The clerk inclined his head while puffing up his entire frame, not unlike a bantam rooster about to snatch a worm from its hole.

"My account amounts to such a trifling." Josie steadied her voice. "It can hardly hold any interest to anyone other than my daughter and myself."

"Oh, no," protested Reuter. "There is nothing trifling about this account. Look, you have all..."

"I really do not understand such nonsense, investments and bonds. I am barely capable of overseeing my expenses, certainly not speculations, no matter how titillating." Josie simpered sweetly. No one could know of her education or their curiosity might become an unmasking.

Disappointment etched the man's face. "Please, Mrs. Broderick, reconsider. You have a tremendous opportunity."

"Even on the best authority, such as yours, I fear I am quite unapproachable. However, I thank you. If I do change my mind, I will notify you first." She offered Mr. Helmut her most charming smile and tapped his arm. "My account book, please." With all the disarming charm she could author, Josie accepted the book without inspecting the statement. "Good day." Hastily, she grabbed Taylor's arm and firmly led her daughter from the bank.

"Momma, are you all right? You are shaking." Taylor's voice trilled unsteady and frail.

"Pumpkin, you are not to tell anyone of our banking business." Josie touched a finger to her lips signaling a secret.

"But, Momma, I already told Mrs. Cos and Mandy about Mr. Mutt. That's his nickname we made up." Taylor scrunched up her face, inviting tears. "I am sorry. We only laugh about his flannelettes and how he fumbles when you look at him."

Josie bent over and hugged the distraught child, then wiggled her nose to nose in a playful Eskimo kiss. "There, there, no harm done! But, be careful how you carry stories of people. A lady never mocks or invents unkindness, her heart's soul is sincere."

"I'll do better." Taylor half-smiled.

"Tell no one else. These savings must ease your way when you enter society. Now, cheer up, we still have our afternoon." Josie buried the statement in the folds of her skirt pocket and promptly dismissed the bank clerk from her mind.

They strolled several blocks back to Seventh Street. Taylor began hopping on one foot, then the other. "Look Momma, at the sidewalk café, a real magician. May we stop, please, Momma, may we?"

Twinkling eyes and delicate laughter gave Josie's answer. Josie loved a show as well. She rushed alongside her skipping daughter, then boldly guided Taylor into the white-fenced café. "Two, please!"

The waiter led them straight to an area at the edge of the café. His choice of table troubled Josie. Propriety demanded unescorted women occupy the center of the restaurant, seating couples and men eating alone on the rim, thus protecting women of refinement from the distraction of passersby, street debris, and being casually accosted.

Only loose women sat on the outer edges. The table did, however, offer Taylor an unobstructed view of the Magician. The waiter hovered expectantly.

"Thank you, this will do." Josie gave her best smile. "A strawberry ice for the young lady. A pot of tea, cream and sugar for me."

Taylor laughed and clapped her hands. When the magician pulled his cart toward their table, Taylor squealed. "Momma, he's coming, he's coming here."

"Of course, be of consequence. What you want will come to you."

Josie sipped tea while Taylor basked in the attention lavished upon her as she easily identified the suits and faces of cards that flashed and fell. The young mother had employed playing cards initially to teach her daughter numbers, later on addition and subtraction, and more recently the advanced computing of fractions and percentages.

As balls, batons, and birds appeared and disappeared, Taylor settled into the role of assistant naturally. Josie beamed, delighted Taylor was enjoying herself and pleased by her enhancement of the magician's show.

After the finale, the magician passed his frayed and battered top hat among the onlookers. The tips surpassed any generosity he had previously experienced. He pranced about the café, his excitement more evident with each clank of a coin.

Finally, he bowed politely to Josie, obviously seeking Taylor. "Madame, thank you for sharing your lovely child. You have allowed my performance to be more entertaining because of her participation."

Josie's attention diverted for an instant to her daughter who talked with a man in military red standing outside the fenced area. In the wheelchair alongside him, a blanket and shawl concealed a slim figure from head to foot. Wisps of long gray hair fluttered from a slight opening at the neckline where the coverings met.

Surprisingly, when Josie started their way, the strange duo hurriedly departed. When she called after Taylor, Josie noticed long bony fingers stroke the top of the spinning wheels, assisting the uniformed man who pushed the conveyance. Extraordinary strength for an old woman, she thought.

Her face still showing her pleasure, Josie turned her attention back to the magician. "Thank you for your appreciation. Perhaps it would be equally generous of you, in return, to compensate my daughter. I can guarantee you that your admirers would be even more appreciative after seeing you pass a few coins to the child's pocket?"

Josie's voice rose ever so slightly. "Over here, Taylor, we have a surprise for you."

Eyebrows raised in shock, the magician fumbled through the change and selected two small coins. Briefly, he drew the gaze of the woman, then immediately replaced the coppers, substituting instead silver dollars. Josie stepped aside so the audience still waiting about could see the coins appear above the head of her daughter then magically reappear in Taylor's dress pocket.

Taylor clapped her hands and squealed with delight at this additional good luck. Applause began as a trickle, then escalated when word passed among the onlookers of the magician's generosity. Several gentlemen stepped forward and dropped more coins into the hat.

Josie stared directly at the bewildered magician and winked boldly, then gracefully led her prancing child from the forum.

The beauty shop of the Grand Hotel, the last stop of the afternoon, remained Josie's favorite. The young apprentices made over Taylor, played at creating fancy arrangements from her long copper curls. Meanwhile Josie selected fancy combs, ribbons, rats of varying bulk to form the fashionable upsweep hair arrangement, and jars of the latest lacquer, along with her usual bottle of brown hair dye. Josie studied several magazines and gossiped with the hairdressers while Taylor reveled contentedly under the deliberations of the jabbering trainees.

Within minutes, a dozen uniformed housemaids arrived, almost en mass. One of the women dragged a small table over to Josie while giving a warning. "Dame Geltice left her charges unpaid again this month. Her youngest son has skipped several appointments." The maid's voice grew disgruntled. "I was counting on those tips."

"Her sister reserved the holidays with us. What do you think?" asked Josie.

"Better collect full payment up front. Family seems to have trouble paying bills lately. You asked about Jorge Schlosser, related to the New Orleans' Schlossers. Good as his word. No black sheep in that family."

Another woman set a wooden box on the table before Josie, then opened it. Inside lay several combs, a brilliant pin, a cufflink, several unmatched studs and some scarves. A muscular girl brought over a lamb jacket with a tear across the chest and a brocade dress with a stained bodice. All the others deposited items or displayed trinkets on their opened palms.

"The concierge approved?" Josie asked. She would not deal in stolen goods. The manager must sign off on the items stating that they had been unclaimed by a guest. Of course, for this service he received a percentage of the maid's award.

Not until each girl nodded in turn did Josie begin to inspect the treasures. "Regular percentage." Josie plucked at the jacket. "This can be mended. The dress will have to be ripped and redesigned. Expenses will be high." Then Josie laid the combs out along the tabletop, one studded with brilliants of an unusual aquamarine color caught her eye.

While they dickered over the possible price of the comb, a blonde beautician spoke up. "The undertaker left early last night. Didn't fare too well. Seems he's making the rounds, collecting on his accounts."

Another turned to Josie. "You don't come to the games as often lately. Lady luck gone the other way?"

Josie's eyes narrowed while she sorted through the plunder. Discussion of her personal affairs was prohibited.

When Josie ignored the question, the blonde continued. "We all borrow from the undertaker at some time. You needn't be troubled. You have many bedfellows."

The attempt at familiarity bore only insult for Josie. No one knew of her arrangement with Sidney Yettes, the undertaker. She struggled to keep irritation out of her response. "Taylor needs so much more of my attention. Besides, absence makes for appreciation. Nowadays, I spread my appearances a little thinner." She resented the impertinence of the beautician and felt no desire to explain her activities to anyone.

The blonde scoffed. "Of course, the Goldenrod is 'the' place to be. Sitting at Mr. Yettes's table tonight, or are you floating?" The woman became snide. "Or do you gauge the purse of the crowd first?"

Josie stiffened appreciably. "Mr. Yettes invited me. Seems to me large numbers of newcomers, rather seedy element up from Orleans, crowd the tables of late. I get somewhat anxious among strangers."

Like a tightrope performer in a circus, Josie treaded a thin line. She was not in a position to let gossip develop that she and the undertaker were at odds over gaming debts, nor could she give credence to the talk that she considered herself above the other's station.

"For me, the riverboats do not seem as safe. Especially when people know a lady attends without benefit of a loyal companion. But, perhaps, I am being too fainthearted."

It had taken years to cultivate these relationships, and they must be kept viable. Besides keeping Costello House updated on their guests' financial situation, Taylor's future depended on the joint profit taking.

At the thought of her daughter, Josie looked over to see a little head nodding precipitously, puffy eyes blinking. She scooped up her sleepy daughter, quickly standing Taylor on the floor when she found herself unable to cradle the long frame. "Goodness, Taylor, you have grown almost as tall as Momma."

Taylor slid down her mother's side, and holding onto the rustling skirt stumbled through the doorway.

After they arrived back at Costello House, Taylor napped while Josie and Mrs. Costello discussed the day, checked the market's delivery and reviewed the accounts.

Afterwards, before dressing for the evening, Josie rested in her small room, resolved to put first in her mind how well life at Costello House had treated her and Taylor. Her thoughts, however, returned consistently to their future after the completion of the new Worldwide Bank. *Would Father come? Stuart manage the bank? Dieter?*

As she lay on the bed, Josie grappled with the complications of keeping her visible position. Serving the fringes of society endangered Taylor. Eventually, an acquaintance or a guest would mention the name Broderick, and someone from Worldwide Bank would make the connection.

That realization would end Costello House's providing sanctuary, a modest income, and the opportunity to mingle with the refined of St. Louis. Josie labored without pretense, knowing she offered no skills warranting engagement in any other position as rewarding.

Why did the world devise such trials for her? Each misadventure tested her judgment and the outcome brought more hardship.

Life had frustrated her. But, not without reward. Josie smiled, feeling sweetness huddle in her heart. Taylor had entered her life. For that reason alone, she forgave François's lifeless bones, whenever she thought of him.

If only Jacob would come back. In eight years, except for those few weeks after Taylor's birth, Josie never gave up hope. If Jacob lived, he would have traced her from Taylorsville to St. Louis. Costello house would be the second place he would visit, after Stuart's townhouse. Unquestionably, he had met with an accident; otherwise, he would be beside her now.

Josie felt certain that theirs was the only love in the world that birthed such passion. She had sacrificed so much. Fate would not be so cruel as to have Jacob purposefully abandon her. For that sole reason, she had begun to rue over the probability Jacob Broderick had met with an unfair death.

Of all her letters of inquiry over the years, a few replies gave her hope. Strangers had penned personal notes suggesting knowledge of Jacob, his whereabouts, or someone who resembled the man she sought. Each suggestion sent her on a new course. The last two years, her inquiries had simply been returned with the brief notation "unknown".

When her plans for Taylor shifted to thoughts of Stuart's presence, Josie's anxiety intensified, fed by the undying fear that weighed on her. Today her dampened spirits sobered more while considering the news that Contessa's winning reputation had thwarted the undertaker's latest efforts to arrange decent races.

With Contessa's potential loss of income, the thoroughbred's ability to earn its own keep was jeopardized, and Josie's meager finances did not allow sentimentality. She had always resisted entering her lineaged horse in second-rate races, but now, she would celebrate any contest.

~ * ~

In a townhouse on The Hill, in the Italian section of St. Louis, Monsieur ducLaFevre rolled his wheelchair across the wooden floor. "You saw her, too, Dupaune. Yes! The truth is known. That child is mine." Françcois rolled to a window. "My daughter. No question. The girl looks just like a young Marianne."

Across the room Stuart poured two brandies, his back to the gushing François. "And, what of Marianne's untruthfulness? You certainly would not want to blame her." He walked to the wheelchair. "And what of Jacob?"

"In all probability, Josefina got back off the ship after Marianne left. As for Jacob, he has nothing to do with what happened here." François took one of the glasses. "He has his own life now."

"Josefina manages the ordinary house where Jacob boarded when he surveyed the coming Bank site. Dieter arranged Jacob's accommodations." Stuart went on. "Josefina's arrival there is connected somehow, although I cannot explain since I was not involved."

"You tread deep water," François warned. "I am still not convinced of your innocence." François spun his cane chair quickly to his left where a solidly built man wearing a red uniform jacket waited patiently. "First, I want this done. Listen to me well, Dupaune, you are the only one I trust, and I will tolerate no halfhearted effort. I want Josefina returned, along with my daughter. Do whatever is necessary to bring them to me."

"Josefina will not come of her own accord," Stuart said. "If we kidnap her, she will not stay. You know that very well."

"She hates everything about you," added the red coated Mr. Dupaune. "From what you told me, I believe she has good reason."

François's scarlet neck arched like a combative rooster. "The bank deposited a portion of the promised money to her account. Mr. Helmut reported she declined to meet with me even after she received notice of the windfall." François shook his bony finger in the man's face. "I want her brought here now, by whatever means necessary."

"If you force her to return, she will only run again," Dupaune said. "The only way for Josefina to return to Taylorsville, and stay, is to allow her no alternative. Then, you may have a slim chance at keeping her and the child."

"What do you think?" François smiled, dancing his arms in the air. "The child is charming, delightful. She will undoubtedly grow into a woman even more captivating than my Josefina. Taylor, the girl gave as her proper name. How clever of Josefina." François tossed the snifter of brandy down his throat.

"Create a disaster." Stuart said eagerly. "Some dreadful catastrophe must befall her, something of permanence."

"A soiling of virtue, a compromising affair?" offered Dupaune.

"Hardly insurmountable for Josefina," snorted François. "A deed much worse. An act so vile it will bar her future acceptance into the society she worships. An encounter dastardly enough to force her to seek sanctuary with Louis or her friends in Taylorsville."

"An accusation of theft, murder." The gut in the red uniform rumbled. "The misdeed must be believable. But perhaps a hoax, one that can be undone with your intervention." Mr. Dupaune massaged his mustache. "With incarceration hanging over Josefina's head, you might act as her savior, François. Come to her rescue before a public airing. From what I witnessed, Josefina unquestionably dotes on the child and would fight separation."

"Yes, yes. Plus, I will dangle a carrot," François shouted. "Papers will be drawn, assuring Josefina protection from prosecution and granting Taylor my fortune." A broad smile softened the angles of François's face. "Dupaune, carry it out. Have Dieter establish an account for your expenses. I must remember to compensate him well for his information. Josefina and my child. It is as if they belong to me already."

Stuart brooded next to the liquor cabinet, a second full glass in his hand. He had made a smart move blaming Marianne, and the girl could hardly protest lest she expose her other scheming. "What did you find out at the house?"

"Decent quarters." Dupaune grinned broadly. "Josefina is well-liked. Passes herself as an abandoned "gold-fever" widow. Has a full retinue of admirers she keeps well at bay. Looking forward to meeting her." He noted François first smirk in a pleased manner, then his face soured at the shown interest. "Stole her firearm, just in case."

Stuart had difficulty hiding his frustration. Damn Dieter. The ingrate had journeyed to St. Louis for the sole purpose of inspecting the construction of the new bank building. Whatever had possessed the timid dunderhead to go to a gaming boat? And why, when Dieter wanted Josefina for himself, had he run to François with the news?

Stuart concentrated. In Father's absence and François's incapacity, Dieter controlled Taylorsville's bank. He had won François's eternal gratefulness, and would have Josefina home again. François's bad health was apparent. Perhaps the dolt was not as stupid as he appeared.

Stuart felt his position eroding. He must decide quickly what part he would play in this reuniting with Josefina. What could he gain? Whatever else, he could not allow her to divulge his thwarted intentions of eight years ago to anyone. But he could not antagonize François; the weasel held too many of his notes.

~ * ~

Josie's blue floral silk lay at the foot of the bed. The white lace she had tatted trimmed the décolleté neckline, bodice and sleeves.

"Tighter, Pumpkin!" Josie took a big breath, sucking in her stomach while she hugged the bedpost.

Yanking on the laces of the corset, Taylor pulled, dwindling her mother's already minuscule waist.

Josie gathered her dark hair into a coil on the back of her neck, then covered it with a lace snood before finishing dressing. A pearl-encrusted watch pin and pearl earrings provided her only jewelry. She poked in the shelf beside for her evening bag.

"Tonight I attend the Goldenrod Showboat. Some guests plan to purchase a home in Forest Park and invited me to meet their business partners and give them my assessment." Josie speculated every contact she made now multiplied ten-fold when she purchased her own ordinary house.

"Will you bring back your bag filled with gold?" Taylor teased as Josie removed an evening tote from the shelf of the night table.

"Remember, we must save our money. One day we will become important people in our own right." Josie hefted the cloth bag twice. "I wager only what I feel necessary to be companionable in the company of our guests."

"One day, when I become rich like you say, Momma, I will buy you the biggest house in St. Louis. Ready made clothes in every closet and cooks and maids to do your every bidding."

"For now, we will buy a share in Costello House. Later, we will purchase another house. If we live frugally, one day we will own an entire city of ordinary houses." Josie patted the bag flat, poked inside, then turned it upside down and shook it over the bed. A perfume tincture, handkerchief, some coins, and a money clip clasping a few bank notes fell out.

"When I am rich," Taylor taunted, "I will buy a pony, like Contessa, and buy Mandy one, too, only smaller. Mrs. Costello will live on the very first floor of our estate and have a water closet all her very own." The words rushed out in one breath. "Poppa will be so pleased when he comes back home. What would he want me to buy for him?"

When Taylor's excitement spilled over into Jacob's wants, the question brought Josie face to face with her guilt once again. Josie did not know what Jacob would want, and one day she would have to tell Taylor why.

The smell of baking bread brought comfort and escape. Josie shooed her daughter out the door. "Go. See if Mrs. Costello needs any help with her baking while I finish dressing."

Twice circumstances had robbed Taylor. François's death came as a result of his own black heart, but Josie knew Jacob wanted to marry her. *Why had he not come back?*

Jacob had never judged her, had accepted her with all her faults. Josie had needed that, and her freedom from those who found her so wanting. She must never give up on him. If she did, Father with all his contemptuous holiness would be right; she would be nothing but another whore.

The beaded purse lay deflated, not a bump showing. What had she done with the gun? On her rides to the country to exercise Contessa, Josie always took the firearm. The practice kept her skills sharp. She never failed to return the gun to this bag. The satchel with the weapon boasting a silver inlaid "T" stayed in one place inside the house, on the rear of the shelf of her bedside table.

For years, since robberies had occurred to several lady acquaintances of hers, Josie concealed the weapon in her purse whenever she ventured to the gambling boats. Everyone knew all the women in her situation carried firearms. Without a husband or companion, a woman alone became too vulnerable. Many times she walked back to Costello House leaving an inebriated or foul escort behind her. Tonight could well be another such occasion.

One of the chambermaids must have charitably cleaned the room. Obviously, in cleaning, the girl had misplaced the gun. The mystery confused Josie. *My room is barred. Why would someone remove my gun and leave the purse?*

Unnerved, Josie focused on the ceiling, staring at the flecks of peeling paint that hung like miniature cliffs along the door. A sense of foreboding tormented her. Since seeing the bank's gapers' fence, Stuart's image had crept repeatedly into her thoughts all day. Months had passed since she had thought of him. She had been extremely lucky that their paths had not crossed again.

The image resurrected Josie's loneliness. She felt the loss of Taylor Estates, her friends, her family. She could smell Mother's roses, and ached for a smile or a pleased touch. Father and Stuart's threat had prevented her attendance at the funeral, prohibited a final farewell. Josie felt in her heart if she had seen Mother again, the mourners, the casket, that might have helped diminish her longings. Some days the separation became too much. Were it not for Taylor and her consuming obligations at Costello House, Josie would choose, as her mother had, to remain alone in her darkened room.

Unwanted, along with these pain-filled thoughts, emerged another odious memory. The image of Father's revulsion and the reverberating words that poisoned her and ate at her soul.

Josie's conclusion always ended the same. In the beginning, she had been too wanting, too young and unworldly, easy prey for François's manipulating ways. As for the events after that, she would not have done anything differently.

Gathering her party dress about her hips, Josie left to kiss her daughter goodnight.

Twenty

The only woman among six card players, Josie sat next to Mr. Yettes at a table on the opposite wall from the Goldenrod's busy bar. The room's arrangement separated the more serious gamblers from the partygoers, funneling the big money to the undertaker's territory.

Laughter and music rocked from floor to ceiling. Scarlet drapes lining the windowed walls compressed the noise, muffling the clamor to a deafening din. Customers pushed or amiably threaded their way through the unusually large crowd. Crystal chandeliers, sparkling pendants dimmed by dust and smoke, dipped and swung with the sway of the steamboat, the musical tinkle of their fragile glass wasted.

Josie noticed a handsome gentleman, conspicuous in a red uniform jacket, smoothly advancing toward the head table. When Sidney half rose and the other seated members nodded their recognition, the easy welcome made Josie feel uncomfortable. She felt outmaneuvered, like a naïve child.

"My dear," said Mr. Yettes as he tapped Josie's bare shoulder. "I would like to present Mr. Dupaune."

A vague apprehension nudged Josie at Sidney's introduction. She kept both hands in her lap and nodded a silent greeting. Josie recognized the man as the one who had chatted with Taylor at the café. She did not like his being here.

What a ninny I have become. Of course, anyone visiting St. Louis would walk the uptown and tour the riverboats. He appeared likable, patrician but not overbearing.

"Join us. Take this seat." Mr. Yettes shooed one of the more penny-pinching players off, motioning the newcomer to the empty chair on the other side of him.

"Here to learn something of financial stratagems for Worldwide Bank, Mr. Dupaune?" The undertaker chuckled at his witticism. The statement drew guffaws and wisecracks from the men around the table. Josie felt the cheer drain from her.

The stranger's name and face were unfamiliar. Eight years had passed, she reasoned. Assuredly many changes had taken place at Worldwide Bank. Dare she ask what she ached to know? Of Father and Stuart? Dieter? A list unraveled in her mind.

Mr. Yettes shuffled the cards, offering the deck first to the stranger to cut. Three deals passed before Josie felt brave enough to ask. "The officers of the bank, have any accompanied you?"

"Only two." The officer's voice was solid, commanding. "One of our directors engages only for very high stakes; the other finds no amusement in playing games for money." His cordial smile addressed Josie. "I, on the other hand, rather enjoy out-guessing my opponent and play for any gain." The man raked in his third pile of winnings.

"Well then," Mr. Yettes smirked, "shall we raise the stakes?" Others around the table nodded in agreement.

As the undertaker dealt the cards, Josie saw a queer thing happen. On two passes, cards came off the bottom of the deck. *Probably the lighting or perhaps my nerves.* She would not let the distraction keep her from her mission.

"Perhaps we have met your associates? Are they here?" Josie's heart pounded. The players casually threw in their cards ending the hand. The newcomer lost a large sum; Sidney won.

Undaunted, Mr. Dupaune placed his ante. "A woman as lovely as you. I am sure they would have spoken of you, Mrs. Broderick. Our high stakes contender, however, just returned to St. Louis yesterday. He'd been assigned to assist at his in-laws' bank in Germany for the past eight years. The other gentleman avoids public houses, a near recluse. I promise, however, once they learn of you, they will both be eager to accompany me."

The coins dropped from Josie's hand. Stuart and Father. It had to be. She must get away. She willed her legs to stand.

"Are you all right?" Mr. Yettes showed obvious interest, but continued to deal the cards. "You paled considerably."

"A slight headache. Nothing of concern, but I should excuse myself." Josie started to rise from the chair when she saw it again. The undertaker dealt off the bottom of the deck. Twice. Three times. "I feel rather faint. Please, if you might accompany me, Sidney. Maybe a breath of fresh air..."

Mr. Yettes lay a small pistol atop his winnings then offered Josie an arm.

The minute they stepped foot on the deck, Josie attacked. "You dealt off the bottom. I saw you, three hands in a row, at least twice each hand. I never would have believed you a cheat."

"And who else would either?"

"I saw you. You deliberately stole Mr. Dupaune's wagers by cheating, and I plan to tell him so, and the others."

"No one will believe you. Such a tale would boomerang. I will simply state that I was the one who caught you cheating, so you made up the lie." Mr. Yettes stepped away. "People are of the opinion you owe me a great deal of money. No one knows of our arrangement. They will most likely decide you are lying to escape your debts, or question if we are in cahoots. Both of us filching money from the poor customers of this establishment." Mr. Yettes chuckled, his good humor mocking Josie.

"I will not aid in your theft from a harmless man. Plus compromising my reputation."

"In that case, perhaps you need a little persuasion to change your mind." Mr. Yettes reached inside his jacket and brought out a fistful of greenbacks. "We will share. Equal partners. Then it would be imprudent if not unseemly to accuse me of cheating."

"I cannot believe you are so vile."

A voice behind Josie spoke softly. "Believe it, Josefina. He stole everything Father advanced me for getting rid of you and your bastard." The voice smacked Josie with instant terror.

The hairs on the back of her neck rose, her skin rippled. Fear bound every fiber of her body as she turned. Stuart stood ten feet behind her, self-righteousness haloing his evilness. His cat eyes narrowed slyly while she watched. With one corner of his mouth dropped in a lopsided smirk, the same cocky slant of his shoulders conveyed the power and disdain Josie remembered.

Taylor. Her daughter took the forefront of Josie's mind. *I must save Taylor. Run. Run fast.* Panic seized Josie. Her mind and body deserted her, rooting her feet to the deck.

Light from the lanterns shone across Stuart's upper body. His arm raised and something in his hand glinted.

Josie dug in her purse. The gun was not there. Of course not; she had forgotten.

I must run inside by people. Stuart stood between her and the door. Mr. Yettes waited a few feet the opposite way. Josie darted toward her friend. A shot fired. A soft thud sounded like a fist hitting a pillow. Then another.

Josie heard the clunk as the gun hit the deck. A skidding noise accompanied its glint as Stuart slid the weapon across to her.

"Pick it up," Stuart ordered.

The silver inlay "T" beckoned to her. Josie unconsciously grabbed the gun. Empty. She turned toward where Mr. Yettes stood. A third thud, sounding as if a bullet struck near her feet, urged her to run.

"Sidney!" Before Josie could reach him, the undertaker crumpled across the railing, wrestling to crawl over the top and escape. Splotches soaked his white shirt, the feeble light made his chest appear muddy colored.

Footsteps advanced slowly from behind her. Josie dropped the gun and reached out to prevent Sidney from jumping overboard. A clutch of her shoulder sent a bolt of terror through her. The fingers tightened, steady and intense, delivering their odious message. At last, Stuart Taylor held her in his grasp. At that moment Sidney Yettes fell overboard, leaving only a scrap of blood-soaked cloth in Josie's hand.

Josie screamed and kept screaming as loudly as she could, yet knowing somewhere in the vacuum of her mind, no one would hear her.

The deck stretched before her, free and open. Josie twisted quickly, jerked her arms up and wriggled free of Stuart's hold. Her legs seemed detached, acting with a mission of their own as they carried her forward along the rail, then tripped crossing the deck. She nearly fell in her winged stumble down the ramp.

Her thoughts sought not Sidney dying in the murky water, but Taylor sleeping peacefully in her bed. Josie ran until she suspected her heart would burst. Each backward glance revealed only darkness and shadows. She ran harder, not stopping until she locked the door of Costello House behind her.

She must get Taylor away, far beyond Stuart's reach. Josie barricaded the door, propping a chair against the crystal knob, shoving a hall tree against the glass inset. Had Stuart followed her charge up Park Avenue? She sobbed dryly. *How foolish, I have led him straight to Taylor.*

She could see no one out front. *Where had he gone to? Where had he come from? Is he here now? Or soon? Does it matter when?*

Twenty-one

Josie crept silently through the dark house. In the dining room, she flattened herself against the wall alongside the window, then parted the curtains using one finger. The sliver allowed enough opening to peek out. Except for the regularly seen lamp warden, Park Avenue appeared deserted.

She dashed up the stairs, seemingly taking an eternity before slipping into Taylor's bedroom. Mandy and Taylor lay wrapped across each other's arms. Taylor gave little sign of rousing before Josie guided the stumbling Mandy up the attic stairs to the worker's cubicles.

Josie quickly returned and kissed Taylor, her hair, cheeks, closed eyes, then dropped down onto the edge of the bed. She caressed her child's shoulders, back, arms, finding joy in the soft skin, calming now that her daughter lay within reach. Taylor's nearness allowed Josie's anxiety to dull. No one had gotten Taylor yet. Still, terror urged Josie to act, to form a plan, do something, quickly, before Stuart crashed through the door.

Trembling and nauseated, Josie entered her own room and perched on the side of the bed. One leg remained extended, ready to run. Curbed fear pulled at her body in wrenching breakers like an ocean tide, relentless, leaving her breathless and wasted. Her mind failed to furnish answers. Anger, good sense, frustration, all faded before the overwhelming strength of her fear.

Doubled over like a newborn, Josie numbly rocked back and forth, the lace edged gown scratching jagged marks wherever it bound. A shiver as sharp as a knife blade sliced across her skin, landing with full strength in the pit of her belly. Shadows danced with evil eloquence on the bedroom walls. Josie shuddered then moaned long and low, fearing a vision of Taylor lying still as a corpse would prove true.

A sound in the hallway destroyed Josie's nightmare. Josie scoured every inch of the nightstand. Nothing. Of course, she had dropped the gun on the Goldenrod. *No, the gun had disappeared before that. Or after?* Confusion tangled Josie's thoughts like iron cobwebs, barring sound judgment.

Suddenly, someone grabbed her and began shaking her violently. Josie twisted and fought against the hands.

"Holy Mother of God. What's wrong?" Mrs. Costello asked. Her hands held fast, pulling Josie to her feet.

While Josie struggled for breath, she saw the dark streaks across the bodice of her dress. The feel of Sidney's blood soaked chest against her exploded in her mind. Josie opened her mouth to scream. A plump hand clapped tightly across her mouth, smothering the noise. Mrs. Cos released her hand when Josie's jaw relaxed.

"Are you hurt?" Fingers traveled Josie's body. "What's going on?" Mrs. Costello demanded. "Who did this?"

Recognizing the voice, Josie calmed some, but began babbling. "Mr. Yettes cheated. We went out on the deck. When I accused him, he threatened me. To expose me as the cheat, have me arrested." Josie's voice rose in disbelief. "Then there were shots."

"Where's your wound?" Mrs. Costello searched frantically. She peeked and jabbed and patted unmercifully.

Josie wrestled with her gown, tearing the flimsy cloth. So much blood, her wound needed to be treated.

"No. Josie, No!" The older woman held Josie's arms firm to her sides, making any effort at discovery fruitless. "The blood is dried. He didn't hit anything vital."

"He's dead." Josie stared vacantly after her voice as it bottomed into a whispered gasp. The admission startled her. "Stuart shot Sidney. Then I ran."

Josie paced back and forth picking at her ripped and smudged clothes. "He pointed a gun at me. I saw it." She twisted her toppled hair through her fingers.

"Who pointed a gun at you?"

"Stuart. No one will believe me." Josie closed her eyes, unable to face the life draining from Mrs. Costello's face. "Even you do not believe me."

Mrs. Costello pushed Josie down onto the edge of the bed. "Your story is so confused. Again, tell me everything."

Josie raced through her explanation. Her tongue selected and twisted the fabric of her story into a tale barely recognizable.

Mrs. Costello attacked the missing details. "Someone must have seen the man with the gun, heard the shots. Maybe found his weapon."

"They would find my gun. We have to find a witness." Josie gasped. "There was someone. A stranger. I remember seeing his red coat in the lamplight."

"You are right in one important matter. We must find someone who saw the accident. Who would believe Mr. Yettes had attacked a helpless woman? He's a responsible citizen. Now Josie, I know something of your less than truthful nature. I question myself why the undertaker would fear you? You would have a hard time destroying his reputation. There must be something else. Think, Josie."

"His body sank in the river." Josie sifted through her thoughts. "He jumped overboard to escape. Stuart shot him."

"Who jumped overboard?" Mrs. Costello asked again, her voice rising in frustration.

Josie's eyes widened with anxiety. "Stuart is coming to get Taylor."

"Who is coming? And why?" Mrs. Costello gently shook Josie's shoulders.

Josie's eyes lost their hopelessness as if a lamp had been lit. "Stuart is my brother. He shot Sidney, and he is the one who promised to kill Taylor eight years ago to keep her from making any claim to our family's assets." Josie began pulling at her hair as if extracting the roots would rid her of the horror. She bawled. "Taylor cannot stay here. We must go." Josie jumped up from the bed prepared to make a dash for the door. But then delayed, confused, unable to make a move.

"Shhh! Quiet, we must not wake the guests," Mrs. Costello directed. "First, we must assess the danger. Decide if you can stay here. Then, if you must, I will help you hide outside of town. At least until we find out what really happened and have time to ready and pack your things."

"I cannot wait. He wants Taylor, then the others will come for me. I know he will put the blame on me for Sidney's murder."

"Give me a minute, please? Maybe you are seeing only a half-truth. Not a lie, but in your fright maybe you don't remember everything. Perhaps, in the confusion, you missed something. Besides, if Stuart shot Sidney, why should you run? Possibly, it was an accident."

"Three shots. I think not. I must get Taylor. We must leave now," Josie insisted.

"Josie, stop. Give us some time. You needn't run until we know for sure what happened." Mrs. Costello spoke firmly. "You can't bundle up Taylor and flee like a criminal in the middle of the night. Especially not having any idea where you're going."

"We must leave. Before Stuart gets here."

"If you must, go to the Riverfront Inn. I can meet you in the morning. I'll bring Taylor and money. And you'll need provisions."

"I have no time. Someone should have missed Sidney by now." Josie's eyelid twitched rapidly as if sending a secret code, the tic warping her vision. Between blinks, she looked up to see terror emanating from Mrs. Costello. Josie closed her eyes, unable to face a fear matching her own.

Wringing her hands as she paced, Mrs. Cos begged. "Is there a chance he wasn't...?"

Josie sobered. "Look at me!" As the two looked down at the bloody dress, Josie tore the tatters from her body. "We must go *now*."

Mrs. Costello shrilled, "You have no money. No food!" She grabbed Josie. "Listen to me!"

"No, we must be gone within the hour." Josie stalked from the room. A flood of memories rushed at her, frightening days and nights of hiding, foul stables, hunger, and loneliness. She stumbled, wanting to weep. She remembered the prostitute's dreary hovel. She could not put Taylor through that.

Perhaps, I should stay, wait for a trial. But, if I lost, I would be put to death or imprisoned for life. And what of Taylor during and after the trial? Who would protect her?

The choices swirled like a cyclone. *Would Taylor be better off left behind? Mrs. Costello would guard her. Ridiculous. No one could save Taylor from Stuart.*

The publicity surrounding the trial would announce Taylor's presence to the world. If Stuart and his conspirators did not know of Taylor's whereabouts now, they would then.

Josie pictured bold black letters of a banner headline PROMINENT BUSINESSMAN MURDERED, smaller script screamed Socialite Josefina Taylor Alias Josie Broderick Sought. The irony of her imagining hit her. She was not a socialite and never would be if she stayed here in St. Louis. And what would Jacob think were he to see the headline?

Josie's body chilled like a quartered slab of beef, heart stilled, blood curdled. Everyone who knew of Worldwide Bank would discuss the news. Word of her wrongdoing would spread like typhoid, frightening everyone whose life she had touched. And the ne'er-do-wells would ruin their best horse for the thrill of being the first to inform Josef Taylor of his banished daughter's fate. Taylor could never be protected well enough in St. Louis or anywhere civilized.

Mrs. Costello had been talking, but Josie had not heard a word. Josie pushed the anxious woman aside and rushed into Taylor's room. Talking as loud as she dare, she coached, "Pumpkin, wake up. Wake up!" One hand shook Taylor; with her other hand Josie grabbed underwear from shelves and dresses off pegs until the wall was bare.

Dark lashes fluttered, then slowly parted as Taylor opened her eyes. Josie ordered, "Put on your dark green dress. I need your help.

There has been an accident. We have to go to Contessa." She left her daughter sitting upright, blinking.

Even though her hands shook, Josie needed no help. She flung on fresh clothes, prodded by the demon named Stuart. She dumped both dresser drawers, crawled under the bed, and rummaged through hidden boxes grabbing necessities.

Cold gripped her belly as Josie remembered the last time Stuart's hideousness forced her to run. She clawed through the pile, making sure she had the warmest clothing she owned. Too soon the nights would become cool. She would rather remove uncomfortable in too warm clothing now than freeze in a blizzard. Finally, Josie tied everything securely in the sheet and the bedspread. Balancing the two unwieldy bundles, she snuck back into her daughter's room.

Taylor sat hunched on the edge of the bed. One shoe on, the other dangling listlessly from her fingers. Little girl belongings lay piled in the center of the bed, including the knickers given to her by Mrs. Costello. When her mother entered, Taylor reluctantly stood and finished dressing.

Josie tied a knot in the bed cover and placed the awkward bundle in Taylor's arms. "You must be quiet and obey everything I say. We must reach Contessa without waking anyone." She placed her finger to her lips, then led the way.

After they sidled down the front stairs, Josie detoured to the kitchen to place an envelope addressed to Mrs. Costello on the table. When Josie quietly pushed open the swinging door, a throaty voice startled her.

"I will not let you leave." A lamp flamed in the darkness. The safety match Mrs. Costello held had broken in two her hands shook so badly.

Josie came nearer her friend and employer.

"Josie, you can't outrun the law." Mrs. Costello's chubby fingers nervously swiped away moisture clinging to her upper lip. "Stay. Let me help you straighten things out!" The anxious, lined face seemed to have aged years in the last minutes.

Josie gave a choking sigh; her eyes stung with unshed tears. She strode over to the comfort of her friend's arms. "Whether I am found innocent or guilty, Taylor will be taken from us. No on will believe me. At minimum, I will be hung or imprisoned for the rest of my life. I have no choice."

Josie debated over how much of her past she should reveal. With all they had shared, Josie felt too ashamed to tell Mrs. Costello the entire story. Probably even such a dedicated friend would not approve. And, Josie would not endanger Mrs. Costello's life by making her an accomplice. "We must leave now!"

When Josie turned to leave, Mrs. Costello darted past and rushed into the hall. She gathered Taylor protectively into her ample arms and stalled, dancing in crazed circles. "Wait, provisions." Lugging the child, Mrs. Costello dashed back to the kitchen and began pulling cornmeal, beans, coffee and sugar from the cupboard. Boxes and bags, large and small dropped onto the counter and table. Pans. Tins.

Josie felt her fear mounting at the same time her resolve weakened. "We have no time. We can barely manage our things now."

Mrs. Costello bent down over Taylor. "Go to the attic. Wake up Mandy. Bring her here." Taylor looked tentatively at her mother. "Now," Mrs. Cos ordered. "Get Mandy and hurry right back. Use the kitchen stairs." Taylor dropped her parcel and flew up the steps.

Josie picked up her bundles and adjusted the load.

"You must be mistaken. People will know it was an accident. Everyone knows you could never kill anyone. Whatever happened, we can make it right."

Josie could not listen to any more pleading. She grabbed Taylor's bundle and started toward the kitchen door. Desperate, the innkeeper grabbed the fleeing woman's skirt, pulling hard enough to make the fabric give. "We can find the truth together."

"You do not understand." Josie stopped, took a breath deep enough to raise her shoulders, then stared Mrs. Costello hard in the eyes. "My Father is Josef Taylor, member of the Worldwide Bank Board and Chairman of the National Land Company, President of Taylorsville Bank. Do you hear, Worldwide Bank, Bank of Taylorsville? Before I arrived at Costello House, he ordered my brother Stuart to get rid of my baby, kill Taylor, however necessary.

Indiscriminate if it caused my death. I know that my Father will never forgive me. I know, too, there are no means to protect Taylor or me from Stuart. I will not endanger your life, too, bringing you further into this." Josie hugged the woman heartily, patting her shoulders."

Dry sobs broke from Mrs. Costello. "Now that I know, I feel even stronger that together we can find the answer. Think, Josie. Why would the undertaker fear a challenge to his reputation by you? He could manufacture whatever tale he wanted. Something else is amiss. I am sure we can find help elsewhere. You needn't run again."

"Thank you for all you have done. I will write when I can. You understand, I cannot let you know where we are." Josie had trusted this kind soul with her life and with the life of her unborn child. Now, she must trust Mrs. Costello's humanity again and extract a hard promise from her.

"Jacob Broderick never came back for me, and you have earned the right to know why. We had pledged to marry, but Taylor's real father is François ducLaFevre. He was shot by my Father, murdered. If Taylor had been born a male, she would be the undeniable heir to a French title and fortune. She is still entitled to some favor from François's estate, with the proof from my best friend Marianne, and also has claim to the Taylor family's fortune."

"If your family is that wealthy, surely, they cannot carry such vendetta against one child. Not enough to kill a little girl." Mrs. Costello appeared visibly shaken.

"I am not aware of their partnership agreement." Josie said. "But I am sure Father benefited in some manner from François's death. And believe me, Stuart will never allow me or Taylor to get in the way of his inheritance."

"Perhaps you are right to flee. But leave Taylor with me."

"I entered into a devil's bargain. Sadly, Taylor bears the burden. She will never find peace from my family. You must never, ever tell anyone the truth of my being here, or of Taylor. Lie if you must, as I have for years."

The age lines at the end of Mrs. Costello's brows deepened, the corners of her mouth sagged as if loaded with buckshot. "I fear for you both. Leave Taylor. I'll find a safe haven for her with my relatives in the country. I'll sell Costello House, and go there to care for her. Without you, no one will ever guess her ancestry."

"I cannot." Josie anticipated more demands. "She is my sole reason for being."

Spittle sprayed from Mrs. Costello's mouth as she argued. "Taylor was born here. This is the only home she's ever known. She has been my child, too. You say yourself I saved Taylor's life and yours." The older woman's double chin wobbled with each pronouncement, like a ponderous weight hammering out her pain. "Leave Taylor with me!"

Josie squeezed the woman's rough hands. "I will write when I can." Her eyes carried the depth of affection in her heart.

~ * ~

Taylor thought her heart would burst. Momma looked so scared, and Mrs. Costello? Taylor had never heard Mrs. Costello holler at Momma. It must be terrible, whatever had happened. No one ever woke her up in the middle of the night and made her dress. The sun hadn't come up yet. All the guests still slept. Whatever it was, it must be awful.

She would be good and help. Do whatever Momma said.

Taylor cracked open the door at the bottom of the stairs leading from the fourth floor up into the attic. Even in the night, heat wafted down like a chimney. Moonlight from the vents at each end of the roof painted faint stripes on the dark floor. Taylor picked her away among discarded furniture and stored memorabilia. Trunks stacked in towers created walls of privacy, but Taylor had visited the attic often and was well acquainted with the live-in worker's tiny cubicles.

She went directly to Mandy and shook her vigorously. The dazed girl protested. "Not yet!" She tried to shoo the pesky hands off. "Go away."

Taylor whispered. "It's me. Get dressed. Momma and Mrs. Costello need our help. We have to hurry."

Mandy bolted upright. "Something bad?" She was awake, ready.

Taylor answered while she retreated. "Come down to the kitchen. Momma and Mrs. Cos need us right now."

In one move Mandy slid the slack cotton nightshirt up over her head, pulled on a faded dress, picked up her shoes then ran behind Taylor down the attic stairs.

Below, in the kitchen, Mrs. Costello and Josie argued in furious whispers. "She's like my own child." Mrs. Costello said, "I prayed for her before she was born. You must leave her with me. You have no idea what's ahead of you, not even where you're going. She'll be safer with me."

The anguish in the older woman's voice was matched equally by the obstinacy of the other.

"No, it is too dangerous here. I will take her with me." Josie felt the old nightmare repeating itself. No one would take away her child. She reached for sugar, cornmeal, a tin of coffee, a can of brown bread, rice, salted pork back, beans, sweeping off everything Mrs. Costello had grabbed, dropping it all into twenty pound flour sacks.

"I know you feel I'm just an innkeeper," Mrs. Costello said. "But, to Taylor I'm her family. All she has. You were just a child yourself when you came here. I protected you, gave you everything you needed."

Josie knew the torturous plea mirrored Mrs. Costello's growing heartache. The good soul did not mean to make things harder. "I promise," Josie said, "if they find me, I will send Taylor back to you. I know you would take good care of her, but she needs more than just taking care of."

"Leave her! I promise. I can keep her safe." The girls' appearance interrupted the argument.

"Taylor, come with me now!" Josie ordered flatly. After giving Mrs. Costello a lingering hug, Josie dropped two bulging sacks of foodstuffs into Mandy's arms before turning to leave.

Mrs. Costello swept Taylor up in her arms, cradling the burdened child while she followed Josie out to the hall. The young body spread its warmth in the folds of her housecoat, but Mrs. Costello shivered, then crossed herself as if the soles of death had scampered across her skin.

With one hand, the other locked tightly across Taylor, the innkeeper dug beneath her robe, her nightdress, her undergarments.

"Josie, take this." She handed over a sizable leather pouch that jangled, then turned to the ladened, round-eyed Mandy. "Do whatever you're told. Then come straight back here. Don't talk to anyone, not one word."

As Taylor squirmed out of her grip, the old woman reached out to touch the departing child, snagging a few copper strands of hair before the small troupe disappeared into the darkness. "I will pray for you." A sob thinning into a quiet wail gave her farewell.

Just as Taylor did every time she left Costello House, Josie stopped to take a final look at the ordinary house. She hesitated, remembering the generosity she had received when she first arrived, frightened and expecting. The plump outline of Mrs. Costello was lost in the darkness now, just as it had been that night.

"Hurry, Taylor!" Josie peered behind her. There was no one. Her daughter raced ahead, not looking back.

Twenty-two

Fortunately for Josie escaping in the darkness, the St. Charles road lay well trod and level. She had no idea how far they had traveled since leaving St. Louis. Contessa raced as if she carried her terrified passengers to a finish line on the horizon. They fled the entire night, pausing only when Contessa needed water and rest while Josie wiped her down.

The road led north almost thirty miles to the summer resort town of St. Charles, an outing Josie had enjoyed on several occasions accompanying guests of Costello House. Her decision to escape this way came without effort; the street alongside the stable fed into the throughway.

One night's journey had not taken them far enough away. A main highway stretched from St. Charles to the capital, Jefferson City, then on to Kansas City. She would parallel this road; thereafter the sun would guide them West, until she either collapsed or was discovered.

Josie's hands ached. The reins had sliced the net gloves into a few imperfect rows and straggling threads. Her eyes watered and stung. The wide brim of a cotton bonnet that had served her so well while gardening offered no barrier against the dust-peppered August wind. She had wrapped one social hat but no extra veiling in the sheeting.

The bedspreads concealed mostly basics, although Mrs. Costello's intervention had prompted Josie to look harder at her needs and for that she felt grateful. Without that nudge, they would be without the canvas bag sloshing with water, the lantern, and the sack of oats from the stable. Josie had left a coin for Peter, near Contessa's crib, for more than the cost of the supplies, foregoing a note expressing her indebtedness for all his kindness.

They began passing farms; the arid dust of butchered grains and sweet smell of field corn taunted Josie with reminders of Taylor Estates, but even the threat of hanging could not persuade her to return to Illinois.

The mottled haze of daybreak brightened to a golden glow, and the countryside stirred. Flitting honeybees swarmed the flowering sorghum and roadside wildflowers unlike the lumbering, fat bumblebees of the city. Birds warbled in discordant song of warning as other travelers began to appear on the road.

Josie veered from the stranger's inspections, seeking the safety of shallow tracks through gloomy woods and overgrown lanes. A breeze swayed the dappled foliage; a bush, then a fallen branch appeared to take on human form. Josie imagined the sheriff, a posse, every imaginable manner of menacing constabulary lurked in the murky depths. She started at the snap of a tree limb. The croak of a bullfrog incited a frenzied slapping of the reins. The leather straps wrapped tightly around her hands demanded sharp, swift direction, spurring Contessa on.

After civilization disappeared, Josie began to fear robbers as well. Her elbow fixed tightly against Taylor's chest as if to bar any intrusion. *Any peace officer or thief who attempts to stop us will find a lively battle on his hands.*

The underbrush of the narrow trail slowed the mare's pace. The tiny troupe became more vulnerable. Josie's head twisted from side to side, eyes squeezed into slits, watchful, straining to see into the shadows.

Midday Contessa showed signs of weariness. Josie stopped. While the horse grazed, Taylor napped, then nibbled on bread, cheese and an apple. Josie stayed alert, always watching, while the sun crossed overhead.

By early evening, the dying heat created hazy drapes that hung like shrouds, taking on queer shapes of monstrous size in the wooded gloom. The ghostly blots plucked at Josie's fear. She grew more frightened.

When dusk arrived the last quarter of the moon hung lusterless, giving notice of its deficiency in the cloudless sky. Before the darkness of sunset came, Josie returned to the well-traveled road. Alone, eerie silence enveloped their fleeting clatter, snaring the pounding of Contessa's hoofs and the rattle and clack of the buggy in a cavity of stillness. The chassis swung to and fro as though rocked by fiendish beasts. Splintering cracks and pops cut the air as if it were only a matter of yards before the entire vehicle dropped into a heap in the middle of the road.

With one leg braced firmly against the well of the buggy, Josie fought to keep her weary body upright and steady, leaning in rhythm with the sway of the vehicle. Her other foot dangled uselessly, banging against the storage bin. If only she had thought to place a trunk or a box in the foot space. But they carried only her small mending tote and tonic satchel, and the lazy bedspreads sprawling their indifference across the floor.

Clouds fathered a moonless night, forcing Josie to concede. She and Taylor flopped on makeshift pads of lumpy gowns and the dainty summer coverlets. The hard ground offered no respite. Knots twisting through Josie's body bound tighter, making her toss from side to side, uncontented, punishing. There seemed to be no reward for their being there.

The night passed too slowly, as if the sun had overslept. The frightening blackness remained as impenetrable as smoke in a closet. Josie felt she would choke on the suffocating obscurity.

At the first splinter of light, Josie roused Taylor. Together they dug through the provisions. One makeshift sack produced an iron pan.

A tin held safety matches, but the nearby wood tested too green. Taylor gathered dead weeds and debris while Josie harnessed Contessa. The feeble flames warmed enough water to soften some oatmeal, but the cereal clumped into a gelatinous glob like bookbinding glue.

The harried band started out again. By midday a spasm yanked Josie's back, then drove its way up to the base of her skull, worming into fragmented painful kinks. Waves of nausea sucked the strength from her arms and showered black sparks behind her eyes.

Totally by will power, Josie froze her arms and legs into their assigned places. The attempt to control her body made mockery of her determination. Beaten, she slowed Contessa to a deliberate plodding. A tiny shimmering sliver peeked through the brush. "We will stop there, by that creek." The effort of speaking sickened Josie. "Stretch your legs, but keep close by."

Taylor's bright eyes turned wary, she stayed within reach of her mother's skirts.

Her head pounding, Josie unhooked the straps on the mare. Her hands slid gently around the taut belly, then stroked the sweat-soaked haunches. The foal inside moved causing Contessa's ears to flicker, her eyes to widen, and a snort.

Josie whispered, "You have had to share my faults." She looked into the huge unblinking eyes, and felt mutual pain, but reassurance, too, as if Contessa promised to get them through it all. "We will wait here, until the churchgoers slack off in the morning." With Taylor tugging on the hem of her skirt, Josie led Contessa to the creek.

While they rested, Taylor wandered aimlessly along the creek, pulling leaves from weeds and watching them float away. The child glanced regularly over her shoulder, needing the reassurance her mother still waited.

A scowl furrowed Josie's brow. Sidney's murder prodded Josie's thoughts ruthlessly. Several minutes went by, she remembered, before she and Sidney got outside. Josie sensed a nagging piece of information, a needed insight tucked away in her memory, just beyond her reach.

Taylor came back and sat down on Josie's skirt, then lay across her mother's lap. Neither had spoken a word since they snacked on some bread and cheese. Taylor quickly dropped off to sleep. Josie gave up on preparing any bedding, closed her eyes, and slept.

She woke with a start. In her nightmare Josie heard a voice. "Unusual night, Mrs. Broderick." Before the outsider sat down at the table, she recalled with surprise, he addressed me. But Sidney had not made introductions yet, and when he did, he did not say her name. Had the others at the table talked with the stranger earlier and told him who she was?

For a seasoned gambler, he set an imprudent stack of notes on the table when he joined them. The others readily accepted him, or perhaps it was the tower of currency. What did it matter? Whatever else had occurred, she remembered the red jacket behind Stuart during the brief moment she held her gun and before the undertaker went overboard. The stranger had seen only half the crime, the half incriminating her.

The black sky brightened to the gray of predawn. Wakened by Josie's jumpiness, Taylor rose and absently began tossing pebbles into the creek, the splashes barely noticeable.

The sounds reminded Josie. A single splash occurred after Sidney went overboard, a noise like a sack of potatoes hitting the water. No scream or struggle to stay afloat came to her mind. Sidney Yettes was undoubtedly dead before he fell.

Josie chided herself for trying to solve a mystery when the answers made no difference. She had made a spectacle of leaving the casino with Sidney, and everyone believed she was heavily indebted to him. No one would accept his death as an accident. Stuart would certainly not step forward and claim his part.

Worldwide Bank was the link between the stranger and Stuart. She felt confused, angry, but less uncertain. She should have warned

Mrs. Costello about the red uniform and to be wary of anyone connected to Worldwide Bank.

Too drained to dig deeper into her supposing, Josie shook her head, hands masking her face. Josie uncovered her eyes and looked down at her daughter kneeling before her. Taylor gripped her mother's arm so tight both fingers and arm paled. Quizzical green eyes looked back, intent on reading her mother's mind.

"Pumpkin, I want you to know why. Some people think I shot someone. It's all a mistake, but we must watch for lawmen, stay out of sight until they find out the truth." The worried green eyes staring at Josie darkened, but showed no panic. *Ah, my constant child.* Josie dared not share her worst fear that some time might pass before the truth surfaced, if ever.

They had endured four days. Josie hated hiding, using the underbrush as a blind whenever someone approached. She jumped at every noise, so edgy the rustle of a falling crisp autumn leaf startled her. She felt like a ne'er-do-well, human refuse that should be avoided, or worse, hunted down and destroyed.

The seemingly endless bumping and tossing hammered bruises, seen and unseen, and left Josie disheartened, as if battle-fatigued. Near dusk of the fifth day Contessa stumbled. Josie saw nothing on the road. Against her better instincts she relented. Josie reached out and shook Taylor scrunched tightly into her corner of the seat. "We must stop soon. Contessa cannot go much further. The pulling might destroy her."

Dark half-moons rimmed the young girl's eyes. Why had she risked her daughter's life, too? "We will stay a few days at the first place that looks safe."

A curse died on Josie's lips, and her temper teetered precariously. If she gave in to her fretfulness her temper would only worsen, and she must not waste energy on what could not be changed. Her frayed nerves quivered like a fiddle too tightly tuned. Bringing Taylor had been a foolish mistake.

Jacob had baited Josie with his praise of the West, fostered exciting dreams with his clever stories of adventure. She and Taylor had not yet encountered the rawness of the Wild West, and already she felt old and spent.

Taylor's voice startled her. "When we stop, will they have more than cheese and biscuits?" Her lips curved sweetly, her voice implored without rancor. She had no idea gritty smudges outlined her eyes like a raccoon mask, that her auburn curls had meshed into a dusty, gnarled nest.

There would be days to come when they would appreciate beans to warm their bellies, a dry place to lie down at night, a safe passage through hostiles. The way ahead of them loomed hazardous, menacing. Josie sought to convey the bad tidings as optimistically as possible. Finding no means of promising such a wish without deception, she remained silent.

By midmorning the next day, their travel slowed. Mammoth limestone bluffs blocked the horizon. They rose like white stone walls above the cedar and pine treetops, shutting out everything except a cramped ribbon of blue sky. Their steady progress across the flat land changed into a series of charges up steep hills and headlong descents, all navigated on narrow, undeveloped lanes. The wheels bounced between boulders that paved the edges of the ridges, tossing the passengers about like popcorn on a hot stove.

For a half-day they clambered to the peak of a staggering hill. Delighted at their success, Taylor clapped. "We climbed as well as any billy goat." After they crossed the crest, a dark chasm appeared, the descent steeper than the rise they had just ascended. The pattern repeated as far as Josie could see.

In spite of the canopy, the sun burned Josie's skin. Blisters sloughed their runny bubbles, releasing sticky liquid and leaving tender milky splotches in their wake. Teensy black no-see-ems stung with swift punctures, then itchy welts marked their visits. Josie swatted continuously at the empty air; the pests assaulted her body without regard. Her stomach cramped in objection to the greasy corncakes, too strong coffee and soured beans.

Taylor's complexion reddened, too. But each morning, yesterday's sunburn faded into a few additional sun kisses apparently causing little discomfort. The nasty insects avoided Taylor, preferring to riddle Josie's broiled complexion.

Squatting on the ground, Josie stabbed at mounds of cornmeal floating in fatback, dodging flames that licked at her trailing skirt, slapping at the popping ash that scorched holes in its wake. Cooking had not been to her liking in a kitchen provided with every need, let alone this. The shiny bottom of the empty tea tin reflected Josie's glower; her one luxury had ended.

Huddled in the cramped buggy the next day, Josie fought her dozing fits, hoping for a better sleep later. That night she lay awake again. No matter how much she swept the earth with pine branches or how many layers she put under her on the ground, one stone would find her. In addition to being sore, she felt vulnerable in the openness, and shabby and unimportant. The field hands of Taylor Estates were the only people Josie had ever known who chose to sleep outdoors.

As the days passed, Josie bounced along increasingly mindful of being frustrated and dirty, along with feeling apprehensive. She slowed their progress, giving the stressed mare longer and more frequent periods of rest. They had been on the run for ten days, their provisions gone. Her fear of capture loomed second to finding food.

As they emerged from a wooded area, Josie spotted a smokehouse and garden a fair distance from a cabin. "I am going to see if I can find something to eat. Sit here quietly." Josie scampered through the grasses, then inched her way around the hidden side of the hut. She opened the smokehouse door, grabbed, and fled. Onions popped from the ground with slight tugs as she snaked her way back through the garden. She found nothing else.

Taylor's stomach rumbled in way of greeting her mother's return. The smell of bacon puffed from the folds of Josie's skirt. Taylor reached over to help her mother up, then quickly ran her finger along the salted rind of the carcass, savoring the fat in a noisy suck.

By the time they fled beyond reasonable pursuit and found a clearing to inspect their cache, Josie's appetite had dulled. She had set another unwanted example, stealing. She should have sought out the farmer, or in his absence, left one of their precious coins in the smokehouse. Josie picked at the stolen treasure, unappreciative of her daughter's wholesome appetite.

Wild clover thrived along the narrow farm roadbeds. Josie picked as many of the fuzzy purple heads as her skirt could hold. When they reached a creek, she brewed a pan of clover tea. After she drank her fill, she pruned a limb of a willow and sliced off strips of bark. Then she ground dandelion heads on a rock with the heel of her shoe before simmering it all in the leftover ruby tea. Josie waded ankle deep into the creek and poured the improvised mixture onto her head.

The brew left red and gold streaks in her hair. The result emerged much less becoming than her daughter's natural auburn locks, but the brassy color altered Josie's fading mousy hair significantly.

The next afternoon they neared an isolated farm. Contessa was spent, dangerously driven beyond acceptable limits. Josie approached the property; confident they had arrived before any news of her crime would have reached this remote area. She felt satisfied, too, that her altered appearance offered a modicum of protection. Regardless, they could go no further.

Josie's chin dropped to her chest as she surveyed the homestead. Her traveling hat sheltered a squint that lacked her normal acceptance. Taylor's curious stare seemed to absorb every discouraging detail of the dilapidated farm.

Long, narrow logs chucked with dried mud formed the cabin, square holes served as windows. No glass sparkled and no flower boxes hung below the openings. A vegetable garden, as large as Mrs. Costello's but badly in need of watering, had almost disappeared among weeds, neglected alongside the little house. A large barn, exposing its need of repair, leaned open and empty. The fencing between the barn and house wandered disjointedly with long sections missing.

Beyond the barn, erratic paths of plowed dirt broke a scorched square of ground. About every ten feet, immense stones jutted into the air. A pile of tree roots dried at the end of the field, waiting to be burned. Josie abhorred the shoddiness, the apparent laziness.

Mother and daughter sat in the buggy, dresses wrinkled and stained, skin splotched and peeling, but with backs straight and heads high as a man approached. Josie picked up a few of his words. "Trade... good mare." Her ankles wobbled when her feet hit the ground, pinpricks stabbed upward, but her words carried steady and strong. "The mare is not for sale."

"Seems a shame to punish a good horse like that. Going far?"

"The horse is not open to any agreement." In a fit of annoyance, she pulled at a coverlet beneath the seat and dumped its contents. Scrunched in a tin crammed with the stolen onions lay Mrs. Costello's leather pouch. Josie knew how many coins were there, she counted them daily. The shiny pieces clunked dully as she poured them out. Too late, Josie realized she had neglected to hide any coins in case the farmer proved untrustworthy. Her hands shook when she glanced at her daughter.

Josie coyly slid a gold piece into her palm, before dropping the purse among the disarray on the floor. "This is one of the most splendid rigs ever made." She seethed at remembering the thrift needed to accumulate enough to buy the smart buggy. Josie gestured as she sauntered back to the waiting farmer. "A fine vehicle for going to meetings."

"Got no need for a fancy buggy." The farmer leaned back on his sturdy legs.

"A woman can feel pleased to be squired around in a vehicle this grand. Everyone could see you're a good provider." Josie squeezed the gold piece with her fingers, rubbing it with a blunt nail before him.

"Ahh, we all get along the same out here. Hand to mouth. But, uh, you throw in another one of them gold pieces you hiding, with the buggy, and you can take that there wagon in the field over there." Josie backed a few steps. "And I'll fetch a pair of oxen from out back."

Josie carefully handed him two gold coins, walked to the buggy and quickly began unhitching Contessa, praying all the while the farmer was honest, not bent on stealing their remaining gold.

Grayed with dry rot, the wagon appeared solid enough. Thick timbers. Iron-clad wheels. Not the light schooner of late, but a sturdy transport. Josie kneaded Contessa's flanks, praising the mare. She had given up some of their cache, but saved Contessa.

Taylor hopped down from the buggy and helped transfer their belongings to the wagon while the farmer led a pair of oxen forward. Their bones protruded from sagging flesh. A woman followed carrying a basket of turnips, carrots and potatoes.

The scrawny animals lumbered west at a snail's pace. Josie hoped their endurance outshone their speed. The slow ride gave her plenty of time to review the problems she had mulled over during her sleepless nights.

Even acquiring a fortune, Taylor must arrive in California with a respectful reputation, not as an opportunist escaping the law. The normal westward trek took four to six months, depending on destination, weather and hostiles, but taking a circuitous route would mean many more months for them.

At the first opportunity, Josie decided to post a letter to Mrs. Costello, direct her to send the money from the Boatman's account in care of General Delivery, Fort Gibson, the last dot on Jacob's map that Josie remembered.

"Momma, how will Poppa find me? He only knows about Costello House." Alarm showed readily on Taylor's face.

Taylor's sudden worry surprised Josie. She had not suspected her daughter would be that concerned. Jacob's return had not been a frequent topic of conversation lately, although she knew Taylor never gave up on someday being with him. "Help ready things. We can talk on the way."

Josie decided the time had come to end Taylor's fantasies and her own. Eight years was long enough. This journey might provide opportunity for her to search for news of Jacob, but Taylor should not waste her life waiting.

"From the moment you could talk, you begged Mrs. Costello and me over and over to tell the story of how you were born." Josie talked softly, as if she were confiding a secret. "Mrs. Cos and I were alone when you came into the world. Poppa had gone to California. You know I never learned why Jacob failed to come back. After waiting so many years for him, since before you were born, Mrs. Costello and I agreed he must have met with an accident. He may never have reached California and his gold mine."

Taylor's eyes grew wide, frightened.

Josie's heart wept with sorrow for what she must do. "Think about what I am saying. With a daughter as fine as you, and a loving wife waiting, Poppa would fight bandits and wild animals to return. Mines are very dangerous places to work, and Jacob's surveying sometimes made him enemies. I think it best we try to accept that Jacob is not going to return. I doubt you will ever see Poppa."

Taylor's brow furrowed, but she did not say a word. Her green eyes showed no expression. Josie wanted to cradle her daughter, tell her everything would turn out all right, buy her a strawberry ice, for she, too, did not want to let go of the Jacob Broderick fairytale.

Josie wrapped her arm around her daughter and held her tight. "During our journey, for the last time, I'll tell you about your Poppa and his dreams." In spite of the throbs pounding her skull, Josie once again told Jacob's tales of adventure, the dreams that had won her heart.

Twenty-three

A few days after giving up her buggy and gold, a rider chanced upon Josie while she watered the oxen and Contessa at a creek.

"Afternoon, Ma'am. From the looks of it, you aimin' West, too?" The voice was polite; his eyes steady.

Josie noted the older man smelled clean. His teeth and clothes showed no tobacco stains, and he stopped at a respectable distance. He wore no guns or badge.

"My husband went into town for information about the roads. He will return shortly." Although she recognized an opportunity to be neighborly and obtain news of St. Louis, she backed away a mite. "Have you been to California? We are in dire need of information."

Taylor stopped tossing pebbles into the water. Her head cocked as she listened intently.

"Don't you worry none. Got no bad thoughts about you or your kin." The man knelt on the ground and began splashing water on his face and neck. "Left Tennessee. Wife died few years back, daughter married, passel of kids. Thought I'd try a little ranching in Oklahoma. Hear there's grass taller than a fence post and sweeter than molasses. Water enough to float the whole country."

Josie's apprehensions eased. "Truthfully, my husband went ahead to Independence to make arrangements to join a wagon train. I stayed longer to visit family in Illinois."

Taylor watched, stirring a fuzzy cattail in the stream.

"Ain't much in the way of wagon trains nowadays. Since the Santa Fe laid tracks clear to Independence. Anybody with any money in their pocket rides the track. Lot faster, don't see so much tho'." The man casually picked his teeth with a weed.

"We brought machinery and tools to make a living," Josie lied. "And livestock we don't care to part with. Merchants, you know." Hopefully, the old coot had not nosed around their wagon back on the road.

"Got the right stuff, can probably earn your way along a merchant's route. Mention Cabot's Trail to your husband."

"Would you tell me what you know? We might not get accurate information from someone else."

He proceeded to tell about a less traveled route utilized mostly by traders and suppliers that followed the Canadian River, crossed Oklahoma and the Texas panhandle to New Mexico. Jacob had spoken fervently about Santa Fe, almost worshipping its natural beauty.

Josie decided if the authorities felt the need to track her and Taylor beyond Missouri, a lawman would never suspect she would choose the more desolate route. In addition, her persistent fear of recognition spurred her to avoid settlements and made the stranger's telling all the more appealing. They parted after he used a stick and mud to sketch a ragged map and names of forts on the wagon's canvas cover.

The day after listening to the stranger, Josie learned from a casual rider that the season had passed for the wagons to push straight through to California. Only weeks remained before winter began. Waterways froze, range feed for the stock disappeared, and winter winds made navigation of the wagons perilous across the open ranges of Kansas or Nebraska. Oklahoma, Josie learned, fared as bad, and northern Texas worse. Snow could form drifts head high on a man, burying anyone who managed to survive by feasting on jackrabbits and hard tack.

The news stunned Josie. Their remaining gold would not last through the winter. As various strangers drifted along with them for a short way, a number of men offered indecent proposals, but a layover in Independence seemed the only acceptable answer. Josie would not risk their lives to the hazards prophesized. At least, if the law caught up with her in Independence or Kansas City, Taylor could be returned safely to Mrs. Costello.

"We will simply stay until the spring thaw," Josie told Taylor. "I will find a sensible post, teaching or tutoring, or as a companion, or clerking in a store." Josie delivered the finest performance of unconcern she could muster for her daughter.

"I can wash dishes as good as Mandy and clear tables, too," Taylor offered.

"I will find a position, something suitable for a lady. There will be no kitchen work, cleaning, or such, for either of us."

More than a week after Josie first heard the distressing news, they arrived at a road marker indicating Carthage. For an unknown reason, the name conjured up references of wealth and influence for Josie. She turned to Taylor. "I will try here. Competition for a position might be less. If not, I will try again in Kansas City."

~ * ~

They entered Carthage on Broadway, a street divided by a parkway clustered with golden sweet fennel, blue chicory, parsley, goldenrod, and chestnut trees. A faint mint pungency of the purple henbit coursing the air convinced Josie people of taste and thrift lived here.

Proud Victorian homes banked the passing lawns. Some stood four floors high, turrets and balconies dressed a few, copper, slate and ornate tiles topped many. The houses grew larger and more complex as they neared the center of town.

Josie stopped in front of a neatly kept merchant's store that appeared busy. After both she and Taylor washed up, Josie entered the store, intent on selling her skills. "Good morning." She bowed her best, as did Taylor. "My name is Josie Broderick." The necessity of using a fictitious name escaped her. My daughter Taylor and I just arrived in your lovely town."

Before Josie could say another word, a man popped up from back of the barrels. The woman she addressed rushed from behind the counter. Both chattered at the same time.

"We had no idea Jacob had returned. Is he outside? Bring him in at once." The man headed for the door. The woman began clucking and tucking strands of hair under her bonnet.

Josie's thoughts spun like a top. Jacob? These people knew Jacob? She felt thunderstruck. "Well, no, Jacob is not with us." Could they mean her Jacob?

"Ah, so he waits for you again in Santa Fe," said the man. "We knew that young man would not give up until he carted you west. He talked of little else, striking gold and coming back for his sweetheart."

The woman's eyes softened. "Why didn't he stop on his way back through? I'm disappointed."

"Probably took the train. Must have hit a motherlode." The man stopped peering out the display window. "Think, Mother. Jacob's settled down, done with his ventures. A man has no time to gallivant around the country with responsibilities and a family waiting. Shame though', he couldn't stop to visit."

Josie fought to make sense of what they said. Her head felt light, empty confusion threatening to dash her sensibilities. "I have no idea why. He must have had a very good reason."

"You're right, husband, probably traveled by train. Bad thing, them not giving us a depot. Well, what news do you bring of your fine young man?"

"Taylor, would you step outside, please?" Josie waited until her daughter shut the door. "My daughter gets quite disturbed when I talk of Jacob. We have been through such an ordeal. Family business and such. Separated from him much too long. Please, tell me of your acquaintance with Jacob."

"He didn't tell you about Carthage? the man said. "There's little to confess. He came here about seven..."

"Now, husband, more like eight years ago. Eight years plus four months, I daresay. Summer, eighteen seventy-nine. Here 'til after the railroad finished. Except for two weeks in St. Louis for that Frenchman's project."

The gentleman bowed his head toward the interruption. "I stand corrected." He pointed at the woman, nodded at Josie. "Please, my Missus, name is Lucy. I am Andrew... Colby."

The ladies half curtsied to each other while he bowed. Then he beamed at Josie. "Jacob drew up the plans for our new courthouse. You can see it through the window there. Going to be the talk of the state. That Frenchman sponsored him, proposed a goodly sum. When that source dried up, well, considering all the veteran's families we supported, the council had little money for nonessentials. After Jacob started receiving your letters, he left."

"My letters? When was this?" Josie felt as if her feet hovered above the floor.

"Around the holidays, in fact he picked several up here that month. Took the train to Santa Fe. Said he was meeting someone there to make his fortune. Promised to come back and visit when he returned to claim his Josefina. Described you down to the penny, well except for having golden curls." The shopkeeper studied Josie's hair.

"Wonderful man," added the lady. " Adventurer, but dependable. Left us some drawings."

Poking his wife, the man spoke. "Mother, get those sketches. You know which ones." He turned back to Josie. "Whole town was sorry to see him go. Lots of widows and debutantes like hounds at his heels. Any one of them ready to do his bidding."

The woman smacked the man's arm as she laid the papers on the counter. The flowing charcoal lines showed Josie exactly as she stood before them. Then another, a colorful watercolor of her standing in a rose garden.

Tears of joy escaped down Josie's cheek. "He certainly caught my likeness." She longed to grab them up, hide them in some secret place and savor their existence. She owned nothing that had belonged to Jacob. "I had some like these, but I lost them in a fire." *God forgive me.*

The man gushed. "Seeing' as they're you, take them. We would be pleased for you to enjoy them." The woman's fingers gripped the paper edges. "Let go, Lucy. We have others. Come, welcome Mrs. Broderick, and bring out the tea. Remember Jacob telling how it pleasures her. Hurry now, woman."

Andrew studied Josie. "Where are you staying? Such a surprise. The Mayor's wife and Mrs. Hill I'm sure fought over your visit."

"No one else knows of our arrival. We had not planned on being detained in Carthage, but we began our journey too late. The wagon masters tell me snow will close the route soon. That I had best wait for spring."

"They gave you the right advice, unless you care to take the train." When Josie failed to explain, Mr. Colby went right on. "You must post Jacob a letter straight out. You'll have your choice of rooms, of course, best not to have him worry. You letter will be picked up tomorrow."

Where to send a letter? Josie had no address. She would ask questions, worm her way to the heart of the matter. Josie literally danced inside her skin with excitement. "Tell me more. First, let me get my daughter. She always enjoys tales about her Poppa."

The parlor behind the storefront filled with greeters and well-wishers before Josie and Taylor had barely tasted their tea. Offers of accommodations came from every visitor.

"How lucky of Jacob to finally marry his sweetheart," someone said.

"Surprising," said another, "since he seemed so discouraged before he left."

Josie eventually accepted a private guest house located on the grounds of a luxurious resort. The officials would take care of all her expenses, a generous gesture for a small payment still due on Jacob's design. Josie felt exhilarated, confused, but mostly hungered for more information about Jacob.

~ * ~

Taylor waited near the door of the store, stone still, her knotted stomach seeming to balance on her toes. These strangers talked of Poppa, as if he were still alive. Momma had told her how dangerous the mines were, that Poppa had not come back because he had been hurt. Momma probably didn't want to make these people sad, tell them Poppa had most likely been killed. They seemed so kindly and happy.

Later, after settling in their cottage, Taylor fired questions at Josie. "Why did Poppa stay here? Why didn't he come to Costello House? Where is he now?"

Josie wanted answers to the same questions.

"Was Poppa killed or not?"

"I have no answers yet." Josie hoped dearly not. She glowed in light of the discovery he had loved her so, to make drawings, and share his feelings with strangers.

And the letters, who had sent them? Josie's efforts around the holidays had been to secure a place to live and safety for her unborn baby.

"Maybe Poppa wasn't hurt too badly."

Josie heard her daughter's plaintiff voice in the distance. Jacob loved her, that was all she could think of now. "What, Pumpkin?"

"Now we can find Poppa, with the whole town looking for him. We should go to California on the train."

Josie knew no one would pay the outrageous sum she had paid for the wagon and scrawny oxen. They were near penniless, and what would they do in California? An uncivilized land of foreigners and pirates. No society. Better to remain here with a roof over their heads and food in their bellies while she scouted for answers. "We will stay here until spring. Poppa will not disappear in a few months."

"What if Poppa's lost and can't find us?" Taylor began to sob, the strain of the journey telling. Josie cuddled and patted her unsettled child. Too many questions without answers for an eight-year-old.

"I do not want you talking about any accident or asking questions about Poppa." Josie's voice vented her concern, her manner turning stern. "We will take our time. Quietly collect all the information we can. Then when we are ready to leave and look for him, we will be in a position to ask the right questions and find the right answers. First, we must assure ourselves they speak of Poppa, our Jacob Broderick."

"Momma, the pictures. Poppa drew them of you." Taylor's lips trembled. "He went so far away and was too busy to come back and draw my likeness."

"Pumpkin, we will do everything possible to find Poppa. But not until spring. For now we will enjoy this lovely cottage and use the time to prepare for our trip."

"I don't think I can wait, Momma."

"We must." Josie dared not speak of the eight years she had waited for Jacob who worked only a short distance away. He had not written to Mrs. Costello seeking information, not sent instructions on where to send the maps, books and plans of François's bank that had been discarded in the attic. She would keep these portraits. Store them where she could exam them each day. She would find the answers, and Taylor would know if the man she knew as her father still lived. *And if Jacob lived, what then?*

Twenty-four

Early the next morning Josie and Taylor strolled through Carthage. They marveled at the impressive homes that stretched the length of Broadway, all owned by the wealthiest people in the state of Missouri who touted the newly created title of "millionaire." The affluence fed Josie's addiction to gracious living.

The homes designed by French and Italian architects sported expansive front porches, gingerbread, and contrived towers plunked atop any story affording a view. A French chateau constructed of pale pink brick with iron balconies, like a pastel cake swirled with white frosting became Josie's favorite. It belonged to the banker, Frank Hill.

Copper roofs oxidized to a turquoise green patina shaded the confectionery appearing structure. The owners referred to the mansion as "their starlight home," because of majestic light fixtures that spotted a white fleur-de-lis iron fence encircling the mansion.

Taylor admired the bronze lampposts separating each flowery fencing section while supporting barrel sized gas lamps aloft. Each glass measured an arm's length tall and several hands across its width. Later that evening, mother and daughter discovered that in the darkness the gas fueled lamps flared like comets, casting firelight pantomimes across the house like a shadow play of giants.

Even though Jacob's profession barely acceded the edge of gentry, the isolated residents had welcomed their well-traveled visitor years ago. And now, his beautiful wife's charm and bearing, hinting at a mysterious regal ancestry, drew the residents in. Soon invitations overflowed the little cottage's silver reception tray. Requests arrived seeking Josie's attendance at late morning brunches, afternoon teas, musical etudes, sewing circles, and readings.

The ebullient young mother dragged her daughter with her everywhere. Taylor suffered daily, from early morning through to excruciatingly boring afternoons, confined to the parlors of pampered women.

For breakfast, they ate a full farmer's plate and sipped strong tea accompanied by scones, cellar peaches or berry preserves and clotted cream. The brisk afternoons brought luncheons with cucumber and dill rounds, peanut and olive sandwiches, melon, a wedge of Brie, pate, assorted crudités and petite fours. Dinner each night became a feast with each hostess attempting to outdo the night before.

Not to lose her standing, Mrs. Hill conducted a newly fashionably imported "High Tea." The early evening refreshment offered hearty soups of corn chowder or beef barley, meat pies, cheeses, garden salad, green tomato cups, fresh apples and cognac infused peach cobbler that rendered the recipients groggy with gluttony.

Late the same evening, after a recital, Taylor contemplated the displayed desserts. "I don't know which to eat first." The tables sagged under the weight of pound cake drenched in apricots and caramel, brownies crowned with nuts and candied cherries, carrot cake, and cheesecake surrounded by raspberry syrup. Her eager eyes scanned the table, alternately landing on cookies and melon.

Josie's face became stern, her voice taut. "Unless you wish to be known as a piglet, sample only one fully. Then if you must, nibble on the others." She worried over the strained seams of Taylor's dress. Absently Josie twisted a curl while studying her daughter.

A flush suddenly swamped Josie. An overwhelming fear of suffocation compelled her to run outdoors, to gulp the cool air. The chin, nose, and obstinacy of François had appeared like a ghost on her daughter's face. Josie closed her eyes. She could feel François's hands on her. Each finger scalded her skin with an imagined touch leaving its sordidness behind. The odor of his succinct tobacco mixed with wine burned her nostrils. The panic left her weak, her heart racing.

Josie inhaled the perfume of a kerchief, and waited, allowing the tormenting to ease. *Taylor belongs to me; she will never know of François.* Josie made one qualification: until the time came to make claim against his estate. The attack passed. Fixing a smile on her lips, Josie rid herself of the harassing panic, and returned to the other guests.

Fall became winter. Two days before Christmas a roomful of gentlemen and matrons sat in critical judgment as Josie performed alongside a piano. The bow poised against the strings of the violin. Drawing her bow down, Josie began an evening of musical entertainment using a borrowed violin that made her long for the Armati she had hidden, fearing question of how she came to own such a valuable instrument.

She felt relaxed, youthful and confident. Her restored platinum hair escaped in springy masses from the severe bun of style. A lovely robés princéssé, the latest fashion she had tatted, looped in cascading frills over the skirt of her blue silk gown. She matched the apron-like affectation with lace trim for cuffs and a décolleté-ruffled collar. She played with the assurance of a well-practiced violinist. She did not know that her childlike charm abbreviated envy and birthed many recitals starring Mrs. Broderick.

The mayor's praises fed her vanity. "My dear, you play sweetly, and look like an angel. Such a blessing to have you here. Your family must be very proud."

Josie bubbled under the much ado, then abruptly stilled. The gentlemen in attendance had quite probably conducted banking business with Father. She withdrew into the cloak of her deceit. "I lost my family soon after Jacob left for California. Only my daughter remains." Her fingers crossed to ward off the devil from her lies. As the days passed, they became almost locked in that position.

January arrived in a shield of ice with additional invitations to card parties and book reviews for the Broderick ladies. February brought sleigh rides, bonfires with corn and potato bakes. The rains arrived and introduced costumed readings to Taylor. She learned that imagination combined with invention proved valued tools to pass the time. An important lesson taught by people of leisure and means.

Only Taylor received Josie's confidences. "As soon as the weather permits, we will leave for Santa Fe. Find Poppa. But you cannot discuss our plans with anyone; they must remain our secret. There are those who still accuse your Momma of misdeeds."

Contessa had foaled soon after they arrived in Carthage, an easy birth. Like the mare, a red, Edwardian script "T" marked the chest of the pale filly. The newborn made Josie the most content she had felt in a long while. The naturally tattooed animal and promise of another breeder delighted her. Josie promptly inscribed Contessa II on the thoroughbred registration documents the Mayor volunteered.

Disappointment crushed Josie's happiness when she realized she could not submit the credentials. Which woman would claim the prized animal, Josefina Taylor or Josie Broderick? Both were sought. Listing of ownership would divulge her whereabouts. She asked the Mayor's wife to put the documents in safekeeping.

Set on establishing their place, Josie began a dangerous practice of reciprocation, inviting the Dames to dine at the resort as her guest. She hired musicians, ordered special flowers, and served unique foods. She thrived on the accolades from the wealthiest men and women of the country, and entertained with the arrogance and aplomb of aristocracy. Josie Broderick was surrounded by the life she revered.

One afternoon the first week of March, the Mayor entered the parlor and set a thick stack of invoices on the table near Josie. After pleasantries, he began, "I need to clarify the town's position. Jacob's talents are well appreciated, and we have enjoyed your visit. But, perhaps you might be a bit more cautious. The extension of his commission for designing the Hall is almost expended. Your mounting charges have consumed a substantial portion of our available revenue."

"I beg your pardon. Are you telling me I have been withdrawing Jacob's earnings? That my indiscretion is toppling your treasury?"

"In truth, that is but a portion, a small amount, but our debt is not infinite. Jacob left before we paid his charges fully. He asked that we invest the balance in municipal bonds with interest. He originally anticipated using the profits, on his return, to take you with him to Santa Fe. Of course, that all changed." The Mayor waited, as if he sought an explanation for the change. When Josie failed to answer he went on. "And now you arrive alone, and since we have not had word of him since his departure." The Mayor waited politely. "I only warn you to be cautious. Not knowing your circumstances, I would not want you without funds."

With all the tact she could marshal, Josie dismissed the Mayor. Her dreams had died in bitter disgrace.

Josie declined invitations and moped about the cottage. Alone with her thoughts, she worked through this turn of events for several days. *Jacob had not claimed his earnings for eight years?* Certainly not a normal behavior from such a responsible person. Nor had he sought her or inquired after her, not an expected step for a man in love. From her earlier ebullience upon learning of Jacob's loyalty, Josie's spirits deteriorated. By the end of her pondering, Josie reached the life-altering conclusion that no chance remained that Jacob Broderick still lived.

The following morning Josie posted a letter to Mrs. Costello. One document gave the innkeeper permission to cash in the savings book, the other instructed Mrs. Costello to send the money to Carthage, Missouri, in care of Josie Broderick. The amount added up to little enough, but combined with the balance the Mayor had exposed, if she practiced frugality, Josie reasoned the future she and Taylor shared appeared brighter than when they had left St. Louis.

~ * ~

Within days of the first March thaw, a young man seeking the Mayor entered the city official's home during a musicale. He waited boldly just beyond the room's entrance until received. A gold crest glistened on a red jacket as the visitor bowed toward "His Honor". Josie's heart stopped.

"Good day, sir. I beg your indulgence. I was advised to contact you about my interest in securing a position." He extended his hand. The initial conversation registered too low to be heard, but the two neared the circle of chairs in the room.

"My reference, from an acquaintance you contracted with before, is contained in this portfolio. My certified license can be obtained from the city engineer of St. Louis within days."

The red coat extracted an envelope, handed it to the Mayor then dropped some neatly rolled drawings across an empty corner of the adjacent table.

Josie felt her life drain from her. The reference to St. Louis carried to where she sat. Her arms and feet refused to move. The red jacket glowed.

The man continued. "I just spent a brief visit in Illinois."

Josie's knees began to tremble. She braced herself against the piano. Her mouth formed unrecognizable noises. "Ahhh, agghh," answered a nearby matron's question.

The Mayor fumbled with the envelope while forcing the direction of the interview toward the young man's endeavors. "I see you recently completed a dam project. Who financed it?"

"Young Durante, for his Union Pacific line. Are you acquainted?" The redcoat man overtly scanned the room.

"Yes, yes, of course, walked one of his bridges myself. How long were you in St. Louis?" Their brief talk of business allowed Josie time to collect her thoughts and judge the genuineness of the young man. She worried if he represented the government; oddly, she felt fear of someone closer, more personal. The red jacket of the Goldenrod taunted her. Only a smattering of the businessmen's words carried above the room's chatter.

Within minutes, the men shook hands. The eager man's voice grew louder. "I look forward to calling at your office. By the by, I am also seeking information about a lady friend of mine. Originally from Illinois, may be injured. Involved in an accident. I am concerned about her well-being. Possibly passed through here late summer with her daughter. A beauty, dark hair, tiny woman. Recently partnered in an inn. Was a regular guest of the owner of the Goldenrod Showboat."

"Most have gone onto Independence to wait out the weather. No strangers here this winter. Unlikely she would stay. Not much in the way of gambling excitement in our town." The Mayor dodged the implication, struggling to bring warmth to his words, but his normal friendly smile sagged. Slapping the young man solidly on the back, the official hurried the intruder to the door. "If you will excuse me, I have guests."

The Mayor fidgeted, watching out the window after the young man disappeared, then turned to the noisy, speculating group. "Some sort of investigator I would suppose. Best lock your wives and daughters in the house. Man seems intent on taking some pretty young thing back to St. Louis with him."

The roomful chuckled, and the men artificially barred their women from attack. "I think this is an opportune time to end the musicale," the Mayor added. "Thank you all for sharing the afternoon." He walked straight for Josie. "Would your remain? I have something to discuss with you."

How could the Mayor have guessed her guilt with such paltry information? The young man seemed rather unsure. Josie feared there was no escape for her.

After the others departed, the mayor pulled a chair near Josie. She sat woodenly poised for interrogation while the Mayor repeated portions of the stranger's conversation unheard by her. His eyes never left hers during the telling. He leaned close to Josie, his body more comforting than intimidating.

"Saw such a pretty and charming girl once myself, in Illinois. Before a luncheon with Monsieur ducLaFevre where he proposed I employee Jacob Broderick. Believe the girl's father was intent on marrying her to royalty at the time. Both the Monsieur and Jacob seemed quite smitten with her. Never quite figured out who won her hand."

Josie's heart stopped. Pins and needles pricked her head and chest. Although he appeared calm, almost cavalier, the Mayor's voice held an undercurrent.

"I genuinely admired Jacob. Didn't care much for that Monsieur, never appreciate Frenchmen. Perhaps, we should alert the local militia of this red coat messenger? Turn the cards on him." Robust belly laughter accompanied his suggestion.

Surprise blinded Josie to any possible deception by the Mayor. His words had dismantled her world. Her fingers reached for a curl. He had known who she was from the beginning.

"What can you tell me of Jacob's departure?" she asked impetuously.

A smile caused puppets of fat to dance on the Mayor's cheeks. "For some reason Jacob decided the love of his life was lost to him. He received an offer to work somewhere out West. I was not surprised when he left, having known his desire for adventure. As I recall, he was to meet with someone, I thought perhaps the Monsieur, to do some building for Worldwide bank."

"Not François. He was killed." Josie felt something further amiss, almost sinister, in what was left unsaid.

"Perhaps the woman, some nature of bank representative, I believe." His Honor stared hard at Josie. "But you are seriously mistaken about Monsieur ducLaFevre. He is not dead. A cripple, bound to a wheelchair, years of recuperation from an accident, but assuredly not dead. Administers Worldwide Banks and the National Lane Company across the country."

Josie fell from the chair in a dead faint.

~ * ~

Josie woke on a chaise in her bedroom. Someone fussed over her. The Mayor's voice boomed instructions. "Out, all of you. The Mrs. and I will see to Mrs. Broderick."

A smile filled the older man's face when Josie's eyes finally focused.

"Gave us a scare." He pulled a chair against the lounge. "Taylor told me much of your history. Partly true as I see it, but I'm sure complete truth to that poor child. Before you confess or deny, let me tell you where I stand." He looked behind him. "Mother, you may go. She is perfectly safe now."

Josie heard a rustling of skirt and the door close. For some fool reason, she felt relieved.

"Mrs. Broderick you may call yourself, but I know when Jacob left here he believed you wed. Perhaps carrying that man's child."

Josie gasped. *Dieter? Stuart? Who had told Jacob such a lie? Only half true.* Her reason begged answer. Anyone within listening of her tumultuous departure from Taylor Estates could have. Half of the people of Taylor Estates.

"Jacob was heartsick." The Mayor waited.

Josie knew he studied her for the effect of the revelation.

Apparently satisfied, he continued. "Other than myself, Jacob kept his own council. His only salvation came from two people. Some male friend wrote concerning François's accident. The letter said the victim could not live but a few years, and that time as a bedridden cripple."

"What accident? My father told me he murdered François."

"Not true. Well, be that as it may, Jacob believed, as François's wife, you sailed to France to register the child's claim to Monsieur ducLaFevre's properties and titles. In light of this news, Jacob accepted a position offered by one of his other correspondents. One, he confided in me, would afford him opportunity to keep abreast of your whereabouts and marital position. And when, or if, you returned to this country."

The story sounded preposterous. So many twists and half-truths. But the Mayor had no reason to lie. "Where is Jacob now?"

"I am not surprised that you do not know. Unfortunately, I do not either. He did not divulge the position, his benefactor, or if he intended to immigrate to California. I know only he expected to join a woman friend on the Santa Fe train."

Woman? It had to be Marianne. Josie could think of no other. But, her friend would have told Jacob about Costello House. *No,* Josie thought, *she would not have. Jacob would have been lost forever to Marianne if he had contacted Mrs. Costello and returned to St. Louis and found his real love.* But arguably, Marianne had sailed to France. Probably a French name that sounded feminine.

Anyway, Josie allowed, Jacob loved her. He also believed her wed to François and living with his child somewhere in France. That would account for his not searching for her. But that had occurred over eight years ago. Long enough, ample time, to begin a hunt, hire investigators, whatever it took to find the woman he supposedly loved. He had certainly learned within that time that François had not left the country. And what about the woman on the train?

"You must leave."

The startling, deep-throated order startled Josie.

"The young man here earlier. A representative of Monsieur ducLaFevre if I am not wrong. Asked too many questions. Offered a reward. Seems intent on surrendering the woman he seeks to a St. Louis constable and taking the child to his employer."

Nausea rose and fell with the pull of an ocean tide in Josie's midriff. The blood drained from her face and pooled in cramping bundles around her heart. Blackness fell. A burning odor filled her nose and burned her eyes. The Mayor swished smelling salts under her nose. Josie's head jerked back quickly. "Shh!" he murmured.

She listened silently, questions bumping each other in her mind.

"I will purchase train tickets through to California for you both," he said. "Withdraw enough funds tomorrow to guarantee your safe keeping after you arrive there. The least I can do."

Josie's hands complained of a chill, although she wrung them without stop. "I cannot take the train without leaving clues to my destination. Besides, I have Contessa, and the foal." A tear wobbled down her cheek. "I have no idea of where to go when we get to California." Her head shook of its own merit as if to deny the situation.

"Go! You must! We will equip your wagon as you planned. Pass Independence and board the train somewhere in Kansas. Disguise yourself and the girl until you reach California."

Josie nodded her head weakly. François lived. He had come for his daughter. The gold and glittery crest worn by the red coated stranger identified her enemy.

Josie could think of nothing beyond protecting Taylor. "We must leave." Josie fought to get up as another fear gripped her. "Where is Taylor?"

Wide hands held her down. "Sleeping, my wife is with her. She will stay with your daughter until you leave. I will stay here, by the door, until the bank opens in the morning. No one will get by either of us."

~ * ~

Before the haze of early morning burned off the next day, an abundance of supplies stuffed the overlander. The Mayor had retrieved the fattened oxen, Contessa, and the foal. Josie qualified their sudden departure with a longing for husband and father to the curious friends who interrupted their departure. Amid sniffling and hasty good-byes, Josie and Taylor set out.

The night before, while the Mayor enlightened her about the railroad and possible places of embarking, Josie had mapped the merchant's trail she had studied since fall. Southwest along the Missouri River then across the plains of Oklahoma, far away from more popular routes. Across the Texas panhandle and into New Mexico.

Hope of joining Jacob would have to wait. First she had to protect Taylor.

Twenty-five

The Mayor never learned of Josie's change of heart. Instead of going north to Kansas City as he instructed, Josie led her band south along the Missouri River to Fort Smith before turning west. She had used the Mayor's money to purchase passenger tickets and freight transport for Contessa and her foal. The fares had been outlandish, but with the decoy, François's redcoats would blunder along a false trail, for a while.

Mr. Reuter's advice on recently discovered gold fields in Santa Fe stuck in Josie's mind. A mining town that profited for the past eight years would assuredly need a surveyor. If luck traveled with her, she might find news of Jacob before he entered California. If his mysterious employer had whisked him away to some unknown place, one more stop would not make much difference.

The rambling wagon traveled singly along the Canadian and Washita Rivers, sticking close to the waterways. On several occasions after filling their water barrels, Josie discovered a carcass, bloated and black with blowflies, left by the current. A silk tie wrapped around the throats of their canteens strained the contaminated liquid whenever they sipped. Josie hoped that would suffice.

She steeled herself to disregard the misfortunes of nomadic life, the insult all the more flagrant since their recent flirt with gentility. After awhile the towns blended together, Silver Creek, Anderson, Fort

Wayne, barely civilized, but accepting of an attractive woman and healthy girl.

On the occasions when they hooked up with a wagon train, Josie found the situation intolerable. The others relished living in each other's armpits while Josie valued her privacy.

Men pinched and patted her at every opportunity, behaved with vulgar and arrogant familiarity. Others grumbled over her lack of a husband to share chores and the added risk of two unescorted females. As long as she divvied her share of the wagon master's charges, he stood up for her, but dissension always accompanied their presence.

Some of the wives resented the attractive, pampered woman. They wore slack, cotton dresses without benefit of corset or hoop and men's work shoes, and cared not a twit about fashion or manners. Some outcursed the men while they drove the mules; others walked behind the cows collecting steamy dung for fuel. Once a woman served as the encampment's butcher, hacking and sawing on a timber attached to the back of her wagon. Few wasted their effort corralling their unruly children.

In each group, however, a few women would step forward to help Josie and were cordial and welcoming, defending those who wheeled knives with the relish of trappers, skinned wildlife and saved the marrow of bloodied corpses. When the women exchanged talk of sod houses with dirt floors, methods of keeping mold from destroying food and clothing in a cave, and the efficient storm-cellar shelters in their anticipation of temporary housing, Josie swore to do better by Taylor. All the women cheerfully carried out whatever chores their men had no time to perform. On no occasion did a woman only simper and watch. All the men read, a few seemed well-educated, only twice did Josie note an illiterate. On one occasion the wagon master sought her assistance with the allotments of food staples, measuring out equal shares after the members pooled their resources.

One afternoon a widower suggested if Josie were to act more civil, he might buy her and put an end to the writhing and preoccupation of the unmarried men. He would give her a mule, a roof, and take in her offspring.

Josie's fury was impassioned. She cursed him, chased him away by brandishing a shovel, then told Taylor. "I swear, I will never reduce us to such meanness." Immediately, Josie bit her tongue; she knew better than to bait the gods.

The land stretched without pardon forever. Off in the distance Josie could see the end, where she suspected in this mammoth emptiness they might fall off the edge of the earth. Huge withered sunflowers bobbed gigantic heads against thunderous purple skies, their seedless centers having provided winter fodder for the wild birds. No buffers appeared to replace the magnificent cliffs and thick wooded valleys of Missouri. Instead, the Oklahoma Territory greeted them with a vista as uninteresting as a slug's back, and moldy grasses torqued by winds into humps of frosted waves.

No matter how far Taylor burrowed into the wagon nest, nor how many layers Josie wrapped around herself, the frigid March winds whistled across the prairies, driving the cold through their flesh.

Spring rains pelted them, swelling the creeks, miring the roads. Jagged bolts of brilliant lightning sliced the sky, touching the earth with hair-raising cracks followed by ear-deafening booms. Plum clouds rolled across the horizon blocking the sunlight, turning day into night as temperatures plunged to bone-chilling depths.

The bare fields supplied nothing more than divots to escape the harrowing winds. On two occasions, Taylor spotted twisters. The black spirals roared across the plains, sucking up everything in their paths, then, when their ferocious appetites were appeased, deposited miles of unwanted debris. Taylor watched as much in fascination as fear. She had never witnessed such power. Luckily, in both instances, the tornado's path ran parallel to their own.

The days became endurance contests of constant jostling and setting up and taking down camps. Some days Josie allowed Taylor to walk with the other children or ride Contessa, freed of the jostling wagon. The children chewed weeds along the way, pretending their bitter juice held the peppermint taste of store bought candy sticks, or the more brazen lit the tips and blew imaginary smoke, copying the grownups. While the oxen plodded along, Taylor wove wildflowers into crowns and bracelets and reigned as queen to imaginary knights or sparred with dragons.

At night, Josie, her hands burned from carelessness at the campfire, set up their camp, cared for the animals and secured their property, sometimes doing record keeping for others while Taylor cooked the meal. It was agreed; Josie scorched the rations much too often.

Two days out from Chouteau's Post in the middle of Oklahoma, having left a wagon train after weeks on the trail, Josie brooded with needle and thread in hand. "I can let out the seams of my blue dress. But, look at you. It is too early for you to be developing." Josie hurried to add an explanation. "That rich diet. I warned you."

Josie felt aggravated with herself; her cantankerous mood had called Taylor's attention to her changing body. She wanted to chastise her daughter's unladylike gluttony, not introduce questions about maturing. Their isolation and poverty grated on Josie's sensibilities; the girl required new clothes, and they needed fruit and soon soap. When they reached the fort, she would mail another letter to Mrs. Costello, have the secret account sent ahead to Santa Fe.

Josie held the dress up against Taylor. For an instant she thought Taylor's pallor more pronounced, but her speculation vanished quickly. The color so flattering to her own fairness cast uncomplimentary chartreuse over Taylor's freckles.

After prayers that night Josie leaned over Taylor. "Good-night kiss?" Dry, rough lips touched Josie's face, and the heat of fever brushed her cheek. Josie hurriedly sparked a flint and lit the lantern.

Captured in the oval of light, Taylor's eyes appeared glazed, her face flushed but drained. Buttons popped as if from a slingshot as Josie's fingers probed her daughter's body. "You should have told me you felt ill." A chill puddled around Josie's heart. No rash, no blisters. "Thank God."

Taylor heaved and wailed with belly cramps. Josie's panic peaked when ragged breathing became the only sound her daughter made. Taylor had never been sick. There had been no nights of walking floors, forcing castor oil, binding wounds or setting bones. Rebellious, spirited, Taylor survived infancy without a whimper and sailed through childhood free of physical difficulty. *Lose my daughter to disease? Impossible.*

By morning Taylor lay alarmingly quiet. The lethargy mimicked Marianne's wrestle with death. Josie's mind gelled into mush, unable to stir beyond guilt and retribution befitting her barnyard conduct while Marianne lay ill, and the other—François's offense. According to church preaching, with its unforgiving laws pointed as pins, Taylor's death would be just punishment.

Josie plowed through their bundles, digging for the household book her mother gave her so long ago. Frantic, she tossed their belongings among the weeds and wildflowers alongside the wagon. She had never needed the book at Costello House. She finally found it, jammed into the bottom of her sewing satchel.

A chart suggested several herbs for fever: yarrow, chamomile, bay leaf, hyssop, and horehound. The names rang familiar to Josie. Mother had insisted she learn to recognize them and know how to steep suitable potions. But Josie's excitement faded as quickly as it arrived. She would need to crawl on hands and knees through the fields for the illusive herbs. The art of harvesting and preparation had occurred within easy reach of mother's well-cultivated herb garden. Josie tossed the book, set a pot of water over a flame then plunged into their rations.

Taylor slept in restless fits. Josie spooned sugary chamomile tea between Taylor's lips and drenched cloths with cool water from their drinking barrel to lay across Taylor's brow. When chills shuddered through the young body, Josie piled all their blankets and clothes around Taylor, repeatedly tucking them in. Snuggling against her sweaty body when the shakes would not let go. Still Taylor's fever climbed with the energy of a well-stoked stove, alternately simmering in a vapor glistening on Taylor's skin and a scarlet bone-dry flush.

About sunrise Taylor pushed the sugary spoon away and fought not to swallow. Her whimpers rasped, chest wheezed. Within hours Taylor ceased struggling and lay unacceptably rigid, still.

Josie groaned, flailed, and cursed God, then herself. Such stupidity—why had she exposed Taylor to such rigors? The murder served as an excuse to resurrect her search for Jacob; she had acted selfishly. She could lose her daughter in the effort. Such sacrifice came too dear. She should have stayed in St. Louis. Mrs. Costello warned the journey would be too rugged for Taylor.

An uninvited thought boldly intruded on Josie's misery, a shocking parasite piggy-backing her anxiety. *Taylor is my key to well-earned riches.* At the appalling invasion, Josie crumpled in a tower of remorse. *Have I no shame?* Josie beat her fists against her head to rid herself of the horrifying Devil who had planted the seed of greed.

Taylor was dying or at least her life was in dire jeopardy, and Josie's sin still would not quit its hold. Self-loathing erased the last speck of respect Josie held for herself and her avarice.

Taylor would survive. Josie brutalized the oxen, whipping them toward the outpost, praying they would reach help. The hard clay provided a good surface for speed. She goaded the team with the flange of a hoe, their corpulent bodies swaying in lumbering strides as they used every gram of energy they could muster. For Josie, the creatures' progress was tediously slow.

Josie raged, her face contorted with panicked madness. "Faster, faster." *I will saddle Contessa. Ride for a doctor, bring him back.* No, she could not leave Taylor's side. Josie's voice sputtered, her throat raw. "Run, you lazy beasts, or I shall have your hides for boots." Josie brushed her forehead, flicking sweaty curls from her eyes. She recognized her own unnatural warmth.

"God, must I beg the Devil's help, " Josie prayed, "to give us a chance." Sour breath tainted her mouth; her stomach rumbled. Ghostly recollections of Marianne near death and calling for her taunted Josie, along with a vision of a laughing François twirling her around the sick room. The old tune drummed through Josie's mind, accompanied by the ditty "as you sow, so you reap."

Whatever she did, alone on the wagon seat cursing the lumbering oxen, sponging Taylor or attempting to feed her, more repugnant scenes bedeviled Josie. Guilt, fear, and hate rode abreast in the wagon, poking and puling at will. Defiantly, Josie struggled to rid herself of the intrusion, calling on long unused petitions of healing. She had no energy to waste on past sins.

While Taylor lay motionless on the wagon floor, Josie beat the oxen into a frenzy, driving them with whip and rod beyond their normal limits. They arrived at the fort by morning, half a day ahead. Taylor lay limp, exhausted. Josie convulsed in shuddering spasms, the fever attacking her body. Still, the guards of the fort heard her frantic shouts for help a hundred yards away.

The military doctor, a rheumy-eyed drunk with palsied hands, made a cursory examination of Taylor. His breath delivered a blast of spirits with each decision. "Powder of Nightshade, let her go peaceable," he directed after glancing over Taylor. He tapped Josie's skull, pulled down the lower lids of her eyes, thumped her back, listened with his stethoscope, then examined the insides of her wrists for spots. He would not dare breach her privacy. "Bloodletting," he ordered the attendant.

Josie flinched. She distrusted the odious treatment. Mother, an oftentimes victim of this misfortune, spoke only ill of it. "For my daughter. Something else. An herb, a purging?"

The doctor repeated, "Bloodletting for you. Only thing I know might rid the poison. The girl's too far removed." Without waiting for approval, he opened his bag and removed a straight razor that had already seen much use and a strand of stained silk cord.

Cradled in a soiled blanket on a straw mat, tears flooded down Josie's cheeks. What had they come to? She rolled her head faintly from side to side, her body jerking like the futile attempts of a downed fawn. Her mouth moved, but no sound came. The spark of recognition drifted from the too brilliant blue eyes. "Save my daughter. I will not lose her." Her eyes closed off the world, barring her from hearing his response.

The doctor shook his head. "Wasted time for the girl. I'll try to spare the woman." The razor sliced a fine line.

~ * ~

By morning Taylor's skin had cooled to the warmth of toasted bread. Rumors of smallpox, cholera, ague, yellow fever circulated throughout the fort. The angry inhabitant's fears rang throughout the enclosure. "Out! Throw them out!" A shield of warriors protected the commandant's quarters while the officers debated, then voted their decisions.

Outdoors, the greenhorn residents protested the most forcefully, ordering the guards to cast out the women. Some suggested the afflicted be set on the range to spread their disease among the redskins. Josie recognized panic in the voices that grew louder, more insistent, then increased in number.

Josie begged. "A gold piece. I have gold. Surely that buys a place." She fought to find the charm that had always won her way.

The Captain apologized. "Sorry, ma'am. Can't have a riot. Maybe have my men fall sick, too."

"Two coins not to put us outside the fort."

The man stubbornly refused, shaking his head without answer.

Josie braced herself on her elbows, barely managing to sit up, but she bargained fiercely. "All the gold I have left is yours. Put us with the animals if you must. Leave food and water. I will care for my daughter and myself."

"By morning everything you have will belong to me anyway."

His response, factual with a trace of courtesy, left Josie no hope.

~ * ~

In the dark of night, four silhouettes entered the room. Hastily, they dropped a litter on the floor. "Get on with it," a voice ordered nastily. Josie wrapped both arms as tightly as she could around Taylor and with her elbows scooted toward the stretcher.

The bad-tempered man spoke again. "Cain't stay here all night." The shadows moved away as Josie neared.

She tugged, crawling up on her knees, using her whole body to push her still child along with her. No one moved to help. Finally Josie flopped onto the stretcher on top of Taylor clinched securely in her arms.

Josie woke to the stink of straw and urea. The hut barely provided enough room to house the two women. Misshapen logs stacked atop each other long ways, notched in the corners to maintain balance, formed the confinement. The door appeared more sturdy, scarred as if kicked and hammered.

Beneath Josie a mattress stuffed with mildewed foliage and spread with scraps of dingy rags occupied most of the packed dirt floor. Its proximity welcomed spiders, toads, beetles and whatever else crawled to explore their feverish bodies.

Dust from the horses and marching soldiers seeped through the perforated timbers in horrible, choking surges, and piled into arid anthills along the log's edges. By midday the sun brought sweltering heat, baking the tiny confinement with foulness and humidity.

Next to Josie on the floor, a scant supply of meal and water covered the bottom of two reed containers. Bubbles and squiggles indicated the presence of unwanted guests. Beside the rations, a misspelled note ordered mother and daughter to remain within the confines of the jailhouse. They had been spared.

Josie fought for the remainder of that night and the following day, using what little strength she had left to minister to her daughter. Some hour in the black of night, the sickness stormed Josie's body, stealing her mind in its invasion.

~ * ~

Midway of the third day, the fever that racked Taylor subsided, she roused thirsty and hungry. The skin on her face, hands and feet began to peel, leaving behind strips of crinkled, transparent flesh. Bloody crusts peppered her scalp and more private parts where blisters had fallen away. Her freckles had faded, taking with them their bloom of vitality. Taylor recovered unharmed, but in the war between the fever's onset and the healing, her childish rebellion died.

While Josie slept, Taylor rocked herself, hunched in a corner, barely cognizant of dawn or fall of night. She abandoned Momma only to retrieve food and water left outside the lean-to door or to doze on acrid straw piled in the corner.

The reaper of death invaded the room, hovering over the mat that offered up the once beautiful woman, then cowered in the dark corners, waiting to be called. Taylor's perseverance began to desert her, leaving behind an empty shell. Her hunger and thirst passed scarcely eased.

As much as her exhausted body would allow, Taylor sponged Josie and spooned drops of water through the parched lips. She used her shoe to pulverize the grain, drowning it in the foul water to soften. Taylor muttered to herself, trying to recite the chanting Mrs. Costello had repeated with her beads over the sick animals.

Josie babbled, shaken with chills then burning with fever, "Father... Please, forgive..." Her eyes too bright, her breathing labored. "... must save... child...."

Taylor attempted to soothe her. "You're safe. I'm here." If Momma died, Taylor might as well die, too. Scant tears formed grimy ringlets on her hands as she chaffed Josie's skin, her touch leaving smudges of caring. "I won't let you go."

Josie babbled on, "...true, ...true." The sun rose to greet a woman who knew neither darkness nor light, then set again before she knew of its visit.

Taylor sapped her own body, crooning to her mother for hours. Reassuring Josie, "I'm here, Momma. Feel my arms holding you?" She clutched her mother to her chest. Drab hair clumped into a lifeless, pale mat. "Momma!"

Josie heard a familiar voice. Someone called to her, a child. Hers? No, that had only been in a dream.

The following afternoon as Josie lay quiet, Taylor rummaged through a carpetbag slung against the wall. She scratched among the belongings and found a hoarded vial of rosewater. She touched drops of the precious liquid to her mother's crowed temples and neck. Taylor discovered a brush and carefully, strand by strand, removed the filthy tangles from Josie's broomstick hair.

A phantom seemed to inhabit Josie's body as she groped to remove the arms moving tenderly about her shoulders. "No, no... You mustn't...not to me...not like this..." Josie felt cool liquid trickle down her throat. Someone was begging her. "Don't leave me. I don't want to be alone. Don't go." Josie felt too tired, too weak, to heed the plea.

"I'm sorry I made you sick, Momma. Please, Momma, stay with me," Taylor cried. Ruddy splotches scarred the paleness of Josie's cheeks as Taylor's dry sobs swelled. The girl exhausted herself seeking forgiveness for an offense the dying woman couldn't comprehend.

~ * ~

Josie's fever climbed; she imagined herself back at Taylor Estates. She sniffed the air approvingly, roses. "Momma?" she called, then rubbed her arms where unseen bruises ached. Sleep of a trance separated the tiring bouts of hallucinations that plagued Josie, allowing no rest.

"Don't leave me. Stay." The voice that called to her demanded too much.

Josie's whimpers bloodied the air when she thrashed her body against the wall. Taylor squeezed herself between Momma and the logs. Using all her strength, she barely won the battle to protect Josie from breaking fragile bones. Her mother's skin peeled like the paint of an abandoned house.

A long week passed before Josie gained a semblance of consciousness. The ugliness of her nightmares stayed with her and rolled over into her reality. Vaguely aware someone held her, Josie pleaded. "Help me. Not safe."

Gentle arms rocked Josie like a baby, held her tightly against a beating heart. A voice bent close, a child said, "You're safe with me. I'll help you. I'll not let you go."

"Never, never go to Taylorsville. Murderers." Josie rose above death to give her warning.

"I understand, Momma, I do. I promise to never go there." Soft, tender lips kissed Josie's brow. "We'll go away together." Before Taylor could say more, Josie dropped into another troubled sleep.

Taylor cradled her mother, leaving her alone only to take care of personal necessities. She sipped rank water and gagged on fingertip bits of meal. For both women, their filthy clothes hung like rags, too luxurious for their shrunken flesh.

The meager water allowance provided barely enough for drinking, its metallic taste nauseating. For two days after the fever subsided, Josie's swollen belly racked with pain. The infested meal passed through her as she ate, adding to her peril. The drain on Josie's remaining energy rendered her almost lifeless. One evening Josie garbled, "Who...?" Sharp, bony fingers searched around seeking clues.

Taylor shook her limbs awake and scrambled to her mother's side. Her hands trembled as she caressed the peeling and furrowed face. "Momma, it's Taylor." She placed Josie's fluttering hands on her own face.

Josie's eyes showed no recognition while her plea continued. "Who is it?"

Taylor hugged and rocked Josie, stroked her hair and patted the clawlike fingers while she whispered courage. As Taylor's rhythmic sway continued, a new resilience filled Josie's question. "Taylor? Born for riches, you are my life."

Taylor sobbed quietly, "Rest, Momma. In the morning I'll make you pretty. We'll have tea." When Josie drifted into an untroubled sleep, Taylor crouched like stone, swallowing her silent hysteria. Later, she opened the door to the blaze of the sun and screamed. "Poppa, where are you? Why don't you come and get us?"

~ * ~

Josie sucked the spoon dry. Oats? Grits? Mush? She could not remember what they called the thick gruel. The few spoonfuls stuck to her ribs and gurgled like a fountain in her belly.

Josie looked up at incredible green eyes hovering above a beautiful smile. Together they had beaten the monsters of her nightmares, won another chance. "You were born for riches, but you gave me the wealth of love. You are my life." Josie vowed to take hold this time with both hands; this second life belonged solely to her daughter.

~ * ~

In Santa Fe, a fat envelope lay ignored in a box crudely inked General Delivery. PERSONAL and PRIVATE slanted in cramped letters above an address To: Josie Broderick. Headed by the crest of the St. Louis Workingman's Bank, the contents consisted of a letter and an authorization requesting a notarized signature and current address.

The store clerk acting as postmaster discovered another ivory envelope for Josie Broderick. Inside, a long handwritten letter sheltered a recent newspaper clip advertising a St. Louis embalming service, including an unkind photograph of Sidney Yettes.

Some time after the mandatory holding days expired, the clerk returned both envelopes stamped with bold letters—UNCLAIMED.

Twenty-six

"I am going to see the commander," Taylor announced with authority. "You need more food and water if you are to get stronger."

She was a handicap. Josie knew her fragile condition predicted more sorrow and burden for Taylor. "I will wait outside." She needed to see if her life was worth living. "I would like to feel the sun."

Two men guarding the dismal hut for the benefit of the inhabitants of Chouteau's Post kicked dust and pebbles toward the emerging prisoners and slashed the air with their guns and knives. Their fear of the pestilence had promoted them all to vigilantes. The first step Josie took outside the lean-to, the watch spread word that the "poxed" were about, before they fetched military reinforcement.

A soldier exercising his horse saw the hostile mob, and by using the barrel of his rifle, prodded Josie and Taylor past the cursing men and hissing women into the post commander's office. Without hearing them out, the Captain ordered the unwelcome civilians to decamp the fort immediately.

Taylor yelled, "We want our money, our livestock, our possessions. We must have rations to live."

"Go to your wagon, or I will turn you over to them." Dirt clods and rocks thudding against the wooden wall punctuated the shrieking and curses that had not lessened. "Your animals will follow." He nodded to a soldier who used the spread of a broom to sweep Taylor out. He denied Josie the chance to prove they were no longer unclean or to beg for mercy by shoving her toward the door, then wiping his hands on his dirty pants.

A squad escorted mother and daughter within stoning reach of children who ran alongside them. The attack wounded Josie's courage as deeply as the rocks cut and bruised her flesh.

Their wagon, deserted outside the fort walls, still held their belongings, only because thieves feared the contents foul. Josie felt grateful the grousers had not burned everything.

Taylor obviously needed weeks of rest, and Josie's less youthful body lacked the vigor to undertake any task above its own survival. Every soul within the walls of Chouteau's Post knew the journey ahead would probably kill the two miserable mortals, and yet they shouted and cursed with spirit, demanding the wretches flee or be burned.

Physically and emotionally savaged by their hard won battles, the two women labored alone to load the sparse provisions and hitch their oxen. Josie had no idea where to go, or how they would manage alone. The attack and labor of preparation had exhausted her too much to allow for worry.

Fortunately, Contessa and the foal had been well cared for by someone. The kindness came in anticipation of her death. Josie guessed the animals would have been auctioned or more probably, confiscated by the officers. In return for this good turn, however, the Captain kept Josie's gold to pay for stabling services and the meager provisions he had issued.

Just before she climbed onto the wagon, the officer tossed a few coins in the dirt, a goodly distance away from the fort's door. Not enough to buy back his soul. The stronghold appeared well sealed off by the time Josie's ragtag band departed.

She felt no hate when she looked back over her shoulder at the sturdy walls. Some soldier's wife's compassion had saved her and Taylor, creating another debt to repay one day. *I must push all fear from my mind, ration my energy, concentrate on surviving. Should I fail, who would care for Taylor?*

The miles stretched forever, longer and more desolate than she thought endurable. They progressed slowly in a series of stops and starts. Taylor rose alone at daybreak and broke camp, letting Josie sleep until needed. Their most arduous effort became the yoking of the oxen, the most rewarding, preparing tea, they felt sure had not been included by the Captain, to wash down the hardtack.

By early afternoons Taylor's strength gave way to her exhausted body, forcing her to give up on the day. They survived on jerky, skillet biscuits and the extravagance of chicory or blue dandelion tea.

Josie took no interest in the surroundings. She dozed on the wagon seat, the reins slipping through her fingers while the oxen followed whatever walked ahead of them. Taylor took advantage of Josie's good days, appreciative of the freedom to ride Contessa and lead the pony. Without priming, Taylor passed from child to caretaker.

The agony of the shifting and bumping of the wagon jerking and slamming her aching body drove Josie to despair. Though she no longer knew or felt her passions, she strove gallantly to master her apathy. Occasionally, her body exhausted, her mental preoccupation reverted to pleasanter times in her childhood.

She tatted yards of lace from unraveled trimmings or played the violin, which the Mayor and his wife had generously packed. She experienced cycles of disorientation with only brief spans of lucidity in between them. Days her sight followed the red head, seldom straying, nights her hands crept to the thin shoulders beside her before dashing away her tears.

They rode with strangers infrequently. The other travelers feared the "touched" woman and reed-like girl who rode the wind on the frisky yearling.

Children played hide and seek in prairie grasses tall enough to hide a goat on the afternoon when word reached them that the Apache leader Geronimo had surrendered. Not since Kit Carson defeated the Mescalero and Navajo Indians a few years earlier had such news been so welcome. The Brodericks joined the stragglers leaving the Oklahoma Territory, pushing toward Santa Fe.

Whenever Josie's energies succumbed, they stopped in isolated towns or way stations until another escort came along to continue their journey. Taylor healed quickly and made friends with the other women, but Josie kept to herself, hoarding her energy for the trail.

~ * ~

In Council Bluffs, Josie rested on a bench outside the general store. Taylor tucked a shawl around Josie's shoulders. "I promise to come right back, Momma!"

"Come here, child."

Taylor walked into her mother's extended arms. A flush reddened Taylor's cheeks when Josie plucked at the flannel shirt and denim pants. "Those Levi's again. Must you dress in pants like a boy?" Josie's hands moved hesitantly around the young girl's body.

"Momma, you know the riders don't resent my win so much if they think I'm a boy."

"You take care riding my Contessa." Josie warned, shaking a finger.

Hands floating with the grace of feathers froze in midair as bewilderment stole the brightness from Josie's eyes. A puzzled frown shadowed her brow, and Josie dropped her arms. "Run along."

Taylor sauntered away, her lanky legs taking long, drawn-out steps, imitating a boy growing into manhood. Taylor failed to understand what confused Momma. She had explained if the townies discovered a girl rode Contessa, they would most probably take back the wagers, steal her horse and beat her with a stick. The winnings paid their way; without that, they had nothing.

~ * ~

The aroma of sweet apple and cinnamon woke Josie. She had no idea how long she had dozed. Taylor stood over her, a slice of pie in each hand. The child always washed up and changed after wiping down Contessa and assuring herself of the disinterest of the other riders, but today she wore a new dress of green and blue print.

"My clothes didn't fit. I bulged out in the front, and the skirt stopped at my knees. I took the winnings and bought this."

Josie vacillated between laughing and crying. Apple round breasts balanced her daughter's thin chest, and her legs had doubled in length. Taylor would turn eleven in the spring, hardly grownup, but not the child of Costello House. The way had been long, too vile, and too confusing for a girl who would become a lady. Miners, soldiers, and 'worker bees,' Josie forgot where she heard that term, thrived on such adventure, but this life was not for women of consequence. This hardship must end soon.

Green fields and clear lakes gave way to red clay. Taylor labored endlessly, doing both their shares of chores alongside the older women. The camps seldom lit fires, but when necessary, they cleared huge pits, draped damp clothes alongside and above the flames to keep the embers from drifting.

The danger Taylor had so wrongly addressed in Missouri at the onset of their flight was justified here. An unconfined fire brought sure death.

When the trail left the grasslands, the red clay changed to a barren beige landscape. Loamy, dry, pebbly soil, too solid to be sand but too fine to form clumps, stretched before them, seemingly forever. They entered and left behind the open land of the hostiles without incident.

The small bands of Indians who approached the wagon train came to trade or beg. Their physical appearance was more miserable than frightening. Few young men rode among the groups, and Josie felt a kinship when she looked into the vacant eyes of the desperate women and children. Josie admired the beauty and softness of the hides.

Taylor admitted, "One day I might be convinced to wear such trappings."

"Absolutely not," Josie said. Her tolerance only stretched so far.

With Josie's need to make camp early in the day and frequent urgency to linger for days at a time to recuperate, two months passed before the bluffs of the Mexican Territory towered on the horizon. Similar in height to the Missouri granite, Josie preferred this brilliant red, stark whites, gold, and blues. The rushing rivers which brought peace and energy twisted through mammoth columns, gouging deep, narrow passageways where only the scouts knew the hidden entrances into the canyons.

Along the way, Josie traded the oxen and a hand mirror for two mules, a sack of flour, four eggs and a half tin of tea. A fortunate decision that enabled them to avoid crashing down the bluffs like many of their traveling companions.

With perfect weather and level trails they covered twelve miles a day crossing the Mexican Territory, occasionally fifteen downhill.

More often, with the need of climbing buttes and fording rivers, they made nearer four miles. At rare times it took the entire day to move three wagons up and across a bluff.

For Taylor's safety, Josie preferred to travel with a merchant's train, stopping in a town until she gained her strength, then joining another group. The queues no longer numbered four hundred or more wagons strung across land; now they averaged less than twenty. Danger lay in the reduced numbers.

Taylor entered Santa Fe riding Contessa while Josie drove the mules. A natty looking man addressed them. "Looks like you're a mite too late." He nodded in the direction of the scores of tents slanting precariously on a hillside. A long line of filthy men waited for food to be ladled into their tin pans. Scuffles erupted where the more brave broke into line and encountered querulous opposition. Other than the pushing and shoving, no one talked. The men concentrated on their growling stomachs, indifferent toward the new arrivals.

Taylor scanned the tents where colorful female occupants leaned out open flaps. "I don't see anywhere for us to stay."

"There's some tents beyond." A scruffy man's eyes raked Josie. "Kinda scrawny, but you might pick up some work if you have a mind to." He nodded toward the dingy windows of the saloon.

Taylor slapped the reins. She hoped if they had to share a tent, the strangers wouldn't poke too much into who they were and where they were going. She didn't have the answers.

The miners worked long tiring hours, drank at sundown and rose at break of day, everyday. As soon as they made any kind of strike, they played it out then left for California. Everyday new blood arrived to be sacrificed. No one was interested in surveying. A pile of rocks and some sticks marked their boundaries; an "X" bought their rights. Jacob would not have found reason to stay here.

After spending several unproductive days in Santa Fe, Taylor hired on with a trail broker who was pressing on toward Albuquerque then onto Socorro along the San Pedro, wanting to reach Fort Thorn and pass through the mountains before winter, and before Geronimo's renegades broke out again.

They spent the summer moving deeper into the Mexican Territory. Taylor washed their clothes in icy streams that flowed down from the mountains, and they shared the drover's meals. She learned to cook, overlook nastiness in men who preferred to be alone, and rely only on Momma and herself. Their personal purchases were functional and infrequent. The two greenhorns stuck with the chuck wagon and avoided socializing.

One afternoon Taylor brooded as she had a tendency to do of late. The men had finished eating and she washed while Momma dried. "Why wasn't I born looking like you, Momma? Tiny, fair, like an angel? I despise my red hair and freckles. And my green eyes, changing color to give away my feelings. I can find nothing to admire about myself."

The barrage took Josie by surprise. Taylor had expressed absolutely no interest in her appearance. Her sudden displeasure gave Josie reason to ask, "Has someone expressed a dislike for the way you look?"

"No. It's just that when we reach California, Poppa would like me much better if I looked more like you."

Taylor's wistfulness tugged at Josie's heart. She had no idea her daughter was still concerned over Jacob's reception, nor that she thought so frequently of him. Josie worried what would happen when Taylor found out the truth.

The two women continued their sporadic travels for much of that year, stopping in towns to race, buy provisions and catch up on the trail gossip. They passed through Albuquerque, San Miguel, Socorro, headed toward Fort Craig or Fort Thorn. The landscape was deceptive. Headlands and bluffs that appeared within reach on the horizon lay days away. Ripples of heat rose, creating mirages of rainfall. The land schooners wedged themselves through the scrubby nettle covered rocky mountains only to face miles of scorching, arid wasteland. They followed the San Pedro River increasing their danger of wild animals and Apache, making their priority the nearness of water.

Twenty-seven

Fall, 1890
Mexican Territory

Josie rambled into Bisbee, Arizona, the southern most tip of the Mexican Territory, as drooped and limp as the six-foot whip towering over her on the wagon's seat. Contessa followed on a long lead rope. Alongside, trusting her animal's instincts, Taylor rode bareback astride Tessa, the three-year-old filly. The four unhurried mules picked their way down the narrow path of the rocky slope then ambled down the main street.

A discreet sign beside the door of a three-story clapboard house advertised Hilltop Hotel. Sick at heart, her spirit too broken to continue, Josie entered the building, stepped up to the desk and waited. A harried woman rotating between diners and kitchen rushed over shortly, apologizing. "We have so many new people arriving in Bisbee, my husband and I are finding it difficult to keep up with our tasks."

Josie experienced a surge of interest. "For over eight years, I managed the chambermaids, kept books, and purchased supplies for an "ordinary" house of note." The looks of the plain, clean woman and the High German Yiddish that salted the woman's polite comments encouraged Josie. "My daughter who has matured significantly since then managed to do a significant array of tasks. Perhaps, after we settle in, you might have positions we could fill to help." Josie penned in a signature. "Please, if we might engage a single, for Mrs. Broderick and daughter."

If, after two plus years, Sidney's murder still invited investigation, Josie just handed the law a prized lead. She saw no other choice. Her cowardly flight from St. Louis had almost led to her death and, with all the furtive skulking about, had encouraged an increasingly rowdy and mischievous Taylor to embrace chicanery. Josie's carpetbag swished softly up the stairs, she hadn't the energy to pick it up and carry it.

The third floor room was tiny but clean, with one narrow bed, a two-drawer side table and five metal hooks. Knee-high above the creaky floor a strip of pale yellow smiled across the rough sanded walls, but elsewhere the clay-laden air had spread an orange glower that turned the room gray.

Taylor quickly volunteered, "Momma, I'll sleep on the floor." The ten-year-old stood a head taller than her mother, her long legs restless at night, her eagerness to be about before daybreak wearing.

Josie, too exhausted to disagree, stood at the window, enjoying a filtered sun that brought warmth to her aching body. Outside a jagged mountain confronted her with its solid impenetrable face, barring escape. A single road rose and fell in a snakelike ribbon that disappeared behind a boulder. Sadly, the landscape pitted its bleakness against her memory of a sassy young girl dressed in blue sauntering across a lush lawn to welcome a handsome engineer.

The carpetbag thudded when it slipped from her fingers and dropped to the floor, a match to the sinking of Josie's heart. Life had come to this, sharing a sleeping room with her offspring in an obscure mining town. She had lost her family, a fortune, the man she loved and almost her life to keep this child no one else wanted. A single tear rested in the corner of Josie's eye; she would never again question her choice.

While Josie rested, Taylor explored the house. She returned spouting news before she fully entered the door. "Six rooms on this floor. One water closet, three doors away. Cold bath five cents for second water, hot bath with new water costs a quarter. I don't mind cold, do you, Momma? One cook and one maid for the whole house.

Do you think I could get work, Momma? Mandy always could wash and dry faster, but I won making a good bed."

Josie listened. She hadn't the cheek to argue in favor of faithfulness to a lady's upbringing. "Keep out of the rooms whenever they're occupied. It's not safe for a pretty girl."

Taylor half smiled. "That's the second time someone's called me pretty. Is it true, Momma? Am I pretty?"

Josie heard the question, her heart so full of her own misgivings she did not answer. She had given up everything she ever valued, everything of significance in her life to save her unborn. But what she had lost amounted to water through a sieve, nothing compared to the love she held for Taylor. Their life had been a constant struggle, so far removed from the luxury she had envisioned. She wanted more for her daughter.

Preoccupied by her thoughts, Josie was slow to grasp the question put to her. *Taylor believed her appearance displeasing?* Josie studied the lightly freckled face and startling honest eyes, thick russet hair and lithe body. She had no words for her daughter. One day soon Taylor would be beautiful, in a manner much different from her mother, but more sensuous than would be safe.

"I'm going to go see Mrs. Wentworth about hiring me."

Before Josie could tell her daughter the truth the girl sought, Taylor, clearly disappointed, closed the door behind her.

The raw mining town squeezed into a narrow canyon that belched sulfur, stewed under a blazing sun year round, funneled ferocious winds with orange tinted snow in the winter and drowned under monsoons in the summer. The weather changes arrived quick and extreme.

Anything dropped into rivulets turned muddy with copper, tools were rendered unusable, clothes orange and irritating. Sacks of potable water came by burro from Mexico; a day's wages bought one bag. Within hiking distance on the far side of the ridge, along the San Pedro River, Mexicans planted corn, tomatoes and beans, and worshiped the green streaked mountain.

Within days Josie hated it all. The vacant-eyed miners, the gruff cowboys, the sulfur smell, the sitting. The days began too brightly, dispatching hot rays that brought no kindness, tormenting her with a blazing sun buffeted by winter winds.

Nights turned cold, often creeping below freezing, blasting draughts of frigid air as the sun set. The weather confused her. She tried to guess the time of day by the warm patches on the bed, testing where the shadows lay. But the sun burst upon her quickly and set in a blink, skewing her timetable, and the light shifted every few weeks as the seasons merged.

Distressing as conditions were, within weeks, saved from the constant bumping and bruising of the wagon and the Spartan diet, Josie's strength returned. Her daze cleared, lifting her out of what had been a mental near-sighted blur. People grew edges, ledgers took life, the weather became almost predictable, and Josie began to hope again.

Taylor bopped in and out of the room constantly, forcing Josie to take walks, along the way introducing her mother to every person, business, building and shanty. On days when Josie could not tolerate the light, her head throbbing and the room spinning like dandelion down, Taylor described the goings on through her own eyes, painting a glorious drama of the town.

In spite of her melancholia, Josie observed what her daughter carefully passed over. The dust of a land that spurned roses itched her skin. Rocks turned a lady's ankle in a street men believed mighty fine. The few people who bathed on Saturdays smelled of castile soap; most bathed not at all. The missing attention of whitewash on clapboard and fences introduced the town's poverty. Josie learned the songs and curses of another language through her bedroom window, from the shouts of drivers parading mules carrying water and wood from Mexico. The tongue so near the lovely French she missed, its masquerade sometimes drove her deeper toward the black void of her melancholy.

It astonished Josie what others repeated in her presence, as if her feebleness rendered her deaf and dumb. She listened to the shuffling feet of tired men, anger in voices, heard the silent absence of women, fingered tables without lace, ate meals of goat meat and turnips, endured manners that did not allow for the scraping of a chair when a lady entered the room, the unapologetic splat of a spittoon missed, all signs of a raw, wild life. Her daughter lied in innocence.

Amazingly Josie flourished in the dark serenity after sunset. She thrived on the spatter of applause from below when she stood at her window drawing the bow across her violin, sharing a common appreciation with listeners starved for more than harmonica and tin can music. Her healing mind worried over another view, however, a girl-woman whose size and features proved evidence of her parentage.

Taylor had grown into a lovely young woman, awkward with the newness of legs that stretched too far and arms that reached their target too soon, but one who could quite capably manage a life on her own if she chose. Josie remembered the snatches of Taylor's love and despair that had forced its way through her dying and pulled her back from death.

A private battle began to consume Josie, to bind her daughter to her side and hold onto her. She fought the melancholy of the isolating fog, the naked fear that consumed her hand-in-hand with the punishing, merciless shadows, and the torment of disconnected memories that threatened to steal all this from her. She recalled the crippling of her mother's isolation and forced herself to stroll around Bisbee, greeting passersby. Each day began brighter, each stroll easier.

One evening as they sat on the windowsill counting the chalky stars, love and well being filled Josie so she could no longer keep silent. Turning toward Taylor, Josie tempted the gods. "Do you know how much I love you?" Josie stroked Taylor's coppery hair. "You are what I live for."

Taylor appeared stunned. A look of confusion, then fear, swept across her face, making a kaleidoscope of her eyes. "Momma, you've never talked like this. Are you feeling worse?"

Sorrow filled Josie's heart that her child would think her ill to speak about feeling such pleasure. "No, Pumpkin." Josie's voice dipped and danced. "I feel myself again." She opened her arms wide to the bewildered girl and hugged her long and hard. "I must hurry. There is much to do before you become a woman."

Taylor made a hesitant giggle. "A woman of consequence, you mean."

"You will be that woman, I promise," Josie replied. "But by our own efforts, using our God-given strengths and wits." Tears tinged Josie's lashes, she dashed them away, too full of joy to tolerate the oft-repeated symptom of her melancholia.

"Momma, are you sure you feel well?" Hope spun a hush around each word.

Josie shook as if freeing herself of shackles. "Such a dreary struggle for you to have to endure, and all alone. I am sorry I took so long." Josie hugged Taylor again, kissing the top of her head, her cheeks, and the long fingers that had cared for her so lovingly. She held the tall precious bundle tightly to her, even after they both fell asleep, content in the comforting nearness of one who loved without judgment.

The dreams that came to Josie were of reward, mountains climbed and peaks reached, roaring rivers crossed with ease, a mother and child whose days and nights filled with happiness.

Some days the despondency threatened to kill Josie's high spirit, demanded she let go, forget her aims, and ignore her yearnings. She willed the despair away. She knew it would come again, so she prepared well. She had given up too much time already, lived alone in her body, and battled the demons that had cursed her soul. No more. She had earned the right to live and prepare the way for her child.

Josie's enthusiasm impressed Mrs. Wentworth. Within days the clerking job in the general store that had been deemed unnecessary suddenly needed filling. Josie undertook the position with spirit and dedication.

After two weeks, proposing the Arizona Quarterly and New York Times be used as an incentive to draw customers, Josie wangled a subscription for the store. She read and digested the financial reports, soliciting comment from the customers, opening their minds to acceptance of her opinions. She courted the more affluent businessmen.

Josie learned that during her illness Congress forfeited hundreds of thousands of acres of undeveloped lands for the continuing development of the railroad system, with distribution under the purview of National Land Company. One of many public acts, she discovered, that benefited the financial giant.

Within a few weeks, her body began to respond with vigor to the labor of stocking and general busy work of the store. She paid attention to the natives' insights, listened for the chirp of crickets and tested the air for the rain that was sure to come.

Soon Mrs. Wentworth became dependent on Josie to process all the purchases, catalogue inventory and eventually to barter with the Indians and traders. The challenges fed Josie's hungry mind.

Within two months, Josie took total responsibility of the books, handled all suppliers, dispatched every piece of correspondence, and in her idle time of evenings and Sundays, acquired two accounting registers of her own. By spring the population of Bisbee had increased five-fold, and the Broderick Accounting firm was solidly established.

Josie subscribed to professional publications, began catching up on the holdings of Worldwide Bank and the published policy changes of land commitments of the government that had occurred in the last ten years.

She enjoyed the prosperity a few weeks before she broached a ticklish proposition to her daughter. "Taylor, your agreement with Mrs. Wentworth frees a monthly charge of $10 for room and a weekly payment of $2 for each of us for board."

At her daughter's puzzled expression, Josie smiled. "We are going to start tithing for ourselves, to secure your future. My monthly pay with the new accounts amounts to $50, less ten percent, still leaves us with more than enough to cover normal expenses."

"Momma, what about the tips Mrs. Wentworth allows me to keep. You can add that to the balance."

"Pumpkin, you are spurting up like a wild weed. Keep that for yourself. Besides, I want to enroll you in a correspondence program through the university." She studied her observant daughter. "Perhaps twenty dollars. Yes, that would be ample to invest."

Traitorous to the scattered silver mines and local copper holdings in the four square miles of Mule Gulch, Josie purchased a ten dollar gold certificate weekly through a Tucson bank.

Her education far beyond the local school teacher's abilities, Taylor contentedly studied university in the kitchen of Hilltop, mimicking her mother's success, serving as kitchen supervisor and graduating to responsibility for the hotel's records. The two often shared similar problems. Mother and daughter grew closer than ever before.

September, 1891, Congress opened 900,000 acres to white settlers, disbursement by National Land Company and financing to be underwritten by Worldwide Bank. In October, the powerful Foresters Association set aside forestlands for Yellowstone National Park. Another million adjoining acres were set aside to be leased to private preservationist if need be. National Land Company acted as custodian.

Adhering to her customary weekly gold certificate purchases, Josie added another weekly ten dollars for a broker to purchase her first shares of National Land Company. She and Taylor could not live on twenty dollars a month despite their free room and board. Josie set about soliciting for her skills. In spite of the hours she spent helping at the general store, expanding her own business and her constant preoccupation with national finances, Josie remained tied closely to her daughter, dependent on her company. That fall their relationship changed.

"Taylor, you seem busy and preoccupied of late. Anything troubling you?" Josie inquired at breakfast. "You are gone so much."

"I met a girl," Taylor answered excitedly, "from Virginia. Her name is Catherine. They call her Cat. Oh, Momma, she's the dearest of friends. Not since I lost Mandy have I found anyone so treasured. She has seven brothers. Her two older brothers Abel and Baxter tag along with us, our protectors so they boast. They're rowdy, but they mean no harm. Her Momma is expecting again this winter. Cat so wants a little sister."

Josie dwelt on the news. She and Taylor had shared as much as many adults; she had neglected the fact Taylor was still a youngster. "I'll arrange a tea, bring your new companions."

"Momma, not for tea," Taylor giggled. "In the evening, after their chores, for coffee and cake." She didn't push for a time.

"Tonight," Josie suggested. "I'm anxious to meet these friends that lighten your spirit." *What a blessing,* she thought, *for my daughter to have found youngsters to enjoy.*

Taylor met her friends on the porch and led them in. Josie sat at the head of the empty dining table. The 'Virginnies' arrived freshly washed, towheads with pale blue eyes, looking like a set of triplets. Abel removed his hat, then kicked Baxter, pushing him to do the same. Cat attempted a little dip of courtesy. Josie knew they displayed their best company manners.

Baxter's prattle quickly outdistanced his siblings. His targeted adventures teeming with ingenious schemes. "Goin' load up the cast-offs. Take me a week or two, then back here to sell. Make a right smart dollar I reckon."

"Cast-offs?" Josie inquired; she doubted it meant more children.

"The goods dropped along the trail, too heavy for the teams to carry. On the mountains, scattered across the desert. Seen some fine cabinets, smithy tools, a stove, pretty boxes."

"I will make you a bargain," Josie volunteered. "Everything you find bring to me first. I will give you top dollar or find you a buyer." She liked the boy's undaunted ambition. Abel hung back, his aspirations hidden.

"And, Catherine, what is it you wish to do?" The girl was pretty, in the used up manner of hill people, older and tired before she had begun a life of her own.

"I wish Ma to make this birthin' in good time. That's all."

Josie caught the understated bitterness, the sharp-edged fear from lack of hope. "I am sure she will come through just fine. We have a wonderful doctor here. Knows modern ways."

"Cain't pay no doctor."

Baxter spoke up. "I'll fetch 'nuff ta git barrels of cash. We'll hire us a doc."

"Ya' cain't go 'til spring. Babe's due sooner."

The little party had taken a sorry turn. "Tell me about your trip here," Josie suggested. "About your home in Virginia."

"Ain't nothin' to tell," Baxter volunteered. "Made it this far. In V'ginny Pa worked the mines. Lungs give out. They let him go. Just bad luck all round."

Baxter's attitude surprised Josie. No anger, acceptance of their bad times, but a strong determination not to let bad luck hamper him, too. A shame his background offered nothing for Taylor; he showed admirable qualities.

Josie had seen what she needed. Too many guests stirred about for her to be concerned about the unsupervised group. "If you would excuse me, I have an early morning. Enjoy your refreshments. Please, feel free to visit as often as you please."

"Ma'am, we come regular-like. Set in the hotel kitchen so as not to spoil the fanciness. You might want to tell us to stay away." The voice was acidic, a dare from Abel.

Josie ignored his bid to be less than well mannered, his envy that leapt out, quite pronounced. She heard promise. He had let her know he was aware of his lack of standing. A young man to be watched.

~ * ~

That winter the gold, silver and copper mines sunk deeper. The blasting powder shook the slat houses as if dragons bellowed beneath the rock. Copper came into its own. Demands grew with the need of wiring for electricity and telephones. The mine whistles blasted night and day. A steady stream of men marched by with red-rimmed eyes and yellow tinted skin. Their bellies ached from the poison, and when they could no longer work, another man stepped up to fill their place. Bisbee grew tenfold.

Shopkeepers and tradesmen came and stayed. Sheds on stilts like invading centipedes crawled up the canyon walls. In the spring, one year after her arrival, the Mayor and his supporters called upon Mrs. Broderick behind the store in a tiny converted storage room she used as her office. Josie pulled up a stool and a bench for the men, she kept the comfortable chair.

"The businessmen of Bisbee have decided to invest in our own bank. We've watched you. We all utilized your accounting abilities in some manner, and although it's quite unique to contract a person of the female persuasion, we would like to consider you to head our bank."

Josie sat silently while the men each nodded their assent to the others. Josie had recently added an assay office to her list of endeavors, buying and selling small bits of precious metals, writing land contracts, acting as an advisor for profits and investments. Her reputation was solid.

"We are inquiring as to your practical background. You exhibit a solid knowledge of economics and the eastern markets."

Josie steadied herself, determined to remain composed. "I am of a banking family. My father provided me with a creditable education, including introducing me to the procedures of his bank and including me in the introduction of their cartel. However, they do not allow women to hold positions of responsibility, so, had it not been for the untimely passing of Mr. Broderick and the welcome of Bisbee, I would now be forming a group commensurate with your intentions, only in California."

Without consulting the others, the owner of Monroe's Mine spoke up. "We would like you to accept a partnership, with a generous salary. We need your skill and ambition to manage our treasury, but we insist on your carrying out an initial demand, a difficult and tricky position. You must approach one of our major celebrities, a Colonel Tuffet, and convince him to join our endeavor. We need a substantial investment on his part to set up the bank and later on might have need of his political savvy."

Josie fought the urge to hug the mine owner, pinch his cheeks, and dance around the room. Whatever Colonel Tuffet, whoever he was, threw at her she could handle, he would never keep her from fulfilling her dream. When she left the cubbyhole, she glided down the street, her feet seemingly never touching the ground.

At Hilltop House Josie's 'hello' in the kitchen went unanswered. She rushed up three flights of stairs, her calls for Taylor brusque, demanding attention. The surprised child averted their near collision at the door of their room.

"Taylor, the Mayor and his committee have asked me to help them charter a bank, to serve as its head. Something I have wanted all my life, never thought possible." Josie stopped long enough to laugh, a robust and guttural noise, carrying from her knees to the crown of her platinum head. "I will be the President." She uttered the title with a capital 'P' and pride.

"What a coup. An enormous responsibility, with a huge increase in income, and status. My responsibility will demand I work day thru evening though. The job must be done perfectly; we will set precedent for women." Flyers supporting women's suffrage often ate up the few pennies Josie indulged on herself. She spun up and down the tight aisle beside the bed, a hum of satisfaction accompanying her dance.

"Our name will be linked with the financial wizards of the West. Respectability. You, my darling, when you come of age, will have your choice of the wealthy and prestigious families of the territory."

"Are we so poor?" Taylor's face waxed between joy and confusion. "What of Poppa?" Taylor indulged her mother's cavorting, but her question demanded answer. "We cannot give up our hunt. I must find my father."

"One does not become a woman of consequence on a clerk's wages or the tips of a housekeeper. We have the opportunity to join the elite, to prosper with the emerging statehood of Arizona, to be listed on the social registry." Josie's words trilled with the joy of a songbird.

"Do you suppose Poppa reads the social registry?" Taylor asked, her enthusiasm decidedly cool.

"Celebrate with me. This is a golden opportunity. We have reached the end of our search."

"And what of Jacob? What about finding my father, showing him how 'comely and bright, what a lady' his daughter became?"

"Ten years now without a word. A mining accident, disease, we know its destruction, something stopped him from returning to us. He has to be dead. We will go from this point on looking forward to your future. Our first step is to stay here. I will accept this position and build a foundation that cannot be dislodged—whatever news anyone may receive."

Twenty-eight

High freight costs, striking miner's protesting wage cuts of fifteen percent, and low silver prices closed many of the principal silver mines. In Idaho, federal authorities arrested dozens of strikers, caging them in newly termed "bull pens". The 1890 Silver Purchase Act had inflated the price of silver such that sixty cents of silver could purchase a dollar of gold.

Anticipating the government's abandonment of silver coinage and switch to a gold standard, the resulting shortage of the glistening yellow metal had created a bonanza for gold miners. The market crashed. Within days of Josie finalizing her contract, pending the Colonel's membership, six hundred banks closed and seventy-four local railroads went out of business. Throughout the western territories, the threatened repeal bred chaos amid a fear of bankruptcy for other miners. This dread reared a head only slightly less frightening than another more real horror—the rapid unstoppable spread of an imported strain of cholera. In those few weeks, Bisbee escaped both.

The winter sun flashed spots of dazzling light through leafless ash and a low-limbed magnificent mesquite when Josie arrived at Colonel Tuffet's place about midday. The meeting had been scheduled for an earlier hour, but the ride took much longer than Josie anticipated, the buggy barely maneuverable on the narrow unmarked trail. Josie worried, upset she had miscalculated so badly, a grievous error in the mountains. If she remained any length of time, darkness would make it too dangerous for her to return to town.

This had to be his ranch. Miles back, before the rock crests surrounded her, an arch of ornate ironwork spanned the road. Human sized initials 'CT' set in the head of a giant hatchet swung from the peak. Thick green vines of bougainvillea wrapped their flower-covered limbs around the posts, the gnarled roots protruding several feet away at the edge of a dry wash.

These same brilliant red and pink blooms crawled up tall, thick adobe walls that hid the home of Colonel Chess Tuffet, a self-made man whose holdings remained a mystery, but whose arm had far reaching effects. Josie expected the Colonel to live in a house of splendid proportion, imported gingerbread, on a hill where his wealth could be exhibited from miles away. She felt gravely disappointed.

This hacienda was domestic, simple, blending in with its natural surroundings. There had been no talk that he was miserly. Perhaps, she excused, his commonness came from the lack of a woman with appreciable taste. She had heard somewhere that he lived alone, a widower, maybe an eccentric hermit. She began to doubt the wisdom of having come alone.

Near the iron gate a leather cord twisted around a bracket dangling a huge bell, the imprinted insignia rusted. She unwrapped the thick strip of hide and gave three good yanks. The gong echoed repeatedly through the basin, bouncing front to back off the protective rocky ledges, the hollow bong carrying further out into the wilderness.

Before the vibrations died, the gate squeaked open. A young man jabbered at her in Spanish, his tongue too quick for her to translate. He gave a hefty pull on the cord. One gong bellowed low and long, after which he clamped his hands across the clapper, silencing the sound.

Without an encouraging word he grabbed Contessa's lead and started through the gate. His muttering carried over his shoulder as he walked away. When Josie didn't follow, he motioned for her to come.

Inside the walls, the cool, damp air delighted Josie, easing away the heat that clung to her. Stones had been laid in ornate patterns across a huge courtyard carefully pruned of weeds. Red bottlebrush, purple verbena, yellow daises, cactus and plants of unfamiliar varieties cascaded from vases of all sizes and shapes. The mix of perfumes was heady. The feathery swish of the fern like leaves of a Palo Verde tree were mesmerizing. The enclosure served as an oasis. Josie responded quickly. She drank the pleasure offered and held onto it all.

Crystal clear windows of remarkable size looked out onto the courtyard, their rainbow rippled glass making an unbroken wall of voyeurism. *Inside must be like living out of doors,* she thought, *with the added enchantment of peering through prisms of shimmering color.* She did not see the door open. A man stood in the shadow of the latched overhang, patiently waiting.

"Good day, Colonel Tuffet. I apologize for arriving late. I am J. L. Broderick. My directions failed to account for a division of the road just past the San Pedro crossing. I mistakenly chose the one well traveled. Seems your side of the fork benefits from more exclusivity."

He stood alone, his hand braced on a fine finished oak doorframe. He was casual, but his voice showed his embarrassment. "I am the one to apologize. When Mr. Wentworth mentioned a banker named Broderick, I mistook you for someone else. Had I known, I would have set aside time to meet with you in town. Be assured, I will escort you back myself."

Josie heard the suggestion under his words. "Well, I am the banker, here to talk of establishing a depository for Bisbee. Your interest is encouraging, because as you know, the town counsel selected me to call on you for your support."

"I am afraid I may take some convincing." When he stepped into the sunlight, an engaging glint in his eye accompanied his teasing response. "Yes, seems to me I'm a far sight away from aiding any effort to start a local bank. Perhaps several meetings before I begin to consider it."

Boulder sized shoulders filled the doorway. His hands splayed thick as a beef roast. At the crown of his scalp a strip devoid of any hair and wide as a belt circled halfway around his head. An inch wide scar stretched a permanent smile up to his ear. He studied her as she took in his appearance without wincing, a mysterious haunting claiming the energy around him.

Admiration took root in the core of his eyes; except for that small encouragement, his welcome remained formal. Josie quickly recognized another wounded soul and claimed acceptance. She knew a glimmer of appreciation flickered behind her eyes. She had carefully noted in spite of his exaggerated western jargon, his words of more than one syllable. "Your courtyard goes beyond imagination. It is beautiful. *Enchante!*" She had not meant to be pretentious.

"*Et tu est tres chic ma jeunne fila. Entrez vous, s'il vous plais?*" *And you are very attractive young lady. Come in, please?*

Her hat barely reached the middle of his chest as she passed, but when she looked up she saw his pleasure that she had understood. So, he thought her young and beautiful. His compliment reached way down and touched a tender spot, melting any resistance she might have had.

After jalapeno tortillas and tomato cheese cooled by a sweet mango punch, they talked of possibilities, listing names, advancing figures, always coming back to his indecision to commit. Both became so engrossed in their agreements and disagreements neither realized the passage of time. The Colonel studied the violet sky. "It is much too late for you to return, the trail presents too much danger. The remaining light will disappear within minutes. You must stay the night. I will arrange to accompany you back in the morning."

Josie sensed capture, a firefly in a jar, her happy glow quickly faded. "I cannot do that. My reputation would suffer, possibly undergo irreparable harm. I must return." She panicked, backed into a corner, her exits barred. She rose clumsily. "I must leave."

"Return if you must, but your journey will take place without me. Facing bobcats, mountain lions, thieves, and hostiles. I value my life too dearly to serve as their next meal or entertainment." His eyes narrowed. He rose, but carefully kept a comfortable distance from Josie. "Stay, I will have my housekeeper remain in the house to protect your virtue. You may choose whichever guestroom you like. No one here will bother you."

Another time, another guestroom haunted her. Josie battled her mounting terror. Weak-kneed, her body trembled. She knew the wildness of this land. Why had she panicked at his kindness?

Josie walked toward the door, aware of the ferns and stones tinted pink by the fading light streaking through glass. Josie closed her eyes, telling herself she could not spend the rest of her life living in another time, allowing François's malice to control her.

The Colonel was right, of course. She would have difficulty finding her way back to Bisbee in the daylight, and assuredly could not find it in the dark. "My apologies, I certainly had no intention of intruding further on your hospitality."

"It has been a long time since I entertained such a charming guest. Your stay will be my pleasure." He came a step closer.

Josie cringed, threatened by his nearness and confidence.

Chess frowned. "I feel as if I have caged a wild doe. One which has been badly treated."

The scar arched up to his ear; understanding warmed his eyes. "Please, feel free to safely move about as you wish. Ask for whatever pleases you, and warn me of whatever does not." He stepped outside the room, long enough for her to collect herself before he returned.

When they finally emerged from his office, the dining table had been set for two. Crystal, lace tablecloth, china and candles. Steam drifted from a silver teapot on a nearby serving tray. A brightly knit cozy lay alongside, forgetting its duty.

The colonel indicated a chair for Josie, then moved to a couch further away. "Tea, first. We can rest and wash, then enjoy a late meal without talk of banks and boards. I want us to become better acquainted."

Late that night Josie marveled at how relaxed she felt and yet how stimulated. They had talked for hours of the territory, possible statehood, the desperation of the Welsh miners, even foreign affairs. Her head barely touched the pillow when she realized he had revealed a great deal of his opinions, but nothing of his past. Nor had she.

Twenty-nine

Bisbee, Arizona
Spring, 1892

    Fog created an illusion of a bridal veil hiding the mysterious face of the mountains by the time Josie left work. Grateful Taylor enjoyed that free time with the Picketts, Josie looked forward to listening to Taylor's giggling yarns describing the eight children's antics.
    "Cat fixed white bean, greens, and onion soup tonight," Taylor explained. "She's so thrifty and inventive. Then I read lessons with the younger boys and recited numbers. Their arithmetic skills are almost up to level with their classes. While Cat, Abel, and Baxter finished their chores nearby, I caught Baxter sputtering while tackling the gist of the lesson. I'm happy you invited them for lunch on Sunday."
    This particular Sunday afternoon the older 'Virginians' were free to share a meal at the hotel, a rare occasion considering how all the partakers waded belly high in newly acquired responsibilities. Josie hoped she hadn't opened a can of worms. Between bites, Abel and Baxter ribbed Taylor and Cat about their approaching thirteenth birthdays. The girls suffered through teasing about their remaining old maids, unspoken for at such an advanced age, past the arrival of menses, an unheard of occurrence in Virginia. They returned equal torment despairing the boys' ability to find a sweetheart, until fresh

strawberries smothering sourdough biscuits arrived; then no one spoke until the forks and fingers emptied.

Baxter pushed his plate away, wiped so clean the swipes of biscuit that had sopped up the sweet cream were invisible. Abel cleared his throat. "Afore the Judge went on circuit this afternoon, he promoted me to clerk. Copying decrees, filing legal papers, and preserving records for court matters while he's gone. Promised me more law learning." The pride in Abel's announcement firmed his shoulders and added a sharp edge to his chin. Two days after their first formal visit to Hilltop House, Abel had persuaded the Judge to hire him. Josie had been right: the boy was to be watched.

A raucous voice boomed through the windows interrupting the other's reaction to Abel's news. They rushed out as one, cramming skirts, sharp elbows, and gangly legs through the narrow doorway. A woman, they supposed, although her bib overalls, flannel shirt, and cropped hair hid the evidence, stood on the bench of a wagon cracking a muleskinner's whip, her deep voice shouting a message. "Got me four chil'uns. Lost my husband four months back. Looking to hitch up with a man don't mind takin' orders." When she spied the unusually sober Mr. Pickett leaning against the saloon, she hollered and snapped the whip toward him. "You got nothin' better to do, I'll take you."

At the astonishment of the youngsters watching, Mr. Pickett grinned as broad as his face would allow and hollered right back. "Ya' got me! Now whatcha' goina' do wit' me." Josie could have fainted right there on the hotel steps.

Three weeks later, when the Judge returned, he married the pair in a riotous celebration that packed all the commotion of a freewheeling, stuporous, Virginia reel. Several hours into the revelry, Taylor and Abel wandered off to the side. Josie watched Abel slip his arm around Taylor's waist and guide her away. They stopped a short distance up the canyon wall, on a ledge of rock dividing a sturdy clump of daisies and blue lupine, and sat watching the dancers and celebrants below her. The two youngsters held hands, their heads close together, faces earnest.

Josie was not pleased.

The bonfire reduced to glowing embers, and the noise of people humming and exchanging noisy banter on their paths home died long before Taylor returned to the hotel. Josie quickly retired upstairs when she saw her daughter coming, then spoke from the shadows of the room. "I saw you leave with Abel. You stayed up on the ridge quite awhile before coming down. You looked upset, or anxious, when I left." Horrible thoughts had rushed through her head all evening. She and Taylor had never shared that all-important talk of men and their needs.

In the silence, Josie heard Taylor's slicking of lips. "Abel is a candidate for law school. He leaves for Chicago tomorrow. This whole year, while the rest of us were playing at life like children, the Judge instructed Abel in law. He recommended Abel to John Marshall Law School, in Chicago, and they accepted his application. If he passes the entrance exams, he will be a lawyer someday."

"Well, an opportunity of this significance should not be kept secret. He should have come down from the mountain, announced his good fortune to the whole party. We all want to congratulate him."

"Please, don't tell. He wants to wait to see if he's accepted." Her sharp intake of breath stalled her words. "Momma, Abel said he loves me. Wants me to wait for him. Promise not to marry anyone else while he's gone." Taylor's tongue caressed the lilting words, accompanied by an eager breathlessness.

"Marry? But, he has nothing to offer. A foggy future at best. The oldest of eight, notably with aspiration, but he has little chance of stepping outside his cast." The condemnation barely escaped her lips before Josie realized her mistake. "A law career shows admirable ambition, sounds promising, but this proposal must be measured against more valued possibilities. A circuit rider barely puts food on the table, and there is little else around here, unless he becomes a company man. A beginning attorney needs contacts, associates to help him buy into an established partnership in a prestigious firm. Where would he find such support?"

Taylor sniggered. "He plans to be governor of our new state of Arizona."

"Well, that is certainly aspiring, but that demands even stronger connections. Well-financed campaigns buy political seats, not good intentions. Officials who administer the territorial wealth owe their lucrative positions to well-heeled opportunists who donate enormous sums to guarantee elections. "A 'virginny', even with a law degree, is a most unlikely candidate. Even if he earns his letters, the competition from old-timers who have fortunes and know the skeletons in the closets will be fierce. Insurmountable in my opinion."

Josie realized a cold hardness edged her voice, the echo as shrewish as her mother's warnings of Jacob. "Plead with him that you are too young. Be firm, but pleasant. Hold onto his friendship, one never knows the turn of events in this untested country."

"It's okay." A kittenish purr hummed in the darkness. "I told him I couldn't think of marrying now. Besides, we might not be here when Abel finishes school. But I wanted you to know he asked, just the same."

Josie sank onto the pillow, relieved. She had not meant to be so hard on the poor fellow. He showed courage and good judgment, and he sought only to follow his heart. She could relate to his need to establish family, sink roots, having lived out such tragedy. However, Taylor required a husband of good background, one fleshed out with a pedigree and an already won fortune. Josie would tolerate nothing less.

Taylor's intake of breath broke the silence. "Anyway, we will probably be in California by then, with Poppa. Won't he be surprised how grownup I've become? Already asked for my hand?"

Taylor's expectant question shattered Josie's complacency. Josie rolled down her stockings, worked the buttons and hooks of her clothes silently in the dark, not wanting to encourage another discussion of Jacob and his whereabouts.

~ * ~

Every day except Sunday, Josie defended her figures and documents to headstrong, pious men in a spittoon pinging, smoke clouded room. She labored arduously, determined to prove her worth. Under her direction, legal arrangements to establish a southwestern banking cartel had been dissected, reforged, and finally accepted, with the exception of one steadfast holdout.

The much-coveted support of an absent and wavering Colonel Tuffet eluded her, even though he enjoyed the profits of Bisbee Bank investments.

In Josie's courting of the Colonel's millions a custom emerged. After church services on Sunday afternoons, Mr. Tuffet would arrive with some unique morsel from his ranch to tempt Josie, and Taylor, if she wasn't with the Pickett children. A tin punched folding screen separated their table from the other guests so they might enjoy a somewhat private meal at Hilltop House, as secluded as space permitted in Bisbee. In spite of Josie's generous sharing of her Sundays, Mr. Tuffet continued a dam in the financial flow, without explanation. Josie seemingly faced a dead end.

Late in March, shortly after the Colonel had departed for his hacienda, Taylor burst into their bedroom. "We can go to California. Find Poppa. We still have time to get our things together to go. Oh, Momma, at last, I can meet my father."

"For heaven's sake, what are you carrying on about?"

"The Picketts and three other families are leaving in four days. We can leave with them. We won't have to travel across the desert alone. Now that you have your strength back there's nothing to stop us."

The surprise of Taylor's announcement caught Josie off guard. She reacted instantly, without taking her daughter's feelings into account. "We have reached the end of our search. We are staying right here. I am very happy with what I am doing. The bank, the friends, we live very well." Josie watched Taylor's eyes cloud with resentment. "You must learn to celebrate the life we found here. Forget the past." Josie's conviction did not beg question.

"But what of Poppa? My father, your husband?" Confusion turned to condemnation. "What of your promise? What about finding Jacob, showing him what a 'lady' his daughter has become?" Sarcasm whipped out Taylor's distress.

"I guarantee you that is not possible. Think, ten years now without a word. He has hopelessly vanished. A mining accident, disease, who knows? We experienced this land's destructive nature. Something dreadful kept him from returning, I am sure. He has to be dead, or he would be with us now."

Josie's footsteps made no sound on the wooden floor when she approached Taylor to comfort her. "We go from this point on, planning for your future. Our first step is to stay here where we have found friends and a lucrative future. I will build a foundation that cannot be dislodged, in spite of any accusations from anyone."

"The Picketts are leaving for California within days. I want to go with them—find Jacob."

"I know you have a strong attachment to these children, and I understand, but my position has handed us an opportunity to return other people's kindness and be accepted in return. Our reward for years of wretchedness. We will be able to establish ourselves, be in the center of an emerging social circle."

"I don't want 'society.' I want to find Poppa. I need family beyond you." Taylor's words crawled out in a bitter and curt lashing. "In spite of our bad luck, I was happy together. I didn't realize you found our life so 'wretched'." Taylor stood straight and tall, head high above Josie. "I know Cat and Baxter will make room for me and help me search for Jacob. I am going to leave with them, whether you do or not."

The brutality and determination in Taylor's challenge eclipsed Josie's ability to think. Her heart stopped, fluttered, then trussed by fear began to spasm. The day had finally arrived, the day she had always feared, the day she must break her child's heart.

Josie gulped an involuntary gasp, ignoring her fear, and prepared to shatter her daughter's trust. "Jacob is not your father."

Taylor's face registered confusion, then astonishment. "I don't think I heard right, what you said."

"Please try to understand. I had no home, no family. A need as simple as keeping the men at arm's length. I had to protect myself, and you, from unwanted attentions, from preying vermin. I pretended to be a wife left behind in the stampede of men going west to find gold. I invented my history. Then when we arrived here, everyone assumed I was widowed. I never said anything to change that idea."

"You lied? You made up a life, the velvet dress with bells, the sailings, picnics...?"

"That part is all true, but, Jacob is not your father."

"Who is? Where is my real father? What is my real name?"

"Your birth certificate says Taylor Louise Marianne Broderick and that is who you are."

"Was there ever a Jacob Broderick? You stole his name? Or, was he invented, too?"

"Yes, no, of course Jacob existed. We were to be married, but he disappeared, then... Well, then I made a very foolish choice, a poor assessment of a man's character."

"Was that man my father? Your foolish choice?" Taylor's eyes narrowed, a tiny wail escaped her throat. "Did he marry you?"

"No, he wanted an heir. That was my gift to him. Then he was to settle a fortune on me. The child would inherit..."

"He paid you?" Taylor's body visibly shook. She toppled, her shoulder banged against the wall.

"No, he never gave me the money."

"But you agreed to bear his child for money?"

"Yes..."

"You sold yourself and planned to abandon me?"

"No, Taylor, it was not like that at all. He needed an heir, a son, to pass on the title to save his family's property."

"And you failed him. I was not the son required, so he did not give you the price of carrying me?"

"That is not what happened, young lady. Now you listen to me carefully..."

"Young lady? I tried so hard to be the lady you wanted, to be just like you." Taylor's slim frame pressed into the corner, face averted. "You lied to me. My whole life is a lie." Tears splashed a glassy sheen over her cheeks. "Who is my father?"

"A man who used me. Who brought heartache to my mother and father and abandoned me before you were born." Josie grasped her daughter's shoulders, fighting to turn her around to face her. *If I can just get her to look me in the eye.* But Taylor fought off Josie's hands. "I kept you. Unmarried and without family, no money, under the most dire circumstances. I protected you, gave my life over to you."

"Why, Mother?" Taylor spat. "Is there a chance I might someday inherit, and you want to make sure you get your money?"

Josie was appalled. Taylor's flushed face and her voice brought back memories of Father and the scene that filled her nightmares. *Is there never to be an end to loves lost? Am I to pay forever for my greed?*

"Get out of my way." Taylor stormed past, a film of tears covering her face.

"Wait!" The strength of Taylor's writhing and hysteria forced Josie aside. "Please, you know you are my life. Since you were born, everything I have done has been for you. Stay, hear me out."

"I never want to see you again," Taylor sobbed. "Don't ever come near me." One arm knocked Josie away, the other flung open the door. She raced down the stairs, not looking back.

The slam of the front door jarred Josie, sending her reeling. Fragments of Taylor's fury jumbled with visions of Father's rage. Josie collapsed onto the bed, drained, empty.

She cried through the changing of the midnight shift, through the chill of the night, with the dawn's greeting of the Mexican water mules, until her numbed body gave way to sleep.

The next day, in the heat of the afternoon, Josie headed straight for the Pickett's cabin. *So like the V'ginnys. First time with a decent place of their own, and they scoot away like stray cats looking for hobbled mice to catch. Well, not with my daughter.* Josie rapped on the front door.

Cat answered the knock. "Taylor don't wanta' see you. And, she ain't even here. She and Baxter went off."

Josie shoulders drooped. What had she expected? "When she does return, would you ask her to come to the hotel? I want to talk with her. She needs to hear the whole story."

"She cain't come. She's leavin' for Californ-i-a with us day after tomorrow."

"You know Taylor means everything to me. My reason for living would end if she left me. Will you help me?"

Cat lowered her eyes. "I don't much mix in other's goin' ons, but she's got no heart for you bein' together. She goin' on her own, for whatever that tells ya."

Washed out, not a crumb of energy to spare, Josie trudged back to the hotel. She spent the day alone, waiting. Taylor never came. The next day she returned to the bank, labored over tedious ciphers and records to keep her numbed mind sane.

The reports of the bank's investments with National Land Company showed hackneyed results. Josie refigured for hours before she assembled a satchel of the disturbing reports for Chess. She hoped he found an error that her overwrought mind had missed.

She worked until the sun slipped behind the canyon wall, depositing blue shadows across the green-streaked walls, well past dinner hour, but Taylor did not come.

Hoping to see her daughter without antagonizing her, Josie kept to the shaded side of the street when she passed Pickett's corner. She cringed at what she saw. Five wagons formed a half-circle around the cabin; bodies she recognized leapt in, out and about with their arms laden. Josie went on, stopping on the hotel's porch and collapsing into one of Baxter's "cast off" spindle chairs. She waited there, rocking until the sun's ray cracked the horizon.

After daybreak, the noise of the sendoff grew louder by the hour. Shortly before opening time for the bank, Josie walked the few blocks to the Pickett house. Pine boughs, cedar, bouquets of daisies, desert lilac, yellow poppies, and ribbon flags of bright cloth decorated the fence posts and an arch of jasmine vines at the gate.

Beyond the colorful array, Taylor and Baxter stood together in the center of a circle of their friends. Hands clasped. Josie recognized the man standing with them, Bible held aloft, as the Judge, only seconds before a black curtain blocked the sight out.

A towel dripped cool water down her neck when Josie opened her eyes and attempted to sit up. The first words Josie heard almost destroyed her world.

"Taylor and Baxter are married." Strong hands held Josie down and checked her fight. "They are staying behind, here in Bisbee, to build up the lumber business. Wait for Abel to come back from the university." Mrs. Wentworth spoke softly, with as little judgment as possible, still kindness cradled her message. "At least, with Taylor here, you have a chance."

The words floated beyond Josie, but the compassion found her; she was incapable of dealing with more. *At least, with Taylor staying, I might have another chance.* Taylor's sudden change of heart and the rent that divided the bride and her mother went unexplained. Josie shut her eyes, drifting into her comforting, hated world of melancholia.

~ * ~

A week after Taylor's marriage, Josie invited herself to Chess Tuffet's ranch, expressing a desire to escape the crowded valley. During the long and tedious ride, fighting to not dwell on Taylor's rejection, Josie forced her mind to peruse the long list of objectives waiting for her at the bank. Most pressing, Josie needed to complete specific purchases of property to ride the crest of the current growth and reach a financial benchmark. Also, she brought with her news of the government's opening two million acres of Crow Indian land, the transactions to be handled by National Land Co. and Worldwide Bank. Josie planned to outbid them for the territory between Bisbee and Tucson.

Her dress copied one of the most recent styles in the newly published Vogue circular. At the fork in the road she stripped out of her skirts and petticoats, unlaced her constricting corset, and snaked into dungarees and a calico shirt. The pants defined her hips and legs, making her feel exposed and vulnerable. The lye-bleached fabric itched; the rivets, straddle and thick seams bound as uncomfortable as any corset.

This better prove worthwhile. Josie felt as public as the women who lounged up and down Brewery Gulch pedaling their wares. But she was ignorant of their alluring manner.

Contessa plunged over a bunker, shifting her heavy haunches in sliding steps toward the moat-like basin of the hacienda. Chess stood just inside the wall, under the shade of the mesquite, rubbing lubricating soap on a silver trimmed saddle.

Hurrying forward, Chess reached up and helped Josie slide from the saddle. He looked her over from top to bottom, and whistled. "I'm pleased you took my advice." The words twisted his tongue. "Come in, freshen up. Aleillo prepared a big meal." He forgot the door. When Josie glanced backwards to see the reason, she saw how flushed his face had become.

"Well, Mr. Tuffet, if you are as right about investments as you are about the benefit of these riding clothes, we should order the iron rails for our railroad this afternoon." She hoped her bright smile hid her discomfort.

"Please, call me Chess. I imagine the town has pestered you about my legal name, but until we're better acquainted, that'll do. I gather Josie is not your birth name, either." His stare barely acknowledged the wince that answered his brazen guess. "After we eat, we'll rest a bit, before we ride my property." At the concern evident on Josie's face, Chess added, "Not all hundred fifty thousand acres, wouldn't want you to wear out the seat of those new britches. Only around the ridge and up the peak."

Josie's unease had not been over the ride, rather his direct reference and stare at her seat.

Later Josie, enjoying Chess's quiet company, rode western style with surprisingly minimal discomfort, solidly seated on a tooled saddle that smelled of new leather.

As soon as they reached a place in the trail wide enough to ride side by side, Chess began questioning Josie. "Explain again to me why we are so interested in stealing such a large amount of land and stock from National Land and Taylorsville Bank. And, more importantly, why you seem intent upon sabotaging Worldwide Bank in the process of profiting for ourselves."

His directness caught Josie short. She wavered, uncertain whether he meant to be honest or insulting. She chose honest. "National Land Incorporated printed thousands of certificates. Promised to repurchase any stockholders' shares on request. They never pledged to meet market rates. Their holdings have matured into valuable properties, but the investors receive only the cartel's discounted price."

"How on God's green earth did you acquire this information? Theirs is a very tight, private association. Are they aware of your intentions?"

"My purpose in my being here is to convince you to participate. I need a person of influence to represent our bank. My previous associations limit me to purchasing small quantities of shares, specifically not enough to call attention. Above all else, the cartel cannot know I am behind these activities, that I intend acquiring control. Not yet."

"You honestly believe you can gain control of National Land and Worldwide Bank?"

"Only a controlling percentage of their assets in this country. Enough to force them to deal fairly with us and those we represent. They have financially raped and pillaged the bank accounts and dreams of a young nation. We have eleven of our own neighbors who face eviction without cause. Their legalese allows them to repurchase property at the original rate, regardless of any improvements and the owner's wishes."

"How do you propose to hide your acquisitions? Our government leaders will demand you legitimize your need to own half the land in the territory. Especially those bickering over statehood. Believe me, I know, being one of the few survivors of their censure. Such a move would make any capitalist, including me, nervous. Invites investigation, and defensive action."

"The railroad I proposed, initially from Bisbee to Tombstone. Then as more investors are acquired, stretch further north, west, and east. Build the needed short side railroads that feed into the major rails. The businessmen of Bisbee guarantee me you have the means. I will provide the knowledge."

Chess tied up the donkey he led and secured the horses. The bundled oilcloth he handed Josie smelled of apple, curd, jerky and Indian bread. A circle of rocks fenced off a pile of brush and logs that he lit before sitting down beside Josie on a flat ledge. "You're a railroad wizard, too?" His admiration showed.

Josie had expected skepticism or sarcasm, not a compliment. She spread the feast between them. "Not a wizard, but I spent a goodly amount of time, probably equivalent to a university year, studying what's required to succeed."

"Look." Chess moved closer, his arm protectively between Josie and a cholla cactus. The sinking sun, eclipsed by mountaintops, brushed rivers of gold, candy pink sashes and violet feathery bursts across the blue sky.

Josie gasped, her soft intake of breath the only sound in the calm. *A cathedral,* thought Josie. The serenity and beauty was more of a promise of God's existence than anything she had seen in her life, outside Taylor. The vision lasted nearly an hour, the vibrancy streaking into a solid flow of intense flaming color as the sun faded, only to be replaced by an inky sky peppered with brilliant studs firing diamond spikes. Sometime during the metamorphous Chess's arm, sharing his warmth across Josie's shoulders, had been enhanced by a wool serape. Josie's shivers came from the beauty, although the temperature had plunged from near ninety to the low fifties. The two had sat quietly, hip to hip. Clouds framed in the gold of the sun's fire, shooting stars, or the howls of lonely coyotes or wolves had brought only a finger point or hushed murmur.

"Time to go." Chess's reluctance matched Josie's. His boots crunched the rocky soil when he stood up.

"Must we?" Josie felt the loss of his nearness keenly. "How do we find our way back?"

"That wilderness song isn't a circus act. Mountain lions and bobcats will be joining the serenade soon. Probably watching our fire." Chess shoveled some dirt with a pan and smothered the embers.

Josie hadn't been aware of how well he had tended the flames. The absolute darkness made their surroundings seem of another world.

"Mule and horses know their way back regardless. Can smell a cat half-mile away. You'll know, too. Hair stands up on your neck."

"And then what am I supposed to do?"

"Can you shoot?"

"Since I was six."

"I'll get out the extra rifle from the pack. Two pistols ready for firing in your saddlebag. Figured you for a lady who's had some experience."

The comment troubled Josie, but through the years her skin had thickened. She no longer fretted about what others knew of her past. And, perhaps, his remark came as another compliment.

Thirty

Josie's friendship with Chess progressed over the next two years such the town treated them as a couple rather than a scandal. Josie felt comfortable and settled into her life, with the exception of her relationship with Taylor.

The hot sun had chased away spring's chill when Josie passed by Pickett House and smiled broadly. Baxter held the hand of his wife while Taylor climbed up onto the bench of their wagon. Josie hurried on to the bank, quickly installed her staff, then while keeping an eye on the clock, checked all the former day's records before rushing out early for lunch, an uncommon event.

She hurried up the steep street that curved behind Pickett House then perched on a large rock overlooking the sulfur fogged canyon road below it. Within minutes two tiny children skipped before her. Aleillo, the Mexican housekeeper, had hustled the children out the back door, pulling the two little ones up the steep stairs of the canyon wall to the flat ledge where their grandmother waited.

Lillian, just past three, looked like a miniature of Josie, tiny, the same look of angelic fragility and porcelain complexion that reflected light like moondust, and identical platinum curls making a halo around her face. The strong-willed child's self-interest reminded Josie of Stuart.

James, not quite two, wobbled on rain barrel thighs and could have been a twin had he not fed a liking for sugared milk and cookies that settled into a teddy-bear belly. He displayed both the jovialness and companionable acceptance of his Uncle Louis. Both children appeared undersized for their ages, Lilliputian, but equipped with an imposing nobleness compared to the Mexican children of the workers.

After his father's departure, Baxter had taken possession of the cabin. During the first year he added more sleeping rooms and enlarged the kitchen. The following year he built a second story and a huge wing onto the continuously occupied boarding house. Pickett House became a landmark.

Much of the treasure Baxter and Josie had squirreled at the lumberyard found a home. Cracked and abused functional furniture alongside antiquities discarded on the trail were refinished; broken mirrors that had reflected centuries of gentry reshaped and installed in heirloom frames; new needlework pads tacked onto hand turned chairs; drawers repaired in heirloom bureaus that had survived oceanic crossings. Every detail displayed unblemished workmanship.

The family's homestead emerged as an inn that won a reputation from St. Louis to California as "the" place to stay when visiting "Little San Francisco" which the travelers had dubbed Bisbee. Each room donned a personality of its own, beautifully done in exceptional good taste. To come upon a vacancy at Pickett House became rare.

Like her meetings with the children, Josie only saw Pickett House in her daughter's absence. These furtive inspections came at the generosity of her son-in-law; Taylor's animosity had not abated. Josie knew Baxter paid a heavy price for his benevolence and felt beholden.

At the time Baxter approached Josie in the bank, James had finally learned to climb, his thunder thighs transporting him to the kitchen and up the counter to the nearby cookie tin. Baxter spoke frankly. "I intend to buy the Baja Mine. Nellie Bly gave me first dibs. The lumberyard and Pickett House et up all my cash. Will you help me?"

"What does Taylor think of this?" Josie asked.

"She holds with anything I do. Leaves everything 'cept the running of Pickett House to me. She don't know much about gold minin'. If I was to miss this chance, might be a long while afore I get 'nother as good."

Josie wavered; ever since their flight from St. Louis had ended in such dismal failure, Taylor had dismissed gold-fever, strongly criticized get rich quick schemes, counseled others to put their minds and backs to more fruitful labors. Baxter's profession of Taylor's unconcerned support didn't ring true. "Let me think on this. Can Nellie wait a few days?"

"I know there's others waitin'. She's wantin' to git her Mescarales to the desert a'fore winter. Won't lose this. Git back to me, two days. Don't wanta git tied up with partners; they'd steal the deal. Will if I hafta."

"Two days. I promise."

When Chess rode into town that evening, Josie presented Baxter's request to him. "I am sure Taylor doesn't agree with this. The bank's approval would require mortgaging Pickett House and the lumberyard. It could turn out disastrous. But, Baxter is so determined. Says he will get the money elsewhere if the bank turns down his request."

"Do you want me to loan him the money? I will."

"No, I am not suggesting anything of the sort, although I appreciate the thought. I am just not convinced Taylor shares Baxter's eagerness. I just wish..."

"Go to her. Tell her the bank requires her compliance. She'll either not talk with you and tell you to leave or give you your answer."

Josie loved this bear of a man, his simplicity. "Of course, I have nothing to lose."

Early the next morning, before the bank opened, Josie let herself into the parlor of Pickett House. The warm cinnamon smell of apple pancakes enveloped her with a nostalgia she embraced.

That was the only enjoyment she received.

After the front door clicked shut Taylor stepped into the hallway. "You are not wanted here. Please leave." Her voice trembled, hostile with anger.

"Taylor, I came to you seeking some advice, wanting to know your feelings. Baxter came to see me yesterday..."

"I won't listen to anything you have to say. It would, no doubt, be a lie. If Baxter has business with you that I need to know, he'll tell me in his own fashion. There is no need for you to be meddling in my affairs. Please go, I have guests to attend to."

Taylor used her height regally, looking down her nose with obvious contempt. Josie admired Taylor's polish, just the right tone, the perfect aloofness to cut her antagonist to the quick, all the while exhibiting exquisite manners. Taylor staged the perfect nuance Josie felt desirable in a lady.

"You are," Josie agreed, impeccable in courtesy, "perfectly correct. It is improper of me to take the Bank's business beyond our doors, to become personally involved." She dared one last try. "I wish only to be assured of your agreement. I would never want a decision I made to cause you harm."

"Mrs. Broderick," the slur of the name and the tone was unmistakable, "you are fifteen years too late."

Josie gasped, fumbled with the doorknob, then dashed away, her tears flowing while she strode numbly back to her office. She had been wrong thinking she had nothing to lose.

Later that morning a composed Josie explained the encounter to Baxter. "I went to Pickett House. My purpose was to assure myself that Taylor supported your venture. She told me to leave." His face remained blank.

Josie slid the papers across the desk, cringing when Baxter hurriedly printed his name. "I am not happy about giving this loan. My hesitation comes not from question of your trustworthiness, but my doubt of Taylor's approval."

"She'll come around. Just wait'll the gold starts coming in. I'll hire people to make the beds, cook, care for the babes. Give us a chance to visit Tucson, maybe even California. She's a strong hankerin' to go to California."

Josie recoiled, feeling as if she had been struck again.

Baxter misunderstood his mother-in-law's fear. "Not to stay, just to stick her toes in the ocean, see Cat and the boys." He ducked around the desk, shook Josie's hand. "Headin' for the general store. Need me a better pickaxe. Gotta find a mule."

His jubilance left Josie unsteady, questioning the wisdom of this god-like power she had pursued for a lifetime.

~ * ~

For the next year, during a time hundreds of banks were failing, Josie mapped a trail of acquisitions that led her board from California to Ohio. Letters arrived with stamps from all over the world. The ink black with analogous petitions demonstrating a willingness to sell National Land stock or to transfer a deed for pennies. Her generosity and fair dealing heralded, Josie sought more investors. Her appeals circulated throughout the financial institutes of the southwest. J.L. Broderick, President of First Bank of Bisbee, quickly developed a more than satisfactory reputation in the western financial world.

Summer monsoons flooded the narrow canyon when Chess returned from California with a briefcase of such papers. After dinner they analyzed the requests. Josie explained, "I've concentrated on the west, mostly southwest. The larger eastern banks have not yet tapped this area. They seem reluctant to deal with cowboys and self-starters. Their unfamiliarity with the wealth here works to our advantage. Tell me what you found."

The hotel had set aside a discreet corner for their noteworthy lodger by installing a wicker-folding screen. A small table topped with a lovely crocheted cloth made their dining area intimate compared to the long open broadsides of the dining room.

Chess scooted his chair closer. "You are more well-known than perhaps you'd like. Your name was already on the bank officer's tongue before I arrived. Already, those who least need to know of your whereabouts have learned of your achievements. This does not come as a welcomed observation, it worries me. Are you prepared for discovery, for face-to-face confrontation? Have you an alternative plan if National Land decides not to protect its own?"

Josie felt her fear as a wobbly indecision that seemed to be without feet. The cartel or Father's bank must intercede. They had never exposed one of their own. Of course, she was not formally one-of-their-own. By blood, by training, but unrecognized, disowned. The wobble grew fists that attacked her confidence, bruising it, slowing its life. Josie fought against the imagined flaying, sent her mind to a place of purple and pink streaked skies and a huge orange moon that promised a future. She would not let the cartel or Father's bank defeat her. They must be forced to acknowledge her. She had made her mark.

Chess grabbed Josie's hands and held tight. "Forget your revenge. You and I can go it alone. You don't need to prove your competence to them. You've already affirmed your ability here. You know deep in your heart the strength of your competence. And, most of the Arizona territory has profited from your skills. Men with more gold in their pockets than they ever anticipated sing your praises from Colorado to Mexico." He bent closer, cupping her chin in his hand.

"Abandon this raid, or at the very least, allow me to provide the finances you need. It would be to my advantage. I've never been in favor of inviting interlopers to participate anyway. You know I have all the cash right here, in your bank. Whatever you need. If that is lost, I have more. There's no need to expose you any further to these vermin."

"I must. For just that reason. I will never be satisfied until they know that I survived. Not only survived, but proved myself. They have to know they judged wrong. I want them to admit their mistake and confront their corruption."

Closing her eyes, Josie again pictured sky-swept pinks, lavenders, fiery orange and fool's gold. The radiance and remembered calm, the link to creation and life revived her floundering confidence. She must succeed.

Within days a stranger stepped off the coach, his red uniform announcing his alliance. Josie remembered. The young man on the Goldenrod and at Carthage. Lost among the fears of that final fateful day in St. Louis had been another scene. The magician distracting her from the red uniform and wheelchair that had enticed Taylor.

Josie searched her memory. An old woman she had thought. Long gray hair, but too tall, she recalled, too quick to add her strength to the hasty departure. Big hands, too broad for a woman. The vision added anger to her stupidity. The cripple had to have been François. He had known from that day. And Taylor, he had met his daughter. Whether by accident or plan he had arrived at the square at the same time they had. *How? Who would have known?* Only Mrs. Costello knew her daily plans. How many months had passed since she had checked Stuart's townhouse?

And now François's agent waited out front. Josie peeked through the door that stood ajar. Composed, well-trained, mechanical, like a windup toy, she determined. The red color his primary attraction, like the male species of the bird kingdom, to draw out the enemy.

Flutters filled her stomach when she opened the office door and stepped into the bank lobby. Her lobby. Bitterness outwardly calmed her at the embodiment of years of struggle and misery that she had faced. Her lungs quivered in an effort to hold her breath steady. Coquettishly, she touched a rose-scented kerchief to her nose.

Josie walked briskly toward him. "You are looking for the President of Bisbee Bank?" With his curt nod of affirmation and before he could speak, she added, "That would be me. May I be of service?"

His attention swept her without a twitch of eye, nothing spoke of surprise. He had known exactly who he was seeking before his boots crossed the threshold of Bisbee Bank.

"Mrs. Broderick, I do believe? May I come straight to the point." At Josie's curt nod he continued. "At the direction of my employer I have a presentation to make to you. He seeks a solution and believes you hold the answer. He has empowered me to make you an offer. An overture he feels you might be open to." He paused. "An agreement he neglected to fulfill some sixteen years ago and feels some obligation to satisfy."

Rage like Josie had never experienced n her life threatened to explode, a fury that promised to destroy. She fought to retain her poise, struggled against profanity and insult. Clinched fingers dug half-moons into palms straining to strike.

Josie wanted to defile the lips that spoke. She was not deaf, not a moron, she heard his caveat. Patronizing, a blatant warning given half-heartedly, without respect. An offer to wipe away her years of torment, a life half wasted, and she already guessed the price. François would offer a life of luxury for ownership of his daughter. Josie began to smirk, then laugh, a low, throaty chortle that would be sensual under other circumstances. All she sought was revenge.

"You arrived too late. A lifetime ago the offer was contemptible, thrust upon a naïve girl who coveted what her manner of life barred. Today you approach a woman who values that which she already has won. Go back to your employer, tell him I have no need of him or anything he has to offer."

The man stood at attention, not moving, as if he had not heard a word she said. She whipped around, her back to the stranger, and spoke to an assistant. "Show him the door. If he returns, go for the Marshall."

The young man squared away to leave. "My employer is prepared to involve the courts addressing theft, false identity and fraud. He invites you to discuss the matter, please feel free to do so at your convenience." His departing words dropped like a bomb. With that he carefully laid a business card on the nearby desk. "If you have need of me? Good day, Miss Taylor."

Josie slammed the door to her office, forbidding the incident entrance to her private domain. *Keep it out, keep it away.* She leaned heavily against the frame, knees trembling, a powdery bitterness fouling her mouth. The water pitcher splashed as she poured. Must wash away the curse that corroded her. The drink only increased the bitter taste.

And what of the charade François played out? In her haste and madness to demonstrate her disdain to the messenger, she may have destroyed any hope of receiving exoneration or the help of father's bank and the cartel. The stolen identity? She had known, of course, Jacob had used J.L. Broderick. But he was long gone, dead.

Josie kept her own counsel on the unannounced visit. With one exception. After years of separation, she sent a letter to Mrs. Costello, telling her old friend about the situation with François and Taylor's unrelenting hostility. She had to leave a legacy. Should she be imprisoned, or worse, someone must tell her daughter the truth. Someone Taylor would believe.

A few weeks later, with the railroad within weeks of reaching Bisbee proper, Mrs. Wentworth burst into Josie's office. "Come quickly. Taylor just came in from the mine. She's crazed, half dead."

Josie dropped her pen, tossed her glasses on the desk and raced out the door.

Taylor was dazed, unable to speak, her movements jerky and uncontrolled. Filth pasted her pants to her legs and smeared her belly. Brambles tangled her hair into untended knots. The remnants of a blouse hung in rags across her shoulders, long rents in the sides exposing cuts, bloody slashes, and bruises.

Taylor sat on the top step of the back stoop, her arms wrapped around James's plump belly, rocking him while she crooned a childish ditty over and over. Lily crouched a short distance away in the grass.

Aleillo, who cared for the children and Pickett House in Taylor's absence, hovered nearby. Lily walked over and leaned against the young Mexican woman, an ornate brush stroking her hair while she looked anywhere except at her mother. Josie flew to her daughter, knelt at her feet. "Taylor, it's Momma. Let me help."

Tears flooded Taylor's red streaked eyes, washing over the swollen rims of dark lashes as if a dam had burst. "Go away. All lies. Go away."

"Please, Pumpkin," Josie pleaded, "tell me what happened. Are you hurt? Were you at the mine? Where's Baxter?"

At the mention of her husband's name, harsh sobs tore Taylor's words. "It's your fault. You sent him there to die. Get away from me."

For over an hour Josie and Mrs. Wentworth worked with Taylor, begging, pleading, trying to get details, any kind of an answer. Aleillo, the only person Taylor allowed to touch her, tended the young mother and inspected her for serious injuries. Taylor had little fight left in her, but she would not release James, droning the ditty over and over again. "Twinkle, twinkle, little star. How I wonder where you are."

Chess arrived and searched the packhorse, tended to Tessa, collecting what clues he could find. He admitted, "Not much. According to the general store, she took supplies enough for two weeks. The packhorse's bags have been emptied, nothing's left, saddle blanket, tools, food. Everything's gone, including her own pack for the return trip."

Josie tried through to the early morning hours to get Taylor to say something, but with no success. Taylor spoke her first coherent words to Aleillo's husband who managed the lumberyard in Baxter's absence. "You must run the lumberyard now."

He coached her carefully. "Did Baxter give you that message? Did you talk with him? Is he ill? Injured?" Taylor ignored his questions. "Did you find his body?"

Taylor stopped rocking. "Baxter's gone. High waters came, washed out the sluice, water barrel. Food buried in tins, his mount wild on the ridge. Searched everywhere." She gave the sleeping James up, examining the cuts and bruises, the fingernails torn to the quick of her banged up hands, suggesting she had used them as tools to dig. *Perhaps a grave?* "Lost. All lost."

Chess stood on a step overlooking the bystanders and barked an order. "Daylight. Here. Bring anyone that can ride. I'll pay day wages and furnish supplies. Plan on at least five days." He leaned over Taylor. "We'll round up every available male in Bisbee, ride to the site and search for Baxter. He knelt next to her. "You'd best clean up now. Tend to the children. Try to get some sleep. I'll need you here at dawn to tell us where to look."

Taylor stared at him as if he were an apparition, then turned to go indoors. Chess immediately grabbed hold of Josie, gently folding her into his arms. "None of this is of your making. The fever caught him up like a passel of other gold-hungry men. He would have found a way without your help." He wrapped his arms snugly around Josie, pulling her toward the Hotel.

"No, I'll stay here. She may need me during the night." Josie prayed. "Maybe I can be of some good to her."

Chess warned, "Don't count on things getting better. Count the blessings you have."

Josie stepped over the threshold, her hope very much alive.

Seven men left the following dawn and returned in five days, spirits defeated, their mounts bone weary. Chess spoke first. "Nothing. Campsite has mud ridge up past the firebreak. Everything smashed that wasn't washed away. Gusher probably came at night, mountain rain rushed the canyon. He wouldn't have had time to run when he heard it coming."

Taylor sat silently in the rocker. She hadn't spoken since the men left. Josie served as eyes and ears. "No chance?"

Aleillo's husband left his wife's side. "Don't seem so. Walked river bottom and banks for ten miles. Climbed the gorges to see if he managed to get up high and over the canyon. Nothing. She buried provisions, left signs for him. Still there, untouched. He's not been back since."

Josie tried to comfort her daughter, to give her a hug. Taylor fought, brushing Josie's grasping hands away. "Don't touch me. Go away."

~ * ~

Fall came suddenly. Leaves piled up against the wood framed inn, grasses began to brown, the dying garden hid squash and pumpkins under their twisted vines, but the fickle sun blazed with a heat that reddened cheeks. Taylor pulled the blanket up from the rocking chair and wrapped it snugly around her shoulders. She stood still, shivering, while Aleillo helped her into the house, teardrops darkening the colorful weave.

Josie waited at the corner of the house until her daughter disappeared inside. Chess's arms clasped her. "I can't leave her this way," she said.

Chess pulled her away from the closed door. "It takes time to heal, Josie. We can wait."

Josie still mourned Baxter's death, still barred by her grieving daughter on the afternoon the Bank held its quarterly meeting.

Mr. Wentworth presented accounts in default. "Baxter Pickett. Mortgage on Pickett Lumberyard and Pickett House. Arrears, six months."

"There must be some mistake." Josie could not believe her ears. Embroiled in the final stages of the land acquisitions, she had not monitored the loan. But Taylor would never allow the mortgage to remain unpaid.

"Sorry, you can see for yourself. The account is in arrears, unpaid for the summer." Mr. Wentworth went on. "We all know the situation.

Sad, pitiful accident. No one expects him to ever be found alive. He would have to be gifted with biblical powers to survive on his own. However, that does not keep us from being generous to his widow. I propose we extend the repayment schedule another six months, adding proper interest, of course. Allow Mrs. Baxter time to organize herself."

A member said, "Thirty days. Foreclosure after thirty days. We already allowed this to remain without payment for six months, that's our rule."

Another clamored, "Sets precedence. Even a board member would not expect such generosity." His statement brought guffaws and loud agreement.

Josie banged the gavel. "How can you be so merciless and unjust? These are hard working, honest people. A tragedy has just taken away the woman's husband. Look to your hearts, gentlemen."

"We're not in business to provide for widows and orphans. Allow it once, it sets standards. I vote we foreclose." Voices clamored as one.

Josie banged the gavel repeatedly. "You know Mrs. Pickett is my daughter. I approved the loan, mortgaged her home, her income. I could never be a party to executing such meanness. If you insist on foreclosing, you force my resignation."

Chess countered, "There are matters other than Baxter Pickett's loan that need our president's attention and support. Without exception, there is no one in this room capable of fulfilling the requirements to successfully complete our projects. I propose that following the vote to extend the Pickett loan we express a vote of confidence in our president."

Every member, with the exception of herself, Chess, and Mr. Wentworth, voted to foreclose on the lumberyard and Pickett House. Every member voted against accepting Josie's resignation. After the count, Chess stood up. "Postpone the processing of foreclosure until the next regular quarterly board meeting. I guarantee the funds will be here to pay the loan in full."

Mr. Wentworth countered. "Suppose we vote to postpone one month, if Josie will withdraw her resignation."

Josie did as they wished, but the whole affair left her bitter and resentful. In honesty she knew, had the case not been Taylor, she would have felt compelled to vote with the Board.

Without discussion, Chess ordered a money draft from his San Francisco account, and convinced the Judge to obtain the legal documents to close the affair.

But the problem did not end there. Judge Truxell walked into her office the next afternoon, his news tragic. "In true tradition of a Virginian, Baxter Pickett appointed his brother Abel to serve as executor and successor of any properties under Baxter's control upon his demise." At Josie's outrage, the Judge argued, "I have no alternative to filing the documents.

Josie sputtered. "You're telling me we can do nothing to secure the home of my grandchildren?"

"The property no longer belongs to Taylor. I will contact Abel Pickett in an attempt to salvage whatever I can. Meanwhile the Bank may proceed with foreclosure, but the legal owner must be notified. It is his obligation to repay the debt, and he must be given opportunity to redeem the property."

Widow Taylor did not own anything, not the rocking chair where she huddled her bereft body, the roof that shed the snows, nor the lovely furnishings that guests admired so. Outside of her two children, the six-year-old mare Contessa II and a two-year-old filly she had crowned Great Pretender, Taylor Broderick Pickett could barely fill a bedspread with her belongings.

The law allowed one lifeline. Taylor, Lily and James would not be forced from their home for the legal period allotted to notify Abel and receive his decision.

Josie's presence agitated her daughter, pushing Taylor further into melancholia. For days after Josie's visits, Taylor didn't eat, wouldn't leave her rocking chair. Sick at heart, Josie stopped coming, relying on Aleillo and Mrs. Wentworth for word of her daughter's health. Occasionally, giving in to her own heartbreak and selfishness, Josie sat on a stool at her daughter's feet. But the dismal effect she had on Taylor brought self-incrimination and a promise not to come again. But try as she might, Josie could not stay away.

The day of foreclosure came and went without word from Abel. Taylor would not sign documents authorizing anyone, especially Josie, to step in with legal action. And Josie's petition that Taylor was medically unsound fell by the wayside when Taylor defended her right to ignore her mother's help to the Judge.

The court began proceedings to settle the matter. The papers Judge Truxell served on the widow lay unopened. The young mother talked of nothing, listened to no one; each day she dove deeper into her abyss, escaping the pain of her surroundings.

Shopping for dolls, wagons, ribbons and candy for the Christmas holidays spared Josie the heartache of watching her daughter slide into the shadowy crypt of Louise Taylor. Josie dedicated her free time to discovering surprises to help her grandchildren enjoy their holiday. She sat alone in her office, inconsolable and defeated, the day she received a fat envelope from St. Louis.

Abel lived in Chicago. She traced another law firm's embossed return address with her fingers for a long while before slicing the edge. The papers crackled like dried chicken bones as she unfolded the layers. On top of a banded pile lay another envelope addressed to her and stamped "Addressee Unknown". She ripped it open, inside lay an advertisement, dated several months after she and Taylor had fled St. Louis. The inset held a black and white picture of a man, a face she recognized. Tiny print under the image stated: "Due to my absence, my associate will complete all service and burial arrangements for a short time. I will return as Director before year's end. I wish to thank the community for their support during my recovery."

Josie's heart pounded. The next item, measuring the size of a playing card, was a newspaper account that explained how the local undertaker had fallen from a slippery deck during a rainstorm and suffered broken bones. Josie read and reread the articles, the papers creasing under the pressure of her grip.

She set the newsprint aside on her desktop and pawed through the bulkier heavy bond papers.

LAST WILL AND TESTAMENT

> *Mrs. Constance Costello, sole owner of Costello House, bequeaths all her properties to Taylor Broderick and Mandy Black to be shared and shared alike.*

Josie read on, scanning the list of personal property her daughter had inherited. The value of the ordinary house had fallen considerably since their departure.

The last piece in the packet was a letter from the legal firm notifying Taylor Pickett of her need to appear in St. Louise to sign documents and take possession. The law did not allow persons of Negro blood to inherit nor control shared properties in the absence of the rightfully acknowledged white owner.

Almost lost on the bottom of the pile lay a square of apple-scented notepaper. It began...

> *October 31, 1888*
>
> *Dearest Josie*
>
> *The enclosed articles appeared on the dates shown. Gossip at my table provided the rest. A stranger mistook the Undertaker for a thief. A struggle occurred on deck, at which time our mercenary embalmer fell overboard. No report on the stranger. No talk of gun shot wounds. Your friend, the supposed assault victim, did, however, purchase several racing horses and indulge in a European tour before resuming his business obligations. Please return quickly, my arms ache to hold our child.*
>
> *Most affectionate regards,*
>
> *Mrs. "C"*

The letter shattered Josie. Crumpled almost motionless in the chair until dark; her emotions boiled to a murderous rage then toppled in disbelief and horror. She had not killed anyone. A struggle, yes, but no shooting. She had lost the companionship and love of a woman she cared for deeply, a life she treasured, on the whim of a monster.

Freed of her fear, she could see that night as it happened. Another red camped young man, the witness, had rushed between her and Stuart's last shot. The undertaker, staggering, jumped away from her flailing arms, teetered dramatically on the railing then fell into the darkness. While Sidney had balanced on the rim of the railing, she remembered running forward, not to harm but to catch him. Stuart threw down the gun that she retrieved in panic. Sidney grabbed her, pulling her into his wooly chest. That was when she felt the sticky oozing on her bodice and bare shoulders. The stranger said, "You killed him. Run, run quickly. I'll hold back the mob." She did as he instructed, all the way to the Arizona Territory.

Josie managed to find her way out of the Bank and onto the street, clutching the envelope, the contents of the entire packet stuffed inside like trash. Stars as bright as any she had ever seen flickered their illusive beauty. Snow flakes large as handkerchiefs floated to the ground, their ivory sisters already dressing the tethering racks, roofs and porches. She wrapped her coat tightly around her, not for its warmth, more from the need to hold herself together.

The whole murder scene had been a sham. A despicable scheme to drive her away, no, not drive her away, to undermine her life. Concocted quite probably in an effort to force her to return home, to beg for help to save her life. *François. He had been the one in the wheelchair that same day. He had undoubtedly arranged the fake murder. With the help of Stuart and the redcoats.*

Through a fog of unreality, Josie gloated. Her survival of the fever's fate, her daughter's determination and skillful chicanery, their welcome to Bisbee had all cheated him of his prize. By two, a woman and a child, who had the will and purpose to thrive.

But Josie knew he would not give up. François wanted his daughter, perhaps to nurture the appetite for avarice he had so admired and manipulated in the mother he abandoned, perhaps to punish them both. *How far did his tentacles reach?* His agents waited, secure that she would need François's help someday. And now two more tiny minds hungered to share life's treasures; besides Taylor, her grandchildren were vulnerable.

Josie walked into Pickett House, straight up the stairs to the bedroom where Taylor rocked before a cold fireplace. Even in the darkness Josie shuddered over the weight Taylor had lost, the eyes sunken into dry sockets, teeth that protruded from slack lips.

Josie recalled having the same feeling when she had found a nest of rabbits. Teeny bodies curled up in dried weeds and leaves. She had watched, hidden in the field corn all day. The mother never returned. Before nightfall she and Dieter moved the puny fur balls to a crate. Used their nest, grass and dirt that might hold the mother's scent to pad the wooden floor. For weeks the two of them tended the bunnies, realizing even as they labored that when the animals grew up they would probably be clubbed in the head for stew.

Josie pulled a stool up to her daughter's feet. "Taylor, you must listen. I did not kill anyone. The murder was a scheme, to force me to return to Taylorsville, make me take you back to my family." She would not tell her of François. To hand her knowledge of her parentage might create a desire to investigate. "We were duped. Forced to leave Costello House, give up our home, the only family you knew to satisfy an evilness."

Taylor appeared not to listen, paid no attention to the words. Josie desperately sought another avenue. "You remember Mandy?" Josie saw a flicker, a raise of a brow. "Mrs. Costello grew very sick and passed on." She hated bringing up talk of death, but it must be done. "She has willed her house to you and Mandy. Because of her color the law won't allow Mandy to keep the house. You must claim the property and share it with her. Do you understand, Taylor? Mandy needs you so she might stay in the only place she has ever known as home."

At the word 'home', Josie thought she saw a glimmer of recognition in her daughter's eye, a spasm in tight lips. "You must dress, come downstairs, prepare the children. You have to go to St. Louis to claim Costello House." Josie grew more frustrated, but she kept talking, of Mrs. Cos and Mandy, the riverboats and their walks.

"Remember the Boatman's Bank and the secret account? Our walks together uptown?"

A brittle voice croaked, "A lie. All lies."

"No, what you lived was real, genuinely happy, please, try to remember more than the lie."

Dawn bathed Taylor in a blush of gold, the sun losing its warmth in the chill of the room. Josie had not succeeded, had only awakened the hate and despise her daughter held onto so religiously. She would come back, try again, keep trying until she reached her only child. Neither of them was safe here. *Were they safe anywhere?*

Josie and Chess spent the days before Christmas at his ranch. She learned to whirl thread around straw drawing the fibers into ornaments, punch holes in tin for candle holders and cut gingerbread into men with raisin eyes and a slice of orange peel for a smile. Chess cut trees and drug them indoors where he and Josie decorated them for the ranch families. Chess could certainly afford more, but the hands preferred the humble decorations, the reminders of their family homes.

Josie had not shared in the giving of her presents to Lily and James. Taylor had been so disturbed since her visit that late night Josie agreed it would be best for her daughter that she stay away as much as she could. Her loneliness locked away, she stood by Chess's side handing out favors to the neighbors and friends who had graciously accepted their invitation to share the holiday. She stayed for the week of celebration until the New Year. She prayed, creating bargains with God of any sacrifice he deemed, if a way could be found to save Taylor and the children.

When Josie returned, the doors of Pickett House were locked to her. Aleillo no longer brought the children to the rocky ledge. Josie never saw their tiny forms walking the street or making snow angels in the brief minutes the flakes covered the ground. After a few days Josie entered the General Store to find an answer. "Harriet, I'm worried. I know Lily and James are not ill, but I have not seen them in the shops or playing outdoors. They seem to be confined to the house. I don't want them infected by Taylor's melancholy."

"Taylor's struggling with a decision to stay or go elsewhere to live. Her rational thinking seems to have returned. She feels she must escape the mountain, the days staring out the window for Baxter to return. She's unable to go on here, and there's nothing left for her or the children."

"But that's wrong. I'm here. Her inn must be kept running. I'm sure Abel will contact her soon and straighten up the matter. A short visit to St. Louis to help Mandy may help her. Chess offered to pay her mortgages, give her a fresh start. I'm sure he'll purchase the house at the auction. Taylor can't leave." The sinking of her heart paralleled the answer she could not face. This is what Taylor wanted, to be rid of her, to be far away from another face that haunted her.

Josie entered Pickett House a second time unannounced. Taylor's appearance surprised Josie. Dressed in a comely dress, the young mother was baking in the kitchen. Josie got straight to the point. "You can't leave permanently. Take my grandchildren from me. It's unfair, to me and to them."

"I don't want you around my children. You've done enough harm. They need to be free of you, and I want to be as far from you as I can possibly manage."

Taylor's absolute rejection laced with almost fanatical hate floored Josie. "This is not entirely my fault. You know Baxter would have gotten the mine some other way. You gave me no objection, avoided discussing it with me when I came asking your opinion. Baxter's disappearance does not rest solely on me." Josie's courage failed her, she could prod no more.

"It's not only Baxter, it's a lifetime of your fraud and deception."

Josie pleaded, "I will tell you whatever you wish to know. I grew up in Taylorsville, Illinois, as I told you many times." Taylor ignored her, folding the dough over, punching it down with the side of her hand. "The man whose seed I carried seduced me, then took me by force. I never wanted you to know the circumstances. I was banished from my home, they threatened to..." She couldn't go on, she could not confide in this tall, vulnerable young mother that her family had wanted them both dead. That an uncle had pledged to murder her. "Do you remember a promise you made to me, that you will never return to my birth place? I expect you to keep that promise. Never attempt to communicate with my family. You must promise me again."

"Why, mother, so I don't find out you're lying still?"

"Just hear me out. If you will do that, I will leave you to your life. If you promise to write Isabelle often, let her know how you and the children are faring, I will step away from you. Give you the freedom you want so desperately." Josie waited, hungry for a word of protest, a sign things were not as hopeless as they seemed.

"I made that promise when I was still a child. When I believed in you, dreamed your dreams." Taylor turned to her mother. "What difference if I return seeking someone you made up? I cannot claim blood with a father or family that is false." Taylor closed her eyes, then turned her back. "I will keep that promise if you will keep yours. Never attempt to see me."

Josie stumbled from the kitchen, the sweet smell of apples choking her. Her cheeks remained dry, the tears swilling to the bottomless pit that held the dark, wounded part of her soul. Loneliness aged her flesh before the door closed behind her. She was not allowed to stay, to help pack, to see the house stripped of its heart. To say good-bye.

Chess would make the arrangements, drop by with enough cash to cover expenses during the trip. She had made her bargain, she would live and die by it, separate from their lives, to never know the mysteries and light and dark of their future. Grief, acceptance, rage, and tenderness blended in a savage, silent wail that deafened her.

She could not turn back.

Thirty-one

Josie welcomed the end to winter. Mired in mud seeping over the edges of her boots she thought of going away, not because of the slippery foothold, but to escape the ghosts that haunted Bisbee. She took a deep breath as she rounded Castle Rock. Below her swarms of people, predominantly coughing orange-skinned men, darkened the canyon floor. She concentrated, trying to pick out familiar faces. Her eyes narrowed, shutting out her surroundings. She did not want to think of Pickett House as she passed.

Taylor was gone. Josie eased away the cold, sunny days mapping out well-defined tracts of land, narrow strips that spread out in landbound octopus tentacles across the country, stretching in all directions from the remote mining town. Maybe if her investments stung a little more, François would spend his time interviewing and chasing down her investors, attempting to decipher her plan, lessening his appetite to search for Taylor.

Chess had gone, his leaving temporary. With the sinking of the Maine in Cuba, he had joined longtime friend Theodore Roosevelt, the Rough Riders and the Negro troopers of the 10th cavalry. Fanned by the encouraging presses of Hearst and Pulitzer, the popular Under Secretary of the Navy and his warhawks waged a lopsided battle. When five thousand Americans died of malaria, the approaching wet season begged an end to the Spanish American War. Chess returned home even more reserved, more content with his secluded ranch house another world apart from the warring field of death and politics.

The daily walk led Josie from the house she had purchased on Clemson Street, high above the valley, to the permanent adobe bank at the opposite end of the valley. From her porch she overlooked the railroad that brought with it a hustle and bustle that answered her need for activity, but she no longer stood outdoors listening for the toot of the whistle, scanning blue skies for the black smoke of the engine's boiler. Nowadays she ignored the comings and goings of the locomotive; the thrill of achieving her first endeavor gave way to a more complex plan.

The morning train had arrived when she elbowed her way through the crowd celebrating the surrender of the Philippines and transfer of Hawaii to the United States. Her greetings to friends and associates came absentmindedly, her mind intent on reaching the sanctuary of her office where she anticipated pushing up her sleeves and swimming in correspondence and research notes about her newest project.

Before joining Roosevelt in Cuba, Texas had been Chess's last trip, investigating grazing land where oil, despised for its unwanted presence, lay in slick jet puddles on top of the ground. The ranchers threw carcasses, unwanted implements, charred timbers, anything unusable into crevices that exposed earth's veins bubbling its crude excess. From the day after Chess left until the morning of his return, Josie perused every publication available. Her enthusiasm stretched into pressuring first Gottlieb Daimler of Germany with his European automobile, then Rock Oil Co., which sold the unwanted sludge for its medicinal qualities and whose owner, Colonel Drake, spouted promise of illumination and energy properties, and finally the Duryea brothers whose bicycle shop had produced a gasoline driven vehicle, to share their garnered sciences. She exchanged her carefully guarded data with other obscure men of invention whom the financial world regarded as inventors or bohemians.

Chess stepped from the train, his posture announcing the pride he felt, the graying along his scarred scalp proof of the price of his mission. His eyes searched the crowd for Josie, the furrow of his brow replaced by that familiar lopsided smile that extended into a wreath of welcome when he spotted her. He sighed with his delight and quickly embraced her. Josie's body sang with an unfamiliar and unwanted response.

Later in the afternoon, by the time Chess digested Josie's orderly, well-presented materials, he agreed with Josie. Deep drilling could unquestionably accommodate this new industrial giant and reap unprecedented rewards for the gamble. Chess added an afterthought; the most efficient means of transporting the volatile liquid cross-country was by rail. He left for his ranch, after approving the investment. Josie felt gratified.

The Bank had dedicated a new wing as a Boardroom with a small portion richly appointed for Josie's office and private meetings. Maps lay helter-skelter on her desk, a table and the floor in anticipation of a full day's commitment. An assistant knocked on Josie's door announcing that a newly arrived passenger sought her attention. She felt no premonition.

Josie smoothed her hair and replaced the combs before removing her eyeglasses and rubbing the ridge that seemed almost permanent. Her elbow rested on the Rio Grand River, the spectacles mid-air when the door opened all the way and a man pushed in.

Handsome. Chestnut hair barely covered his ears and tapered across the back of his head. Tawny eyes willed her into their depths while examining her from head to waist, their lure ripe with admiration. "It is you. I had no doubt, but I could hardly believe you here. So near." Jacob strode toward Josie as he spoke, his arms outstretched, pulling her up easily from the chair. "Just as I remembered."

A radiant smile plumped laugh lines that stretched to crinkles wrapping his eyes like a cherished comforter. He twirled her in an engulfing hug that hooked her heart, swamping her with affection. "Tell me everything. Josefina, you have no idea how much I have longed to see you again. I've missed you since the minute I left." Jacob stopped, laughing joyously. "I have hardly given you a chance to breathe, my Josefina." He released her slowly, his eyes drunk with joy as if he held ambrosia in his arms, his smile hungry.

Dazed, Josie's welcome threatened to die before being born. "Jacob, how nice to see you. What a surprise." The etiquette drummed into her for a lifetime served as her salvation, an instinctive response of polite manners. Not a single appropriate thought came to her. Her knees gave out like quicksand. Her body stopped responding in an instant, suspended, waiting for direction. "When did you arrive?" Her blank mind sped along a track of inane questions.

"Chess didn't tell you I was coming? We met in San Francisco before the holidays. He happened to be having lunch at my club. My friends had been tormenting me about this imposter, J.L. Broderick, buying land, paying top dollar for National Land stock. My brokers wanted to know why I kept holding out on them, masquerading as a competitor but foolishly using my own name." He chatted on, filling the silence with background while she struggled to gain control of herself. "They blindly invested a great deal in your promotion, believing I planned something big, possibly a takeover of the bank."

"My club" and "my investors", thought Josie, *and a familial reference to "The Bank."* So, Jacob had financial power, enough someone thought him a potential threat to Worldwide Bank. He had gained considerable bearing since last they met. Jacob had said "Chess" as if they were long time friends. Josie's mind sponged up his words, tucking them off in a fog of bewilderment, to be examined later. She could not think. Her mouth attempted unsuccessfully to make sounds; instead she stared and listened in silent amazement.

Jacob held her at arms' length. "I do believe I have struck you speechless. Please, forgive me. I had not planned on such an invasion, but immediately upon learning of a Mrs. J. L. Broderick." Jacob dwelt on the Mrs. "A fascinating and beautiful woman who appeared to be related, and of a daughter of very fine quality, I couldn't wait for Chess's invitation." His words nudged each other, like beads on a string.

Jacob placed his fingers under Josie's chin and gently cupped her face up toward his. "Come, come, my Josefina, you had a great deal to say last we spoke. Although we both were somewhat distracted." He teased her, with the affection of an old friend, an easy acceptance she had coveted a lifetime past. The intimacy and glow emanating from him prompted her to recall that frenzied last meeting, to relive the past.

She remembered the eagerness of his hands, his firm, ravaging lips, caresses that fired her desire. A hunger too long buried, passion Josie thought dead came to life. A blush heated her face and carried down her throat, across her breast. Seemingly well aware of his effect, Jacob rattled on while Josie's body remembered.

He hugged her into his chest. The fabric of his suit merged into flesh that had loved her. Holding her chin in his fingertips, Jacob lightly brushed his lips across hers. "A welcome." He took her elbow, lightly guiding her toward the sofa against the far wall, where her shawl, casually draped over the armrest, seemed to belong to someone else in another world.

"Sit, make yourself comfortable " he instructed. "We have a great deal to discuss. This conversation will not end until I know everything." Josefina looked up, grateful her clerk had quit the room before Jacob began his commentary.

After she had arranged herself on the cushion, Jacob leaned forward and took both of her hands in his. "Josefina, you have always been in my thoughts. Tell me, how did I lose you so many years ago?"

"I hardly know what to say, although the answer is simple. When we returned from St. Louis, you had gone."

"We? You refer to François and Marianne?"

"Yes, of course. Well, you wouldn't know. Marianne became ill, so we were quarantined for several months. Then it was weeks more before she could travel. When we returned Father and Dieter said you had moved on."

His question jumped into the middle of her telling. "And the child, when did I father the child?" His question probed gently, but barely cloaked his agitation.

Josie studied the tension in Jacob's face and decided he had come seeking revenge. She must be through with it. "You know my daughter is not yours. When I announced my condition, the scoundrel denounced me and disowned his child. After I told Father the situation, he sent me away." There she had said it, the truth was out.

"That is when you went to St. Louis. Stuart threatened to sell the child to a workshop? But you escaped, saved the child?" Jacob's eyes narrowed.

How did he know? "Stuart promised a much worse fate for my child and for me. My brother planned for us both to die." Cold ripples chased down her spine at sound of the words spoken aloud. "How do you know this?"

An odor of tobacco came from Jacob as he drew nearer. "Is that when you took the name Broderick, claimed to be my wife, to protect yourself and your child?"

The same tinsel fear danced through Josie, she could taste its salty sting. "I was desperate. Unmarried, penniless, with a bastard, where could I go? Costello House offered food and shelter, supposedly for a short time. I sincerely believed you would come back for me, that you would not give up until we were together." Jacob's rejection had lived in her mind for a lifetime—dark, fragile, a cocoon of suffering finally opened.

"You said your next position would be in St. Louis, so I stayed. Each spring I thought you would return." Josie's voice began to fade, to haltingly expose her wound. "Mrs. Costello saved my daughter and me from the poor house, and possibly even from death. She was all we had. She loved Taylor as her own." The truth of her admission brought Josie fresh pain.

"And what happened to change all that?" Jacob's words turned sharp, his voice deepened as if he spoke from the bottom of a pit. "If you were so well off, why leave?"

Indeed. Dismissing her own vanity her position at Costello House was as common as the housemaids, but Josie heard danger in his question and hedged. "An accident." She cleared her throat. "No, the truth is I believe François staged a murder, a scheme that put me at risk. He hoped to force my return to Taylorsville. But I fled West instead, still hoping to find you."

"And so you have." Jacob spoke brutally, knife sharp words that cut off her dialogue. "I know François fathered your child. That he has conspired for all these years to control our lives. To force both of us into roles we chose not to undertake voluntarily."

Josie realized his deduction was perfectly logical, but it still surprised her.

Jacob moved closer, their thighs almost touching. "Did he ravish you? Or did he dangle a carrot?" He looked steadily into her eyes, the golden depths reaching for her soul. "I must know."

Josie wanted to lie, to say what would please him. "François claimed he needed an heir. When I revealed my love for you, he offered a contract. If I would bear his child, he would provide protection and seclusion for me until the child was born. A trip abroad with Marianne, not uncommon for a debutante. A secret birth. If I did not learn to care for him during that time, he would settle a fortune on me. Hand me the means of marrying you in the luxury I desired." She felt immoral and unclean. "I did not say no."

Josie looked away, afraid to see the condemnation in Jacob's eyes. "I hoped that you and I would become secretly engaged. To deceive you about the child. When I returned, I would bring ample assets to marry and go West in comfort." She could not stop. "When François came to me I cried out your name. Pretending you were the one in the bed was no match for his brutal taking." Josie longed to cry, punch, undo the pain of the remembered torment, instead, her shoulders drooped in defeat.

Jacob spoke quietly, consoling. "Ahh, my Josefina, you had too little faith in me. More so, you were born to luxury and trained to lead, to wield both riches and power. Your seduction came not of sin, life taught you to take your advantage." Jacob sat silently looking at her. "Hearts broken, lives destroyed, a financial kingdom in abeyance, there must be easier ways to win a cause."

He stood, looked about the orderly, but charming, office. The tender invitation in his eyes waned. "Those papers. Whatever you are laboring over now, is it possible to free yourself? I brought my wife for the sole purpose of meeting the other Mrs. J.L. Broderick. Would you take the time, for me? I think we are both in need of that."

He paused when Josie made a small sob, then continued. "We're lodging at Pickett House. Quite a remarkable place, in many ways reminds me of you. Has a charming style. A quiet elegance that puts guests at ease."

The beat of her heart stilled, Josie was unable to boast of her daughter's talents. Jacob had said "my wife," casually, as if she were an item on a shopping list. Wife... wife... repeated with each thump as Josie's heart pounded. He belonged to someone else, had loved and married while she pined for him.

"Please? Come with me now. This can't be avoided." Gently, without coercion, Jacob pulled Josie to her feet and started for the door. "Do you usually wear spectacles?"

"An illness, left me almost blind." Josie apologized. "I'm afraid print jumbles together without them." Good graces, a lifetime of habit, corseted her in calm.

"And people, must you wear them to distinguish features? I want no mistake when you see my wife. I would prefer your captivating eyes uncovered. She must share the pain she caused when she faces you."

Josie's knees bowed, out of control. She stumbled. Her hand twisted a wayward curl as Jacob steadied her. Josie knew in that moment who waited. Her stomach burned as if poisoned by his words. She wanted to escape, hide in her private darkness. Sink into a dark hole that swallowed her up.

How could this happen? They had all ceased to exist so long ago. Her life had gone on quite nicely without them. The black ache came again. She wanted them dead, buried. The coffin closed. Josie pulled away, prepared to flee.

Jacob's hand tightened on hers while his eyes searched her face. His lips brushed her cheek. "Trust me. Your anguish is no greater than the misery I have lived in since discovering the truth. I will stay by your side as long as you need me, I promise."

Her fingers tugged hard, fighting to pull away. Her secret screaming warned beware of his promise.

For Josie the walk down the rock strewn street passed in a nightmare of unwanted shadowy visions. But, the familiar green streaked mountains, sulfur air, nude wintering gardens, the place she had once slighted, brought sanity. A breeze tiptoed down the canyon walls and cooled her heated cheeks. The sun's rays funneled a hug down the canyon and warmed her quivering shoulders. The strange language she had mastered spoke to her of home. The noise of thousands of people carrying on with their dreams played like the pull of a bow across a violin, pleasing music carried her body along on a gentle wave.

Castle Rock loomed at the crook of the street, half shrouded by storefronts and billboards claiming to be the best, of anything, of everything. She avoided going this direction since Taylor had left, Josie thought. She must have lost her way.

Jacob kept his arm tight around her waist, with his other hand he guided Josie up the hill, as if they skated a waltz on an icy pond. Across from the towering landmark, Pickett House stood like an alien fortress. Baskets of strawflowers scattered along the porch brought to mind an English garden, their carefree inconsistency a decoy. The white shutters appeared chalky, the stairs steeper, everything in extreme.

Josie stood apart and watched as her body moved up the steps, crossed the threshold, indifferent to Aleillo's surprised greeting. Her mind became a box, a toy, she stood atop a bouncing spring, a jostling jester clothed in bright colors to entertain.

What she saw when she entered was a lone woman sitting at a table set for tea. Thick auburn hair bunched in a matronly French twist beneath a plain burgundy hat. Dark gloves covered long fingers that fussed with the teapot and repeatedly rearranged the sugar bowl and creamer. A rosewood rosary had been tucked in the belt of a dark wine dress devoid of any ornament, plain, pleated to cover long legs.

Josie struggled not to scream, claw, run away and avoid the face that turned to look at her. She could not accept the message her eyes delivered. Her body stalled, spent and vulnerable. Her mind attacked every detail, inspecting, seeking to find a fragment that didn't fit and therefore made the picture false, willing a mistake. But the image remained as it was.

Regal, imposing, a lady of consequence with green eyes and powder that failed to cover russet kisses from the sun. Josie fought to hold herself together, to accept the reality that faced her. A vision of Taylor flashed through her mind, the elegance of her daughter sat before her. But then Josie recalled a loving young girl, dressed in boy's trousers, burdened with the care of a mother who struggled to stay alive, a child without home or family. A spirit wakened within Josie, a fierce dark warrior with the tenacity of ironwood.

Marianne watched with the steadfastness of a general whose battle had already been won. The light of her eyes dulled, empty of emotion. The gloved hands picked up a fork and wiped it on a napkin, then replaced it perfectly aligned with the table setting. On the floor, a rug, an oriental of exquisite design threaded a path of brilliant reds and golds. When Josie and her escort reached its colorful center, Marianne stood up.

Josie wanted to wail and cry, beat her fists on the body standing before her. Marianne resembled Taylor too much. The pain exploded, its fragments bringing more wounds. Josie's hands pawed the air, seeking something to stop her collapse. Jacob snatched a nearby chair and guiding Josie, gently helped her sit down.

Marianne asked, "Are you all right, 'Little Jos'?" Concern barely masked the indifference of the green eyes as she sat.

The hated name brought Josie back. "Tell me! All of it."

"Would you like tea, or a scone?" A rise at the end of Marianne's lips outlined an attempt to smile.

"Tell me now, Marianne. I must know the whole story."

Jacob placed his hands on Josie's shoulders, his thumbs touching the bareness of her throat.

Marianne clasped her hands in her lap. "It is very simple. Jacob chose you. François needed an heir, and secretly desired you. My illness gave him that opportunity. When he told me later of your resistance, I told him your protests were of no consequence, that you had been intimate with Jacob that evening in the stable. My lie became his truth. François believed the child Jacob's. I did it knowing that without help you would go to your father, and he would send you away, then Jacob would be mine."

"Then you left me, abandoned me. My unborn child and I a target of François's insanity, a threat that still exists." Josie's anger boiled, gathering strength.

"I had to know of your plans. If your son survived, he would be François's heir. I could never desert a legitimate successor. François arranged clients for Jacob in California. He always knew Jacob's whereabouts."

Marianne's nose tilted up, her shoulders shrugged, as if it was all of little matter. "When you faked Jacob's note, I knew, of course. I returned to Taylorsville and watched over François's affairs until he began to recover. I sent spies to St. Louis often, bringing me reports about you. After your daughter was born, I joined Jacob. François didn't learn the girl belonged to him until years later. When his scheme to force your return failed, he invented another, and hired agents to find you."

"He lost you for some time after Carthage. Fearing you both dead, François became quite despondent, more reclusive. Then, your audacity exposed you. You became too full of yourself. Did you not see that appropriating my husband's name would eventually attract attention?"

Josie looked over at Jacob. "You knew of all this?" Jacob tugged at his earlobe, his eyes averted.

"Not until Colonel Tuffet visited San Francisco this past month," Jacob replied. "Then much of what had been told to me fell into holes." When Jacob came around and knelt before Josie, Marianne stood, her back to them. "Early on the morning after the banquet François dispatched me to Carthage on a matter of urgency. I came back after I thought you would have returned from St. Louis, but no one knew where you were. I kept my promise and asked for your hand in marriage. Your father discharged me on the spot, threatened to do away with me if I did not vacate Illinois and the vicinity immediately. I left letters at the Chateau explaining everything, one for you and one for François. On my ride back to Carthage, I stopped and told Dieter the whole situation. He promised to help you find a way to join me.

When I arrived in Carthage, government contracts with an advance had arrived for the project I had estimated. I returned to St. Louis once, briefly, hoping to discover for myself what had happened to you. I learned nothing. For months I received no other word. Finally, I received correspondence from both Marianne and Dieter that François had fallen ill and you had gone on ahead to France before your pregnancy prevented your traveling." Jacob's narrowed eyes scanned his wife. "Marianne sent me confirmation from the ship's registrar indicating you had sailed to France, supposedly to register François's heir. Everything documented that you had decided to live abroad, and François would join you when his strength returned. When I learned François's health did not appear to be improving, I drug the Carthage project out for a year, hoping you would return and I could see you one more time. And, a blight upon my soul, making plans if François should not recover from his illness."

Marianne remained standing, her imposing frame dominating her seated rival. She turned and faced Josie. "Jacob and I lived quite contently until your devilishness began to unravel old lies and unearthed truths better left buried. You managed to develop into quite the financier. I doubt, however, your daughter knows of your sins. My brother is quite prepared to educate her."

Josie blanched, but her eyes never wavered from Marianne. Color warmed Josie's cheeks as her body began to stir.

"Marianne," Jacob said, "you may excuse yourself. I think you are quite through here." Suddenly, Jacob barred his wife's way. "First, in your presence, I will tell Josefina what I told you on the day we exchanged vows." Jacob turned back towards Josie. "If I married her, it would be with her acknowledging that I could never love another as I loved you." He turned back to his wife. "She agreed to the contract."

"I believed you would learn to care." Satisfaction settled on Marianne's face; her catlike eyes flashed. "And you have, for the world I afford you."

Josie's curiosity shriveled as she listened, sapped by the memory of tinkling music and the same bold seduction François had used. Marianne had bludgeoned Jacob's spirit, rejected his dream. She had carried out an identical plan to François's.

Underneath all this carnage a common bond appeared. It did Josie's heart no good to learn Jacob's integrity had succumbed, as had her own.

The tall, imposing woman glided away, her fingers clicking away on the gifted beads. Riddled with wishes, Josie sat as if posing for a portrait, the torture of revealed events cascading in agonizing 'what ifs'.

"Are you feeling well enough to share my company?" Jacob asked. "I don't wish to impose on you any further. But now that this ordeal is over, I have need of nourishment, a drink, conversation. I want to hear every detail of the past sixteen years." He moved another chair close to Josie, crossed his legs and leaned back. "You know you delivered the impact on National Land and the Bank you intended. Tell me of your next move, I'm captivated by your success."

Josie talked and sipped, unable to eat. As she told her story Jacob nodded and smiled, his encouraging touches light and possessive, as she remembered them. Aleillo cleared and replenished his wine glass, the teapot and service several times. As the hours passed, Josie grew comfortable introducing her acquired knowledge, and less heart struck by her virile companion. She nibbled on dilled cheese and crackers, pushing orange segments around her plate. She laughed at Jacob's recounting of the hysteria that greeted her identification as the interloper at National Land Company and the Bank.

Neither of them saw the man with the smiling scar peer through the glass of the front door or walk past the window at differing hours.

Josie declined Jacob's offer and walked home alone, fearless of the miners and foul hustlers who strode past her. She did not sleep. She laid awake dreaming scenes of longing with Jacob devouring her with the hunger of years of physical famine, the need to unite his body with hers, passion remembered and cherished. Memories of loving and being loved dissolved the splinters of broken heart that resisted, opened the core of her passions. Josie still lay awake when the sun rose, wrestling with emotions that pleased and displeased her in alternating segments.

When she arrived at the Bank the clerk stopped her. "A Mr. Broderick is in your office. Just arrived."

"Thank you." The clerk's curiosity marred his steady expression. Her staff, friends, clients, all wondered who Mr. Broderick was. Well, she would announce it for all to hear, shout down the canyon's green walls, toast him at dinners, toss his cards from her porch. Jacob had returned.

He sat alone on the sofa they had occupied. "I cannot stay," he said. "Marianne insists we return immediately to San Francisco. I am afraid she fell ill. In spite of her shameful behavior, the wrong she has done us both, she is my wife. She has earned my consideration."

Josie's spirit tumbled; her mind protested. Things were not finished. She had not had her chance to demand accountability, to seek retribution for the damage done. He said he still loved her. No, she argued with herself, that was wrong, he had not said any such thing. He had fawned over her, mesmerized her, collected all the stories of the past and sieved through her future. He had turned her life inside out and upside down. He had not told his history, had not said he still loved her. Now he prepared to leave, without her again.

"Yes, yes, of course," she responded. She had nothing else to say, the accusations on the tip of her tongue, the anger that smoldered, the need to know love, all dissolved into polite, charming rhetoric. "It was so good of you to come. The relief of knowing these misdeeds were not born of my avarice brings me new life. As for my success, your congratulations are appreciated, and I extend mine to you." Jacob leaned in as if to kiss her good-bye.

Josie held him at bay. "I do have one concern. The question of my daughter being an heir, has that then been dismissed?" She must know how close he was to François, and perhaps Stuart, how united the front.

"Upon François ducLaFevre's death, his daughter will become wealthy within her own right, but not entitled to property. Even though the aristocracy lost its formal recognition during the revolution, the government ruled that only the male line inherits property under French laws."

The hated name rolled off his tongue with ease, an inflection of worship, adulation beyond respect colored his reference to royalty.

Josie's features wore the most beguiling mask attainable. Her eyes blazed with admiration, her shoulders opened in welcome, her mouth purred. "Well, then, I have no worries. Will you give my regards and my forgiveness to Marianne? Please?"

Jacob neared, his eyes hungry, his hand involuntarily fingered the lace that corseted her chest. "Yes, yes, such generosity, you are a wonder and always have been. I will tell her. By the by, is your group still in need of a surveyor? I saw a publication. Perhaps I might fill that position. For a short time. The arrangement would free me of the bank and give me an excuse to spend time on the range, an opportunity to get reacquainted with the territory," his voice deepened, "and you."

Josie teased with the allure of a hussy, lashes lowered, voice throaty. "Your credentials would need to be approved."

Jacob slicked his lips, beads of moisture glistened on his brow. He bent his head to hers. "Look for me, Josie. I will be back."

Josie stood on tiptoe, her breast nuzzling his arm. His lips closed on hers, then pressed hard, the kiss long, liquid. When his arm loosened Josie fought to remain standing. Her body dizzy and weak, trembling inside with the fragility of a flower in a spring breeze. She backed against the desk, her weight propped against the wooden edge.

Josie locked the door the instant Jacob's boot crossed the threshold. Silent tears flowed as they never had in her life, a flood of grief and self-pity, despair and self-disgust, finally igniting a rage that seared every longing that had surfaced from her soul in the last day. Indeed, where Jacob was concerned, all the ardent sparks of love he had ignited in her disintegrated into ash.

When Josie left her office later, she stopped at her clerk's desk and dropped a stack of letters on the corner. Josie pointed to the proposals. "Put two of our best people on this now. I want an offer telegrammed to every prospect within an hour. Use my office for privacy. Before sundown make any final offer needed, threaten government intervention if you meet any resistance. Bring me the entire list yourself by midmorning tomorrow, not one name omitted. Double check any property not acquired. I will be at the Colonel's ranch. You can tell anyone looking for me that I have taken leave, a respite if need be. There is to be no exchange of information with anyone else of this business or its urgency."

The sun already hung at midday. Once out of sight of the bank, Josie raced for Clemson Street. Her hat flew off into the muck, her freed chignon dropping pins as it spilled undone. She ran faster. Once in her bedroom she tore off her clothes, jammed both legs into dungarees, and wiggled into a blouse while searching for her western hat. She had to reach the ranch before nightfall. Her eyes were too weak to perceive anything beyond buildings after dusk.

Contessa pawed impatiently at the water tank, sensing the tension flowing from her mistress. Once the reins grew taut, the mare galloped with the vigor of younger years, willing the cooling wind and setting sun to a daring race. They finished the run without stop. Before the streaks of pink and purple scrolled across the sky, a blending of rider and horse arrived at CT Ranch.

Josie knocked, then rapped harder at the door, rushing her way through when the door opened from her pounding. Chess was striding across the room. His eyes filled with anxiety as he headed toward her. She reached him first, pounded on his burly chest and screamed. "How could you? You knew. Traitor. Bringing his vileness. You are no better than a liar, hypocrite." Josie sobbed her condemnation, driven by anger and outrage. "You betrayed me, and I allowed myself to trust you."

Chess grabbed both her wrists in one hand, his other arm held her tight against his chest. "Calm down, Josie, whatever's wrong, I'll make it right. Think of what you're saying. I've been here beside you. Whatever it is, give me a chance to explain. You know in your heart I would never do anything to hurt you."

Josie buried her tear-streaked face into his shirt, mumbling her disgust. Unsure. Quieted by his concern.

"Josie, I love you. Do I need say more?" Chess smoothed his hands across her back, caressing her with gentle strokes.

She drew away from his touches at first, angered, confused, then realizing the hollowness of her accusations melted into a sagging, spent being.

They stood together for several minutes. Neither one speaking, their breath bound into one rhythm. Finally Josie broke away and stumbled to the couch. "Jacob came. Marianne and François conspired to keep Jacob and me apart. She was here. She married Jacob while I struggled to survive, provide an existance above the level of a beggar and save my daughter's life."

Josie rose and began pacing like a caged animal. "He still attracted me. Dreadful, insane disease this lust I carry." She talked to the walls, the ceiling, as if all the objects in the room listened. "He most likely will return." She turned on Chess. "You met him, knew he would come. Not warning me was unfair, you had no right."

"Josie, I didn't know he would come. I suspected, but I'm glad it's done. When I met him, I realized he was your Jacob. So near. Never looked for you. I wanted you to meet him, but on my terms. We both needed to find out what he still means to you."

"You had a duty to warn me. Give me time to prepare. The pain and humiliation you subjected me to went beyond contempt." Josie faced Chess, frustrated, unable to show him the depth of her anger.

"And do you still care for him? Was this a girl's first love or the cherishing that comes of admiration and respect that binds and lasts a lifetime?"

Josie fumbled with her hair, pulled her spectacles from a briefcase. "I've brought you enough reports to arrest Jacob and François with criminal charges."

"That is not the answer I'm looking for."

Josie leaned toward Chess, her feet wide, hands on hips. "Besides the public scandal, they have looted Taylorsville Bank and National Land Company cartel for years. They have pushed the bank to the brink of receivership and seem intent on ruining Father in the process."

Chess leaned forward, elbows on his knees. "Josie, be certain of the accusations you make."

"I would gamble my life on what I have discovered."

"And so you are."

"I believe my seduction was part of François's plan, to guarantee I would never act against him." Josie shouted her words. "Help me. I must find the trail leading back to when François toyed with me."

"What do you need?"

"I want an independent company established, above reproach, funded for the sole purpose of crucifying the ducLaFevre's. Reports, witnesses, dates, places. Start with tallying the accumulation of stock we now own. Improve and solidify our holdings. Sometime, I must contact Dieter, then Father." Josie's thoughts moved with the force of a whirlwind. "We need better communication then telegraph. A telephone, for us to communicate firsthand. What will it take for you to have a line brought here?" Her voice softened into irritation, as if she talked with herself. "Modern conveniences, we must join the twentieth century." Josie strode off, her demands trailing behind her as she glided up the stairs.

"Chess, have tea made. Bring a pot and sandwiches. I have an idea how we can bring the wrath of Hell down upon their heads."

Thirty-two

For four tiring months Josie composed appeals requesting incriminating dates and documents concerning Taylorsville Bank and the cartel. Her buggy, pulled by Contessa's offspring, traveled every peak and valley of the Cochise territory, eventually targeting banks further afield, occasionally straying across the border to nearby Mexican banks.

Her unannounced visits initially served as decoys to sort out allegiances and degrees of susceptibility, later prying substantiation of associates tied into the more confidential upper tiers of the organization. At day's end Josie jotted down memorized facts too confidential to be allowed out of clutched hands. Towns far removed from stagecoach lines and telegraph brought forth surly bankers and tight-lipped clerks whenever they encountered the unusually marked thoroughbred and the petite blonde with the obstinate spirit.

Chess searched separately. He penetrated the Tucson and southern California enclaves, enlisting associates to fake offers of investment into other suspected associate land companies, climbing through tiers of an heretofore impervious beast to the head of the financial dragon. Detailed reports arrived from around the country of millions of dollars diverted from public trust funds into bonds to finance phantom investment companies then resurrected in François's accounts. The estimated skimming, chronic recidivism of land purchases, and inflated interest charges bulged the deep pockets of François's secret conspiracy.

Hushed confessions uttered from behind hands shielding identities, exchanged in darkness, shared under false pretenses, faceless voices that identified fraudulent investments, provided names of colleagues who denied affiliation when questioned.

Chess divulged the scandal to the officers of a nearby unaffiliated bank. Since he held the largest margin of the bank's stock, their cooperation was quickly promised. A skeleton team serviced customers while the senior associates compressed weeks of normal investigative schedule into a miraculously short period. After four solid days of sending and receiving wires steadily, a basket of telegrams provided names, dates of deposits, and more shocking, periodic withdrawals and transfers from the cartel and associates of Worldwide Bank to private accounts in Swiss and Brazilian Banks.

By early spring Josie squealed her delight. "I have them."

Chess protested vigorously. "In spite of all our efforts, the damning evidence stops several levels below directly implicating François. I'm afraid we've reached the end."

Josie tugged at a curl. "Then I will go to Utah, the largest depository in the west is centered in Salt Lake City. They must be informed, we can surely gain their support."

"You cannot expect help from the financial brotherhood, even if you had undeniable documentation of conspiracy. I will admit withdrawals and matching deposits directed to various false accounts exist, but no clear line of theft leads to François. An insider, a male, would have precious little chance of breaking loose a mustard seed of information that could prejudice the financial beds of this country."

"Then what can I do? The evidence shows a huge embezzlement and François's increasing wealth. The implication is unmistakable that he is defrauding the public and the government. I see, we have not penetrated the uppermost swindlers. The culprits become more illusive the closer to the top our inquiries reach. Whoever physically funnels the capital from the cartel's accounts stirs about like ghosts."

Chess's troubled expression reflected Josie's own feelings. "You've accomplished a great deal. You cannot expect to march into their offices and in turn be invited to destroy them. I feel as deeply disappointed as you do. I had hoped this would put an end to your fixation."

Only half Josie's mind listened. One other person remained who might hand her the proof she needed. "San Francisco Bank, aligned with Worldwide, maintains the ledgers for every transaction west of the Mississippi. Jacob's bank. He possesses these documents. I have no alternative. I must convince him to join us."

"And what do you plan to give him in return?" Chess slammed his papers to the desk. "He has to have been party to every suspect deed that transpired. If not by direct participation, than by not tackling someone else's abuse of the authority given him. The sin of omission is not exempt from prosecution. Josie, be reasonable, everything we know indicates Jacob's involvement.

"Tell me why he would give up his position, his wife, open himself to personal and professional assassination to help you. Recall St. Louis? The threat to you and your child. That was no apparition. These people are thieves, embezzlers and frauds, perhaps murderers. They will be under tremendous pressure to prove their innocence, perhaps just to survive. They targeted you before and assuredly are again, adding to their degree of retribution as we proceed. They have no conscience, no morals, employ brutality and treachery without remorse."

"Jacob must be convinced. We have no other." Josie's chin jutted out with the steadfastness of a cornerstone on a church. Her eyes stormed with the turbulence of a winter sea.

"You expect this man to deliver himself to the authorities without offering him compensation for his self-ruin. You had best find another alternative. Either try those who supplied your original indictment again, or at best, promise of pardon for the sacrificial lamb." A livid blue outlined the scar that always remained, casting a corpse-like tint from Chess's mouth to his temple. "Or do you have your own reward in mind?"

Josie snapped. "Don't be preposterous and crude. If National Land or the Bank dissolves in wake of fraud and dishonesty, our investments are lost with it. And be forewarned, Josef Taylor may have exiled a daughter he felt unworthy, but the woman that stands before you today is not so easily cast aside." The ugly words flung at her years ago ripped through her mind, deepening the bitter byways that had been etched years ago and never healed. "I will pack this afternoon, take the morning train for Tombstone."

She had not voiced her desire to go alone to California, and before she found an opportunity, Chess invented a cause and accompanied her. In three days, having uncovered more damning evidence in Salt Lake City, Josie arrived in San Francisco, determined to persuade Jacob to align his loyalties with her.

Their hotel towered at the center of the major merging of arteries of San Francisco. Within walking distance of the end of the railway, the mission style building looked down upon an aqua ocean that engulfed the horizon in shimmering waters. The lobby was regal; crystal chandeliers hung in massive canopies, their glitter dripping in fist sized pendulums. Red carpets divided the terra cotta floors into private seating arrangements; each division furnished with period pieces reflecting Spanish influence. Silver urns overflowed with fresh flowers, silver trays held glass boxes filled with sweetmeats, delicate candies and cakes. A hand bell in the center of each tea set brought a pot of hot freshly brewed liquid at anytime, mint juleps for afternoon, and whiskey or tequila for evening.

Chess nodded to the concierge as he crossed the massive lobby, then led Josie to a single door shielded by a huge palm.

A young man hurried past him, opened the door to a cage capable of lifting a small party. "Please, madam?" He assisted Josie over the bars dividing the floor and into the implement, then waited for Chess to enter. As the elevator moved Chess chuckled. "You are either the best actress that has ever enjoyed this contraption or your experience bests mine. Is it possible, my silent Josie, there is more to you than a Dutch-country banker's daughter?"

Josie smiled. "My father installed a lift after my mother suffered one of her early collapses. I grew up pulling those ropes. Later, Taylor squeezed herself into the silent butler at an ordinary house where we lived. I always knew when the tea arrived cold that she had been playing games on it." Pale lashes flicked at instant moisture.

They stepped out into a short hall where Chess produced a key that opened an enormous pair of double doors. Inside oversized mahogany furniture nestled with dainty brocades and satins, the contrast inviting and simple. Costly silver lamps sat amid delicate china burners and copper miner's boxes, brutal military paintings in somber oils hung next to water brush florals and oriental silks.

Leaving Chess at the door Josie sped through the rooms, picking up various objects in admiration. "Such a collection, all so beautifully displayed. So worldly, almost of museum quality, the hotel has my congratulations." The eclectic mix enthralled Josie. "Where on earth would one obtain such fascinating possessions?"

"As you said Josie, around the world, everywhere." Chess watched, his eyes alight with interest. "Glad you approve."

Opened doors led to sleeping arrangements on opposite sides of the room. "Perfect. The suite is absolutely stunning." A bell captain arrived leading an entourage carrying trunks and valises. Chess quickly directed them. "Put these two in this room," he pointed to his right. "The remainder can go over there."

Josie felt disappointed. She had not expected to share sleeping quarters with Chess, but now that the opportunity had risen she would have liked to at least have had the chance to tease a little before denying him access to her. His apparent disinterest in her proximity displeased her.

After they each had unpacked their private articles and settled down over refreshments, hers tea, his port, Chess laid out the terms he felt appropriate for enlisting Jacob's aid. "The initial meetings must be private, without arousing suspicion, secluded, away from trumpet ears and tintype eyes. We must get Jacob's cooperation before anyone discovers his participation." Chess gazed around the opulent room, fingers fussing for a stick match in his vest pocket. "I will engage a separate room, something less ostentatious, under a fictitious name. The houseman can send Jacob straight up, make it appear an appointment to consider a large investment."

Josie protested. "He would be inclined to bring others of importance who have had dealings with you. Even if you expressly indicated you wanted it kept secret. He would question your position. Better yet. No one here knows me. I would be better suited to contact Jacob initially." Josie spoke almost as if she talked to herself. "I must meet him in a public forum, someplace quite common, but proper for a lady to conduct business with a gentleman."

Jacob would come alone. She must insist on public arenas where her own weakness could not be tempted. She could not allow any personal longings to betray her. A tea house, of course. Perfectly respectable, no opportunity for an unpleasant incident. Satisfied, she turned to Chess. "I'll meet him near the wharf, at a public tea room."

"You feel you must do this yourself? Our pressure has already demoralized him. Look at the manner in which he is selling off his stock, taking advantage of your spirited offer. I have no doubt he has dismissed his loyalty to his wife's family. Our caution concerns his associates suspecting betrayal. Why should we add concern over propriety? Unless you suffer fears of testing your own attraction?"

Josie rearranged the flowers in a vase, plunking the largest in the center, striping the others of their browned blossoms and tossing the thorny stems into a nearby container. She hadn't the courage to protest his insight. "This hotel could certainly do with tighter standards, perhaps I should offer training for their staff." She flung the still fragrant petals into a stationary drawer.

Chess chuckled. "I'll speak to my manager." At her expression of shock, his robust laughter waffled through the room. "You can be quite charming when you are confused. It is not often surprise shows so plainly on your face. Yes, this hotel belongs to me, and others of equal grandeur."

The edges of Josie's teeth spit shock waves as they banged closed. She felt ridiculous, like a catalogue girl at a debutante ball. He displayed his standing without mean spirit, never flaunting it, usually admitting to ownership only after she had caught an error in the presentation of one of his properties or weakness of a financial holding. After she settled this situation, she would uncover the extent of his wealth.

Chess's jovial tone turned serious. "You see, my little Josie, I have a very plausible reason to appear at the local men's clubs, collecting gossip and adding a bit of my own theory. Trust me, no one wastes speculation on my purpose in prying into the stability of Worldwide Bank or my questioning the trustworthiness of its board of directors. However, I will relent to your meeting with Jacob, but that I feel is necessary for another reason." He held up his hands as if to ward her off. "Do what you must do. Meanwhile, I will monitor the stew you already have boiling."

The note to Jacob was prepared, her artistic pen announcing her arrival in black and white, inviting him to join her. Her fingers traced his name, so similar to another note she had sent, one that had been returned, but this signature reflected another person entirely. Josie pulled the bell cord for a courier.

Late that same afternoon Josie entered the teahouse alone. "A table for two, please? May I have the one in the back, near the kitchen?" She had arrived early, but her skirt still needed arranging when Jacob greeted her.

"Now my day begins. Our separation lasted much too long." His bow introduced a string of questions. "How long are you staying? Are you free for the evenings? Promise me I may escort you to supper? Tonight? Every night?"

Josie exhaled slowly, suddenly aware she had been holding her breath. Her heart beat like a clock wound too tightly, skipping rapidly. She must act composed, not let him see his effect on her.

Josie extended her hand, trying to think of everything else but his lips lingering on her fingers, moist warmth that invited more intimate exchange. "I missed seeing you arrive. How fashionable you look. It must be satisfying to have access to the best tailor. You must give me his name." A flush warmed her throat and cheeks, she began to perspire.

Jacob slid into his chair, holding tight to her fingers. "You didn't come all the way across the Arizona territory and halfway up California to ask for the name of my tailor 'Little Jos'." He smiled, a supplication that offered sweetness and admiration. "And I do not care to concern myself with why you came, only that you are here."

Fear gripped Josie in a paralyzing clutch, fear of believing him. Her heart stood on edge, ready to break. "You may be sorely disappointed when you learn of my cause. I have a matter that must have your immediate attention. A situation of such grave concern to me that I risk your dismissal and rebuke for even presenting it to you, but I must." She need not pretend her affection, or her dread that he may well send her away, she felt the fear of his rejection travel from her curls to the soles of her doeskin clad feet.

"If your cause exists for any other reason than to become reacquainted with me, I shall be miserable. I shall cast myself into the ocean, a victim of your charms." His eyes penetrated hers with the heat of warm liquid on a cold day, reaching to the core of her soul, offering the attention and vigor her body had long denied. "Whatever the reason, Josefina, your wish is granted. Anything you desire to keep you near me."

She felt dizzy, her skin twitching with remembered caresses, a gentle friction that had heated the very being of her so that no other touch was welcome. She must hurry. "Jacob, I speak of François. He has embezzled funds, more than half the treasury of the bank and cartel. If he is not stopped, exposed, Taylorsville Bank will be ruined, along with my family. You will be judged an accomplice. My investors will be bamboozled; my reputation ruined forever."

Jacob dropped her hand as if scalded. A frown creased his brow. "Why would you utter such false accusations? A lie of enormous potential. Whatever provoked you? Who put you up to this? Your talk could start a scandal of such proportion it would destroy us all. Ruin a goodly percentage of the financial world."

Jacob looked about the room, searching faces for familiarity. His chair grated as he scooted next to her. "You must not spread such rumors. What prompted you to bring such an attack? To speak such abomination. Surely you don't think such a recrimination on your behalf would ever win you favor. Is this a ploy to restore your rights with your father, secure your inheritance?"

His breath tingled on her cheeks. Josie could smell his tobacco. "I brought documents with me. Concealed in the reticule at your feet. I only ask that you take them. Read them today, as quickly as possible. Meet with me tomorrow and tell me if you can dispute their accuracy." Her head filled with the scent of his tonic as she took a deep breath. "If you find fault with my presentation, I will destroy the documents and return to Bisbee without speaking to another soul. I do this to save myself, and to save a you, an honest man who has been wronged as badly as I by the accused."

Jacob's face paled, chalky fissures lined the lips that had been so warm just minutes ago. Josie wanted to crush him to her, reassure him it all would be righted. Instead she stood, extending her hand; her knees curtsied. She spoke in a natural tone. "You have my regrets for tonight. An appointment tomorrow, lunch at the Blue Heron, two o'clock."

Josie regretted her words immediately, but his eyes did not blink, his attention elsewhere. Her skirts swished in a lazy swirl as she strolled slowly around the length of the room, making sure he picked up the leather case she had laid against the table leg. She latched the door behind her just as he tucked the thick portfolio under his arm.

~ * ~

Chess ordered wine and dinner brought up to their suite. Dressed in his evening attire he waited impatiently for Josie to emerge from her room. He had not wanted her to go alone to meet Jacob. A disaster, as he had suspected. She had not spoken a word other than to assure him Jacob had received the parcel. This mission of Josie's might well lead to his losing her, not through lack of effort on his part. Her passion glistened like fool's gold; she had not forgotten her first love. Worse, she assigned to Jacob qualities the gods of mythology would envy. Resentment plagued him, weakening his interest for a memorable evening, but he could not let her know.

Josie stepped from her room, covered from shoulder to toe in a glistening gown of sapphire crystal, nipped at her waist, bustled in the back with a sweep that called attention to her firm derrière. She pivoted, pleased with the display. "You are satisfied with my choice? You acted such a dog in the manger about my shopping, pleading an engagement."

"I had no idea I would share such exquisite beauty. You are, Josie, without question a siren brought back from history to cause men to dash into the sea with the exhilaration of your nearness. I ordered dinner sent up. May I suggest an alternative? Play for me, Josie, a soliloquy on your violin, then we'll parade the dining hall, the flower garden, the veranda, perhaps see a show and visit a club. I will show San Francisco a real lady."

The chimes struck one when Mr. Tuffet and Mrs. Broderick entered their suite. The night had seen them pursued by the highest officials, foreign dignitaries, a prince, with introduction to the elite of San Francisco. Josie courted the successful and ended the evening crowned a member. Chess's boasting of her multiple achievements and references to the expansion of his own fortune drew requests by the dozens for advice and a place on her list of investors. Her heady exhilaration remained until they faced the stacks of documents neatly piled on the library desk.

Chess spoke first. "We enjoyed tonight, a taste of more to come. Tomorrow, another test of Jacob's willingness. Soon the whole charade will be ended, one way or another." He raised her hand to his lips. "Good night, Josie, as an earth bound goddess you were magnificent. Only thing better would have been if I had been able to introduce you as my wife." He turned without waiting for a response and entered his bedroom.

Josie walked around the large sitting room for a long while, fingering the objects d'art, admiring awards from places she had never heard of that hung on the satin pinned walls. The parting remark was the closest Chess had come to a proposal. He was an enigma, a mystery, a man of many dimensions, and without question a man who loved her deeply. And she depended on him, shared her heart's desires and hurts with him, needed his admiration and support, but she feared, in the darkness, alone, her dreams would return to Jacob's touch.

Josie hung the splendid gown in the armoire and threw on a chenille robe, drug a chair to the balcony and sat in the cold, wishing she could care differently about a man who offered her the romance and love she coveted before her solitary fight to survive had begun.

~ * ~

The next day the lunch whistle brought lads and maidens holding hands, strolling past fishermen filleting their midday's catch, mothers with almond eyes calling to hidden children with shrill clamors in a language Josie did not understand. Seamen sipped ale while downing their fish and chips. All the while her chowder grew cold. Jacob was not coming. She twisted and fidgeted, tasted and sipped, smiled at innocents and snubbed those of foul intent; she could not eat. Chess lingered on the wooden wharf that edged the ocean. He would not chance her leaving the eatery unescorted, despite its reputation of soundness.

Josie decided she waited in vain. Counting out the required payment she signaled the girl. Over the server's thin shoulders she saw an uneasy, tired, lackluster Jacob enter.

"A quart and a bowl for my brother," Josie said, then squared herself on the bench. The back end of the room was dark. False portals opened to the smell of musky waters and shrieks of gulls, she thought of Costello House and Taylor. Of the better life they had been denied.

Before Jacob sat down Josie began; anger edged her haste. "The documents were in perfect order, just as I promised. There is no question François set about to ruin my family, used Father's own trust to weaken him. Slicked the profit off the top like cream from milk and plans to bankrupt the cartel, leave soured curds behind for my father to explain."

The girl set down the ale. Jacob, his body whipped like an abandoned mongrel, landed on the seat solidly, lifeless as a mannequin.

Josie took a deep breath. "Jacob, I am such a fool." He looked across at her, his eyes red rimmed, seemingly surprised at hearing her voice. "I gave you no chance to speak your mind. Please, forgive my urgency. I have lived with these documents far too long. They have taken possession of my sensibilities. I must give you opportunity to search your own mind, ask questions, share your opinions with me. Perhaps I have rushed too hastily to a faulty judgment." She folded her hands primly in her lap.

Jacob sat with his eyes trained on a bubble in the ale, then traced the path of solitary drips each time they slid from rim to bottom. "No," he snipped, "your judgment is sound. If these papers are as authentic as they seem, François's fraud is indisputable. He has perpetrated a crime against every person with whom he has ever crossed paths."

"I worked all night in a futile attempt to prove your claims inaccurate. I prayed for them to be false. I juggled every record and digit I could to find a fault, to no avail. The man is guilty." Jacob raised his head, his lips thinned to a thread, "as is my wife. Marianne used my position and facility to bury receipts in multiple layers of fictitious accounts. Whenever the sum reached some foreordained level, her draft shifted the funds to accounts in France, bureaus controlled solely by the ducLaFevre name."

Josie vacillated between a need to scream her assent and a longing to comfort. Her throat rasped with tightly controlled emotion. "You have a fortune at stake, as do others. What would you suggest we do?"

The thread relaxed into a grimace. "Burn them at the stake, hang them by their heels, throw them overboard. Whatever we do will not be enough. I wrestled with our chances of righting this and found no answer. Who are we? An heiress who has been disowned, the courts would discount your witness as greedy discontentment. An itinerant engineer who married a wealthy foreigner and soon shared the fruits of her stealth. Our cause is beaten before it begins."

"There is a way," Josie interrupted. "A friend proposes to present the documents and indict François on conspiracy to commit fraud on the United States government, but we must have more proof. Legal descriptions of property stolen, deeds granted to fictitious investors, records of the deeds and profits retitled solely to the ducLaFevres. They must exist in your bank somewhere."

Jacob nodded. "Tomorrow, near the wharf. The transfer must be concealed, completely innocent appearing. I may already be suspect." He looked straight into Josie's eyes. "Marianne has left me. My connection with the ducLaFevre family can end." His gaze transferred to the sky, then the sea, following sea gulls battling over bits of floating carcasses. "I will bring what you need."

"Jacob, if the deed is too costly, perhaps someone else might be willing to help. I would be a fool were I not to tell you I worry about my part in destroying you. That was not my intent. With the proper documents presented, a proof of cooperation, a pardon may be forthcoming, but there is no guarantee."

"Josefina, my love, you share your meal with a ruined man. Whichever way it goes, I am riding a blind horse."

~ * ~

The ocean slapped the shore like a mother's hand spanking a baby's bare bottom, leaving behind an imprint that quickly disappeared, never scarring the wonder of living canvas. Josie relished more the roar further down the sandy beaches, where the wind and water joined bodies, their entwined strength crashing upon the cliffs, eroding man sized holes in walls of stone, leaving hollows for earth bound gazers to track the path of the sun and moon.

While she and Chess waited the next day, Josie dipped her toes into the ocean, then mouthed her chill. "Brrr. Too cold." But she ventured further out, until she felt the slimy, wet seaweed attaching itself to her legs, as if it proposed designing a gown more appropriate for her visit. Foam clung to her knees like gauzy scarves; her bravery lost, she scurried for land.

Flocks of women dressed in wool bathing dresses lounged on the sands, their bodies protected from voyeurism by the heavy, dark fabric. Men strutted about, their hairy bodies turned into underfed chicken breasts or overfed barrels, few with the attraction a well-padded suit coat and girdled pant advertised.

The sun cast long shadows by the time Jacob plopped onto the forgiving sand, a box sufficient to hold a picnic banquet by his side. "Here they are, a sampling of the documents you need to indict François. Straw corporations, hidden assets, layers of disguised companies, everything." He stuck his hand out to Chess, not seemingly surprised at his presence. "I sure skinned my own hide."

Chess assured him, "All the proof we collected points directly to François. It began before you ever arrived in Taylorsville. Assets were hidden in banks overseas before François and Josie's father reached American shores. Their comradeship developed during the people's revolutions in Austria and France when hidden funds were a necessity. Only one of the partners never gave up."

Josie countered. "I carried a lifetime of guilt for how my greed caused such misery for me, you, my daughter, ruined every chance of happiness any of us had. My salvation is that out of it all I have Taylor. François had prepared since my birth to generate my fall from grace. Indeed, his avarice thrived and eventually bore fruit, and Marianne was not without blame."

Josie's voice crackled like sand strewn on paper with the mention of Jacob's wife's name. "I pray this puts an end to all the deception." She felt there still remained a dark shadow, an unknown hand with an unidentified print they had not yet matched.

Chess quickly examined half a dozen specific dates. "Embezzlement. A pattern repeated each time a new investor joined the National Land Company. A portion of the investment disappeared. The remainder became a legitimate holding with the Bank, or it too passed into a fraudulent land company then into the same accounts."

Josie realized, the year her eyes set on a debut that would free her to roam and her eager heart to troll for a vagabond engineer, she had unknowingly trod on the toes of the world's financial power. François had chosen her as much for her ability to avenge his partner as for her appetite and love of luxury, a judgment she both denied and valued. Now, Josie planned to be the lady of unwanted tidings that crumbled François's kingdom.

"Will you be safe here?" Josie asked. "He will know immediately that you provided these documents." She wanted him to need her, and she wanted to walk away freed. Never, she belonged to him.

Jacob beamed at her, excitement flashing in his eyes, "Worried about me?" He casually hugged her shoulders, his arm remaining. "If

I find times too dangerous here, I have friends and business partners I warned of the disaster that is to come. They are most grateful for my forbearance, willing to share my burden. Other than their support," his honey-colored eyes met hers, "when this is finished I expect to find a position waiting for me, or a new endeavor, perhaps Broderick and Broderick Corporation."

Chess barreled out a rumbling laugh before removing Jacob's arm, ostensibly to shake his hand. "You are a smooth one all right. Can see how you come in so handy. Charm the fuzz off a peach. But I am putting you on notice. I have asked Josie to marry me. She has not said no. You come to Bisbee, you are treading on my ground."

Jacob stood still, then his shoulder nudged Josie. "Well, I am sure we both know, we can always count on Josie to know her own mind."

~ * ~

Chess turned the evidence over to the California federal courts, learning it would be weeks before they could sift through all the documents. The trio would need to remain nearby to answer questions; meanwhile National Land and the Bank remained free to conduct business without restraint.

Within days a new representative of Worldwide Bank arrived, relieving Jacob of his position, snatching away his authority. His desk was moved to the open area of the street floor, outside the private office arena and far removed from earshot of inner workings, his keys requested. He retained no responsibilities.

After weeks of interrogation and explanation to the court Josie and Chess returned to Bisbee, more certain then ever their efforts would be corrupted. Josie began her next project.

That summer brought further collapse in the stock market, silver dropped in value to forty five cents on the dollar, six hundred banks closed. By spring, seventy-four railroads had gone out of business and another eighteen were convicted of rate fixing in violation of the Sherman Antitrust Act. Broderick Investment Corporation grabbed some up for a penny on the dollar.

Almost two years passed before the grand jury read the indictment. By then the dummy companies had been dissolved, the identity of their creators scratched. Monies invested in secret annuities suddenly bore the name of National Land Company Bank, layers of covert businesses appeared justified for security sake. Although scandalized and censured, its prestige slandered, Worldwide Bank and National Land Company survived. Josie's only reward amounted to the huge sums of money her investors now possessed and the increased value of the shares she held.

Not a single sign of recognition came from Josef Taylor. Neither letter, telegram, nor any grateful word of mouth from any National Land, Worldwide Bank or Taylorsville Bank associate found its way to Bisbee. Outside her circle of local supporters, no one acknowledged the splendid efforts of the Bank of Bisbee's President.

Josie's wounds festered.

Thirty-three

Chess's telegram sent Josie scurrying on a train ride from Bisbee to St. Louis. Emerging from Union Station, she quickly hailed one of the horse-drawn taxis lining the walk. "Park Drive." Her first call would be at Costello House. Mandy's letters sent meager news of Taylor, Lily, and James, little more than they were well and safe. She knew the little family had moved from The Landings, but perhaps face to face with Mandy, she could garner more than in a letter.

On the way the carriage passed stores Josie had frequently shopped years ago, but now their murky windows displayed tacky merchandise. Further on, when they entered the residential area, the houses showed visible neglect. It was midday and people lounged on the porches, unconcerned with the weed crowded gardens and unkempt lawns surrounding them.

The deterioration dismayed Josie. The drain on her emotions, if Costello House reflected such deterioration, would prove too debilitating, and she wouldn't be able to see Taylor either. Her attentions must concentrate on her upcoming appearance. Josie tapped the driver's shoulder. "Turn around, please, take me back uptown to the Villa Olivia." She had heard the décor was elaborate, the service lavish. Costello House could wait until after she dealt with Father and François.

The decision proved inspired. The lobby of the hotel nourished Josie's need for elegance, surrounding her in all the luxury and pomp her tottery confidence sought.

Four months after the government's too lenient settlement of the fraud and conspiracy charges against the cartel and Worldwide Bank, Josie prepared to travel to Taylorsville. Small fines and a directive to reorganize under new leadership amounted to no more than a royal snub to the cartel. Josie wanted full restitution to the investors and the reputation of her family restored.

"Well, J. L. Broderick or Josefina Taylor, however they think of you, this is it." Josie twirled before the mirror, seeking assurance. "Maybe, the bright candy-stripe would look better, less like I was attempting to curry favor?" Josie preferred the blue silk, and Father would appreciate its reserve. If he chose to favor anything about her.

Father had inhabited his private world and that of the "thou shalt nots" for an additional twenty years after her escape. Josie did not wish to invite Father's or the Elders' immediate disapproval, thinking she mocked them with vulgar display. A platinum curl twisted through her fingers.

"Josef Taylor, mean-spirited as you are, will think what you want, regardless what I wear." Josie smiled. She felt good, had slept well. The nightmares had evaporated months ago, pushed away by the strong man who normally accompanied her, anticipating her every wish.

Chess remained in Washington, lobbying against the Elkins Act. In spite of his efforts, Senator LaFollette and his cronies labored to pass a law deeming railroads in violation if they rebated a portion of the cost to their better shippers. Even before Chess's telephone call, Josie sold their shares not involved in transporting oil and invested the profits in what she felt would be the next mode of transportation to win American's hearts, Henry Ford and his Model A.

She diverted a small portion, as pure speculation, with a gentleman who had in the past collaborated with Thomas Edison. Mr. Edwin Porter had produced a moving picture film, twelve minutes long, "The Great Train Robbery." She found it entertaining while visiting Los Angeles, spending a dime to view the miracle dozens of times. After eavesdropping on the exhibitors, Josie wired Chess to make arrangements to view the new amusement.

When she and Chess had returned from San Francisco, Chess bought a cottage within an easy stroll of Josie's house in Bisbee. He soon filled her days and evenings, and the ache of Taylor's absence became less distressing. An untiring man and unfaltering friend, Chess dealt with Josie's demons, listening, encouraging her to end the torment that hampered the happiness they had found.

Josie missed him by her side this trip, and still felt annoyed he considered his task in the Capitol too important to accompany her. She had set about to settle the matter herself, but she had expected Chess would come with her to face Father.

I should motor to Taylorsville. Think of the excitement of operating the first mechanical machine to travel the roads of Taylor County. What an opportunity to experiment with an automobile. Take a day. What about a breakdown? So what? I have no set arrival time. They know only I will attend the meeting. Who would come to my aid? No, best rent a horse and buggy.

The possibility of a breakdown came as a hidden wish. No automobile mechanics existed, and she knew nothing of machines. Stuck along the road, she would on all counts miss the meeting. Josie was many things, but not cowardly. Besides, it would not do to shock the Elders much more. A proper carriage, driven at her normal speed, would be enough to announce her arrival.

The road stretched furrowed and powdery, packed hard by a cloudless spring. Dust covered toads croaked in the ditches, calling for rain. The pristine farms and flat acres of green veiled earth brought an overwhelming nostalgia that fed Josie's homesickness. She faced her romanticizing. *Remember the last time I traveled this road. And why?*

Memories came of racing recklessly, blinded by rage, filled with fear. Not knowing the faithful companion sharing her bench buried betrayal beneath a ruse of friendship. No comparing this beautiful day with the snowstorm she and Marianne had weathered or the finish to that forced flight with the expectations Josie held now. Oddly, she felt revived. The memories had lost their impact, seeming more like a tale taken from everyday folk stories. Understandably, Josie thought with satisfaction, she was not the same woman of that tragic day.

Queen Ann's Lace, golden yarrow, and blue primrose led away from long banks of daisies. Josie enjoyed the ride, elated and comforted—until the carriage entered Taylorsville's square.

The wheels stopped before the granite building whose stone edifice proclaimed Bank of Taylorsville, like some mute, mythical beast. The glorious brass door eased open at Josie's touch, as if magical.

A ping vibrated up from Josie's heel when she crossed the brass threshold. So many normal things brought strong feelings of regret. The slender tucks that wreathed Josie's chest puckered as she took a deep breath. She felt dizzy, woozy.

Perhaps I should freshen up, come back later. No, I am here now. May as well get through the first encounter.

Josie approached a marble counter, its edges worn smooth where customers had leaned over palm-sized books, adding to or taking from their history.

The shaded carpet separating public and private areas looked new. Electric lamps brought a tasteful glow to the lobby, without the gaudiness of falseness. Most probably, Josie speculated, glowing from the bank-owned generating plant. A telephone bell chimed, another addition most probably installed under Father's direction. All modernization nonexistent such a short time ago.

But, the tantalizing smell remained.

Josie inhaled. The elusive, notable aroma of gold that pulsed through her veins offered a robust welcome Josie had not anticipated. She looked about, seeking the cause of the awakening of the worship of wealth that filled her. *Could I have remained the same?* No, Josie battled her irritation. She recognized the power of wealth, but no longer coveted riches for its own sake.

The clerks' desks stood in the same orderly rows, old nicks forgotten alongside the prominence of new scrapes. The years of customers' touches had softened the bright brass of the cages into a browned patina. Astonished, Josie studied the stairway rising before her. It seemed not nearly as steep, nor as broad. Her feet trod with a peppery step she had forgotten.

"The blue of your dress falls short of your beautiful eyes."

Josie gasped. The years fled, the voice dropping her into the scene of years ago. "Dieter, must you sneak up on your victims?" Josie stared at hair still gold as flax, a slight paunch that seemed only to lend stability and affluence. Dieter stood half-hidden in the shadows of the stairs. Raising her arms, Josie extended them in welcome. She did not see Dieter rush into them, only felt the crush of his body and the kisses that wet her cheeks.

Finally he stopped and took a few steps away. "I have been waiting impatiently since your telegram arrived. Seems an eternity. Actually, I have waited a lifetime, and more than twenty years for your return." He did not let go of Josie's hands. "Too much time lost, Lil' Jos. You should have come to me right away. You knew I would make things right for you."

"Father would have had nothing of your efforts. Probably sent you packing with me." Josie looked about, not expecting to see Father, but uncertain. "Where is he?"

"You do not know, Josefina? Your father has not come to the bank since shortly after you left. Well, not once since the day your mother passed over. Conducts all his business at Taylor Estates. Both he and François left the day-to-day management of the bank to me." Dieter stopped, smiling proudly. "I promised you someday we would direct the bank together."

The fact Father's signature had not appeared on any of the documents had led Josefina to believe he was not involved in the corruption. That he had handed over his power had eluded her. Perhaps so, perhaps more brilliantly, he moved behind the scenes, schooled to have others incriminate themselves.

"Dieter, you have accomplished so much."

"Then you will stay. Marry me. Govern the cartel and bank. I know you have never married. François agreed to sell me the Chateau when we marry. I know you admired it, and..."

Josie interrupted. "Dieter, I have a bank of my own. A following, a home, friends I could not abandon. I have a new life. Too many years have passed."

"I told you," Dieter's voice grew anxious, "you should have come right back, come to me that very day. I would have protected you." Dieter dropped his hand. "What kind of friends?"

"I have business associates who depend on me. Families who have taken me to their hearts." Josie could not stop the smile spreading across her face, knew her eyes sparkled. "An intelligent, caring man who supports my ambitions and sees that I am well cared for." Thinking of Chess brought reassurance and an unexpected longing.

"Your father is at the Estates." Dieter sounded mean-mouthed, beyond sullen. "He seldom leaves there now. He has been dying a little bit each day since the morning you deserted us all."

Josie thought her Father still controlled Bank of Taylorsville, although she had noted Dieter, Jacob and François had signed the documents, deposits and transfers.

The wicked gleam of Dieter's narrowed eyes pulled his smile into a sneer. "You are genuinely surprised." He backed away. "Perhaps you should go directly to your Father."

He stepped down the stairs, then turned back, his face a blank canvas. "I have always wanted you, Josefina, for my own. Seems in spite of all my best efforts, I have lost again. My congratulations to whomever you have chosen." He turned on his heel, making a little clicking salute as his shoes touched. He did not offer his hand in good-bye.

"I must go home directly." Josie spoke aloud to no one. Her reference to home spoke the strength of her fear. Her feet stutter-stepped.

Nonchalantly, Dieter stopped his descent. "Perhaps you should go to the hotel? It's near dark, and our roads will be unfamiliar, dangerous for you to travel alone. After all, you are a stranger to our community. After a good night's sleep, you can arrive rested in the morning."

Josie scowled, the forced pinch clearing her mind. "Tomorrow?" That was prudent. Still, she felt haunted by an unaccounted fear. "Tell me what you know of my father?"

Dieter stepped back up, slipped Josie's arm in his. "You really should rest. Gallivanting around the country, alone, is difficult for anyone, especially a lady of your inherited delicacy. Let me escort you to your room. We can share dinner."

She had no appetite. Her body felt sluggish, cinched about the chest, as if she had swallowed an entire meal whole without stopping. She had heard Dieter's reference to Mother's preoccupation when her mind had begun sliding into murky waters. "You are right about my resting." Her voice was listless and distant.

When they entered François's hotel, memories of years ago haunted her. Jacob had supervised construction of The Chateau, why he remained in Taylorsville. The reason she had time to learn to want him.

"Eating will have to wait. I could not swallow. I prefer to stay in my room, avoid any confrontation," Josie said.

Dieter showed his understanding and ordered a light supper sent up to her. She ignored the overfilled plates and crept into bed. The nightmares returned, waking her with muffled shrieks and tearless sobbing.

In the morning she slid easily across the satin bedspread, tumbling from the bed to jam a shoe on her foot. She would have preferred to play possum, crawl back under the covers in the empty room and sleep, then take the hired buggy back to St. Louis without ever facing anyone. She would not. The people of this "thou shalt not" place held her future happiness hostage, and perhaps the lives of Taylor and the children, too.

If Father is in trouble, I must help him first. How full of myself I am. Josie brooded. *Fath*er *does not want my help, over twenty years without any contact.* Only Mandy kept her family alive, and that correspondence told about Taylor and the children. But lately, Mandy had not revealed what Taylor was doing, or where she was, only post cards saying Taylor was well.

Josie considered that Taylor had promised, *on my life,* she would never visit Taylorsville. Josie, arms clasping her legs, began to rock back and forth. Her daughter must never come here, on threat of her life and the lives of their entire family. Josie could imagine Chess scolding sternly. "Let's set things straight right now, madam. Nobody owes you a thing. Taylor is a grown woman, free to make her own decisions." Josie noticed she was humming. A vision flashed of Mother sitting on the bed, rocking and droning impassively. The image distracted Josie. Abruptly, she drew her dress over her head and walked toward the water closet. Of course, Chess was right, and that only made the situation tolerable, not what she wanted.

The physical effort of commanding the buggy brought some contentment for Josie. A triumphant return in an automobile, no matter how much she promoted the invention, would have been too unnerving, for her and the Elders. The swaying vehicle and horses whipped past the fields, the field hands rising from their work to watch her fly by them. Josie chuckled inwardly at their visible objections.

The wide, slicing leaves of corn plants covered the fields, their development past the brilliant green of seedlings. Prohibited spring nourishing because of drought, the ears were undeveloped, caught between genesis and harvest, stunted by lack of nurturing beyond their control. Father had abandoned the temperamental tobacco and rice crops.

The trip took much longer than Josie remembered before she faced the narrow country lane. Before turning, she stopped for a few minutes and surveyed Taylor Estates. The countryside looked the same, as if she had never left.

She was again Josefina, who served the tyrant that lay at the end of this path. She had not favored coming, but could not stay away. Her need was singular, the revelation that would set her free. Had she transgressed or was she the one wronged that fateful morning?

Josie slowed the pace, peeking around trees shaded by the gray of a cloudy sky. Workers bobbed and squatted along the lane, their curiosity momentary.

The mansion bludgeoned Josie with its sameness. Except for the absence of the roses, everything looked as it had the day her curses poisoned the air. The frenzy of rage leading up to the profane behavior simmered deep within her, the words lingering for all to hear. "Damn you both to hell. I shall never give up my child."

Baskets of red and pink geraniums hung from the porch eaves, creating a canopy of color.

The flowers at Pickett House had delighted everyone else with their cozy charm. Now Josie knew why the display had offended her so.

A lone figure sat in a rocking chair, the rockers still, their back to the approaching visitor. A shock of gray hair. Corpulent flesh hanging on diseased bones disappeared into a shawl draped to the floor.

The reins slid from Josie's hands. Her arms shook while she watched Father.

The old man stood with trembling feebleness, the shawl sliding to the floor. His cane wobbled as he shuffled in an unhurried turn. "Is it you, Josefina?"

Josie hopped down and went to Father, hugging the thin shoulders, not daring to kiss more than the top of his head. Her heart wept with the feel of his knobby body in her arms.

Josef Taylor fell back down into a wicker chair at the end of the porch. Head riveted, his cobalt eyes locked on Josie. "I expected to never see you again. I forbade you to ever return."

"I am here, Father." Josie sat on a spindly settee next to the chair. "I go by the name of Josie Broderick, conduct business as J.L. Broderick."

"Whatever you call yourself, you are still the whore I sent away." His eyes narrowed, the pupils pinpoints in their sea of blue. "Josie Broderick, you say? You did not marry him."

This was not the manner in which Josie anticipated meeting her father. "A name I appropriated to protect myself. I am sure you know the reason why." Father's body had aged beyond its years, but his mind had not slipped.

Watery eyes, dulled with pain and anger, leaned toward Josie. "It matters not to me what your reasons were. Nor will your lies please me. I did the best that could be done for you."

Josie sat very still, her sapphire eyes thundering, locked on Father. Her lips moved, but the immodest retort stayed in her throat.

The odor of the stables assaulted Josie. The pungent smell scalded her nostrils, or was the wounding of another stable memory? "Tell me, Father. How you did your best." The words were cautious, solicitous, as if Josie asked someone to pass the cream at a family dinner.

Josef turned to his daughter, dangling his hand across the wicker arm. "You were to care for me, care for your mother. When we needed you, you were gone. I am alone now."

Tears spotted a dark path down Josie's silk dress. Her choked sob stopped his words for a moment, but his look remained steady. His voice was strong, confident. "Perhaps, one day I shall have the strength to forgive you." He started to rise.

"Now, Father. I deserve forgiveness now." The words issued a command. Josie sat straight, shoulders steeled. "Tell me everything, now."

Josef pulled his chair nearer, scooting along with a leg that seemed not to bend. "I am not sure, Josefina, that you wish to hear it all."

Thirty-four

Josef bulled his diseased body out of the chair and staggered toward the entrance door. "Go inside." At Josie's astonished look he added, "No need to involve the entire community any further in your sins."

The library had not been aired recently. The smell of the leather bindings lining the shelves turned Josie's stomach upside down. She shuddered, her limbs wooden, stiff and disconnected, walling off a crumbling spirit, a puppet waiting to feel a heartbeat. Fear oozed from her in an acrid sweat that made her more uncomfortable.

Sultry air pillowed the room when a single, silent outcry exploded in her mind. *Whore!*

The condemnation preceded a recollection of a promise and hazel eyes swimming with desire, tender touches sweeping over her, and the relief of pending freedom. The swift, powerful passion enveloped Josie for less than an instant before being eclipsed by the insult of François's savagery. The scars pulsed and pained over the trust betrayed and innocence despoiled. Cold fury swept over Josie, until she thought of Taylor.

Josie envisioned an unwitting sole-eyed fawn venturing eagerly from its den. Shot for sport, then ignored, lifeless. Blameless. Destroyed nonetheless, food for vermin. Was the animal Taylor? Or herself?

Sunlight nuzzled the glass of the French doors, warming the transparent panes Josie had seen so easily shattered. The wooden frames barred a rage that waited on the other side, threatening to burst in, an ugly wrath swooping in to crush truth and love. Josie squinted, expecting to unearth a glistening shard buried in the carpet. There must be one, she mused, smeared with the venom so viciously spilled that day.

A pen rested untroubled in its hollow, the gold clip advertising its richness. A lamp, pewter, unbreakable, without the brilliant reds, oranges and blues of artfully arranged stained glass, anchored itself on a corner, the milk glass shade embarrassed in its plainness. Had her life passed with the only evidence an elegant masterpiece replaced by a common lamp? A measure of time, from sunrise to sunset, a span going to and from, gone, Josie felt suspended, as if she had never been.

The evilness that brought nightmares and threatened her child stalked this room, a tyrant that belched filth and had cast her out. Was he now reduced to this old man, lonely, starved for compassion in spite of his vileness that had bled her of joy and denied her hope for her child?

Josie was startled when someone entered the room, goblet in one hand, the other clutching a pitcher and draped with a lace edged hand towel. The elderly "sister" mumbled Deutsch words deep in her throat and ambled along with marathon effort. Ice chips slopped against fragile crystal, tinkling with each shuffle she made. "Ahh, we knew you would come back, Josefina. Who could stay away forever?"

Josefina stood.

The woman poured the cold liquid, pushing the filled goblet toward her. "Here, a cooling drink. You need to be refreshed."

Dimpled fingers patted Josie's cheeks after setting the pitcher on a table. "Absent from this house far too long. He feared you would never come." The woman preached in her best English, arms folded across her apple-dumpling belly. "Is good you come home." Ignoring Josef, she latched onto Josefina. "We will prepare a celebration of homecoming for you."

Josef waited until the door closed after his housemaid before settling his bulky weight in an armchair. "I loved your mother above all else. When you came to me with your confession about François, I thought first of the pain Louise would endure at his betrayal. I became so enraged I acted without thought of consequence.

"That day has been my cross to bear. I arrived at the chateau fully tasting the bitterness of your tale. François stood alone, dousing his head under the well pump. I bore down upon him, bellowing my rage. I recall standing in my stirrups, thundering churlish warnings. 'Debaucher. Bounder. I will have my revenge.'

Josef closed his eyes. "François ducked behind the watering trough, then attempted a run to the house. My first shot struck a glancing blow at the temple. He staggered in a zigzag dash as though he dodged multiple shooters. I thought I had missed him completely. His shouts carried back to me. '"A lie. No truth to her claim."'

Josef's eyes popped open, glacial and tormented. "Up to that point I had not considered a truth other than your confession. I closed range, firing my pistol again, striking him in the back. He immediately fell." Joseph sighed. "He lay there, shouting his denial, red gore as bright as pulpy tomato where his flesh lay opened."

Josef covered his eyes with his hand, bowed his head. "All the years of trust we had shared smacked me of loyalty. Doubt pierced my rage. Perhaps he was innocent? Maybe, I had misunderstood you. My thoughts whirled like blades of grass thrown from a cutter. How could any sort of misunderstanding occur when he had misused you? He had embraced us all; we accepted him as family. Had I erred so badly in my allegiance to him?"

"François persisted with his hue and cry. 'She lies,' he yelled repeatedly. 'She lay with Jacob in the stables. The child belongs to him.'"

Josie paced the thick carpet, her steps silent.

"Do you understand, Josefina? His words delivered the salvation I sought. The cause was my own weakness. I knew his self-interest, his obsession with Louise, his leaning to show me as less of a man, but you, he doted on you. My arrogance could not face his betrayal, that I had misjudged him, endangered you. I jumped down to kneel at his side, never questioning how he knew of your accusation that very hour."

"His defense turned more vicious as he lay there. 'I know too,' he rasped, 'of your misdeeds.' He strengthened in his mock anger. 'Devoted to you, kept my silence. If you fire again, my proof will be unveiled. You will see your wife and daughter die in a workhouse and you imprisoned.'"

"'What cockamamie bedevils you?' I asked."

"François's breathing became labored, words choppy. 'Expose you. Have evidence of your thefts.'"

"His threat and accusation wiped away the importance of your allegation. I leapt to defend myself. 'Embezzling, fraud, how dare you speak such contemptuous lies? There is no truth to such invention.'

"'Just,' François moaned, 'as there is no truth to the slur that brought you here.' I felt the life slipping from him." Josef sighed heavily.

"His play-acting befuddled me. Distorted my perceptions, redirected my concern to my innocence in the charge he leveled against me."

Josefina sat in the chair next to Father, recalling François's seduction and how his sincerity had won her over. She had remained loyal, while he swilled deception like a pig and dishonored his promise.

"I thought," Father said, "if François would pledge? 'You swear on your life that Josefina lies, that you did not assault her.'"

"'She,' François jeered, 'laid with others.' I raised my pistol, prepared to fire another shot to stop his filth. François looked beyond me, tried to rise up. 'Ask Marianne, she...' Then he fainted."

"An agonizing shriek came from behind me. Marianne raced toward us. I held her back in her attempt to reach François. 'Did Josefina engage in sinful acts?' I asked. Marianne stared at me as if she were deaf to my question. I demanded. 'Did Josefina meet Jacob in the stables? Did they bed?'"

His hands shaking, Josef tentatively touched Josie's fingertips then let his hand drop.

"Upon my word, Josefina, François's charge of my dishonesty rendered me hapless. I fell completely into his scheme, aligning my guiltlessness with his."

Josef's eyes brimmed with anger. "Marianne screamed at me. 'Yes! Yes! Yes! She laid with Jacob.' " Her dazed state altered, seemingly resurrecting her senses, her words slashed as viciously as a madman's blade. 'Jacob sought to marry her,' Marianne said, 'but he only did so as a gentleman. A misdirected attempt to salvage Josefina's honor.'

"I said, 'I cannot believe this.' I wanted to attribute her tale to an oversight, some error in judgment. My confusion distorted my thoughts.

"Marianne stood before me, eye to eye, and swore. 'On my life I speak the truth. Dieter saw Jacob bed her, too. He can attest to Josefina's scandalous conduct.'

"My pride perished, bludgeoned by her indictment. Everyone there heard. The brotherhood knew my daughter a trollop. A saber through my vitals would not have wounded more." Josef's cheeks ballooned as he blew out a deep breath. "The foreman arrived, so I turned Marianne over to him. Then I carried François indoors myself, administered to him until the physician arrived.

"With what I imagined his last breath, François made a demand. 'Banish her. Send her away. All lies. She deceived us both.' His command fell in with my need to salvage my self-respect.

"Years ago, when I unwillingly rescued François at your mother's request, I feared his unhealthy greed. I prepared you to withstand François, to preserve our wealth and the Taylor family rights. My faith in your piousness was weak. Within minutes their lies convinced me you had betrayed my intent.

"With little encouragement on my part, the servants attested that the shooting had been accidental. By this time François lay unconscious. I believed I had committed murder for the sake of your already sullied name.

"Now, I must tell you, I too had discovered discrepancies in our Bank's dealings. Earlier, I had leapt upon Dieter with evidence that pointed to his ineptness or of someone's corruption. When Dieter persuaded me of his fault, not of greed or misappropriation, rather of stupidity, I kept my silence. That morning I believed François had discovered the same problem. Thinking me the culprit, even though sorely tested, I believed he had remained loyal to me. I felt duty bound to reward François's allegiance.

"My suspicions of François did not die, but on that morning the Bank controversy ranked secondary. I rode to the Vandemere plot with Satan hounding my heels. When I cornered Dieter he upheld Marianne, confessed to having witnessed your wanton behavior. Your scandal, attested to by your closest friends, drove any sane thought from my mind.

"Their lies became my truth." Josef rested his hands over Josie's. "Rage and shame colored my desire to contact you. By then, I had lost all courage to face you. Your sacrifice had been too dear.

"Father, the time never passes for forgiveness."

"Then, Josefina, ask forgiveness of me and all those you know. You blasphemed the teachings of our Elders. Dishonored me, sent your mother to her grave, and begat a bastard, all out of greed and ambition. Were there more than seven deadly sins, you would accomplish them all."

His turnabout stunned Josefina, but his words rang true. In her willful quest, she had hurt them all. Had there been a better way? He was, foremost, an Apostle and Elder of the church.

"Why did you return? To receive my blessing for the disgrace you created then and the unrest you bring with you now?"

Josie knew she had one opportunity to win Father before his pious indignation overruled his compassion. "Mother requested something very dear of you when I was a child."

"Your mother's memory is all I have. Do not dare!" Wild panic filled his eyes.

"Mother asked that I be educated in all the aspects of the banking business. She cared a great deal about François, more than normally acceptable." Josie held down Father's forearm as he began to huff and puff. "But she feared him even more so."

"How do you know this, Josefina?"

"Mother told me that she could never tolerate being under François's keeping, and she promised to see to it I was prepared to prevent that from happening. She both admired and distrusted him beyond explanation."

Josef's features vacillated between sadness and anger. "I will ask again. What is it you came back for?"

"It was mother's wish, and now I am asking for your support. Sign over your shares and authority in the Bank of Taylorsville and the cartel to me."

"Your lust still lives. Wealth... power..."

"What lives is my desire for retribution. François must pay for his betrayal of you, and of me, his part in mother's untimely death, and your honor, the family's honor, must be restored. I will accept no less."

Josef folded his hands as if in prayer. "In spite of my pain, Lord, I do not give up to death, because there is too much yet to be atoned for. Is this my purpose?"

Father's features were chiseled, cold. "When your mother passed over, I blamed you for that, too. My arrogance would not accept any part of the fault. As the years passed my body and spirit acquired the passion of a stone. My mind wandered without thought, as if it could not accept the insult of your betrayal. My duties at the Bank went ignored, no longer of importance. With no one to protect my empire, to appreciate the burden, no one who relished the fight, I found my duties too heavy a burden. I relinquished all, gratefully, to Dieter. For me, the years inched by with the quickness of a snail, every day wakening to your sins and the loss of my Louise."

Josef produced a kerchief and wiped his eyes and nose. "I truly believed Stuart when he produced verification of a ship docket documenting that you had boarded a steamer to New Orleans and reserved tickets for a sailing from New York to France. The last known record of Josefina Taylor."

Josie recalled the day after Marianne set sail. The tall girl who resembled her lost friend so dearly that Josie felt almost compelled to waylay her. Had she but followed through on her instinct.

Father continued. "My body succumbed to a seizure that excused my absence to the Board. I tended my gardens, bred my mares, and watched over the families that depended on me. Until the morning the local bank board stood on my porch as a whole, demanding explanation of the part J. L. Broderick had played in the impending takeover of World Bank. They ordered me to determine how an employee, a traitor, wielded such power within the cartel and to punish him.

"Initially all my inquiries led to San Francisco and Jacob. With that came the knowledge that he and Marianne married some years ago. I had mistakenly accepted Marianne's tale that you had died in childbirth abroad. I gave no thought to the existence of a child."

"About the same time as my investigation, a Colonel Tuffet requested an informal inquiry through the United States Attorney General. The President, an ally, summoned me, to warn me how and why he must distance his cabinet from the implication of my wrongdoing. He identified two separate people to me, both J. L Broderick. The outsider, a woman of beauty and financial wizardry. Both had sought fraud charges against my bank.

"I knew at that very moment the woman had to be you, alive and well, prepared to battle for your inheritance. You cannot imagine the amazement when I cheered his appalling announcement. He was stupefied, thought me crazed, feared I had toppled over the edge. He did, however, accept my additional donation, a considerable sum to support his legal fund. I pledged complete cooperation, encouraged the investigation." Josef's mouth tipped up in one corner at the memory.

Josie's stomach fluttered and her heart rose into her throat; she wallowed in Father's words. Never before had his respect and admiration addressed her. And yet, he spoke casually of what she thought a cardinal feat—her survival. "Did you know Dieter worked in tandem with François and Marianne?"

The color drained from Father's cheeks. "Not until you flushed the traitors from the cartel." The fervor of Josef's eyes danced, his mouth twisted a grin. He skipped over the question of Dieter. "When the inquiry committee delivered the evidence, I knew only a person intimate with the inner details of my holdings could prepare such damnable proof. I dwelt on your every detail, proud beyond reason of the merits in your case."

Father's smile broadened, then faded. "About that time I learned about Taylor Pickett. Dieter said to me, 'I believe sincerely that

Taylor is the daughter of Josefina. She is the right age, and she could be a twin to Marianne, you remember, Josefina's best friend—François's sister. I would swear on the Holy Bible. François ducLaFevre bedded Josefina. There is no doubt.'"

Joseph Taylor began to cough, consumptive tremors rolled from his chest to his temples, his jowls quivered. "Lil' Jos, my Josefina." The hushed name escaped his lips in a whimper.

Josie took a sharp breath, her own wail awaiting life as a baby's cry during birth. Father had opened his wound, plunged her into a shriveled soul starved of spirit, and she lived his pain. A soundless keening swept Josie, a dual howling for lost souls. The tears wetting her cheeks flowed from the shared anguish.

Josef paced for a moment, his leg obviously pained, until his composure returned.

"Unknowingly, Dieter's well-meaning had pushed you and your child deeper and deeper into meanness. Meanwhile, confident you had survived and would someday look to your child's inheritance, he kept careful secret records of François's theft. Secure about your hatred of François and me, Dieter supposed your pride would lure you back. Like lancing a boil after a speck of sand filled it with poison, Dieter planned to help you burst the pus sac of the cartel. As your hero, he believed he alone would be capable of giving you what you had always wanted."

Josef bent toward Josie. "Forgive me, I cannot warm to you. I have tried to write to you." He would not look his daughter in the eye. "Not only am I a fool, I have become cowardly. A barrier exists I cannot pass. My conscience punishes me with constant reminder of the torment and grief caused you. That yoke bears too much weight to ease by taking advantage of your giving ways."

Josef pulled the kerchief from his coat, dabbed at eyes and nose. "I have one more burden for you, daughter."

Josie spoke first. "I can resurrect our good name."

Josef's recriminations disappeared; arrogance salted his words. "I prepared you to administer the Taylor family's interest in my absence. That was not your mother's wish alone. You have proven to me the breadth of your capabilities. Your coming is providential. François may die within months."

Josie tried to feel some sadness for François. No remembered joy filled her mind. She recalled music and whirling then pain. "Can you tell me, Father, why François did this?"

"Long ago, he loved Louise and lost. He wanted to destroy me. I think by ruining whatever I valued most."

Sorrow for Father, for her own lost youth, for Taylor's loss rode a huge shudder that rid Josie of the vapors. "Neither of you know of the appalling life we endured because of your jealous war."

"Dieter and Louis came to me. There was no mistaking the genuineness of the misery they described. Louis is particularly heartbroken."

"And they know of all this duplicity? The deceit and betrayal?"

"They know only that my pursuits, as well as François's, are in a state of chaos."

A memory pecked at Josie, a reminder of the shredding of her heart another time, in this room, by this man. She listened for glass shattering. "And you propose what?" Josie's voice trembled. Her western boots became powder puff slippers; whalebone stays of a corset she had long given up poked her ribs. On this cool day, sweat trickled down her sides.

"You have a daughter entitled to her happiness. Can you forgive and accept those who contributed to your misery?"

Josie would not be victimized again; the grit of conviction cleared her throat. "Knowing of François's powers first hand, I would guess that he has already manipulated Dieter into a situation of trust, if not endearment. Assuredly lied about his part in my downfall. And you would suggest I sabotage any hope of an alliance with my daughter someday." Her voice rang clear as struck crystal. "I think not."

Hope brightened Josef's face. "When Dieter informed me you were coming, I vowed to live until you arrived. I, too, have waited these many months for revenge. I would not ask you to make another sacrifice, especially one you deem imprudent. No, the burden I propose comes from another offender. That you forgive Stuart. Bring him back into the bank."

Josie would not, could not forgive her brother. His part was to provide the needed solace; instead he proposed murder. "Too much has occurred."

"Stuart suffered much because of his misguided loyalty to François. His desire for wealth and power differed very little from yours. François and Marianne duped him, claimed I supported their schemes. You are safe now. I expect you, in the interest of your decedents, to make a fresh beginning with Stuart."

Josie could find a place—at the bottom of the deepest coalmine in Taylorsville County, never to see the light of day. *Father had not ordered Taylor's death, nor my own disfigurement, that threat came of Stuart's own desire. He was as evil as François.* Dare she speak?

"That is all I ask. We are going to battle. There is a place for all our soldiers."

Josie sidestepped the request. "Do you expect Dieter to visit this morning?"

"No, men are arriving from all over the world, some seeking out François for information." Josef's voice turned nasty. "Vultures waiting to pick the bones, further their illegal profit." A tone of respect picked his words. "François depends on Dieter. He works diligently for him. He will not come until the meeting is ended."

Disbelief obvious in her voice, Josie asked, "They are that close?" Josie could not believe her friend that blind. François had twisted all their lives. "Not long ago, I saw Marianne again. Taylor, the granddaughter you have never known, is that of a twin as Dieter said."

Josef ignored the reference to his additional oversight. "François is an impotent old man, as am I. He seldom leaves his estate, excepting extraordinary circumstances. Lives like a recluse surrounded by military-like attendants. His few ventures carefully controlled. No one he encounters would dare demean your daughter's likeness."

Josef blew his nose, the handkerchief carrying the distinct perfume of roses. "Believe me, even in my rage I protected you." His self-protesting came unnaturally, was unbecoming, still he offered his self-respect in hopes of her approval. "I had no inkling Dieter harbored the devious nature to sit side by the side and watch the conspiracy as he did, nor that he had dedicated his life to claiming you whatever the cost."

Josie let go of Stuart's murderous intentions so long passed. What use would her causing Father more pain serve? She leaned toward her father. "Why does Dieter still head the Bank?" Her question addressed her distrust.

"The investigation. The evidence pointed to François and me, which precluded either of us from gaining control of the bank. I was unable to prove François's theft. In absence of an alternate authority, the cartel committee requested Dieter administer all affairs until the government approves our new appointment. All our holdings, with the exception of minor personal affairs, must be conducted through him."

"And the agreement you signed to financially underwrite my new venture?" At his puzzled expression Josie explained. "The authorization I obtained from the government to form an exclusive trust for communication and electric energy?"

"A forgery," a brittle voice boomed from behind her. "A promising profitable investment, Lil' Jos. However, neither your father nor François knows of the agreement." Dieter closed the French doors behind him, the glass casting beams of color as brilliant as holiday ornaments. "I knew you would follow the corruption; find your way back to me. You have the most ingenious mind of us all. Do you understand? I had to leave you exposed to François's hunt. Jacob was taken. You already detested your father, with François dead, which will occur soon, that left only me to save you."

Josefina shrunk into the delicate fabric of the chair.

Dieter's voice softened. "You have always been loyal to those you cared about. I had not bargained on your finding another." His knees met Josie's skirt before he retreated. "Did you ever care for me at all?"

His nobleness had lost its way in his obsession of her. His life dedicated to building an ark that would provide them with shelter from the floods had failed. Josie opened her arms wide and reached up to him. "You have always been a dear friend. I am only sorry you never met someone who would love you so richly in return." His body nestled alien and strange in her arms, reluctant to move away.

Josie let go and stood up. "There is a matter unknown to all of you that may change your opinion of me." Her eyes meet Father's briefly before she looked away. "In return for bearing his heir, François presented an agreement to me, a stipend sufficient to live in luxury and allow me to marry Jacob."

Josef raised his head. "I would not be surprised if you agreed to his offer." His eyes narrowed, mouth thinned.

Josie cringed. "I did not say no. I fled from him, ashamed he believed my character so weak. When he overwhelmed me with gifts, and with the thought of a fortune plus having Jacob, I succumbed." To Josie's ears all sounds died, with the exception of the exhales from Dieter and Father, their acknowledgement of her sin done.

Josef recovered first. "Nothing can be gained from second guessing what has passed. You were but fifteen, a child of strict parentage, never free to debate your own choices. Any freedom you enjoyed came at my pleasure, even your rebellion tolerated by my need to test your strengths. No, Josefina, François contrived to take advantage of you, then failed to honor his debauchery as revenge on me."

Dieter added, "Even after he learned of his child, he monitored your miserable existence and still plotted to force you to do his bidding. Conferred no respect on you, the child, or anyone else involved."

Josef came close to his daughter's side and reached out as if to stroke her. "The church law I parroted could not override your willful spirit. I closed my eyes to your ambition. If blame falls on any other than François, it rests with my indifference to your need." Father stood over her, his hand balanced midair, as if blessing her.

Thirty-five

Josie L. Broderick entered Taylorsville Bank's board chamber appearing confident and in command, but within the sinews and bones of her body, the Josefina of twenty-two years past who had made the choice to escape these forbidding confines quaked. In spite of the numerous speeches Josie had made before other stockholders, the Bank's imposing boardroom, which had doubled in size since her last visit, intimidated Josie and still made her feel she had been born of Lilliputian and lacked the prowess of the harrying Goliaths surrounding her. She willed herself to parade before them with the assurance of a Herculean.

The huge conference table had been forfeited for rows of wall-to-wall male-fitted chairs, barely allowing their occupants knee space, certainly not offering room for the ruffle of petticoats. The stink of spittoons was absent, the vile receptacles nowhere in evidence; instead an aroma of bay rum edged cigar smoke.

While Josie fought her way to the head of the room, "She ... She ... She ..." pulsed in edgy whispers, countered by robust shushing. Smiles, scowls, and snubs of indifference scattered among the otherwise blank faces that greeted Josie. She stepped up onto a box behind the dais, gavel poised, encouraging the chatter to subside.

Astonishingly, once the gavel was in her hand Josie felt completely calm, controlled, decidedly alien from the willful girl of before who had taken this same spot and endured Father's humiliation.

A red-coated attendant, how could he be missed, wheeled François through the opened double doors. His sudden appearance startled Josie. For a moment fear overwhelmed her, her hollow stomach rolled. What if François had succeeded in bringing about an alliance hostile to her? His arrogance traveled before him, buffing the edge of the self-confidence he flaunted.

He had aged, however, his jacket exhibited surprisingly broad shoulders above a solid chest. She suspected them well padded. The redcoat stepped aside, and François's arms pushed effortlessly, his breath barely altered by the strain. He smirked, aged eyes serpentine and unwelcoming. Midway the room, he observed Josie with a nonchalance reserved for beggars and small animals, nothing of value, looking through her, ignoring her existence.

Josie smiled confidently in return, wasting the charm for appearance sake. François had opened up one truth for her: she was born with a will of her own, a will to wield power, and today he would discover how well she had learned to do just that. Without his help.

Josie banged the gavel three times before the murmuring stopped. "Gentlemen, I am known to you as J. L. Broderick. I stand before you prepared to officiate this meeting under the auspices of the United States Justice Department. Our chairman, Josef Taylor, signed authorizations yesterday granting me his holdings, rights, and all authority for Taylorsville Bank and the National Land Company cartel. Together with my Bank of Bisbee holdings of seventeen percent of the cartel's offerings, thirty-seven percent of the shares allotted and the proxies of an additional twenty percent now within my control, I represent the single largest block of shareholders."

Whispers zipped back and forth around the room, the male buzz uncharacteristically high-pitched with anxiety. Josie's voice carried over the din.

"Many of you met me over twenty years ago at the inception of this cartel. Since then I have become a banker, a financier, an investor, an enemy. For two years I gathered evidence of corruption and fraud among you and uncovered a scheme that shifted funds from this brotherhood and other monies designated for the government's treasury to private accounts. I exposed this skullduggery, then sought indictment of your officers for fraud and embezzlement."

François maneuvered away from the wall of men hugging the sidelines and rolled within ten feet of the head table. His cutting, steel gray eyes never wavered from Josie. "What started you on this destructive, self-righteous path?" His voice boomed gruff and churlish. "And tell us, does your authority recognize you as Josefina Taylor, daughter of our Chairman, or under the immoral, self-elected credentials of Mrs. Josie Broderick, or the illicit alias J. L. Broderick? You are not above throwing stones about deceptions and dishonesty."

François's arms locked, pulling his torso up from the seat as if he expected to get up and walk. He sank back on his chair, a smirk slashing his face. "You have returned to us as a renown woman of finance. Well done."

"Thank you, Monsieur ducLaFevre," Josie demurred.

"And you accomplished this without the tutelage of any of the acclaimed masters of money in this room." He grinned. A glittering object suddenly dangled from his fingers.

A glare of fractured rainbows appeared at the side of Josie's eyes, like blinders on a racehorse. Josie knew instantly—the sapphire robin's egg of years ago. Its gold chain circled the jewel in a smooth oval mirroring the ruse of a hypnotist's ability to control your thoughts. All these years she felt cursed by the brilliant gem, and while she watched, the dazzling blue stone swing to and fro, its magnetism emptying her mind.

"You can have much more Lil' Jos. All you're entitled to; all you've earned." François's voice was caressing, his words inviting.

A big mistake, Josie thought. He should never have called her Lil' Jos. She was not her father, nor his counterpart. She was her own woman.

"You are out of order, sir. As appointed Chairman of the cartel, I order you to remain silent until all business of this organization has been brought to the attention of the membership."

François's eyes blazed. "We will not allow a woman, certainly one of your repute, to preside over us." François blustered his mortification. "Take your profits and hanger-on's while you flaunt your stolen power, inscribe your false signature where needed, then leave us to our tasks. This cartel will remain in the hands of men of experience. Men, I vouch, whose errors of judgment have been rectified."

"What Monsieur ducLaFevre says is partly true. The thefts have been repaid. Under threat of imprisonment," Josie added. "After restitution, the federal government commuted the incarceration penalties. I have here, on the table for all to see, the resignations of all but one of those involved."

François edged his chair nearer.

When a handsome, but weary looking Jacob reached the end of the row nearest her, Josie's heart filled with appreciation. She had thought him on his way to the Klondike. He stopped within François's reach, barring the agitator's ability to come nearer.

Jacob's presence did not surprise Josie unduly. He had contacted most of the members, expressed regret for his involvement and promoted allegiance to her. Josie knew, too, he still carried affection for her in his heart.

A commotion drew Josie's attention away from Jacob. A red-faced Chess wedged his barrel chest through the knots of gossipers left in Jacob's wake. Chess elbowed his way forward, appearing to the onlookers as a well dressed but raw, perhaps dangerous man, his jagged scar pulling his mouth into grim, lopsided contempt.

Josie yearned to leap across the table into Chess's arms. He had not abandoned her, had not left her behind to protect herself among the wolves, unlike others of this place in years past.

The admiration and refuge he exuded filled Josie with a love and assurance she had not accepted before this moment. Soundlessly he telegraphed his oft-repeated appeal. *Love me, I love you.* His presence impacted her more than she would ever have imagined. Her world seemed almost complete, the decision she had wrestled with for months astonishingly made without thought.

She answered his message with her eyes and smile. *Yes*! Together they would face Taylor, and Josie would unburden herself. Josie knew whatever the consequences, with Chess by her side, the pleasures would multiply. Her thoughts kited to Jacob and that brief history, then she smiled, content, and returned to the battle at hand.

François had not finished with her, Josie knew that, but she had her own wits to depend on and the support of the man who had weathered the test of time and the contest of her will.

"I expect the immediate, full cooperation and resignation of the remainder of those involved. We must elect a new board and chairman before the end of the day."

Josie's glance swept the room, seeking a bond with the men listening intently. "I have been appointed by the federal justice committee to guarantee such corruption does not occur again." Her gaze repeated the circuit, measuring each man one by one. "I propose we vote. Allow the newly installed officers to conduct the remainder of today's business." Josie sat down, her battle of many years ended.

Voices clamored for attention. A chant began. One word. Initially, Josie heard the heckling as a derisive booing, then she deciphered the word. "You! You!" A single handclap began at the table and multiplied until applause filled the room.

"Stand up," a voice said. Another. "Stand and receive your well-earned due." The urging grew louder. Josie rose, inclining her head in recognition. She had done the impossible, inspired them to allow a woman to participate, not just that, but lead them.

The first ballot sanctioned Josie's election. She made quick work of the business at hand. "In light of Mr. Vandemere's unstinting loyalty, I feel he is qualified to remain— as President of Taylorsville Bank. Since the two financial interests are so entwined, I put it to a vote to place him on the board of the cartel as vice-chair." Josie felt Dieter's obsession with her, although misguided previously, had not weakened. He would never again allow anything to occur that would cause distress or reflect badly on her.

"Second, I recommend Stuart Taylor be designated to represent the bank and the cartel both in Germany and the Antilles. Josef Taylor has resigned. Monsieur ducLaFevre, you alluded to submitting your resignation. In light of your poor health? May we expect that today?" What she said was not true. François had made no such overture.

Josie, in fact, had not received any contact from François since her arrival.

François rolled up to where Jacob guarded the podium, produced an envelope sealed with his gold coat of arms and thrust it at a third party. Having outmaneuvered her protectors, François threw a parting jab at Josie. "Be assured I have seen to it that no one will ever seek investment with this cartel again. And between you and I, I am pleased your daughter is lost to you. I have seen to it she will never seek your presence for the rest of your life." The red-coated aid retrieved François and wheeled the chair away before Josie fully absorbed his words and could reply.

She had lost her daughter forever, he said, but how had François known? What did he know now that guaranteed Taylor would hate her? There could be no question François had done something. Secure in the love of the scarred man watching, his body poised for action, Josie searched her soul, drawing from the laws of her childhood and her generous nature. She acknowledged François's imperfection. He had sinned, not unlike she and others who took the reins of life in their own hands. Taylor's conception and the dishonoring of Father were offenses of human frailty, the fault hers to bear. She could leave François to his dying, knowing she had done everything possible to protect Taylor from his evilness.

But, Josie knew she would never be fully content in her life without the love of her daughter.

~ * ~

Chess relaxed his arms that had been folded across his chest as a buttress. An angelic appearance adorned this complicated woman whose mind was capable of out-guessing most men in the room, including him. Her vulnerability lay in her heart.

Women beaten by some of the most prestigious men in the territory, widows and orphans of copper poisoned miners, wives and children of drunks, Mexican families fleeing the brutality of guerilla wars, and more, survived on Josie's freely given financial resources. Her more prized commodity, time, she spent at his ranch, overseeing the construction of wards and schools for these "banished angels," in particular the dark-skinned babies left behind by deserting buffalo soldiers.

He had seen her suffer many times before, but never the boomerang elation and despair he witnessed here, today. She had garnished her charm well and exhibited the staying power of an accomplished actress, but she could not remain here—if he had to hog-tie and kidnap her to get her away. He loved her too much to let this place destroy her.

~ * ~

After receiving congratulations and promises of support, Josie approached Chess. "I will never be a typical wife, can you accept me as I am?" she asked.

Chess took her hands in his, brought them to his lips. "I will always love you just as you are."

The lingering kiss tingled Josie's fingertips; she longed to float adrift in the love filling his eyes.

Jacob urged the few remaining men out of the room, allowing Josie and Chess a few private moments to collect her belongings.

Someone spoke Josie's name. A chill shivered across her shoulders and woke the hackles of her neck. She turned and stared up into green eyes damp with unshed tears. At first, her heart thumped. *Taylor*!

"Zee pain I caused you is unpardonable." Marianne's French accent had grown more pronounced. "Please believe my betrayal never came with a willing heart." Marianne weighed her words. "My selfishness severed our friendship. Can the rent be repaired? Is there enough kindness in your heart to forgive me?"

"You destroyed my life," Josie accused her long ago friend. Anger, love, and distrust fought to be addressed in unanswered questions bursting in Josie's mind. *My Judas! The puppeteer aiding François's evilness.* Josie stared at the troubled woman, unable to detach herself from softer memories that plugged her anger. *Not true. The choice was mine. Marianne did no more than take advantage of my ambitions.*

"I beg you, Josefina... Josie."

"...deserted me, at a time I needed you most," Josie whispered.

"You cannot be so unforgiving. That is not the Josefina I love."

Josie turned her back, dwelling on the persuasive words. Marianne was right. The childhood lessons of the "thou shalt nots" taught one to take responsibility for the doors opened and closed in life. The hardships she had suffered started with her reckless need to exercise her own will, satisfy her wants; the misdeeds of others came secondary. *I took from life what mattered to me.*

Josie faced Marianne. "I cannot place so much importance on your betrayal. To do so lessens my passion for life and the significance of other souls touching mine." Josie sidestepped Marianne's outstretched arms by clasping an extended hand and numbly lowering her head in a half-curtsy.

Turning quickly toward Chess, Josie beamed with a broad smile. "Except for having my daughter near, I have everything I want from life. And I feel one day soon, she will return to me.

Meet Nancy Minnis Damato

My neck and shoulders have that semi-permanent bow, and sometimes ache, familiar to avid readers who devour all the print their busy schedule can manage. Late nights, early a.m.'s, and stolen hours of reading give me so much happiness, heartbreak, and compassion, the tales a huge influence on me. Courage, determination, ambition, basic survival, vanity, betrayal, greed and thousands of other attributes and flaws of characters become easy lessons about life, broadening my world, strengthening my own character. When I began to write, it was with the same intent—as a gift to my readers to enhance their own lives, to suffer and celebrate vicariously.

Born in Illinois, a graduate of the University of Illinois, a Midwesterner most of my life, home gave me a basis to appreciate the additional beauty and blemishes of other places, the differences of speech, the conflict of opinions, the challenge of intolerances.

Divorced mother of two, remarried and blending offspring of six, my time became more precious. Still, I found myself driven to read and to satisfy my yearning to write. Sentences, paragraphs, eventually short stories squiggled down between assignments at work brought me enormous satisfaction—also got me fired. Substitute teaching and eventually starting my own insurance agency opened up more writing time.

Finally, my day has arrived to fulfill a lifelong dream—you have *The Pawn*, the first book of a family saga. Enjoy.

Let me know at <u>www.nancydamato.com</u> what you think. And look for *Belonging*, book two in the history of the Taylors.

*VISIT OUR WEBSITE
FOR THE FULL INVENTORY
OF QUALITY BOOKS*:

http://www.wings-press.com

*Quality trade paperbacks and downloads
in multiple formats,
in genres ranging from light romantic
comedy to general fiction and horror.
Wings has something
for every reader's taste.
Visit the website, then bookmark it.
We add new titles each month!*